S EAN

ISBN 978-0-7653-6687-0

50799

9 780765 366870

$7.99
($9.99 CAN)

TOR® Fantasy

T-170-218

Rave Reviews for Recent Xanth Adventures

"The Xanth books constitute Anthony's longest and most successful series. . . . They are intended to be kind-spirited, fun reading, a series of wondrous beasts and beings, and most of all, an endless succession of outrageous puns."   —*The Wichita Eagle*

"Classic Xanthromancy! *Air Apparent* sends a company of adventurers on a quest through multiple Xanths, encountering absurdities, danger, and romance, but also finding themselves unwittingly involved in extremely complex intrigue."   —*Booklist*

"Profusely punning his path through his twenty-sixth Xanth fantasy (*Up in a Heaval*), the prolific Anthony focuses on a contest between Demon Jupiter and Demon Fornax, reviving to great effect the dueling-demons theme from last year's *Swell Foop*. . . . As they crisscross Xanth, they encounter many of the characters featured in Anthony's previous works. Anthony's latest offering is certain to please fans."
                     —*Publishers Weekly*

"*Jumper Cable*, the thirty-third installment in master raconteur Piers Anthony's popular series, is a tale of friendship, duty, honor, love, and betrayal, liberally spiced with his characteristic wordplay; an essential addition to any library's fantasy collection."
                     —*Library Journal*

"Here we go 'Adventuring' in Xanth once more! Xanth remains a land of happy endings, however, and readers can expect the usual amount of enjoyment from this thirty-fourth Xanth tale."
                     —*Booklist* on *Knot Gneiss*

TOR BOOKS BY PIERS ANTHONY

Piers Anthony

LUCK OF THE DRAW

A TOM DOHERTY ASSOCIATES BOOK
NEW YORK

This is a work of fiction. All of the characters, organizations, and events portrayed in this novel are either products of the author's imagination or are used fictitiously.

LUCK OF THE DRAW

Copyright © 2012 by Piers Anthony Jacob

All rights reserved.

Map by Jael

A Tor Book
Published by Tom Doherty Associates, LLC
175 Fifth Avenue
New York, NY 10010

www.tor-forge.com

Tor® is a registered trademark of Tom Doherty Associates, LLC.

ISBN 978-0-7653-6687-0

Tor books may be purchased for educational, business, or promotional use. For information on bulk purchases, please contact Macmillan Corporate and Premium Sales Department at 1-800-221-7945, extension 5442, or write specialmarkets@macmillan.com.

First Edition: December 2012
First Mass Market Edition: October 2013

Printed in the United States of America

0 9 8 7 6 5 4 3 2 1

CONTENTS

LUCK OF
THE DRAW

Xanthin Box

Bryce smelled a rat.

He sighed. He knew what it meant. He would have to clean up the garage. At least until he found the dead rat.

So he started in. He was eighty years old, and increasingly absentminded, so if he encountered something that needed doing, he generally did it immediately, lest he forget. The stench of the rat would not ease on its own if ignored. The body would be there somewhere, buried under or behind assorted junk. If he could get at it.

It had been some time since he had shaped up the garage. In fact he had mostly stopped coming in here, since he gave up driving, and things had pretty much accumulated on their own. But in time it would need to be cleared out, when the house was put on the market, because—

Because Bryce had between one and two years left to live. His doctor had given him the word: he had type two diabetes because he had grown too fat, and his blood vessels were three-quarters clogged because he had eaten too many fatty snacks, and the formerly inert prostate cancer was beginning to become assertive because, well, just because. He had to exercise, reduce his weight, and stop sleeping so much in front of the TV. He needed to get out and interact with other people, becoming more social. He needed to challenge his brain instead of being a mental sponge. Or else.

Bryce had lacked the gumption to do any of those things. Exercise was too much work, and his fading eyesight made it harder to recognize people. So he was faced with the or else. That meant he would die, and his house would be sold in the process of putting his estate in order. It wasn't much of an estate; forty-odd years of office work had not paid any fortune. The two of them had been comfortable, however, not requiring much.

Then Bev had died, and any remaining ambition Bryce might have had had dissipated like windblown smoke. He existed; that was most of what was to be said for him. Their sons had expressed concern, but they had lives and families of their own, as did their grown children, his grandchildren, so they mostly left Bryce alone. His increasing grouchiness of age might have had something to do with it.

He got to work, slowly, because he did not have a lot of energy to spare. He might have to do the job in installments, until he penetrated to the rat's nest, wherever it was. Too bad odor was not more specific, so that he could orient on it efficiently and be done with the distasteful chore. As it was, he would soon be grimy, because layers of dust covered everything. Roaches and silverfish skittered away, resenting the disturbance. Bryce grimaced; he should have donned gloves for this dirty work, but naturally hadn't thought of it. It was just too complicated to go back to fetch them from the house, assuming he could find them.

Almost immediately he had to fight off a wave of nostalgia. There were things here dating back decades, to when the family was more active and ambitious. Useless things that he had not been able to throw out, because that would have been like discarding part of his wife, or a son, or a friend, or his own youth. He knew it was foolish, but he just couldn't do it. So the junk accumulated, reminders of hopelessly faded memories.

He had lived a mediocre existence, and not entirely because he had to. He had made obvious mistakes of judgment and passion, and paid for them. If he could somehow live his indifferent life over, he would be a lot smarter about that. He would do the right thing instead of the convenient thing, the decent act instead of the selfish one, the prudent decision instead of the reckless one. He might not be richer or better known or respected, but he would be a better man. That would count for a lot, personally.

For one thing, he should have made more of his ability to sketch. He was no artist, and had never worked with paints, but if he had a pencil and paper he could sketch anything he saw, accurately enough so that others could immediately recognize it. He still liked to draw things; the house was piled with old pencil pictures, and he always kept a stubby pencil and a little notepad in his pocket. It was his sole creative expression, and it made him feel good. Had he taken art courses, who knew what he might have made of it? So he would definitely follow up on that.

And a fat lot of good that resolution was, at this stage in his wasted term! It was easy to make fine resolutions when there was no prospect of having to follow through on them.

But he was woolgathering, one of his bad habits. It was time to get back to work.

Here was an old push-lawnmower, overwhelmed by cobwebs, as dated in its fashion as Bryce was in his own. There was a similarly old circular rattan chair, once a comfortable novelty, but in recent decades useless because Bryce knew that once he sat in it, he would not be able to get back out of it. It was piled with junk: a bucket of dry-rotting wooden clothespins for laundry that no longer got hung out to dry in the sun, a bag of tattered clothing that Bev might once have worn, an empty picture frame that could have pictured his present empty life, several battered paperback novels that would never be reread, and a bright yellow box.

Bryce didn't recognize that last. Could a granddaughter have left it here? But no granddaughter had been here in the past decade, and this wasn't the kind of thing to be left and forgotten. It was too pretty: it almost glowed with a xanthin luster. Also, there was no dust on it, so it couldn't have been here long. Yet who could have left it here? The garage was locked from the outside, and the neighbors were not the kind to intrude. It was as if it had simply floated in on its own and found a place to perch.

In a moment he realized something odd but surely significant: the dead-rat odor emanated from the box. Such an awful smell from such a lovely object! Could that be coincidence? It had the one fragrance that was guaranteed to make him search it out promptly. So it must have been placed for him to find.

He picked it up and opened it. Inside were three objects: a tiny pillbox containing a yellow capsule, a small vial of yellow fluid, and a bound yellow notebook. Each had lettering on it. The pillbox said FBU NF, the vial said ESJOL NF, and the notebook said SFBE NF. What did it mean?

Bryce had never been any genius, but in the old days he had diverted himself with newspaper word puzzles. That repeated NF looked like a two-letter word. There were only so many of them. Suppose the letter B were substituted for the letter A? The letter F for the letter E? A childishly simple transcription.

And just like that he had it. The pill said EAT ME, the vial said DRINK ME, and the notebook said READ ME.

Like Alice in Wonderland. Who knew what effect such things might have on a person? Nothing magical, surely, but they could be candy—or poison. It was best to leave them alone.

Except that someone must have left them for him. Why? He had no close friends anymore; they had all died. Similarly, he had no enemies. What possible reason could any stranger have had for such an obscure contact? This was curious indeed.

Well, hell: what did he have to lose? He took the pill and swallowed it.

Nothing happened. So much for that.

He unstopped the vial and drank its few drops of golden elixir. It was neutral in taste. Again, nothing. What had he really expected?

So he opened the book and started reading. It was in the same code, so he had to change the words letter by letter, tediously. It was a curious, probably nonsensical message.

THIS IS A SECRET ONE-WAY PORTAL TO THE LAND OF XANTH. TO ACTIVATE IT, SPEAK THE MAGIC WORDS

He paused. What magic words? It didn't provide them. This must be someone's idea of a joke. Bryce tucked the book in a pocket and went on with his cleanup, since he was now well into it and had nothing better to do.

He discovered his old recumbent tricycle, buried under more junk. He hauled it out and brushed it off. The chain was oil-caked but seemed serviceable. The tires were solid rubber; he had gotten tired of repairing punctures and switched to these ones that might wear out in time but would never go flat. The trike should be ridable despite its long neglect.

And what about him? Could he still ride it? Balancing was tricky on such machines, because the rider was low to the ground. He had learned the art, but his old reflexes might not be up to the challenge. Still, the trike should be secure against even his clumsiness. It was a bike, not a trike, that required balance. He had been confusing the two, in true senior moment fashion.

Well, hell, again. He opened the garage door and hauled the trike out onto the pavement. He would try it, and if he crashed, well, that was the luck of the draw.

"Ruff."

Startled, Bryce looked up. There was a dog. Female, healthy, older, with short black and white hair, fairly solid, with somewhat floppy ears. He was generally familiar with dogs, but did not recognize this one. "Well, what breed are you?" he asked.

She shrugged, obviously unable to answer the question.

Bryce left the trike and approached the dog. "May I? I want to look at your tag." It was always best to approach any strange canine cautiously, though this one seemed friendly.

She shrugged again. Taking that as a yes, he petted her shoulder, then reached for her collar. There was none. Evidently there had been one, but somehow it had been lost along with the tags.

"You must be lost," Bryce said. "And maybe hungry and thirsty. Let me fetch you some water and whatever else I can rouse up. Wait here."

He went back into the garage, glancing back. The dog lay down in place, doing what he had asked. That was a good sign.

He entered the house, found a pan and some leftover pie, and brought them out. He set them down before the dog. "Sorry it's not more. It's all I have at the moment."

She merely looked at him. "It's okay," he said reassuringly. "Drink. Eat. Then we'll see what we can do for you. Maybe there's a bulletin out."

She got up, put her head to the pan, and drank thirstily. Then she ate the pie.

"So I was right. You're lost and haven't been fed in a while."

She looked at him and seemed to nod. She perhaps understood the essence if not the words.

He looked at his trike. "I was about to try riding this, just to see if I could. Let me make my attempt, then I'll pick myself up off the pavement and bring you inside so I can try to locate your owner. Okay?"

This time he was sure she nodded. This was evidently a smart dog.

He oriented his trike, settled onto it, put his right foot in the webbing on the right pedal, and pushed. The trike started to move, rather wobbly despite its third wheel. He brought his left foot up and pushed that pedal, gaining speed and balance. He was doing it!

Then he was out on the street, not by choice so much as because that was the only place to go without crashing. Fortunately there was no traffic at the moment. He turned right and moved along the pavement. "Damn!" he said, pleased.

Then he saw that the dog was running along beside him, keeping him company. He liked that too. Loneliness had been his chief companion in recent months. "I'll loop around the block and return home," he told the dog.

She glanced at him and nodded. She probably recognized the word "home."

He laughed. "I guess I said the magic words."

He looked at the street, ready to make the first turn around the block. But there was no turn. In fact there were no houses. He was suddenly on a strange street. Not even a street; a path. It wound through a quiet forest. How had he suddenly come to this parklike avenue? He had been distracted only a moment, and there was no such park in his neighborhood.

The dog still ran beside him. She looked surprised too.

Then the path tilted down. Before he knew it he was picking up speed. He squeezed on the hand brakes, but they were ineffective. That was what must have fallen apart with disuse: the braking mechanism. He was out of control. All he could do was steer and hope for the best.

The dog kept pace with him, but he suspected she was questioning his judgment, speeding like this on a strange path.

They rounded a curve—and there was a great old-fashioned stone castle. The path led right up to its sturdy wood dungeon door. But the door was closed.

He tried again to stop, and could not. "Swerve aside, doggie!" he cried. "We're going to crash!"

But she only drew closer to him, as if trying to cushion his crash with her body. It was way too late to stop.

Bryce closed his eyes and braced for the worst. They crashed.

Bryce blinked. He was sprawled beside the dog in an empty stone chamber, obviously not his cluttered garage, and the trike was gone. But that was only part of it.

He had double vision. Whatever he looked at seemed slightly blurred. Was he suffering a stroke? "What are the symptoms?" he asked himself rhetorically.

"Yes?" the dog asked.

"You talked!" Bryce said.

"Yes," she agreed, looking surprised.

"Did you talk before we got here?"

"No."

"Something very odd is happening. Maybe we both died in that crash, and this is our afterlife. You think so?"

"No."

Bryce sighed. "I guess that would have been too easy an answer. But right now I have another problem: double vision. Let me have a moment."

"Quiet," the dog agreed.

He stood perfectly still, and his vision cleared. Then he moved, and it blurred again. He discovered that if he closed one eye, things were clear. So it was a nuisance, but did not seem dangerous. He felt fine.

In fact, he felt great. He looked down at himself, and discovered that his overgrown belly was gone. His arms and legs were lean and muscular. His eyesight was pre-ternaturally clear. It was as though he had imbibed a youth potion.

He smiled tolerantly. Could it have been in a yellow vial?

Then what about the pill? Had it caused his double vision? If it was another magical gift, it did not seem to be very convenient.

He looked at the dog. "What's your name?"

"Rachel."

"Are you feeling as healthy as I am, Rachel? Especially considering we should be close to dead?"

Rachel checked herself, surprised again. "Yes."

And she had not eaten a pill or drunk from a vial. Something else was in operation here.

Then someone entered the stone chamber. Someone? It was an animated skeleton!

Rachel moved protectively close to Bryce, picking up on his reaction.

"Do you see a skeleton?"

"No."

Oh—maybe this was a horror house, with scary figures being dangled to impress the visitors, not visible from every angle. Or something.

Bryce shut his left eye, and the apparition disappeared. But a few seconds later it reappeared, this time in the right eye. What kind of horror house effect could account for that? He wasn't wearing glasses. He needed them, but was forever losing track of them. Rather, he *had* needed them, until now.

Rachel growled. This time she was seeing what he was seeing. "Attack?"

"No," he said quickly. "It probably isn't real."

The skeleton saw them and paused. "Who are you?" it asked with evident surprise. Now Bryce realized it had spoken before, but in his confusion he had tuned out the sound. So the thing talked, or at least there was a speaker somewhere to make it seem to do so despite lacking lungs or lips. Such effects were standard in amusement parks.

"Just an old man suffering a hallucination," Bryce replied, playing along. "And his friend. Who are you?"

"I am Picka Bone, proprietor of Caprice Castle. This is supposed to be a secure chamber. That's why I investigated when I heard noise here." His words seemed to repeat themselves about ten seconds later. Bryce focused, trying to tune out the extra voice, and succeeded reasonably well.

"I can't explain how I came here," Bryce said candidly. "I was riding a recumbent tricycle, and suddenly we were in an unfamiliar setting."

"I'll ask Dawn," the skeleton said. "She will know. Please come this way." He turned and departed the chamber.

This was weird, but it was easier to continue playing along. Bryce and Rachel followed the skeleton out the door, up the stone steps, and into a rather more ornate section of the castle.

Soon they were met by an astonishingly beautiful young woman. She had bright red hair, green eyes, and a figure a movie starlet could only dream of. She must be Dawn; indeed, her presence was like the rising of the morning sun.

Dawn approached Bryce and touched him. "Ah," she said. "This will require some explaining. Please come this way."

Bryce and the skeleton followed her to a pleasant family room. They sat opposite her. Dawn talked.

"I am Princess Dawn, wife of Picka Bone here. I must explain that I am also a Sorceress. My talent is to immediately know anything about any living thing I touch. Thus I know about you. Bryce, you are freshly from Mundania, a land almost bereft of magic." She smiled, and the room seemed to brighten. "There are traces of it, such as your rainbows that can be seen only from one side, and perspective, where distant objects hurry to keep up with close ones without actually moving. But aside from such minor effects it is a remarkably drear world. This is the Land of Xanth, which in contrast has magic everywhere. It is for my taste a much preferable place to live." She grimaced. "Except, perhaps, for the puns. But we are doing what we can to reduce them."

"I never was very good at puns," Bryce admitted. "But my companion, the dog—can you check her too?"

Dawn knelt before the dog and put her hand on a shoulder. "And you are Rachel, a German short-haired pointer highly trained as a Service Dog. But your master died, and they were going to put you down, so you left. Bryce reminded you of your owner, in that he needed help, and you really like to help, so you befriended him. Now you can talk, or at least say the few words you were trained to obey, but you understand many more."

"Yes," Rachel said.

"The point is that both of you will find it strange here, especially at first. But you will acclimatize, and you are welcome to remain here in Caprice as our guests until you do."

"Until we return to Mundania, as you put it," Bryce agreed.

"Until you are ready to live on your own in Xanth. I don't believe you can return to your own realm. Not by your own choice. You passed through a one-way portal when you spoke the magic words."

Bryce was astonished. "You mean those were the magic words the book told me to utter? 'The magic words'?"

"Yes. You are unusual in that you did not die first."

"That won't be long," he said. "A year or two."

"No," she said firmly. "You surely have a good sixty years ahead of you, before you fade out, if you stay clear of dragons and other dangers."

He shook his head. "I am eighty years old, and in poor health." He glanced down at his body. "Or I was, until I mysteriously arrived here. I assume I'm dreaming, and my real body remains a wreck."

"You are mistaken. You have been gifted with four magical things, and Rachel with three, and you have no choice but to work through them as well as you can."

She seemed very certain, so he didn't argue further. He ticked them off on his fingers. "A youth potion. Blurred vision. A pass to this magic land. There is another?"

"A youth potion that makes you age twenty-one, physically," she agreed. "And healthy. The illnesses you had in Mundania are gone. The blurred vision is actually a magic talent, second sight. You can see, hear, and feel ten seconds into the future with your left side, while your right side is normal. This is nice magic; it could be quite useful on occasion, such as if a dragon were about to pounce. It will give you that time to take evasive action, possibly saving your life. Because you are young, not immortal. All you need to do is take a few days to attune, so it no longer confuses you. You are correct about the pass to Xanth."

"So what is the fourth gift?" he inquired skeptically.

"You have been imprinted with romantic love for my younger cousin, Princess Harmony."

Bryce laughed. "I am long beyond love, let alone for a young princess. She must be a teen."

"Sixteen," Dawn agreed.

"Younger than my youngest granddaughter. Believe me, I know better than to get romantic about a child."

Dawn glanced at the skeleton. "Picka, dear, please bring a mirror."

A mirror?

The skeleton got up, walked to a wall, and took down a hanging mirror. He brought it to Bryce. He looked in it, and was amazed.

It did not reflect his face. Instead it showed a pretty girl with brown hair and eyes, as well as a matching brown dress. "Well, hello Harmony," he breathed.

She looked startled. "Who are you?"

She had heard him! What magic was this?

"It is a magic mirror, of course," Dawn said. She raised her voice. "Harmony, this is Bryce from Mundania. He will be courting you."

"He will be what?" Harmony asked, astonished and not entirely pleased.

"I suspect it is a Demon wager to select your ideal man," Dawn said. "You being the only remaining unattached princess of your generation. It is the most feasible way to account for the rather special effects I have noted associated with Bryce Mundane here. There may be other suitors. We must meet in a few days to consider this."

"I'm not courting any teen girl!" Bryce protested.

"Well, nobody asked you to," Harmony retorted. "I'm not ready for courting or marriage yet, and certainly not to any Mundane."

"But he loves you," Dawn said.

"I do not!" Bryce snapped. Then paused, frozen in place.

Because he did love her. Utterly, hopelessly, eternally. He didn't know her, but he was overwhelmed with romantic passion for her.

Dawn had made her point. That was some imprinting.

Picka removed the mirror and the contact was broken. But Bryce was left with his sudden love.

"And you, Rachel, seem to have picked up some of the magic because you were with Bryce when he invoked it. You are now young and healthy, you can speak, and you have a more subtle magic talent of finding useful things. You have been imprinted with love for a dog you have not yet met, though your loyalty to Bryce might be considered similar."

Bryce exchanged a glance with Rachel. Both of them were confused but impressed.

"What's this about a Demon bet?" Picka asked.

"It is the way they operate," Dawn explained. "They like to make wagers on random things, such as how a given mortal will react to a particular stimulus. Such as this."

"So Bryce may have been summoned from Mundania to compete for the hand of Princess Harmony, who is the only one of that naughty trio who remains unspoken for."

"Exactly. Princesses are not expected to remain on the market long."

"That's right," Picka agreed. "Melody will marry Anomy in due course, and Rhythm will marry Cyrus Cyborg. That was quite a scandal when they got together. She was only twelve."

"But we have to give the little twerps some credit," Dawn said. "They did save Xanth from Ragna Roc."

"So Harmony is left," Picka concluded. "A suitable focus for a Demon contest."

Bryce had been tuning out of their dialogue, caught up in the marvel of his sudden love, but this brought him back. "What is a Demon?" Because, oddly, he heard the capital.

"Demons are immensely powerful spirits associated with assorted galaxies, planets, moons, or substances," Dawn said. "For example, the whole of the magic land of

Xanth derives from the trace leakage of the magic of the Demon Xanth who snoozes deep below the surface. The leakage from the Demon Earth is experienced on that world as gravity. Demons seldom pay attention to the endeavors of mortals, but they do vie for status by making wagers that sometimes involve the unpredictable actions or reactions of mortals. You appear to have become one of those. Your entry to Xanth was facilitated, and you were given certain things you will need, such as youth and a magic talent, plus the imperative of courting Harmony. Your entry at this place was probably to be sure you received some necessary background information promptly, so you would not get eaten by a dragon before you got started. So your presence here is no coincidence. If that is the case, the Demon who selected you will not play any further part in your life. He or She will merely watch, and win or lose based on your performance."

"I'm a toy of a supernatural spirit?"

"Yes, in essence."

"But I don't believe in the supernatural," he protested.

Both Dawn and Picka laughed. "You'll get over that soon enough," the skeleton said.

Indeed, if this was not a dream, there was plenty of evidence for the supernatural, beginning with the animated talking skeleton. "I just realized that it probably was not the yellow box with the three items that changed me," Bryce said, working it out. "The instructions were merely labels, a protocol signaling my readiness to participate. The youthening, magic talent, and love for Princess Harmony were all done by the Demon when I spoke the magic words. Because Rachel happened to be in the vicinity at that moment, she was affected too, entering Xanth with me, getting youthened to a lesser degree, and getting the magic talent of being able to speak the words she knew."

"Exactly," Dawn said.

"So assuming that I must participate, regardless of my choice in the matter, what is my best course of action?"

"You are sensible," Dawn said. "You both should take a few days to familiarize yourself with Xanth and its local customs, as well as learning to use your talent effectively. Then you should go to see the Good Magician Humfrey, who will advise you how to proceed. I suspect he won't charge his usual exorbitant fee, considering that this must be a Demon incident."

"What exorbitant fee?" Bryce asked warily.

"He normally charges a year's service, or the equivalent," Picka said.

"A year's service! I just want to go home!"

"Do you?" Dawn asked gently.

And Bryce realized that he had nothing to return to except old age, illness, loneliness, and death. "No. I don't know what I really want." He looked at Rachel. "Do you?"

She wagged her tail. "No."

"You want to relive your life, this time making better decisions," Dawn said. "This is your chance."

"I suppose it is," Bryce agreed, amazed. "Crazy as it seems."

"And to do that, you need to remain here in Xanth and perform your Demon-inspired task."

Bryce sighed. "This is the kind of channeling I would prefer to avoid. Throughout my mundane life, others made key choices for me: my mediocre residence, my indifferent schooling, my dull job, even really my wife. Oh, she was a good woman, and I loved her, I'm not complaining about that, but I really did not choose her myself. My family thought she'd be good for me and guided me rather forcefully toward her. They were right, but it would have been better if I had been able to make my own decision. Now some Demon is channeling me similarly, and some Good Magician, and some teenaged princess. Who knows, I might have loved her on my own, if I could ever get over the immense disparity in our ages and stations, but I wasn't given the chance. I was potioned or magicked into artificial love. Where are my choices? What is the point, as far as my personal life is concerned?"

"He's got a point," Picka said. In that moment Bryce found himself liking the skeleton.

Dawn frowned as if addressing a willful child. "In Mundania, even if you had been granted complete free will, your choices would have been severely limited. You would have had to choose a residence similar to the one you had, and get an education similar to the one you did, and labor at a job similar to the one you got, and you would have had to marry a woman who might not have been as good as the one your family found for you. So if you could live your Mundane life over, what would you do, really?"

Bryce looked at her. "You don't come across like the starlet model you resemble. You are making uncomfortable sense."

"I have had my own struggles with realism," she said with a wan smile. "I did manage to break the mold that my royalty and appearance set for me, to a degree. I married for love rather than status, unlike my sister Eve. That's why I wed Picka."

They were married? Oh yes, she had said so before. "If I may ask, is it usual for a princess and a skeleton to marry?"

"No. And that is the point. The constraints on a princess are considerable, but I managed to find a way to express myself regardless. You can do the same."

"I can?"

"You are faced with a new situation, with new rules. Learn the rules, then discover how you can forge your own way despite them. Isn't that what real choice is?"

He nodded. "I suspect it is. And if I understand correctly, the first rule is that I must win the Princess Harmony if I want to remain here in Xanth for any length of time. If I fail, my Demon sponsor will have no further use for me."

"There are worse fates than marrying a pretty princess. Once that chore is accomplished, you should be able to choose the rest of your life more freely. Harmony is not a domineering girl, though she can be mischievous. And if you fail, having tried your best, chances are your Demon sponsor will simply leave you where you are, here in Xanth, and forget about you. Then you will truly be able to live your life over. But if you deliberately fail, you could face the wrath of an angry Demon." She shuddered evocatively.

It was a persuasive case. "And most of my choices will be more subtle personal ones, such as how I treat others. I am beginning to like this game."

"However, Xanth has its darknesses," she cautioned him. "Do not take anything here for granted until you understand it. You will need guidance."

"I surely will," he agreed. "But I'm not sure who will relish the task of guiding me."

"Woofer and Tweeter will show you around," Dawn said.

"Who?"

A large dark mongrel dog entered the room, with a brownish parakeet perched on his head. "Woof!" he said.

"Tweet," the bird added.

Introduction enough. "Hello Woofer, Tweeter. I am Bryce, from Mundania, and this is Rachel."

Woofer eyed Rachel. "Woof!"

Bryce could have sworn that Rachel blushed, and a little heart-shaped dog bone sailed out from her head, though that was of course impossible. Or was it? Woofer must be the dog she had been spelled into love with.

"They are from Mundania too," Dawn said.

"Oh?"

"They came with a Mundane family, which returned to Mundania. But later they rejoined us here in Xanth. They are among my closest friends."

"You will get to understand their speech before long," Picka said. "They are nice folk. You can trust them."

So he was being handed off to animals. But if this was one of the rules of this realm, he could handle it. "I shall. What's next?"

"Woof." The dog turned and dog-trotted out of the chamber, still carrying the bird.

Bemused, Bryce and Rachel followed. Evidently Rachel had no better notion how to handle her magic love than Bryce did. She was being appropriately diffident. The animals led them to an upstairs chamber where a bed was laid out. Beside it was a plush dog blanket. "Is this for us?" Bryce asked, surprised. Dawn had said he could be a guest here, but he hadn't thought it would be in the castle proper.

"Tweet." It sounded like yes. Was it his imagination?

"Picka said I would come to understand your speech. Did he mean that literally?"

"Woof." That was definitely a yes.

"And it is evident that you understand me. So where do we go from here?"

"Tweet." And this time it sounded like "First shower and change."

So he did. Rachel waited, not needing to do those things. There was a very nice bathroom, complete with a well-appointed shower. He stripped and used it, feeling invigorated. When he emerged and toweled himself dry he paused to gaze at himself in the full-length mirror.

He was a supremely healthy young man, more fit and muscular than he had ever been in real life. But would it last? He decided to take the best possible care of this new body. It did look like him, as he remembered, but better. The Demon had given him an excellent start.

His old clothing was gone. In its place was a clean bright shirt and trousers, together with shoes. He put them on, and they fit perfectly, including the shoes, which were the most comfortable he could remember in ages. "It must be magic," he said.

"Woof."

He hadn't realized that the castle dog was right there. But why not? It wasn't as if he was desperate for privacy. Woofer must have been communing with Rachel.

He combed his hair, admiring his youthful features in the mirror. "A man could get to like being young," he murmured.

"Tweet."

"What, you two are youthened too?"

It turned out that they had indeed grown old in Mundania, but were returned to their young primes when they came back to Xanth. They did understand.

Woofer conducted him to a banquet hall where an impressive meal was laid out. "I really don't need anything half this fancy," Bryce protested. Then he saw the strange man. "Uh, have we met? I'm Bryce from Mundania."

The man smiled. "We have met. I am Picka Bone, your host."

"But Picka is a walking skeleton!"

"One of the conveniences of Caprice Castle is that we are able to alternate forms when we choose. Ah, here is Dawn."

Bryce turned to meet her—and discovered a female skeleton. "Uh—nice bones," he said uncertainly.

"Yes, I am Dawn," she said, possibly smiling. It was hard to tell with her barefaced skull. "And these are our children." She indicated a baby carriage containing an infant human baby and a similarly sized skeleton, side by side.

"My son Piton," Picka said proudly. "A chip off the old block, as it were."

"And my daughter Data," Dawn said. "A calculating female."

Then as Bryce watched, the skeleton boy became fleshly, and the fleshly girl became skeletal.

"They are learning early," Picka said.

So it seemed.

A very nice repast was invisibly served, the new platters appearing and the used dishes disappearing. Bryce tried to catch it happening, but somehow the changes were always just when he wasn't looking. Another convenience of the castle. Woofer and Tweeter had dishes of their own, similarly replenished. So did Rachel. Bryce could see that she was trying to mask it, but she loved being near Woofer.

"You said I would learn to understand Woofer and Tweeter soon," Bryce said. "I believe it is already happening, unless I am imagining it. They woof and tweet, and I understand whole sentences."

"It is true," Dawn agreed. She wasn't eating, as it seemed skeletons did not need to, but was tending to the babies. They were assuming human form for a gulp of milk from a bottle, then turning skeletal while the other took the bottle. They seemed to have the system worked out well. "When you feel fully conversant, you can go out punning with them, as practice in Xanth."

"Punning?"

"Collecting puns," Picka explained. "This is what we do here at Caprice Castle. Xanth has entirely too many puns, so it is our job to fetch them in and store them safely so they can't escape and infest more terrain. It's a challenge."

What next? "I will do my best," he said bravely, and Rachel wagged her tail. And wondered what other surprises awaited him in this odd new land. Very little seemed to be as he might have expected.

"That will surely be good enough," Dawn said.

Bryce hoped so.

PUNFEST

In the morning after breakfast Bryce and Rachel reported for duty. "We have no idea how to proceed," he admitted.

"A couple of weeks of pun duty should have you more than ready to visit the Good Magician Humfrey," Dawn said brightly. She was in flesh again, radiantly beautiful, which seemed to be her normal state. Picka Bone stood nearby in his skeletal mode.

"I am not clear on this. Exactly why do I need to see this magician?"

"He will enable you to define your Heroic Quest," Dawn explained patiently.

Bryce smiled. "I'm no hero." He was distracted by a vision of her doing something he didn't understand. It was his left-eye future vision. So he closed that eye.

"You don't have to be," she was saying. "You simply have to tackle the Quest, so as to become worthy of the hand and heart of Princess Harmony."

"Oh, that," he agreed. "The teen girl. I think I should simply leave her to a more worthy suitor."

An expression hovered in the vicinity of Dawn's face that was deceptively similar to mischief. "You do not wish to pursue her?"

"Apart from the magic love spell, which I assume will wear off in due course, no. She's younger than my youngest granddaughter."

Dawn took his hand in hers. Hers was like a caress of an angel, wondrously cool and delicate. "If she holds your hand like this, and beseeches you to reconsider?"

"No. It simply makes no, if you'll excuse the term, mundane sense."

"And if she embraces you like this," Dawn asked, putting her arms around him, "will you still deny her?"

He was abruptly conscious of her formidable feminine appeal. Never in his life had he held a woman as lovely as this. "Common sense says I must." His unbelievable left-eye vision was coming true. He determinedly tuned it out, but he couldn't stop the following reality.

"And if she kisses you like this?" She kissed him on the mouth. Pastel-colored light shone and music sounded. He seemed to be floating, conscious mainly of her divine lips on his.

It took him two and a half moments—it seemed that such things could be quantified in this magic realm—to recover his physical footing and his emotional equilibrium. He realized that he had not imagined the music; the skeleton had removed his clavicles and was using them to play the "Wedding March" on his ribs. These folk kept surprising him! "I will politely explain why it would not be fair to either of us."

Her features seemed to shift, coming to resemble those of the princess he had seen in the mirror, complete with big brown eyes, lustrous brown hair, and a cute little crown. It was of course another illusion, but an effective one. "Please, Bryce dear, marry me."

He steeled himself, playing the role. He felt he had to, to make his point. "Princess, I can't do that."

Big tears ran down her cheeks. "But I love you!"

The love spell smote him. He felt himself melting. He wanted to hold her, reassure her, agree to anything she wanted. That would doom his resolve. Only the fact that he knew this was an act, and that it wasn't really Harmony, prevented him from capitulating. "But she's unlikely to choose me," he said somewhat lamely.

Dawn reappeared. "But now you know you must do your best to win her, and not merely to secure your place in Xanth. That love spell will not relinquish its hold until you complete your Quest. If she selects another suitor, then the spell will dissipate and you will be free."

"Then I will be free," he agreed, accepting that he was truly bound. The Demon had not brought him here and given him a magic talent without making sure he would perform. Meanwhile he focused on what his right eye saw, to avoid further confusion. He was getting better at that.

"You can control your second sight," Dawn said, understanding his thought because she was still in contact with him. "Simply utter a spot personal spell: Second Sight Tune Out. You will have to do that once each morning, and it will not bother you for that day. When you expect to need it, merely tell it to Tune In."

"It's that easy?" he asked, surprised.

"For you, yes. But you should practice with it, become comfortable with it, because it can save your life."

"When I have time," he agreed. He concentrated on his left eye. "Second Sight, Tune Out." The shadowy image faded. His eyesight was normal again.

"Tune it in whenever you are in any kind of new or challenging situation," Dawn said. "So as to have its full benefit."

"I will. Thank you."

"Now for your first day collecting puns," she said, immediately businesslike. "This will be perplexing at first, so I will assign a castle maid to assist you."

"Oh, I don't want to be any trouble."

"She finds castle housework supremely boring. She is more than glad to go with you." She made a moue. "Also, there are dragons, and other dangers for the unwary."

Because this was a magic land. "Oh. In that case, yes, I'm sure I can use the help."

"Mindy," Dawn said without raising her voice.

A young woman entered the chamber, evidently alert for just such a summons. "Yes, ma'am?" She was of average height but somewhat pudgy. Her hair was blond, and she wore glasses, the first glasses he had seen in Xanth.

"This is Melinda, or Mindy to her friends." Dawn turned to the girl. "You will go out with Bryce here, and assist him in punning, and in adapting to the Land of Xanth."

"Adapting?" Mindy asked, glancing shyly at Bryce.

"He is Mundane, and unfamiliar with our ways, so will need constant guidance at first."

"Mundane!" Mindy exclaimed.

"Sorry about that," Bryce said apologetically.

"*I'm* Mundane!" Mindy said, suddenly friendly. "Or I was, until I came to Xanth a few months ago. I know all the tricks Xanth has for a newcomer, because I walked into them myself." Then she looked embarrassed. "Was I talking too much? Sometimes I do that."

"No, no Melinda!" Bryce said. "You're ideal. When I blunder, you will understand." Also, he realized, she was not a beautiful princess, so he would be more comfortable and feel free to ask her questions and talk with her.

"I sure will," she agreed, smiling. She had a nice smile that began with her eyes and extended down to her mouth. "Call me Mindy."

"Mindy," he agreed.

She turned to Dawn. "Thank you, Princess, for giving me this chance. I promise to keep him as safe as possible."

"I'm sure you will," Dawn said, with a faintly obscure expression. Bryce hoped there were not severe penalties for errors that ordinary servants might make.

"We will leave you to it," Picka said. He and Dawn departed, leaving Bryce alone with Mindy and the two dogs.

The girl was silent, shy again. That was understandable, because she didn't know him. He looked like a twenty-one-year-old young man who might be thoughtless or aggressive. He needed to ameliorate that.

"I may not look it, but I am eighty years old," he said. "It seems that magic made me young again. Think of me as someone's grandfather, essentially harmless. Because I am."

"Oh, they youthened you," Mindy said.

"Youthened, yes. It seems I am supposed to be a suitor for the hand of Princess Harmony, and my real age wouldn't do. It's not a role I sought or am comfortable with, but I seem to be obliged to fulfill it to the best of my ability. So perhaps you can appreciate the awkwardness of my position."

Mindy smiled. "I never was a grandfather, but I guess I can see it. I wouldn't like being a grandmother and having to court a teenaged prince."

"Exactly. So Princess Dawn was not fooling about my needing guidance."

"I guess not. I'll help you all I can." She smiled. "And I'm twenty. You really are of my grandfather's generation."

"Thank you." She seemed to be more at ease now. "But before we start, there's something I'd like to do, if you don't mind," he said. "I rode my trike here, but it didn't make it inside the castle. I'm afraid it wrecked outside the wall. I'd like to check it, and repair it if I can. I might be able to use it here, and if I can't, at least I can give it a

decent retirement as a loyal machine." Then he paused as
Mindy had. "I'm foolish that way. I personalize things. I
don't like to mistreat objects any more than animals or
people."

"That's all right," Mindy said. "Machines have feelings
too, here in Xanth. Some of them are characters. Like Com
Pewter. Some things, too, like Fracto the malignant cloud."

Bryce decided not to ask about the odd entities she
mentioned; he would surely pick up such information in
due course if it was relevant to his situation. "So if we
can perhaps walk around the castle to see if my tricycle
is there . . ."

"Oh, yes," she agreed. "Just follow Woofer."

Woofer seemed to have been chatting in canine language with Rachel. Now he jumped up and led the way
out of the chamber. They followed him through a minor
labyrinth of halls, stairways, and rooms, and soon emerged
from the castle.

"If it is here, it should be near the dungeon door," he
said. "The door loomed so quickly I crashed right into it.
Or through it. I don't really understand what happened,
as I don't seem to be bruised, and neither does Rachel."

"Caprice Castle admitted you," Mindy explained. "It
is very choosy, and no one can enter unless it wishes it. It
must have known you were sent by a Demon."

"There's that capital again. Is that significant?"

"Oh, yes! Regular demons are mainly nuisances, like
Metria, but Demons are vastly more powerful."

A puff of smoke appeared before them, roiling rest-
lessly. "Did I hear my cognomen?"

"Your what?" Bryce asked, startled. He was talking to
an animated cloud?

"Appellation, nomenclature, personage, denomination,
alias—"

He got the gist. "Name?"

"Whatever," the cloud agreed irritably. It expanded and formed into the shape of a marvelously sultry woman whose scanty clothing was two sizes too tight. "I am the Demoness Metria, just now summoned. Who are you?"

He tried not to stare, with imperfect success, as this new young body was highly attuned to feminine charms. Two of those charms seemed about to burst out from her over-taxed halter. "Bryce, from Mundania. I just arrived here."

"That explains that," the demoness agreed. She turned to Mindy. "And who are you?"

"I am Melinda, also from Mundania, six months ago. I work here."

Metria shook her head so that her long hair flung out and dissipated into smoke at the fringe. "I should check Caprice more often, but it keeps me out except by invitation. But naming me is an implore."

"A what?" Bryce asked.

"Beseech, appeal, supplicate, entreat, plead, petition—"

"Invitation?"

"Whatever. So I got an avenue. What's your business here?"

"That's not your business, Metria," Mindy said sharply.

The demoness eyed her appraisingly. "So you have been warned about me."

"Yes. I wasn't supposed to say your name, but I forgot. Now go away before you get me in trouble."

"Nuh-uh, girl. You can't get rid of me as readily as you can invoke me. Now that I'm here, I mean to fathom all coverts."

Bryce opened his mouth. "Don't ask her!" Mindy snapped. "She uses her speech impediment to draw innocent people in."

"Her what?"

"Undisclosables," the demoness said. "Undivulgeables, clandestine, hidden, hush-hush, confidential—"

"Secrets?" Bryce asked.

"Whatever," Metria agreed crossly.

"He wasn't asking you about your word," Mindy said.

"That's right," Bryce agreed. "I was asking about your speech impediment. You seem to have a considerable vocabulary. Why can't you get the right word on your own?"

"I got stepped on by a sphinx eons ago," Metria said. "It fractured me into three parts: D Mentia who's a little crazy—" She re-formed into an even more provocative form, a demoness wearing a tight polka-dot bodice whose dots lacked material, and no skirt.

Bryce heard a snap by his ear, and found a hand before his eyes. "What happened?" he asked, confused.

"She flashed you with her naughty panties and you freaked out," Mindy said. "I just brought you out of it. It happens to men, not usually women. Don't look directly at her."

Bry : obediently gazed over the demoness's head. "Seeing panties does that?"

"You bet it does, chump," Mentia said. "You really are new here, aren't you!"

"I really am. You were telling me about the sphinx."

"And to the young Woe Betide," Mentia said, and formed into a cute little girl. "Who honors the Adult Conspiracy."

"The what?"

"I thought you'd never ask," the child said. "It's the Adult Conspiracy to Keep Interesting Things from Children. I'm not allowed to know any bad words, or exactly how people signal the stork, or anything else interesting. It's unfair!" Her little face screwed up into tears, which danced before her before splatting into the ground.

"Get on with it," Mindy said with resignation.

"And to Metria, whose vocabulary caught the brunt of it," Metria said, reappearing. "It's always the right word that's lost. Anything else you want to apprehend?"

"No!" Mindy said sharply before Bryce could ask. "No, he doesn't. Now go, or I'll call Princess Dawn."

"You wouldn't dare," Metria said.

Mindy opened her mouth and inhaled.

"Oh, bleep," the demoness said, and faded out.

"Woofer, is she really gone?" Mindy asked.

Woofer sniffed the air. "Woof!"

"No," Rachel translated.

"That's what I thought. You can't trust that demoness any which way. I'm calling Princess Dawn." She took another breath.

"Woof."

"Now gone," Rachel said.

Bryce was learning things almost too rapidly to assimilate. Treacherous demonesses who flashed panties, the Adult Conspiracy, suspicious speech impediments. This truly was a different realm.

"We were looking for your tricycle," Mindy said.

Woofer, reminded, resumed motion. They walked around the outside of the castle. And there, before the big wood dungeon door, lay the trike, overturned.

Bryce greeted it like an old friend. "Are you all right?" he asked, setting it back on its three wheels. "Let me try you." He settled down on the seat and put his feet to the pedals. The machine rolled forward.

It was working! He pedaled on around the next curve of the castle wall.

And charged into a patch of sand and brush he hadn't seen. He was about to wreck again. Right when he could have used his future vision, he had suppressed it, and been caught by surprise. He needed to learn to manage it better. "Tune in," he muttered belatedly. The slightly out-of-sync left eye came on. He ignored it, except for a low-level awareness in case it should show anything alarming.

But the trike continued on through the brush without pause. It was handling it! It should have stalled in the sand and foliage, but it moved on as if still on pavement. He steered it around and pedaled back to where Mindy and the two dogs waited. "Amazing," he exclaimed. "Not only is it undamaged, it can handle off-road terrain."

"It must have caught some of the magic you and Rachel did," Mindy said. "So you could use it here."

"That Demon must really want me to succeed!"

"Demons can do magic ordinary folk can't," she agreed.

"So I'll use it in the field," he said. "It's really nice to have this bit of Mundania with me."

"Let me fetch a carpet, and we will head out punning," Mindy said. "Wait here." She hurried back into the castle.

"What use would a castle carpet be out in the field?" Bryce asked.

"Woof."

"You will see," Rachel translated, amused. There must have been an explanatory paragraph in that single woof.

In three and a half moments Mindy was back, floating about a yard above the ground. She was sitting on a small carpet that seemed to move under its own power. Tweeter Bird was perched on her shoulder.

"A magic flying carpet!" Bryce exclaimed.

"I'm Mundane," Mindy reminded him. "I don't have magic of my own. Maybe eventually I will, but for now I have to borrow magic to get along. Princess Dawn lets me use it for punning."

"I see," Bryce said, impressed anew.

"You will need a pun bag," she said, handing him a cloth bag with a drawstring closure. There were several more piled on the carpet.

"Thank you." He put the bag in one of the panniers at the rear of the trike.

"Show the way, Tweeter," Mindy said.

"Tweet." The bird flew up, spiraled several times, then oriented on a distant patch of trees.

"You don't know where the puns are?" Bryce asked. "I thought you had been doing this before."

"Yes, and yes. We have been punning every day, but each day we have to explore anew to locate the thickest pun fields."

"Oh—because you deplete an area and have to move on?"

"No."

"Because the pun fields move?"

"No." She was amused.

Faintly annoyed, he let it go. He would surely find out soon enough.

Tweeter returned. "Tweet!"

"Oh, no," Mindy said. "That bad?"

"Tweet," the bird agreed.

She sighed. "We'll just have to get on it. Lead on, Woofer."

Woofer bounded out in the direction from which Tweeter had returned. Mindy's carpet followed. Bryce and Rachel paced her.

"I feel there is something I should tell you," Mindy said as she floated beside him. "I don't really belong here."

"Neither do I, of course. Were you summoned by a Demon also?"

"No. I committed suicide."

"You what?"

"Self-murder, hara-kiri, seppuku, suttee, croaking—"

"Metria, get out of here!" Mindy flared.

Now Bryce saw a small dark cloud pacing them. The verbally handicapped demoness had reappeared.

"You're not in or near Caprice now," the cloud said. "You can't repel me."

"Bleep!"

"Oh, what you said! And you're supposed to be a nice girl."

"Look, this is not my business," Bryce said. "Let's change the subject."

"We'd better," Mindy said. "Look—here come Midrange and Erin. They often help with the punning. It makes it easier when there are supportive friends."

"They're boring," the cloud said, and faded out.

Bryce saw the two cats. One was a large dark mongrel male, the other a lean tawny female. They came to greet Mindy and Bryce with a Meow and Mew.

"This is Bryce, from Mundania," Mindy answered their evident query. "He will be helping with the puns, as long as he can stand it."

Satisfied, the cats moved on.

"Midrange?" Bryce inquired. "That's an odd name for a cat."

"They were originally three pets in their family, Woofer, Tweeter, and Midrange. As in a mundane sound system."

He laughed. "That does make sense."

"Then Midrange met Erin, and split. The three remain close friends, however. Now maybe it's Woofer's turn." She glanced across to where the two dogs were running side by side. Rachel was staying close to Bryce, but evidently did not mind Woofer's company.

"You were telling me something," Bryce reminded her. "But I have to say, you certainly don't seem dead to me. Were you speaking figuratively?"

"Not exactly," she said uncomfortably. "It's that I died in Mundania, and am here only because of magic. So in that sense I'm not really real."

"I was near the end of my life in Mundania," he said. "I had only a year or so left to live. Maybe I did die there, pushing my feeble limits, so I'm really dead too. I don't know." He smiled. "I want you to know I have no prejudice against dead folk."

"I'm not sure you understand. I am not what I seem."

She seemed to have a certain nagging uncertainty or inferiority complex. His grandfatherly experience came into play. "Can we stop moving for a moment?"

"If you wish." Her carpet slowed to a halt.

He braked his trike and got off. He walked across to Mindy. He put his arms about her shoulders as she sat on the carpet, and kissed her on the forehead. "You are who you are, Melinda, inside. I am satisfied with that, and you should be too. Okay?"

She looked stunned. "Okay," she agreed faintly.

"Now let's get on to the doubtlessly serious business of collecting puns."

"Kiss me again."

He paused. Had she misunderstood his gesture? "I have a granddaughter about your age. I was trying to reassure you as I did her on occasion. I forgot for the moment that I am now in a young body. I did not mean to offend or alarm you."

"I understand. Kiss me again."

This seemed odd, but if that was what she wanted, it was simple enough. He leaned down to kiss her forehead again, but this time she lifted her face and caught him with her lips. They kissed mouth to mouth.

He drew back, shaken by the sudden impact. That had been no granddaughterly kiss!

"Thank you," she said. "Now I am reassured."

"Uh, yes," he agreed, disgruntled. She had to know he had not had any designs on her, because he was in love with the Princess Harmony. Why had she kissed him woman to man? How could that reassure her?

He concluded that she didn't like to be patronized, so had sought to set him back. She had done it. He would not treat her like a child again.

He got back on his trike, and they resumed forward motion. Soon they came to a shallow valley surrounded by trees.

Rachel halted. "Umph," she grunted, pointing with her nose.

"She is a pointer," Bryce said, halting. "I'd better see what she has found." He stopped and got off the trike.

The dog was pointing to a small path that wound into a section of bushes and spaces. When he set foot on the path, she moved along beside him.

"We will let you experience it yourself," Mindy said, standing back with Woofer. "When you find a pun, stuff it in the pun bag and move on."

"It is possible to handle puns physically?"

"They generally have physical components."

Bryce shrugged and walked along the path. In barely a moment a twig fell on his shoulder. Rachel's head turned to point to it. "It's just a twig," he said, brushing it off.

The twig landed on the path and righted itself. "Humph!" it said, and walked away.

"Walking stick," Rachel said, pointing again at it with her nose. "Pun."

Oh. Bryce reached down, caught the twig in his hand, and put it in the pun bag. One down.

Bryce walked on. A swarm of flat, round bugs flew up. Rachel pointed her nose at them. There had to be a pun. Then he saw one that looked like a small zipper. "Button flies!" he exclaimed, holding the pun bag open. Obediently they flew in, commanded by his identification. "Zipper fly." And the zipper followed them in. Two down, maybe three.

He resumed his walk, and soon Rachel pointed again. It was a swarm of ants wielding hammers and saws, cutting wood to build a tiny village. "Carpenter ants," he said, and put the bag down for them to enter.

"You're catching on," Mindy said.

"As puns go, these are nothing special," he remarked. "I was never good with puns, but these are pretty obvious. Why do folk regard them as mind-rotting?"

Rachel shrugged. So did Mindy.

They walked on. Soon Rachel pointed again. It looked like a giant lima bean, the biggest he had ever seen. There were indents on the side that looked like steps rising to the top, where there was a pile of what looked like saddle blankets.

"This one I don't get," he said. "Is it a has-bean?"

"No," Rachel said.

"Then what kind of a pun is it?"

"Don't know."

Mindy kept silent. Bryce had the feeling that she was waiting for him to run afoul of a really egregious pun.

"It wouldn't fit in the bag anyway." He tried to walk on by, but the bean blocked the path and there were brambles on either side blocking his progress. It seemed he had to fathom one pun before going on to another.

Bryce considered. "Well, let's get to the top of this," he decided. He put his toes in the indents and carefully mounted the steps. He discovered that he was being unnecessarily cautious; his young healthy body had no trouble handling this feat. Still, he was not about to become careless; body notwithstanding, his mind was old and experienced.

He got to the top and sat on the blankets, which roughly resembled a saddle and were comfortable. But he still didn't see the pun.

"Come on up, the weather's fine!" he called to Rachel.

She ran up the steps, scrambling, and made it to the top, joining him on the saddle blankets.

"Giddy up!" Bryce said.

The bean broke away from its vine, sprouted little root-like legs, and started moving.

"Oh for pity's sake," Bryce said, finally getting it. "It's a Carry Bean! It must take root in a new spot once it has carried someone to where he wants to go."

Rachel made a sound like upchucking something foul from her throat. They had encountered a really foul pun.

But how was he to get it into the pun bag? There had to be a way.

They passed a large plant that bore sunflower-like disks. No, they were baked pies! Curious whether they were actually edible, Bryce reached for one.

"No!" Rachel barked, nosing his hand away.

"No? What's the matter with it?" But his left eye was warning him too.

Then the pie he had almost taken exploded. Rats flew out, landing on the bean. One nipped at Bryce's left hand.

"No you don't!" he cried, making a fist and knocking the rat off the bean. "That's my wedding ring! What are you, a pirate, trying to steal gold?"

Then he groaned. "Oh, no! That's sickening."

Rachel looked at him.

"I got the confounded pun," he said. "These aren't pirates. They are pie rats, that lurk in pies until something worth stealing comes along." He took a breath. "Pie Rats of the Carry Bean."

Rachel gazed at him as if he had emitted a noxious stench.

But now the bean was shrinking, bearing them down to the ground. He quickly opened the pun bag. "In!" he commanded. "Pie Rats and Carry Bean."

The bean and rats entered. Two more puns had been captured.

"I think this is enough for now," Bryce said. "I have come to understand why pun collectors suffer burnout."

They walked back along the path to rejoin the others, who had stood back. "I got a bellyful," Bryce called to Mindy, heaving up the bag.

"We thought you might," Mindy replied. "Do you want to quit now?"

"Quit? Now, we've barely started. There must be dozens more puns in need of suppression."

"Hundreds," she agreed. "If you have the stomach for it."

"Let's find out." Bryce did not care to admit how sickening that last pun had proved to be.

Now Mindy joined him, wading into the thicket of puns. But almost immediately she got caught up in vines that lifted her steadily upward and forward. "Escalate Her!" she cried, opening her bag. The vines crawled in and she landed back on the ground.

Meanwhile Bryce was attacked by a hedge that had sharp shears on its extremities. "Hedge-clippers," he said, and packed it in.

Woofer dug in the ground. "Woof!"

Mindy went over and looked. "I recognize that," she said. "I knew a girl once who could make stone out of sand. One of her creations must have wound up here. Sand Stone." She packed it into her bag.

Rachel abruptly retreated in fear. Bryce checked. It was an old bottle of shampoo. Then he got it. "Flee Shampoo." He put it in his bag, and Rachel relaxed. Naturally, as a dog, she had been terrified of it.

Bryce approached a large-trunked tree. It did not seem to be made of wood, and it also seemed to be chewing something. What could it be?

"Gum Tree," Mindy called.

Oh. A tree made of gum that chewed things. What else? He opened his bag, and the tree shrank and went in.

Then Mindy found a translucent jacket. She tried it on, and it accommodated to the contours of her body. "Cool," she said. Then she frowned. "Uh-oh. It's a Water Jacket." And the water lost its cohesion and soaked her. Bryce politely refrained from looking. But she commanded it into the bag, and she was dry again. She had after all had some experience collecting puns.

Bryce approached what looked like a huge onion. It had to be a pun. He peeled off a thin layer, and discovered a plaque on its side saying TERMS OF LOANS. That gave him the clue. "It's a Credit Onion!" It condensed to normal onion size and entered his bag.

"Ouch!" Mindy exclaimed. "Something bit me!"

"I hope it's not poisonous," Bryce said, approaching her.

"What gives you the right to have an opinion?" she demanded sharply.

That gave him the clue. "It's a Heretic. It makes you question another person's point of view."

They got it in the bag, and Mindy's bad attitude faded.

Woofer found a pair of human shoes. Bryce tried them on, cautiously, and was immediately ready to embark on a spiritual journey. "Souls!" he said. "Their souls are heeled!"

Rachel pointed. There was a mossy stone rolling down a slope. Or rather the slope was moving up, because no matter how much the stone rolled, it did not reach the bottom.

"That's an illusion, all right," Mindy said. "Because a rolling stone gathers no moss, and this one is entirely mossy. But is it a pun?"

They considered, and concluded that it wasn't. "So not absolutely everything in Xanth is a pun," Bryce said.

"Right. Some is merely crude humor."

Now they came to a pumpkin patch. No, they weren't exactly pumpkins; they had stupid smiley faces with eyes that winked. "Punkins," Bryce said. But they did not fade, so evidently he did not have the whole of it.

Then something else entered the patch. It looked like a chicken, but it was translucent. It was a chicken spirit, the ghost of a chicken. It moved through the patch, pecking at punkins, which flinched but weren't actually damaged because the chicken wasn't real. It flapped its wings and made a clucking sound.

Then Bryce caught on. "It's a poultrygeist! A noisy mischievous chicken spirit."

Mindy groaned. She was evidently getting close to her limit for the day.

At that point he was able to bag both chicken and punkins.

The path led to an ocean shore. Rachel pointed. There on the beach lay a saw. Bryce picked it up. It seemed ordinary. Where was the pun?

Then he got an idea. He took the saw to the water and started sawing. Sure enough, it cut through the water as if it were wood, and in due course he was able to lift out a wedge of water, leaving a hole in the sea. "Sea-saw," he explained, putting it in his bag.

Mindy and both dogs were looking faintly ill, but Bryce was enjoying this. He seemed after all to have a talent for identifying puns, not a magical one, just a mental one. Maybe this was another aspect of his entry into this weird world.

Rachel, seeing his determination to continue, pointed to another pun. This was a small house and garden, fenced, with a sign saying KEEP OUT—THIS MEANS YOU.

"That's clear enough," Bryce said. "But what's the pun?"

The dog shrugged. She did not know what the pun was, just that there was one there.

Bryce walked along the fence, which he discovered was barbed wire. Embedded in it at intervals were fruits, such as red cherries and green pineapples. He reached for a cherry.

"No!" Rachel exclaimed. "Bad!"

"Poisonous?"

"No." But she didn't know exactly what was bad.

Mindy came over. "Oh, don't touch that," she said. "It's a cherry. And next to it is a pineapple."

"So I noticed. What's so bad about such fruits?"

"In Xanth, they're explosive," she explained.

Oh. Cherry bombs and grenades. The proprietor *really* didn't want company. He moved on.

Rachel pointed to the sign by a little gate. GNOME ANNE. So the proprietor was a gnome, like a small person, who wanted to be alone. Still no pun.

Then a light bulb flashed over his head. He actually saw it. It represented his bright idea. "This is Gnome Anne's Land," he said. "No Man's Land."

He opened his bag, and the property closed in on itself and piled in. There wasn't really a gnome named Anne; it was all a pun.

It continued, as they encountered a group of animals having a party—party animals—until rain deer joined in, and it got rained out. There was a cat and a horse who tried to steal their things, a cat burglar and a horse thief.

Finally even Bryce had had enough, as his queasy stomach indicated. Their bags were full, and their patience exhausted. It was time to go home.

"You did very well," Mindy said.

"I was too often clumsy, and slow to catch on."

"I was way worse, my first day. It took me several days to recover my peace of mind. I had a bad case of pundigestion."

"That's a pun!"

"That's what happens when a person associates with puns. They infect her, and she starts emitting bad puns. Nobody could stand to be near me until I recovered."

Back at the castle, Bryce saw how Picka and Dawn carefully poured the bags into secure vaults and stored them in the dungeon. The magic of the castle prevented any puns from escaping. It had been a good day, and they had pretty well cleaned out the area.

"So you should be catching up on the job," Bryce remarked. "We did not leave many puns behind today."

Dawn hardly glanced at him. "There will be another day."

What did that mean? He decided to let it be. There was still too much to learn about this remarkable land, and he could well afford to learn it at its own pace.

"Mindy says you did well," Dawn continued as she worked.

"I tried," he agreed. "But without the help of the others I would have been sadly lost. Everything here is almost completely new to me."

"I'm sure you will soon adjust. If you have any questions, just ask me."

"Actually I do have one. I note that Mindy wears glasses, as she must have in Mundania. But no one else here does, and I no longer need them. Is there a reason?"

"Not a physical one. They are simply part of her personality. In time she may discard them, when she finally accepts that she no longer needs them."

"Thank you."

Thereafter the day was routine. He was glad to retire to his room with Rachel. He needed to sleep, not so much because he was tired; this young body was remarkably hearty. But because his mind needed to sort out the many things he had learned, so that he would function better tomorrow.

"Do you find this all as new and different as I do, Rachel?" he asked as he lay down.

"Yes," she agreed, and closed her eyes.

That was perversely reassuring.

3

TOUR

Next day they went out again, Bryce on his trike, Mindy on her little carpet, the two dogs afoot. But immediately Bryce paused, astonished. "Mountains!" he exclaimed, and Rachel shared his surprise.

"True," Mindy agreed. She seemed amused.

"They weren't here yesterday!"

"Yes they were. *We* weren't here yesterday."

"I don't understand."

She smiled. "Maybe we forgot to tell you something about Caprice Castle."

"It didn't change. The landscape did."

"Caprice travels," she explained. "It fades out at one location, and appears at another, carrying along everything within it. Picka and Dawn had an awful time catching it, before they persuaded it to accept them as residents. It seems to be somewhat random, but they can direct it when they choose. Mostly they let it travel as it likes." She looked around. "I'm not sure exactly where we are now, but it hardly matters. There will be puns."

"That's what Princess Dawn meant. I said we had cleaned out the puns, and she said there would be another day. This is another day, and we are where there will be more puns."

"That is true. Puns are all over Xanth, so we have to travel to get them all, or at least as many as we can. We'll never catch up completely, but at least we can detoxify things somewhat."

"So the castle travels. Live and learn."

"That we do," she agreed.

"Let's get to it," he said, resuming his pedaling.

Soon they came to a small lake in a mountain valley. There was a pier projecting into it. "Woof!" Woofer said.

Bryce looked. "There is a pun? All I see is an almost mundane scene."

Rachel went closer to the pier. She pointed at it with her nose.

"I don't get it," Bryce said.

"Neither do I," Mindy agreed. "But the dogs are seldom mistaken."

"What's the pun?" Bryce asked Rachel.

"Forgot I can talk," she said. "Sorry about that. The wharf."

He moved closer and inspected the planking. There was an eye. Farther along was a mouth. "It's a creature!"

"A mouse," Mindy agreed. "A big one."

"No, a rat," he said, the light bulb flashing over his head. "A huge rat in the shape of a pier. A wharf rat."

Mindy groaned, and both dogs howled. Bryce opened his bag and sucked in the rat.

The business of the day had begun.

They soon spotted another oddity. It was a large spiderweb that seemed to have eyebrows. This time Mindy got it first. "A Web Browser," she said, putting it in her bag.

The mountains gave way to hills. Some of them appeared to have wheels, so that they could move about.

"Rolling Hills," Bryce said, taking them in.

Then a group of socks came hopping toward them. "Sock Hop," Mindy said, catching them.

Beyond the mountains were a number of small settlements. "I don't trust this," Bryce said. "We're in a thick pun region—a pun thicket—and we can't be sure that anything we encounter is not a pun."

"I agree," Mindy said. "Let's examine them more closely."

They came to a sign. WELCOME TO N.

"That's a pun?" Bryce asked. He glanced at the dogs, but they just shrugged.

"It doesn't seem to be," Mindy said. "Ah, here are some direction signs pointing to different villages."

Bryce read them off. "Tice, Velop, Joy, List, Act, Able, Amor, Case. I still don't get it."

Mindy approached the first sign. "Oh, I want to go there!" she exclaimed. "It really attracts me."

"The path to Tice attracts you?"

"Yes! There's just something about it."

Now Rachel was pointing to the sign. There was a pun there.

Bryce got an awful groaner of an idea. "We can do it," he said. "But let's first examine the second sign."

"If you insist," she said impatiently. She walked to the next direction sign, Velop.

It extended to the sides and wrapped its edges about her. "Eeeek!" she screamed so piercingly that he heard all four E's.

He rushed to her assistance. "Envelop!" he cried, opening his pun bag.

The sign dissolved into mist and drifted into the bag.

"Thank you," Mindy said, disheveled but recovering. "But why did that word stop it?"

"These are all N words," Bryce said. "N Tice attracted you. N Velop enclosed you." He looked at the others. "N Joy will please you, N List will make you join it, N Act will do something else, as will N Able. You will really love N Amor, but get boxed in by N Case." As he spoke, the signs dissipated, their puns expended, and coursed into his open bag.

"N puns," she groaned. "And I fell for it."

"Such things aren't necessarily obvious, until a person gets the key."

"Now their villages are gone, too," she said. "I hope we didn't wipe out a lot of innocent people."

"They were illusion, to help set up their puns." He glanced back. "Except for the first sign, which it seems was just a sign."

"It's changed," she said.

"So it is," he agreed, surprised. For now it said WEL-COME TO V.

"I will collect these," she said, opening her pun bag. New direction signs had appeared, and she read each off in turn. As she did, the signs dissipated and floated obe-diently into her bag. "V Ear makes a person turn away. V Toe prohibits things. V Ickle—" She paused, not get-ting it immediately.

"Vehicle," Bryce said. "You can ride in it."

"Thank you. And V Gan will avoid all meat."

They waited, but the sign did not dissipate, and its vil-lage did not disappear. That was curious.

"Go on to the next," Bryce suggested.

But the next sign said N. "I thought we already han-dled that letter."

"Maybe it's the town of N in the V section," Bryce suggested. "V N."

"Or N V," she said. "Envy!"

Now the sign dissipated.

They had cleaned up all the puns except V Gan. Had they gotten it wrong?

"Could it be a real town, not a pun illusion?" Bryce asked.

"Why don't we go see." They walked down the path to the village. It did indeed seem real.

There were even people in it. An ordinary man and a lovely woman were sunning themselves in deck chairs near an outlying house. "Oh my gosh," Mindy breathed.

"A problem?"

"Not exactly. I recognize them. They're famous in Xanth. I will have to introduce you."

"As you wish." He had met so many people he doubted he would long remember two more.

Mindy forged ahead with unusual energy. "Hello!" she called. "I am Melinda, Mindy for short. A servant at Caprice Castle. Maybe you remember me."

The two looked at her, then at each other. "Maybe we do, Melinda," the man said.

"Mindy," the woman agreed.

"This is Bryce, recently from Mundania," Mindy said. "So I, as a former Mundane, am showing him around. We are collecting puns for storage in Caprice Castle."

"How do you do, Bryce," the man said. "I am Bink." Mindy, evidently flustered, had forgotten to introduce them to Bryce. Just how important were they?

"And I am Chameleon," the woman said. "In my pretty phase."

"You certainly are pretty," Bryce said.

The dogs, bored with this, settled down for a nap.

Bink smiled. "My wife is a woman of cycles. In the course of each month she gradually shifts from lovely and stupid to ugly and intelligent, passing through average in each respect. Today she is beautiful, but not much for dialogue."

"You like me better this way than when I'm smart," Chameleon said accusingly.

"I like you every way," Bink said, taking her hand and squeezing it. "In different ways."

"But you manage to keep your hands off me when I'm smart."

"We have been through this before, dear."

"Oh, have we? I'm sorry. I don't remember."

"Bryce was an old man in Mundania," Mindy said. "Now he's young. Maybe you could help him adjust."

"Ah," Bink said. "How old were you, Bryce?"

"Eighty," Bryce said. "Now I seem to be twenty-one."

"He's part of a Demon contest," Mindy said. "He has to compete for the hand of Princess Harmony. He is not easy with that."

"Ah, I see," Bink said. "Let me reassure you, Bryce. Age is no barrier."

"But she's only sixteen!" Bryce said. "I have granddaughters older than that."

Bink smiled. "So do I."

"He is the Princess Harmony's great-grandfather," Mindy said.

"But he can't be over thirty-five, if that."

"Thirty-four," Bink agreed. "And Chameleon is twenty-nine. But we were youthened over a decade ago. Our chronological ages are ninety-four and eighty-nine. We are of your generation, and beyond."

Bryce simply stared at them, having trouble believing this.

"This is Xanth, not Mundania," Mindy reminded him. "Youth happens here."

"We were twenty-one and sixteen when we were youthened," Bink said, gazing fondly at Chameleon. "The same age as you and our great-granddaughter Harmony."

"That seems right," Chameleon agreed.

"The princess and I have no relationship," Bryce said quickly. "It's just a game by the Demons. We won't be marrying."

Bink focused on him with renewed interest. "Because she rejects you, or you reject her?"

"Both, I'm sure. She's not interested in marrying anyone at present, least of all an old Mundane. And I know better than to get involved with a teen girl."

"But this teen girl is a princess."

"We don't have royalty where I come from, so I'm not much impressed. I have been imbued with an artificial love for her, otherwise I would have no interest at all."

"But you don't really know her," Bink said.

"I don't. But I suspect she's a spoiled creature, not my type at all regardless of age. And she would find me an old fogy regardless of my apparent age."

"The girls are Sorceresses," Bink said.

"There's more than one?"

"Harmony is one of triplets: Melody, Harmony, and Rhythm. They sing and play music to invoke their magic. Any one of them is as formidable magically as any other Magician or Sorceress. Any two of them square that power. The three together cube it. They tend to stay together, and sometimes they do marvelous things."

"They made Castle Maidragon," Chameleon said. "You must see that."

"And they tackled Ragna Roc," Bink said. "That was foolish, but showed real courage."

"We may see Castle Maidragon," Mindy said. "Searching out puns."

"I know nothing about it," Bryce said. "But the fundamentals remain. This is not a likely match."

"I am not sure of that," Bink said. "All five of my great-granddaughters are strong-minded and mischievous Sorceresses. No man is likely to oppose them long."

"Five?" Bryce asked. "I haven't yet assimilated three. I didn't know the princess had sisters."

"The other two are Dawn and Eve," Chameleon said. "Twins, cousins of the triplets."

"Dawn runs Caprice Castle," Bryce said. "I have encountered her."

"Did she tease you about Harmony?" Bink asked.

"She did," Bryce admitted. "She thinks that if Harmony should want me, I would be unable to resist her."

"Dawn is surely correct. It's her talent to know about any living thing."

Bryce shrugged. "It's academic. Harmony has no interest in me."

Bink and Chameleon exchanged another glance. "How can you be sure of that?" Bink asked.

"Well, it just makes sense. She'll have far more appropriate suitors. Why should she bother with me?"

Chameleon shook her head. "I am stupid now, but I can still manage Bink. Harmony may have more interest in you than you think."

"And no Sorceress is to be trifled with," Bink said. "You seem to have little notion of her potential."

"So maybe she's a nice girl," Bryce said, nettled. "Maybe she can do magic. But I don't see her out doing useful work like gathering puns. What use is she, really?"

Mindy seemed to choke.

Bink smiled. "Your assistant evidently knows Xanth better than you do. One does not question the use of a princess."

"And you don't want to annoy a Sorceress," Chameleon said.

"I guess it's my Mundane background," Bryce said. "I'm just not much impressed."

"That will change when you formally meet her," Chameleon said.

Bryce shrugged. "I can wait."

"We need to get on with our job," Mindy said. "Thank you for talking with us, Bink and Chameleon."

"It is no burden," Bink said. "We thought it would be nice staying in a village that uses no meat, but actually it's a bit dull."

V Gan. There was the confirmation of the name. Vegan. Bryce suppressed a groan.

"Do tell him more about Xanth," Chameleon said. "He needs to know, before he gets into trouble."

"That's why I'm along," Mindy said. "So far we haven't encountered any real dangers."

"Tangible ones, you mean," Bink said, giving her a hard look. "Keep his ignorance in mind lest he annoy you."

"I am," Mindy said.

They moved on. The dogs roused themselves and followed. "If I have annoyed you, I apologize," Bryce said. "When I spoke of teen girls, I was thinking of the princess, not you. You're twenty."

"I understand."

They came to a sandy spot. A number of what appeared to be human posteriors were sticking out of the sand. Rachel pointed at them. "Beach Bums," Bryce said, perversely glad to be back in business. He opened his bag, and the posteriors floated in, though one did make a dirty noise of protest.

They came to a wall that was covered with yowling cats. "I think I've got it," Mindy said. "Caterwaul." And wall and cats dissolved and entered her bag.

A large fly buzzed them. "Have you seen my son, the flyer?" it asked them.

"A talking fly?" Bryce asked.

"Magical," Mindy said. "And your dog is pointing."

Then he got it. Bryce groaned. "Pop Fly."

They encountered a copse of huge-trunked trees with patterns of tightly fitting boards. "Those look like beer barrels," Bryce said.

"They are. Except these ones are alebarrel trees. Tap them and you get ale. But they're standard; no pun there."

"Still, Rachel is pointing."

They followed the direction of the dog's point. It looked like a small mint plant growing next to one of the trees. "I don't recognize this," Mindy said.

"A mint," he said. "Next to an ale tree. An Ale Mint. Ailment?"

The plant dissolved. He had gotten it. But he remained dissatisfied. "May we take a break and talk?" he asked.

"By all means," she agreed, settling down with her back against one of the ale trees. "What is your concern?"

"This business of five princesses, all Sorceresses. I had no idea!"

"There's a reason. Back in the early days when Bink was young he managed to do the Demon Xanth a favor, and Xanth specified that all Bink's descendants would be Magicians or Sorceresses. And when Bink's son Dor married Magician King Trent's daughter Irene, all those descendants were royal. So when Dor's son Dolph married Electra, their daughters Dawn and Eve were both Princess Sorceresses. When Irene's daughter Ivy married Grey Murphy, their three daughters were all Sorceress Princesses too. It's really quite simple."

"Simple as relativity married to quantum mechanics!" Bryce said facetiously.

"As what?"

"Mundane theories of the fundamental nature of things that make no sense to the ignorant common man or to each other. You didn't encounter that in Mundania?"

"I guess I wasn't paying attention that school day," she said, blushing. "Please, tell me about them."

"I'm a common man. But that little I understand of it is that all things are relative, and this unifies three of the four fundamental forces in the universe, but not the fourth, which is gravity. Quantum mechanics addresses the fourth, but is incompatible with relativity. So the struggle has been to find a way to reconcile the two theories and make one unified Theory of Everything. It is mind-bendingly difficult even to conceive the problem, let alone the solution."

"It sounds like Demon magic."

"Maybe it is; that would explain a lot."

"Xanth gets its gravity via a cable connected to Mundania. Mundania gets its magic similarly from Xanth."

"There is magic in Mundania?"

"Very little actually. Things like the Rainbow."

"Oh, yes. Princess Dawn told me about that."

"Each Demon associates with a particular force. For example Demon Earth has Gravity, and Demon Xanth has Magic. So Mundanes don't know about Magic, but they ought to know about Gravity."

"Mundanes refuse to ascribe a magical basis for it."

"That must be their problem. What else could it be, except a kind of magic?"

"What else, indeed," he agreed wryly. He took a breath. "There's another thing."

"I'm here to help you as much as I can."

"One of the things I am skeptical about, as a non-magic Mundane, is coincidence. I don't believe in unlikely things working out conveniently. There's generally a reason."

"A reason?" she asked innocently.

"Caprice Castle travels randomly about Xanth, and we collect puns wherever it lands. We have not yet encountered anything dangerous, like a dragon or evil magic. So we go out in the country, and just happen to meet the helpful and informative great-grandparents of Princess Dawn, at whose castle I am staying, and of Princess Harmony, whom I am supposed to court. I doubt that was really coincidence."

Mindy gazed at him assessingly. "You're pretty savvy."

"It's just common sense. You led me to them, via a safe route."

She nodded. "Dawn told me to give you the Tour of Xanth without making a formal thing of it and without putting you in danger. Because there's a lot you need to know before you can hope to win the princess. It wouldn't be fair to throw you into that competition unprepared. You'd get killed, or flub it. I think that's why the Demon Earth arranged for you to go to Caprice Castle. He knew Dawn would take care of you."

"The Demon Earth arranged this? I suspect that does make sense. Certainly someone set it up, with the smelly message and all, and the way I landed right at Caprice instead of in a bog. But there must be a considerable random element, because I am hardly the ideal Mundanian for this quest."

"We are not equipped to comprehend the motives of Demons. They wager on the most devious and inconsequential things. They do what they do, and we just hope they don't mess us up too badly."

"So maybe I was selected *because* I'm an unlikely prospect? Too old and ignorant. Maybe that too makes sense."

"I don't think you're ignorant."

"Of magic," he said. "In that respect I'm an absolute dunce."

"But you are learning. You caught on about the guided tour."

"Even magic has to have some common sense. And Rachel," he said, and the dog's ears perked up. "She was selected too?"

"She must have been. To help you cope."

He reached out and patted the dog. "She does help."

"Woofer likes her too."

"Woofer's originally from Mundania," he said, remembering. "So he would naturally like a—a female dog from Mundania."

"A bitch," she agreed. "It's not a bad word here. Otherwise it would come out bleep."

"Bleep?"

"Try saying a bad word. Like if you dropped a rock on your toe."

"Bleep!" he said. And paused, surprised. "That wasn't what I said."

"There's a girl and two nice dogs present. That's why the Adult Conspiracy cut in."

"But they're adults and you're no child."

"I'm two days shy of twenty. Or was, before I came to Xanth. But you're right: I'm old enough. The Conspiracy extends only to age eighteen. So we don't know why it struck."

There had to be a reason. Bryce filed the minor mystery away for future reference. He had too many important things to learn without struggling with incidentals. "Well, let's get back to work, before any puns escape. I'm trying to earn my keep."

"Yes."

They resumed pun collecting. They soon encountered a stag walking disconsolately along the path. Rachel pointed.

Bryce approached the stag. "Why so sad?"

"My name is John," the stag said. "I try to court the does, but all I get is sad letters. It's depressing."

There had to be a pun here. What was it? "May I see one of the letters?"

"Here." The stag lifted a forefoot, and in the split of his hoof was a letter. Bryce took it, opened it, and read the first line. DEER JOHN.

Bryce groaned again. "It's a Dear John letter!"

The stag dissolved into vapor and entered the pun bag.

They came to a small cave. Rachel pointed, so they entered it. It seemed to be an animal's lair, with straw on the floor and blocks of metal stacked at the back. What was odd was that everything was yellow.

"A gold den!" Mindy exclaimed. "Golden."

The cave dissolved into her bag.

So it continued. When they got hungry they paused by a pie tree and ate fresh hot pies and drank milk from milkweed pods. By day's end they had full bags. "Do you know," Bryce said as they walked back toward the castle. "This may be an arranged tour, and the puns are egregious, but I find I am rather enjoying the scenery and the challenge. And your company. You are answering my questions without becoming impatient or superior."

"Thank you," she said, coloring. "I wanted to get away from the castle. I like adventure."

"This must be rather tame adventure for you, with the only challenge being the unriddling of puns."

"I like your company too," she confessed.

"You told me you committed suicide. Forgive me if this is not a question you wish to answer. Did you have a reason?"

"Not really. One of my friends did it, and then another, and I was depressed, and I just did it. Looking back now, I wish I had had more patience. Things weren't as bad as they seemed at the time, and if I had thought about the likely effect on others, such as my family and friends, I wouldn't have done it. I just wasn't thinking straight."

"Your situation differed from mine," Bryce said. "I didn't have many real family or friends left, so there weren't many to hurt. All I faced was increasing discomfort, pain, and certain death anyway. But it wasn't something I wanted to do."

"And here we both are in Xanth," she said. "It's better for me, and maybe for you too."

"Definitely better for me," he agreed. "Despite this foolishness with the princess."

They reached the castle, got their bags of puns processed in, and relaxed. Another day was done. Bryce hadn't gotten nauseous. He was adapting.

The next day there was an elegant castle in sight, with many turrets and flags. "That's Castle Maidragon, that the triplets made," Mindy said. "I understand King Trent and Queen Iris are visiting there now. They are the other great-grandparents."

"What's their magic?"

"He is a transformer. He can change any living thing into some other living thing. She's the mistress of Illusion. They ruled Xanth for a long time before retiring."

"They want to check me out, just in case?"

"Just in case," she agreed. "I think the way the other princesses found their partners was unsettling, so they are watching the last one more carefully." She looked around. "Where are the dogs?"

The dogs appeared. "We stay home," Rachel said. "If okay."

"Woof," Woofer agreed.

This was unusual. "You sure?" Bryce asked Rachel.

"No. But Dawn says."

"She wants me to get more experience on my own?"

"Yes." Rachel was obviously uneasy about this, but Princess Dawn's word was evidently law, here in Caprice.

Bryce shrugged. "So be it."

He and Mindy went out with their pun bags. "What's this experience I am supposed to get today?"

"I think you are supposed to learn to use your talent effectively."

"Oh, that. Then I'd better turn it on." He focused, as it were, on his left eye. "Second Sight, Tune In."

Immediately he saw a tree about twenty paces closer than it was. That was where he would be in ten seconds. He closed his left eye, then reopened it cautiously, schooling his mind to orient on the vision of his right eye. The alternate vision of the left eye remained, but now he ignored it. Only if it showed real danger would he take it seriously. Most of the time he neither needed nor wanted future vision. Ten seconds was after all pretty limited.

He saw a large yellow flower. No, it was a cup filled with butter. "Buttercup," he said, plucking it.

The cup dissolved, its pun expended. But now two of his fingers, actually his finger and thumb, the ones that had touched the cup, had become bars of butter. He could not use them in the normal manner.

"Oh, no, you've got butter fingers!" Mindy said.

The butter dissipated, and his normal digits returned. She had fathomed the second pun.

They walked on toward the other castle. There was a gully, which became a cleft in the land, deep and dark. They paused at the brink. "I've seen something like this before," Mindy said. "But I can't remember exactly what it was."

"That's because you're duller than an ogress, and almost as pretty," a voice called from the depth.

"Now I remember," she said. "It's a sar chasm."

The chasm evened out, becoming a mere dip in the ground. But now several monkeylike creatures appeared, evidently evicted from their home in the depth. "What a bag!" one cried. "That's not a bag, that's her face," another said. "And look at the idiot who's with her," a third said. "He gives ugly a bad name."

"And these are the sars from the chasm," Mindy said grimly. "Making sar caustic jokes."

The sars, exposed, dissipated.

They came to Castle Maidragon. A dragon raced around it and bore down on them. It was an impressively fearsome creature, with spreading wings and puffs of fire from its snout. But Bryce, seeing ten seconds ahead, realized it was about to stop without attacking. He held his ground, as did Mindy.

The dragon stood before them, considering. It had bright green scales, a purplish tinge at the end of its wings, and of course a fearsome toothy snout.

"I am Mindy, serving at Caprice Castle," Mindy said boldly. "This is Bryce, a suitor for Princess Harmony. Princess Dawn sent him to interview King Trent."

The dragon became a girl with blond hair and brown eyes. "And I am Becka, caretaker of Castle Maidragon, for the three princesses. It is my job to protect this castle from unwarranted intrusions. Do you have better identification?"

"Not exactly," Mindy said. "But I believe King Trent will recognize me."

"Wait here." The girl turned and walked into the castle.

"Castle Maidragon," Bryce said. "Maintained and guarded by a maid who is also a dragon."

"Yes. The three princesses have other things to do, so they aren't here much, but they want it kept in good order."

"If I married Princess Harmony, is this where we'd live?"

Mindy was startled. "I thought you had no intention."

"True. It's an academic question."

"Yes, probably you would live here. Her sisters have other things in mind."

Becka emerged. "Magician Trent will be out shortly, with Queen Iris," she said, impressed. "Princess Dawn must have mirrored him about your visit."

Mirrored: contacted him via magic mirrors, which could be much like visual telephones. Xanth had facilities similar to those of Mundania, only powered by magic instead of science.

"Thank you," Mindy said.

"Do I know you?" Becka asked. "You seem somehow familiar."

"I'm just a maid at Caprice Castle. Before that I was—elsewhere."

"I guess not," Becka said. "Well, back to business." She transformed back into dragon form and ran off.

"A literal dragon girl," Bryce said, amazed. "I am still being surprised by things."

"There are surely more surprises in store. But we'll try to get you safely through them."

A man and a woman emerged from the castle. He was tall, stately, about thirty-nine, with a commanding presence, wearing a formidable-looking sword. She was a breathtakingly lovely thirty-seven.

"Bryce?" the man said, shaking his hand. "Trent. This is my wife Iris. I understand you're from Mundania."

"Yes, recently. I'm still adapting to this remarkable land."

"I spent twenty years in Mundania. I remember it well. But I was in a different time."

"You are going to marry Harmony?" the woman asked sternly.

"No!" Bryce said. "I mean, this isn't my idea. I'm older than I look, and she's a virtual child."

"How old are you?"

"Eighty."

"I am a hundred and fourteen, youthened to thirty-nine. My wife is a hundred and ten, youthened to thirty-seven. So we're a generation beyond you."

"I have to believe it," Bryce said. "Because it happened to me. But I am amazed regardless."

"Magic does change things," Trent said. "Let's get out in the field where we can work on your talent."

"My talent isn't much. One eye sees ten seconds ahead."

"That's enough," Iris said. "Stand where you are. Orient on me. Use your talent."

What was she up to? Bryce stood and watched her.

In half a moment his left eye saw her clothing become translucent, then transparent. He saw right through it to her bra and panties. They were excellently filled. Then she turned around, and he saw her panties from behind.

Fingers snapped near his ear. "Snap out of it," Trent said. "Your second sight won't help you that way."

"I—I must have freaked out."

"Exactly. She flashed her panties, and you were gone. You have to learn how to protect yourself from that. Otherwise a damsel and a dragon could wipe you out without even a token fight. Do you think dragons associate with damsels out of mere niceness? The damsels earn their keep."

Obviously true. "How can I protect myself?"

"Put your second sight in second mode. Damp it down halfway, so that the panties lack sufficient detail to freak. Then, forewarned, avoid the view with your right eye."

Bryce had tried to do something like that before, but with inconsistent success. They worked on it, and Bryce began to gain the control he needed. Then Iris tried him again. This time when her clothing faded, so did his vision, fuzzing the details. When she turned around it was almost as if she were wearing tight pants; they impressed him without freaking him. When it started with his right eye, he simply gazed at her head, no lower, knowing exactly what to avoid.

"But I must say," he said to her, "you have a most impressive figure for your age. Either age."

Iris laughed. "It's all illusion. I was never that sexy in real life."

"Illusion?" He had been told, but somehow had not really picked up on it. In Mundania illusion usually meant sleight of hand.

"Remember, she is the Sorceress of Illusion," Trent said. "She can make anything appear. We shall be seeing more of that soon."

"I am impressed, regardless."

"Thank you," Iris said.

"We will start with illusory threats," Trent said. "When you can navigate those, we'll try some real ones."

"I appreciate your effort," Bryce said. "But I can't see why I am worth your attention."

"Two reasons," Trent said. "Retirement gets dull after a few decades, so we don't mind helping out when needed. We also value our offspring, and all five great-granddaughters are remarkable girls. Harmony is perhaps the most practical of the triplets, and we hope to help steer her right."

"The others went wrong?"

"Eve married Pluto, the Demon of Hades. Dawn married a walking skeleton. Oh, he has a good skull on his shoulder bones, and he is Xanth's most talented musician, but perhaps you can appreciate the social awkwardness."

Bryce did not want to criticize his hosts. "They seem to have made a compatible family."

"Indeed, and those crossbreed children are cute. But we had some worried moments."

"We certainly did," Iris agreed. "It's hard to fathom what the latest generation is coming to."

"Melody took up with the Dastard, a despicable man," Trent continued. "Fortunately she has converted him to decency, but it was ugly for a while. Rhythm took up with a cyborg, a perfectly decent man/machine, but she was only twelve years old at the time. Her mother, our granddaughter Ivy, nearly freaked out."

"Understandable," Bryce agreed. He was finding Trent's attitudes compatible. "The Adult Conspiracy—if it prevents even bad words from being uttered in the presence of children, it must really be appalled at the notion of a child being romantic with a grown man." Such as a sixteen-year-old princess with an eighty-year-old man.

"It is. But a willful Sorceress finds loopholes, and Rhythm did. Harmony has at least avoided that sort of thing. There's been no awkwardness or scandal associated with her. It is part of the reason we assorted elders designated her to be a future figure of importance. But this Demon Contest business threatens to mess her up too."

"She can't simply opt out?"

Trent, Iris, and Mindy laughed together. That was answer enough.

"Well, I hope she gets a good man," Bryce said.

"Remember," Iris said. "That girl is a Sorceress. It is dangerous ever to underestimate one of those."

"So I gather. But I believe I was selected mainly to round out a suitable roster, and I will wash out soon enough."

"Don't count on it," Trent said. "We are assuming that you are viable, and that Harmony will be interested in you."

"We want you to be the best that you can be," Iris said. "Just in case."

"I can never be of her generation, regardless of my physical body."

"Yet if she chooses you," Iris said, "you must be ready. She has already shown an interest."

"We met only briefly, via a magic mirror, and she was not pleased."

Iris looked at Mindy. "What do you think, dear?"

"I think she was not pleased to be put up like a prize for strangers to claim," Mindy said. "It had nothing to do with Bryce personally."

"But if she has to choose from several contestants, it is possible she would choose him."

"It is possible," Mindy agreed.

Then a flying dragon wheeled in the sky and stroked directly for them. Bryce saw it with his left eye. It wasn't Becka in dragon mode. This one was larger and uglier, and it was blowing out huge puffs of smoke. It was going to collide with them!

"Get out of the way!" Bryce cried, trying to push them to the side. "We have only ten seconds!"

It wasn't enough. The four of them fell in a tangle without getting clear of the dragon's path. The monster crashed into them.

And nothing happened. After a moment Bryce lifted himself off Mindy's legs where he had landed, and Trent and Iris untangled. There was no huge beast, no smoke.

"But I saw a dragon!" Bryce said.

"It was illusion," Mindy said.

"Mine," Iris agreed. "Your protective instinct was commendable, but you did not handle the threat well."

"An illusion threat," Bryce said. "You did warn me. I did not make the connection in time."

"A real dragon would have smoked and eaten you," Trent said. "That's why you need to learn how to use your talent."

"I surely do," Bryce agreed.

"We will go through this again, in repeat motion," Trent said. "Look in the sky. Do you see the dragon?"

Bryce looked. "Yes. It is flying well to our right."

"Use both eyes together."

"But that will make me giddy! They are ten seconds apart."

"Try it anyway," Trent said. "Coordinate the two images."

Bryce tried. "I see two dragons, one flying ahead of the other."

"In a straight line?"

"No, curving, as if they are points on a larger circle."

"Curving toward us," Trent said.

"Well, yes. If that continues—and of course it will—they will circle around to come here." Bryce paused, a bulb flashing over his head. "So I can see it coming well before ten seconds!"

"Precisely," Trent agreed.

"So we should move out of the way now. Avoid it, get under cover."

They did so. The dragon completed its curve, oriented—and failed to spy them. It shook its head, belched out a disgusted ball of smoke, and flew away without landing. It might be illusion, but it was realistic throughout.

"So I can triangulate, and anticipate a threat in time to handle it," Bryce said, pleased.

"If you are properly alert," Trent agreed.

Suddenly a ground dragon burst out of the ground right before them. "Get back!" Bryce cried.

But his ten-second warning was not sufficient. The dragon had emerged too close. Its head shot toward Bryce, jaws gaping.

And the dragon became a giant caterpillar whose jaws were suitable only for chewing plants. It was so close that it still collided with Bryce, knocking him down. It was no illusion!

Bryce scrambled up and away. "What happened?" he asked breathlessly.

"I had to use my talent," Trent said. "I am a transformer."

So the Magician had transformed the dragon into a caterpillar. That was impressive. "My talent didn't help me," Bryce said.

"That's why you need to get a sword. That could have made the dragon pause." Trent patted the scabbard of his own sword.

"I have never used such a thing," Bryce protested.

"Learn."

"I guess I'll have to."

"We can return to the castle now," Trent said. "After I restore the dragon."

"Restore it?" Bryce asked blankly.

"It would not be kind to leave it as a caterpillar." Trent walked to the huge green insect. "Stay away from humans," he told it. "Some of us are dangerous." Then he gestured, and the dragon reappeared. It shook its head, understandably confused, then turned about and dived into the hole it had come from.

They walked back toward Castle Maidragon. "I am impressed," Bryce said. "Not only with your evident talents, but by the fact that you have taken the trouble to help me like this."

"We are doing it for Harmony," Iris said. "If she chooses well, and avoids the kind of scrapes the others have gotten into, she will likely one day be King of Human Xanth."

Mindy choked. "Harmony?"

"If," Iris repeated firmly. "She has the potential, as all of them do, but must avoid squandering it as the others have."

"Oh. Of course," Mindy agreed.

Bryce wondered why she questioned it. Mindy's position as a servant girl was unlikely to be affected regardless of who ruled. But he had a question of his own. "Wouldn't she be queen, not king, being female?"

Trent smiled. "It is Xanth custom to have kings. So when a female rules, she is a king."

"Oh." He decided not to question it further.

Outside Castle Maidragon they bid farewell to the Magician and Sorceress, and walked back toward Caprice. "I must say, Princess Dawn has set me up with some interesting contacts. I never thought that ex-kings would give me the time of day."

"It's afternoon."

Which he supposed was about as specific as it needed to be, here in this magic land.

4

PRINCESS

The next day Caprice Castle was settled near a far more elaborate castle. "What is that?" Bryce asked, peering out a turret window.

"That is Castle Roogna," Mindy said. "The capital of Human Xanth."

"Human Xanth," Bryce repeated. "I have heard that term before. Are there other races here?"

"Many. Every species has its royalty or equivalent. So there's a Dragon King, an Elf King, a Gnome King, a Goblin Chief, an Ant Queen, and so on. We treat them all with due respect. It makes it easier to get along."

"I should think so," he agreed. "Animals have more status here than they do in Mundania."

"Mundania is backward," she agreed.

But when they checked with Princess Dawn, she had other news. "We are near a humongous clot of puns," she said. "We need all available hands to fetch them in before they escape. Bryce has a prior commitment, so must go to Castle Roogna. But all others must stay, including the dogs. Today you can't guide him, Mindy."

"But he needs me," Mindy protested.

"He needs guidance. That's not the same."

"The castle is right in sight," Bryce said. "I should be able to cross to it alone readily enough."

"We cannot be sure of that," Dawn said. "Xanth still has too many surprises for you. I have arranged for other guidance."

"Who?" Mindy asked suspiciously.

"Piper."

"But he's the best pun collector of them all! You can't spare him."

"He and Bryce can collect puns as they travel. That should be almost as efficient."

"But can he protect Bryce from danger, just in case?"

"Oh, yes," Dawn reassured her, seeming amused.

Mindy opened her mouth, but Dawn shut it with a look. "Piper it is," Mindy said.

"You will find him outside," Dawn told Bryce. "Now be on your way while we organize. There will surely be puns left over when you return."

Bryce obeyed. What else could he do?

He wheeled his trike outside the main gate. There was a handsome young man. "Bryce?" the man inquired.

"Yes. Piper?"

"The same. What is that device?"

"My recumbent tricycle. I brought it with me from Mundania, and it works well enough here. I simply push these pedals, and it moves. Do you have transportation of your own?"

"I have the equivalent: a duplication spell. With your permission, I will copy your machine."

Just like that? "Be my guest."

Piper brought out a small sphere. "Stand clear, or the spell will duplicate you too."

"Can't have that!" Bryce said. He got off the trike and stepped away from it. Could this really work?

Piper flipped the sphere at the trike. It struck the seat and flashed.

And there were two identical trikes.

"Thank you," Piper said, getting on the second.

"The brakes are on the handles," Bryce explained. "You move the handlebars to steer it."

Bryce got on the first and pedaled. He moved forward. Piper pedaled too, pacing him. They moved at a good clip. "I like this machine," Piper said.

Before long they approached Castle Roogna. It was surrounded by orchards and gardens.

"Uh-oh," Piper said.

"There is a problem?"

"This is illusion."

"Illusion? It looks real enough to me."

"Ride into that bush."

Bemused, Bryce did. He passed right through the bush as if it were fog. "Illusion," he agreed.

"Only the Sorceress Iris could fashion an illusion of this magnitude. She must have been practicing, and forgot to delete it when she went home. Caprice Castle oriented on it instead of the real Castle Roogna. I can find it, as I know the general lay of the land, but it won't be conveniently close."

"Can we get there using the trikes?"

"Yes. But there may be mischief."

"Mischief?"

"Did Dawn tell you much about me?"

Was the man changing the subject? Bryce played along. "Nothing."

"I am not exactly what I seem. I am a monster in human guise. I mention this so you won't be confused if I should have to assume my monster form."

"Okay. As long as I know you don't mean me any harm." Then Bryce caught something with his left eye. Now it was his turn to say "Uh-oh."

"There is a problem?"

"Goblins are pouring out of the illusion, or they will in ten seconds. I think we need to get away from here."

"That will not be feasible. Now I see them. Obviously goblins infested the illusion, hoping to ambush some unwary travelers, and we are those. They will have us surrounded."

Bryce looked behind. There were more goblins closing in. "They do."

"They will not be kind to us. I must become the monster. When I do, throw the trikes on my back and jump on yourself. Then try to help me spot the most dangerous ones. I can see well enough, but it helps to have guidance, especially if there are attacks from several directions at once."

"I'm not sure I—"

"We'll let them get close. They won't throw spears or stones because they want to capture us undamaged so they can properly torment us. Then we'll act."

In hardly more than a moment the goblins closely surrounded them. They stood about half human height, were raggedly garbed, and stank of garbage. They had large ugly heads, small bodies, and big ugly hands and feet. "What have we here?" the chief said, rubbing his horny hands together with anticipation. "Fresh entertainment and fresh meat, by the look of it."

"Beware," Piper said. "We are on a mission for the Princess Dawn. We can defend ourselves. Disperse without hostilities and there will be no trouble."

"Har har har!" the goblin laughed, and his horde laughed with him. There was nothing funny about it; this was pure cruelty. "You must be entertainers."

"Actually I am," Piper said. "I'm a musician."

"Oh, yeah? Show me."

Piper brought out a pipe and put it to his mouth. He played a melody. Bryce was amazed. It was the most beautiful music he had heard in decades. The man really *was* a musician, a fine one.

But the goblins were not impressed. "That's all? You're not royalty? No big hostage payoff?"

"We are unusual folk," Piper said. "But not royal."

"Strip them," the chief said.

"I advise against this," Piper said.

"Har, har, har!" the goblins repeated. They put horny hands on Piper and Bryce, reaching up to tear at their clothes.

"Last warning," Piper said calmly. Bryce couldn't figure what he had to be calm about. These goblins were pint-sized brutes.

The goblin chief punched Piper in the belly, which was as high as he could reach.

Piper dissolved. He melted down into an oozing black mass. It spread outward rapidly, gaining in volume. It surrounded the goblin chief, enclosing him knee-deep in the tarry substance. Piper had not been fooling about changing into a monster!

"Yowch!" the goblin yelled, trying to yank out his feet from the clinging sludge. "It stings!"

Then he started descending into the glop. Bryce realized that the stuff was dissolving his legs, eating him away. "Help!" the goblin screamed.

His minions tried, but now the gooey substance was coming after them too. They stabbed at it with their spears, but all that did was dirty the points. They cut at it with their knives, and got the blades hopelessly fouled. They bashed it with their clubs, and the clubs stuck in it and became useless.

Yet, oddly, the black goop did not advance on Bryce. It detoured around him and the bikes, going after only the goblins. It was consciously controlled.

A musical note sounded from a vent in the monster. That reminded Bryce, and he hastily tossed one trike and then the other onto the spreading surface. They did not sink in; the upper skin seemed rubbery, at least back from the caustic fringe. Then he jumped on himself, hoping his feet wouldn't break the surface tension and sink in like stones through mud and get consumed too. They didn't; the surface had a thick rind that gave way without breaking, like canvas. Still, he decided to get on his trike so as to have no further direct contact.

The goblins were neither stupid nor cowardly, and there were many of them. But they were practical. They retreated, abandoning their chief to his fate, and picked up stones.

"To my right!" Bryce shouted. "They've got stones!" Though he didn't see how that information could help.

Another vent opened. Harsh music sounded. Then a fireball burst among the goblins with the stones, singeing them. They retreated, their clothes on fire. So *that* was how the information helped.

But there were more goblins, unfazed. "To my left, farther away," Bryce called. "A catapult!" Indeed, that cat was about to spring.

Another vent opened. Another note sounded. Another fireball burst, setting the catapult on fire.

Bryce remembered how Mindy had asked whether Piper could protect him. Dawn had seemed amused by the question. Now he understood why. This was one seriously deadly creature.

"That's all for the moment," Bryce said, finally having time to be amazed. Piper had not been fooling about being a monster. Bryce was glad the thing was on his side.

The monster forged ahead, and the goblins retreated before them. Soon they were alone.

Bryce glanced at the sky. A dark cloud was looming. "I fear there will be weather," he said. "That could rust the trikes. Maybe we should seek shelter."

A vent blew an affirmative note. The monster continued to flow forward at a good clip. Bryce hung on, satisfied that Piper knew where he was going. Meanwhile the storm was rapidly blowing up. It almost seemed to be orienting on them.

They came to a sudden crack in the ground. In fact it was a crevasse. "Watch out!" Bryce cried. He had been distracted by the looming storm and hadn't seen the crack before, even with his second sight.

He was too late. The monster flowed over the brink and into the gulf. But they didn't fall. Instead they slid along the vertical cliff, the trikes and Bryce remaining fastened in place. This was another surprise. The wind gusted angrily, but the monster was like a giant slug, firmly stuck.

Then, just as the first raindrops fell, they cruised into a cave. The rain crashed angrily against the entrance, but could not get at the dry interior. They were safe from a drenching.

Bryce got off the monster's back, and removed the trikes. "That was an impressive demonstration," he said.

The black goo drew together and formed into manshape. Piper reappeared, complete with clothing. "Thank you. You did well, calling out the goblins' attacks. That spared me some bruising."

"You had told me how." He glanced at the mouth of the cave, which now looked like a sheet of water. "We may be stuck here a while."

"Fracto's rages usually pass within the hour. We'll be delayed, but not unduly."

"Fracto?"

"The storm. Cumulo Fracto Nimbus, king of clouds. He likes to rain on parades and anything else interesting."

"Our fracas with the goblins must have interested him."

"Fortunately I know of this offshoot of the Gap Chasm, inaccessible to most nonflying creatures."

"Gap Chasm?"

"Yes. I gather you are not yet conversant with much of Xanth."

"True."

"It is a giant crevasse that crosses Xanth, patrolled by the dreaded six-legged steamer the Gap Dragon. It has a number of offshoots that diminish and finally fade out. You will likely get to see it someday; it is impressive."

"Surely so. I have been learning things at a phenomenal rate, but it seems I have hardly scratched the surface," Bryce said. "If I may ask, how is it that Princess Dawn was able to call on you to babysit me on this trip? You are evidently no ordinary person."

"It is a long story, simply told. I was the former proprietor of Caprice Castle, a superior musician collecting puns for storage. But I was betrayed by a woman who let them all out. Demon Pundit was not pleased. He rendered me into the monster you saw. Later I saw Princess Dawn, and realized that if I could court and win her I might make her mistress of Caprice and recover my position. But her interest was in the walking skeleton. In the end he and I battled for her hand and the castle."

"How could a mere skeleton ever stand up to a creature of your powers?"

"He was a musician. He learned to conjure fireballs and other things, matching me in that regard. We challenged each other musically, and in the end he won, proving himself to be Xanth's finest musician and worthy of Princess and Castle. I was on the way down to Hell when he interceded with the Demon to save me. I am not unappreciative, and will never betray his interests. Normally I collect puns, but when the princess needed this service, I was glad to oblige. I can't touch her or enter Caprice, but I prefer to retain her favor, though I have another girlfriend now."

"Girlfriend?"

"Granola Giantess. She is a fifty-foot-tall invisible giant, a friend of Dawn's. You will surely meet her soon, if you haven't already."

"An invisible giant? I don't believe I have seen her." Oops; he hadn't been trying to joke.

Piper smiled. "When she enters the castle she becomes a normal human woman. In fact that is where I came to know her. She is quite a girl. We had a tryst, before I was banned. That relationship has continued thereafter."

Bryce shook his head. "I am having trouble visualizing this. She is fifty feet tall?"

"Here is another item for your background information: there exist what are called accommodation spells that enable widely-diverging creatures to indulge in romantic trysts if they wish to. Such as human beings and little elves, or dragons and damsels. Or a human man with a giantess. The effect is temporary, only an hour or so, but that normally suffices."

"An accommodation spell," Bryce repeated. "I will remember."

"The storm is passing," Piper said. "We can resume traveling. I will have to return to monster form to get us back to the surface; then we can ride the trikes."

"Yes. I don't know how I would get out of here on my own."

Piper changed, Bryce loaded the trikes and got on, and they slid out and up the sheer face of the cleft to the surface. Then they changed back, and resumed riding the trikes. But the castle was some distance.

"This is too slow," Piper said. "We need a boost."

"A boost?"

"Granola is near. I will ask her."

"The invisible giantess," Bryce said.

"Hello, dear," Piper called.

"Hello, Piper," a female voice boomed from the sky.

"This is Bryce, from Mundania. I am conducting him from Caprice to Roogna and back. We are running late. Will you help us?"

"Of course."

It turned out to be weird but easy. Huge invisible hands lifted their trikes with them aboard and carried them rapidly forward thirty feet above the land.

In due course they arrived at the true Castle Roogna, which looked exactly like the illusion copy, but without the goblins. The giantess set them gently down. "Thank you, dear," Piper called.

"Welcome, Piper."

"I will wait outside," Piper said. "You will find me here when you emerge from your interview with the princess."

"I'm sorry to make you wait. Won't it be dull?"

Piper smiled. "You forget: Granola is here. We will find a private spot."

Oh. "Thank you. I will look for you later." Bryce raised his voice. "And thank *you*, giantess."

"Welcome," the invisible voice answered.

Bryce nerved himself and walked bravely to the castle. He came to the surrounding moat. Caprice didn't have a moat, because it had no fixed location. This was a broad circle of water that looked serene.

Then a huge serpentine head rose out of it and oriented on Bryce. The moat monster!

He stopped. That snakelike neck could readily extend over that drawbridge and pick off anything on it.

Suddenly three pretty girls wearing little crowns appeared before him, one of whom he thought looked familiar.

"Hello, Bryce," the first girl said. She wore a green dress and had blond/green hair and blue eyes. "I'm Princess Melody."

"We are glad to see you," the second said. She wore a brown dress and had brown hair and eyes. "I'm Princess Harmony."

That was the one he had recognized. She was adorable.

"In fact we've been expecting you," the third concluded. She was in a red dress, had red hair and green eyes. Apart from those features, the three were quite similar, being of even height and structure, with their hair similarly styled. "I'm Rhythm."

"I am pleased to meet you," Bryce said politely. "All of you. However, it is only Princess Harmony I have come to see."

"Okay, we've done our little act," Melody said. She hummed a little tune and disappeared.

"He's yours," Rhythm concluded. A little drum appeared, and she tapped that and vanished to its beat.

Bryce stared at the places the two had been. They hadn't walked away, they had simply stopped being there.

"Come to my room," Harmony said.

He focused on her. "Is that proper? I mean, shouldn't there be a chaperone?"

She laughed. "It's not proper, and there should be. But we're naughty girls, and more than capable of defending ourselves. Come." She took his hand and led him onto the drawbridge. "It's okay, Souffle!" she called, and the moat monster's head sank back underwater.

Bryce tried to hang back, but the love spell on him wiped out his resistance, and he allowed himself to be led. Her sweet little hand was so precious!

He was hardly aware of the details of the castle as she brought him through halls, up stairs, and to what was evidently her bedroom.

She shut the door behind them. "Now kiss me."

"Now I *know* that's not—" But he was cut off by her kiss.

Light flashed in a heart-shaped pastel blend. He felt as if he were floating toward the ceiling, drawn by her precious lips. Her slender body was against his, her delicate arms about him. He might have resisted, but his willpower was totally swamped. Yes, she was a teen girl, younger than his granddaughters. At the moment he was unable to care about any of that. It was sheer rapture.

She broke the kiss, and he dropped several inches to land on the floor. "Ugh!" she exclaimed, wiping her mouth with her hand. "I'm not the first or the second! Who kissed you before?"

Half stunned, all he could do was answer. "Princess Dawn, when she was teasing me about you. Her maidservant Mindy, to shut me up, I think." She could tell his recent history just by kissing him?

"Well, stop it. You're supposed to be courting me."

"I am," he agreed apologetically. "Inappropriate as it may be."

"What's inappropriate about me?" she demanded sharply.

"Nothing, Princess. It's me. I'm really an eighty-year-old Mundane grandfather. I have no business with a girl your age or station."

"Oh, that's right: the Demons summoned you for their contest. But bleep! This is nothing I sought or wanted. I want to make my own decision, in my own time, not have it dictated by chance or Demon."

"That's understandable. I feel much the same way."

"You do? You mean you're not hot for my body?"

"Not by my own choice. I was brought here and dosed with a love spell. That's hardly the same."

"So you wouldn't be interested if it weren't for that love spell?"

"I'm your grandfather's age!"

She looked at him cannily. "I don't think you answered my question."

She was right; he had spoken evasively. "I believe I would not be interested."

"Even if I kissed you and begged you?"

"Are you trying to tease me?"

She laughed. "Yes."

"Well, I know the difference between young fascination and mature love."

She became serious. "What is the difference?"

"I would have to go into a dull personal history to clarify that. I doubt you'd be interested."

"Tell me. I'll stop you when I get bored."

"I'm still not sure—"

A small harmonica appeared in her hands. She put it to her mouth and played a note. Bryce's knees felt weak.

"What are you doing?" he asked.

"Pacification magic. You're being resistive, so I'm nullifying that."

"By playing a harmonica?"

"Yes. We triplets are general-purpose Sorceresses. Whatever we do to the sound of our music becomes real. Melody sings, Rhythm beats her drum, and I have my harmonica. Any two of us together can square our power, and all three together cube it. But for this purpose I don't need their help." She played a melody, and she was good at it, apart from the magic. He was enchanted in the aesthetic as well as the literal sense. He had not expected this level of skill.

She was right. He did not want to argue with her, or even raise reasonable objections. He just wanted to do whatever she wanted him to. So it was magic. So was just about everything else in this fantasy land.

She paused. "Oh, please don't stop," he said. "I love hearing you play. You know how to use that instrument."

"Thank you," she said. "I do get pleasure from it. Sometimes the three of us get together and play just for the fun of it. But I do want to hear your personal history."

Bryce shrugged. "How about a compromise? I will tell my history, while you play background music."

"I like it!" she said, and resumed playing, not loudly.

"When I was young I loved a beautiful girl, and she loved me. We wanted to marry, but her folks did not approve of me and my folks did not approve of her. They had ways of enforcing their preferences. So I had to marry a young woman I did not love, and she did not love me. She had had her own boyfriend. We were both stuck with it, and knew it, so had to make the best of it."

"Like me being caught up in a Demon contest." Her harmonica had disappeared, but the background music remained, as did his desire to do her will.

"Yes, actually," he agreed, surprised. "So we married, and we had children, and life was reasonably good, apart from that lost love. But along the way I learned something. I saw the girl I loved marry elsewhere, and have her children, and grow older. She wasn't much of a personality apart from her beauty, and she lost much of that appeal when she got fat. She also lacked integrity, something I valued. I had not realized she lacked it when I dated her, maybe because I was blinded by fascination. Whatever passion I had had for her dissipated; in fact it was difficult to see what I had ever seen in her. Then I realized that the woman I had married was actually better for me, and not just because she aged well and was a better intellectual companion. She was honest and supportive, and really helped me in myriad little ways. We were simply more compatible. So later in life I did come to love her, and she loved me. Her prior boyfriend had turned out to be an opportunist who avoided serious work; she said she was glad she had not married him. We had true love, based on long familiarity and experience. We were both realists with few illusions left. I truly mourned her when she died. My first love was fascination, and that marriage would not have been a happy one. That's the difference."

Harmony smiled. She was dangerously pretty when she smiled. "I love it, and I am not bored. It's so romantic."

"But there was really nothing flashy or impressive about it. Neither of us was anything special. It was simply a quiet relationship that worked out well. Sometimes the small details of routine interpersonal interaction can in time become more important than the more obvious things."

"But you couldn't know it when you were young, could you?"

"I lacked the sense to know it. Had I been more objective, I might have seen it; the signs were there. But I was young and foolish. I am not that way anymore, I trust, thanks to considerable life experience."

"I am young but I hope not foolish. How can I know what is best?"

Bryce spread his hands. "I don't know. I was speaking for myself. You are a different person, in a rather different situation."

"Well, make your best guess."

He considered. "You are to be courted by what, half a dozen men? You are a princess whom your grandfather Trent suspects is destined someday to be queen of Human Xanth."

"King," she said. "It's a long story."

"King," he agreed. "The suitors will be aware of that, and desire you for your position as much as for your flesh, though they will surely covet that too. They will say whatever they think will please or flatter you. If you could somehow study them each before you had to make a commitment, so as to know their real natures when they weren't trying to impress you directly, that might help."

"I can do that."

"I'm not sure how."

"Let me show you something." She gestured to a large tapestry hanging on the wall. "This is the Xanth Tapestry, woven long ago by a marvelously talented Sorceress. It shows everything in Xanth, now and in the past. I can watch whatever I want."

"Anything?" he asked, amazed again.

"Almost anything," she said with another smile. "We have not been able to watch folk summoning the stork, because the Adult Conspiracy forbids. That has been most frustrating, because we have always been most curious about what is most secret. But I am now at the age where I can begin to get half a notion."

"Then maybe you can observe the several suitors. I suggest that you do so. Someone among them may emerge as the man you could love and appreciate for the long term, regardless of the way he may impress you today. That insight could be invaluable."

She eyed him with that canny expression. "And if it is not you? Will you be jealous?"

"You're teasing me again, you naughty girl. Once this Demon contest is over, as I understand it, the rest of us will be relieved of our artificial love for you and thus not be jealous. Regretful that we were not chosen, perhaps, but not hurting in the manner of rejected lovers."

"But right now, if you saw me kissing another man?"

"Right now I'd be jealous, despite understanding its foolishness. I am trying to be objective here, drawing on my perspective, and give you sensible advice. You aren't helping."

"You're honest."

"I try to be."

"I like you."

Bryce sighed. "And I like you, Princess. But that is to be expected, in the circumstance."

"What is this word you used, perspective? I thought that was part of the limited magic of Mundania, where distant things race to keep up with you."

He had to chuckle. "This is of course how you would see it. But this word has a figurative as well as a literal meaning. What I mean by it is that I have a lifetime of experience that enables me to see and allow for some of the follies of the moment, such as loving and desiring a teen princess. I know, as I did not when I was a teen, that this is a kind of fascination, not true love."

"You think I will be dishonest and get fat?"

"No, actually. Here in Xanth people do not seem to get fat unless they choose to be. But there will surely be constraints that would similarly turn me off, in time."

"You would not want to be a princess or queen consort?"

"It is not what I seek."

"What do you seek?"

Bryce considered for a good two and a half moments. "I don't actually know, given my unfamiliarity with this magic realm. Perhaps some genuinely useful employment, and the love of a good woman close to my own age, as I had before."

"Not power, glory, notoriety?"

"Definitely not those. I'm not an adventurer."

"Passion?"

He smiled ruefully. "That I would like. I am after all a man. When you manage to fathom the Adult Conspiracy, you may come to understand that aspect."

"Passion. I could give you that, I think, once I learned how. I don't really need to understand it."

"Princess, that isn't what I meant!"

Her clothing faded, so that she was standing nude. She was not shaped like the mischievous voluptuous Demoness Metria, but she was absolutely lovely in her modest nubility. "This isn't enough?"

"Harmony, cover up!" he said.

"You don't like me?"

"I love you! That's the problem. You are freaking me out."

"But I'm not wearing panties."

And panties were magical, causing male freak-out, as he had discovered. "I spoke figuratively. Please."

Her clothing reappeared. "Did I do wrong?" she asked plaintively.

"Yes. You flashed me. A proper young woman does not do that."

"Dawn and Eve do it all the time. It's a game with them."

"You're not the same as Dawn and Eve, are you?"

"No," she agreed thoughtfully. "I'm sorry. I just wanted to know if I could be passionate."

"Passion stems from the mind more than the body. When—when you wish to be passionate, when the situation is right, your body will more than suffice."

"Thank you."

Bryce shook his head. "This interview isn't going at all the way I expected."

"What did you expect?"

"I expected to find a snotty spoiled teen brat. I did not."

"What did you find?"

"A smart, sensible, lovely, occasionally naughty but somewhat innocent girl."

"And I expected to find a crusty old Mundane in a young body, who might give me good advice. I did."

Bryce laughed. "So it seems we understand each other."

"Bryce, I really appreciate your perspective, if I have the word right. It is a valuable gift. You have told me things no other man would, and given me a plan to handle this darned Demon contest I never asked for or wanted. Now I have direction I lacked before. I want to give you something in return."

"There is no need, Princess."

"This is not need. It is—desire."

Her term was not quite appropriate, but he got her meaning. "As you wish, Harmony."

"What do you need?"

Bryce laughed. "Magician Trent told me to get a sword. I am not at all sure I want to do that."

"Castle Roogna has an armory with many swords."

"I would hardly know what to do with a sword," he protested. "I'm no warrior. What he meant was that I need something to buttress my second sight in case of emergency."

"Ah yes, you have that."

How did she know? Princess Dawn must have told her. "Yes. But it may not always be enough, at such time as I get into the adventurous hinterlands."

"Some of the swords are magical," she said. "So that a novice can readily wield them."

"I suppose that would help. But really my reflexes are not of that type. I'm more the cerebral type. Luck of the draw."

"The what?"

"It's just a Mundane expression. It derives from mundane card games, where one is dealt or allowed to draw cards to play, and some are better than others. It's a matter of pure luck what hand a player is dealt. I meant that I have what amounts to a hand of information and skills that apply only randomly to the challenge I face here in Xanth. Some may help me, others won't."

"Oh. Then it's not about drawing lucky pictures?"

"It is not," he agreed. "Though I suppose here in Xanth, where so many things are literal, it could have been taken that way. Anyway, for me, the pen is mightier than the sword."

"The pen?"

"A writing instrument. I meant that sometimes what a person writes with a pen is more effective than violence with a sword would be."

"Yes." Harmony rummaged in a chest. "Here it is." She held up a pen and small tablet.

She had misunderstood again. "I meant—"

"Shh. I know what you meant, that time. This is a magic pen. I can't use it effectively, but maybe you could. How good are you at drawing?"

"Well, I'm no artist, but I did take classes in mechanical drawing in my youth. I did seem to have a talent for that. I could draw an almost perfect circle without using a compass, or make other stylized little figures. Much good it did me; I never used that skill in life."

"You can use this pen, then," she said. "Luck of the draw." She handed it to him, together with the tablet. "Draw something."

"You want a little picture?"

"Yes."

He shrugged, and drew a little sword. He showed it to her. "There."

"Now invoke it."

"Invoke it?"

"Say the word."

He humored her. "Invoke."

The sketch slid off the page. The sword bounced on the floor, expanding. In a moment it was full size.

"That's the magic of the pen," Harmony explained. "What it draws becomes real. I can't draw a good sword, so mine would be warped and stunted. But yours is nice."

"Magic," Bryce echoed, staring at the sword. "Amazing."

"Try something else."

"What about the sword? I shouldn't leave it just lying around."

"You can revoke it, or invoke a new drawing, at which point the old one will fade."

"Ah." He drew an ice-cream cone. "Invoke."

It slid off the page. He caught it as it expanded.

"Chocolate eye scream!" Harmony exclaimed. "Thank you, Bryce." She took the cone and licked the ice cream.

"Um, is that actually edible? What happens when I revoke it?"

"It vanishes." She licked it again. "That makes it non-fattening."

"I see." He decided not to eat any other drawings, because he did not want to be deceived about their food value. "Thank you for the pen, Harmony. I'm sure it will be useful."

"You'll need to practice with it," she said. "Maybe set up several drawings you can do rapidly at need."

He had another thought. "I'm not sure I should really accept this."

She frowned, and he caught just a hint of what it might be like to anger a Sorceress. "You are rejecting my gift?"

"It's not that. It's a fine gift. It's that this could be considered as you playing favorites in a contest that should be objective."

"Then I will give gifts to the others too, when I meet them."

"That may do," he agreed. "I probably should go now."

"Yes, Piper and Granola are done now." She laughed at his expression. "No, I can't see what they're doing. For one thing, she's invisible."

That had not been the precise focus of his surprise, but he let it go. "Then farewell, Princess, until such time as we meet again."

"Oh, don't be stuffy!" She flung her arms about him and kissed him again. Once more there was the pastel heart and the floating. She was lovely and that love spell was potent.

Then he found himself outside, walking away from the castle. He must have walked down the stairs and through the halls and out, but he remembered none of it. Princess Harmony might be only a girl, but what a girl!

He realized belatedly that he had seen no other people in the castle, after Harmony's triplet sisters left. That must have been by design. There was so much magic, in so many guises!

Piper was waiting for him. "Was it a good meeting?"

"It was amazing," Bryce said. "She's a remarkable person."

"Sorceresses are. Did she enchant you?"

"Yes. Figuratively and literally."

"They do."

They got on the trikes and the invisible giantess picked them up and bore them swiftly to Caprice Castle. What a day he had had!

$$\overline{5}$$

PEN

Next day Caprice Castle looked out on a remarkable landscape. It was ordinary immediately around the castle, but not far distant a towering cliff rose up. Two cliffs.

"We're in the Gap Chasm!" Bryce exclaimed. "Piper told me about it."

"We are," Mindy agreed. "Just be glad we're not in the Gas Chasm; it really stinks. Rogue puns are everywhere. You will have to meet the Gap Dragon before you start, though, so he won't steam you."

"Steam me?"

"There are several fundamental types of dragons, chiefly the fire-breathers, the smokers, and the steamers. Stanley is a steamer."

"Stanley Steamer," he agreed, amused.

"It's not funny. He's dangerous."

"I didn't mean to imply that he's not. It was a private thought."

In due course they exited the castle and stood before the front gate. Bryce heard an odd whomping sound. Then he saw puffs of steam rising in the distance. Then the dragon hove into view: a green six-legged creature with vestigial wings and a great ugly head. The steamer.

Dawn stepped forward. She hugged the dragon's hot snout. "Stanley, we are here to forage for puns today. We have a new member of our household: Bryce, from Mundania."

The dragon eyed Bryce as if he wanted to steam him. Nervous, Bryce quickly sketched an ice cube. Could he control its size? He tried.

"And Rachel Service Dog, also from Mundania," Dawn continued. Rachel stayed close beside Bryce, ready to defend him in whatever way she could.

The dragon did not seem to like her much either. He puffed up a lungful of steam. Bryce knew that steam could cook them both in place.

"Invoke, large," he murmured. The cube slid off the page and expanded to a yard square. The dragon's steam would have to vaporize that to get at him, giving him and Rachel time to get away.

The Gap Dragon considered the cube. He breathed out a seething jet of steam. It exploded into a cloud of vapor as it struck the cube. In barely a moment the cube was gone, but so was the steam. There was only a roiling rising cloud of vapor. The dragon nodded, satisfied, then lifted an eyebrow.

"Princess Harmony gave me this magic pen," Bryce explained. "I am learning how to use it."

The dragon nodded again, then turned and whomped away. "He likes you," Mindy said.

Or did not care to admit he had been balked. "Because of Princess Harmony, maybe," Bryce said, relieved.

"Perhaps," Dawn agreed, with one of her obscure smiles. "Harmony's mother, King Ivy, befriended him long ago. He wouldn't hurt any of her children, or their friends."

"That is reassuring to know." If the dragon had merely been testing them, it had been a dangerous test.

"Now we will split up and go pun questing," Dawn said. "We'll meet at noon here at Caprice for lunch and storage, then go out again. It should be routine." She glanced at Bryce. "Mindy will accompany you and the dogs, of course. But because there may be unforeseen dangers, Skully and Joy'nt will also be with you."

"Who?" Bryce asked.

Two more figures emerged from the castle: walking skeletons he hadn't seen before. "They are part of the household. They've been foraging for puns elsewhere." She hugged the female. "Joy'nt Bone, Picka's sister, and her friend Skully Knucklehead. They will help you practice with your pen."

"Thank you," Bryce said, taken aback. There were so many people to get to know! But his session with Magician Trent and Sorceress Iris, working on his second sight, had satisfied him that he did need practice handling magic things. The second sight had turned out to be considerably stronger than he had supposed. Maybe the pen would too.

The group split, with Dawn, Picka, Woofer, and Tweeter going west, and Bryce, Mindy, Joy'nt, Skully, and Rachel going east. They spread out and searched the brush.

Rachel pointed, and Bryce went to pick up two linked sticks. "I'm not sure what these are," he said. "They look like nunchaku, a mundane weapon. I don't see the pun."

"I don't know either," Mindy said. "Weapons aren't my specialty."

"Those are none-chucks," Skully said. "They will prevent a mortal person from vomiting, should you feel the need."

"Ouch! None chucks. A pun, sure enough." He put them into his bag. Then, since Skully was near, he asked the skeleton a question. "How did you come to be in Caprice?"

"I was stranded on a sunken ship until Dawn's party rescued me. Then I fell for Joy'nt's nice bones, so I stayed with her party. When Picka won Caprice, we all moved in and helped out. Puns don't bother skeletons as much as they do mortals, maybe because we can't get nauseous."

"Eeek!" Mindy exclaimed. She had come up against a boulder that turned out to have eyes and whiskers.

Skully's arms became swords as he went to her rescue. "What is it?"

"It—I think it's a monstrous mouse."

Bryce got it. "An enor-mouse," he said, bagging it.

They continued bagging puns. Meanwhile Bryce tried to practice with the pen, which he kept with its tablet pad in a breast pocket. He realized that if it was to be useful for him, he would need to have a number of sketches rehearsed that he could draw and animate rapidly, in under ten seconds if possible, so as to coordinate with his second sight. Yet without more experience of Xanth's dangers, it was hard to do.

"Sk lly can help," Mindy murmured, fathoming his thought. "You saw how he can make his limbs into weapons."

He had indeed. "Skully, could I ask a favor?"

"You need someone to pretend to attack you with a weapon," Skully said immediately. These folk were evidently attuned to his needs.

"Yes, so I can figure out how to deflect it. If you could make a sword or two, and come at me slowly, maybe I'll figure it out."

The two swords formed again. Skully approached him with measured steps, slowly waving the swords.

Bryce got a notion. Quickly he sketched a crude shield. "Invoke." The shield slid off the page, expanding. He put his left arm through the holding straps behind it and held it up just in time to block Skully's slow attack. Both swords clanged off the edge of the shield.

"You'd have been skewered in real life," Mindy said. "You took too long."

"I did," Bryce agreed. "Also I'm not sure this shield is my best defense. It's heavy, and it doesn't disarm him, merely balks him momentarily."

"True," Skully agreed. "Had I swooped over or under the shield instead of striking directly at it, I could have lopped off your head or feet."

"Let's try again," Bryce said. "Revoke." The shield disappeared.

This time the skeleton approached faster, and Bryce drew faster. The shield was not metal, but cork. The swords bit into it and stuck.

"Well, now," Skully said. Then he yanked harder, and got his swords free. "That is better, but not perfect."

"Let me try another." He revoked the shield, because he needed his left hand to hold the pad so he could draw the new one.

The third time he drew a shield made of taffy. He found he could define some of the details mentally, as he drew, which helped.

Both swords stuck in the taffy and would not come loose; the shield merely deformed and stretched as the skeleton yanked. "That will do," Skully said.

Bryce revoked the shield, and the skeleton's arms were freed. "I wonder whether I can draw something in advance, ready to be invoked when I need it? That would save me time."

"But suppose you turn out to need something else?" Mindy asked.

That was a good point. "I'd better practice different drawings, so I can do any rapidly, rather than be precommitted to any single drawing."

They searched out more puns, routinely bagging them, while Bryce mentally rehearsed several more sketches. They had to be simple, yet accurate enough to be effective. Suppose, for example, the Demoness Metria appeared and tried to freak him out again with her panties?

A ball of smoke formed before him. "Did I hear my nomenclature?"

"No, you did not hear your name, Metria," he snapped.

"Odd. I was sure I heard a thought about me and panties." Her voluptuous figure formed.

"Oopsy," Mindy murmured. "It is dangerous just to think of her. She was probably tracking you, hoping for a pretext."

So it seemed. Well, now he could test his notion. "Yes, I am concerned about your panties," he said.

"Coming right up."

His second sight confirmed it. Her clothing was swirling into vapor, slowly exposing her brightly colored underwear. He sketched feverishly: a kind of doubled board.

"Ta-daa!" The last of her outer clothing dissipated. She turned grandly to present the rear aspect of her panties.

Bryce invoked his drawing. In half a moment it was in his hand. He swung it, smartly striking those panties with the flat of it. It made a loud thwack!

The demoness was so startled that she puffed into smoke, ruining any effect her overstuffed panties might have had.

"What was that?" Mindy asked.

"It's an old mundane device called a slap stick. It makes a loud noise when it strikes, without hurting the person hit. The sound is from the second board banging into the first board."

"And you whacked her right on her meaty bottom!" Joy'nt said. "She must have thought something was exploding, like a pineapple, and dissolved."

"What a way to thwart a freak-out!" Skully said.

Then they all dissolved into laughter. Skeletons might not have flesh, or freak out when it stuffed panties, but they knew it when they saw it.

"Let's try that again," Metria said, re-forming. This time her clothing puffed off so rapidly that there was hardly time for him to draw anything. She was wearing a bright blue bra and red panties.

But Bryce's second sight had seen it coming, and it seemed that his left eye did not freak out. He hastily sketched a tube. He invoked it as her full undergarments flashed. He squeezed the tube, hard.

A stream of white paint shot out. It splatted against her body, soaking both bra and panty, nullifying them and dripping down her legs.

"Oh, bleep!" she swore, trying to brush it off with her hands. All that did was smear it further, along with her hands themselves. That really set her off. "Bleepity bleepity BLEEP!!" The foliage in her vicinity wilted and browned, and a scorched smell rose from it. The sound might have been bleeped out, but the corrosive essence remained.

Mindy and the skeletons actually fell down laughing. Even Rachel seemed amused.

"BLOOP!!!" Metria said, and literally exploded into a roiling cloud of smoke. The local vegetation was flattened, and tongues of flame flickered.

"There's no Adult Conspiracy for plants," Mindy explained between gasps of laughter. "So they got the full brunt."

"There will be another time," the smokeball said, and floated away.

"Keep that sketch," Joy'nt said. "It should be good against monsters, too."

Bryce was pleased. He was learning how to use the pen effectively.

They resumed gathering puns. Then Bryce walked into something new. It was a swarm of coin-sized bugs with rounded pincers. "Are these puns?" he asked.

"Those are nickelpedes!" Mindy cried. "They gouge out nickel-sized chunks of flesh. Get away from them."

Instead Bryce drew another sketch. He invoked a small vat of liquid tar. He poured it on the nickelpedes. They were immediately mired, unable to attack or escape.

"You are really learning to use that pen," Mindy said admiringly.

"I want to be prepared for any danger I might encounter, at such time as I don't have friends to look out for me."

They continued with the puns. Then Bryce misstepped and slid into a pit he hadn't seen. Suddenly he was in a cave whose opening was too high for him to reach.

He sketched a ladder, invoked it, and used it to climb up and out. He was really getting to like the magic pen.

But his confidence made him careless. When he came to a small river he did not carefully jump over it, but waded through it. He shouldn't have.

The water was deeper than it looked. He sank in up to his waist, then was swept off his feet. Before he could properly react he was carried into a hole and down into the ground. He was caught in an underground river!

There was air above it so he could breathe, but the sides were smooth and slippery so that he could get no purchase. He was carried along through the darkness at what felt like breakneck speed. All he could do was hope that it would end soon. The involuntary ride seemed interminable.

Then abruptly he shot out into space. Before he could scream he plunked down into a great pool of water. Pool? This was the ocean! The river had carried him right out to sea.

"Arf!"

He looked around. "Rachel!" She had followed him. She must have dived in after him, and been carried along too. "You risked your life for me!"

"Service dogs do," she said.

"Well, let's get out of here. I doubt the deep sea is safe for ignorant Mundanes. Which way is the shore?"

She pointed with her nose. There was the cliff, with the water-spouting hole that had spewed them out. But the wall lowered to the north, where the Gap Chasm met the sea. How they had entered the river at the base of the chasm, then emerged above it he couldn't say. "We'll swim that way," he said, pointing himself.

He stroked and she dog-paddled. They were making fair progress. Then a horrendous head lifted from the water between them and the shore. "A sea monster!" Bryce exclaimed, appalled. "How can we avoid it?"

"Arf!" Rachel pointed to the side. There was a tiny island with one tree and a yard of beach. That would have to do.

The sea monster oriented on them and swam swiftly toward them. But the islet was close by, and they managed to reach it just before the huge jaws snapped. They sprawled on the beach.

The monster could readily have picked them off the sand, but it simply looked at them, shook its head, and submerged. Why had it given up the chase?

"Why not us got?" he asked the dog, turning to her. And paused, for two reasons.

First, it had not been his preferred phrasing. He had spoken in a guttural growl, and he had made a stupid rhyme. Neither was his style.

Second, the dog was not with him. Instead there was a naked woman with short black hair and heavy nails.

"You're an ogre!" she said, drawing back as far as the limited beach allowed.

He looked at his own body. He was hairy and muscular throughout. He still had his pen and pad, so he quickly sketched a hand mirror and invoked it. Yes, he was an ogre, huge and ugly. He had been somehow transformed.

Then, realizing what else must have happened, he handed the mirror to the woman. She took it and looked at herself. "Oh, ugh!" she cried, dismayed. "I'm human!"

"So true, for you," he agreed. "Some spell, Rachel."

They discussed it, and concluded that this was an enchanted islet. Whoever landed on it was transformed into something else: a dog to a girl, a man to an ogre. That was why the sea monster had let them go; if it touched the isle, it would have changed into something else, and it didn't care to risk it. That had saved them—but at what price?

"Maybe it's temporary," Rachel said. Her vocabulary had improved along with her form. "Maybe when we leave, we'll revert."

"Maybe," he agreed. "Let's see." He was still rhyming, which it seemed was what ogres did.

"I will try." She slid into the water.

Two things happened. First, she reverted to canine form. Second, the sea monster's head lifted from the water not far away. It was lurking for them the moment they left the safety of the atoll.

"Get back! No slack!" he said.

She scrambled back to the beach, and became the woman, walking on all fours. Embarrassed not so much by her nudity as by her form, she lay on the sand, doglike. "We're stuck in these awful shapes."

"No be sad, you not bad," he reassured her. Indeed, she was attractive.

"But I've lost my fur! I look like a plucked chicken."

He decided not to argue the case. "Maybe night, we take flight."

"I have a better idea. You draw a gun to shoot that sea monster in the snoot."

Draw a gun. Would it work? Everything else had. But he was not eager to kill a sea creature who was only trying to get a decent meal. He preferred to escape without harming it. Still, maybe that was feasible, if he used his imagination appropriately. "Me think, make stink."

"Not on this little isle, please," Rachel said, wrinkling her nose.

"Relax her; for monster," he said, frustrated by the limitations of ogre vocabulary. He sketched a picture of a stink bomb, but did not invoke it.

"Oh. Very well."

"Who are you?" a new voice demanded.

Bryce looked around, trying to spy the source. Rachel pointed, but her pert human nose was not very effective for that. "There," she said, directing him with her gaze.

It was a face amidst the ripples of the water just offshore, surrounded by floating hair. It seemed to be another girl.

It seemed simplest to answer. "Bryce me, can see," he said, thumping his big hollow chest. "Rachel she, canine be."

The girl rose out of the water, catching on to a hanging branch of the tree. Her upper section was human, her lower section a fish or dolphin tail. As she touched the edge of the beach, her tail split into legs. She was lovely as only a nymph could be. "Well, I'm Sela Sea Nymph, and you're on my isle. Go away."

"Unsafe we, swim in sea."

"We were threatened by a sea monster," Rachel said, translating his limited explanation. "We had to escape it. We can't leave until the monster does."

"Oh, that's Semi Sea Monster," she said dismissively. "He forages around here. I don't care about him. I just want you off my isle so I can relax."

That of course was not feasible at the moment. "We team, not what seem."

"We were transformed in shape when we boarded the isle," Rachel clarified.

"Well of course you were," Sela said. "I enchanted it so no intruders would bother me. You'll revert when you depart. Now get the bleep off. The only ogre I want to see is Eli."

"You—who?"

"Don't go calling your dim-witted friends! Just get off my isle."

"He meant who is Eli?" Rachel said.

"He's an ogre who lives on the moon," Sela explained impatiently. "He makes Moon-stir cheese by stirring honey and green cheese pools. He brings me some when he visits. It's delicious."

"Moon-stir cheese," Rachel repeated, groaning. Now that she had nymphly form, she could appreciate the true awfulness of the puns.

"I'm losing my limited patience," Sela said. "Now *go*, you ludicrous excuses for creatures."

This was not going well. "Me man. No can. She dog. No slog."

Rachel had to translate again. "In his natural state Bryce is a human man. In mine I am a dog. Neither of us dares enter the water while the sea monster lurks."

Sela considered. "It might be fun to have a pet dog and a pet man. A dog could bark when anyone came, and be petted." She eyed Bryce. "A man could tell stories, and be fondled."

Bryce did not like the way this was developing. "We no. Must go."

"When I say so," Sela said, as determined in her change of mind as she had been originally. "You can't oppose my will on my isle. Kiss me."

Why did the girls in this land always have to kiss? Yet he found himself responding, compelled by her magic. She did have power here. Somehow he knew that if he kissed her, he would be subject to her will indefinitely, regardless of who else he loved.

He got an inspiration. "Must refrain. We Mundane."

"Mundane!" she exclaimed. "Disgusting! Get off my isle now!" And his feet started walking toward the sea.

Hastily he erased the stink bomb and sketched a toy canoe with a paddle. As his feet touched the water he invoked it, and it splashed down before him, expanding to full size. He climbed in as he reverted to his natural form. Rachel waded into the water, reverted, and jumped in too.

He stroked vigorously with the paddle. They were on their way.

Then the sea monster reappeared in his left-eye sight. He had forgotten it, but it hadn't forgotten them. Now what were they to do? If he drew another picture and activated it, the canoe would vanish.

What could he do? "Sorry, Rachel. We're about to be dunked." He quickly sketched the stink bomb.

The monster appeared to his right eye. Bryce tried to dissuade it. "Go away, Semi! We don't taste good."

The huge head tilted back and laughed. Then it oriented and plunged down toward them.

"Invoke!"

The canoe ceased to exist. They dropped into the water. But Bryce caught the little bottle that replaced it. He braced himself in the water as well as he could, and hurled it upward into the gaping maw.

It was a clean shot. It flew right inside and fragmented against a rear tooth. Purple vapor puffed outward.

The monster choked. It tried to spit out the bomb, but it was too late. The stink was already filling its mouth. As the creature inhaled, the vapor entered its lungs.

The monster coughed. Vapor shot out of it like steam from the Gap Dragon, spreading the putrid stench. The head plunged under the water, but the miasma bubbled up from it, smirching the very sea. Indignant waves rose up, trying to wash it out. The monster forged away, trying to escape it, but of course it carried the noxious smell with it.

Bryce treaded water while he re-sketched the canoe and paddle. Fortunately the pad didn't seem to be affected by water. "Invoke!"

The canoe reappeared, and they scrambled back in, wet but happy. The stench color had faded, since the bomb no longer existed. "Let's hope the monster doesn't catch on soon," he said.

"If returns, pineapple," Rachel said. She was back to her more limited vocabulary.

An explosive pineapple certainly would deal with the monster. But Bryce still hoped it wouldn't come to that. He really wasn't much for violence. He paddled desperately for land.

They made it. They reached the end of the chasm safely and stepped out on land. They were dripping wet, but satisfied. They had escaped assorted dangers; that was what counted.

Bryce sketched a recumbent trike. He got on it and started pedaling. Rachel ran along beside him. Now it was just a matter of time before they rejoined the others.

"I hope we don't have any more adventures like that," he told her. "We survived, but we were lucky."

Then Rachel slowed, stopped, and pointed.

Bryce halted and got off the trike. "What is it? A pun?" He got his bag ready.

"No," she said. "Danger." She continued to point.

He looked, but saw nothing. She seemed to be pointing at empty space. He started to pass his hand through the area to see if there could be something invisible there.

She made a small growl. He jerked back his hand. "Dangerous to touch?"

"Maybe." She continued to point.

He bent to look more closely. Now he saw it: a sort of twisted worm hanging in the air about a foot above the ground. He passed his hand over it to find the supporting thread, but there was none.

"Hmm." He passed his hand under the worm to find some unseen support. There was none. Finally he tried around the sides. Nothing. The thing was unsupported. It seemed to be magically fastened in place.

"This is curious," he said. "But how is it dangerous?"

ZZAPP!

Startled, he looked. The worm was gone. What had happened to it?

Rachel took a few steps forward and pointed again.

Bryce checked. There was a rounded rock with a worm-sized hole in it. Had that hole been there before? It smelled faintly scorched as though it had been recently drilled.

Rachel moved forward again, and pointed. Bryce looked. There was the worm, suspended in the air, as before. Could it really be the same one?

He went back to the stone and sighted through the hole. There was the worm, right in the line of sight. It could have passed through the hole. But who or what had drilled the hole?

ZZAPP!

He checked. The worm was gone again. Now, in the same line of sight, was a small tree. With a neat hole through its trunk. Beyond it, in midair, was the worm.

"I am getting a surprising suspicion," Bryce said. "Maybe I can verify it."

He went ahead of the worm and quickly sketched a spade. He activated it and the trike faded. He used the spade to dig several spadefuls of dirt, making a mound in front of the worm.

ZZAPP!

And there was a hole in the mound, with the worm hanging beyond it.

"That worm is making those holes," Bryce concluded. "It must be zzapping like a bullet and drilling them itself. I can see how this would be dangerous to anyone standing in its way. But one little worm can't do much damage if there's nothing much in its way."

ZZAPP!

"Uh-oh," Bryce said. Because that sound was behind him, not in the same line as the one he had been investigating. "There's more than one of them. Where there are two, there could be more. That could indeed be dangerous."

"Yes," Rachel said.

"We'd better check with Princess Dawn. She can touch it and know everything about it." But they didn't know exactly where the princess was. It might take some hours to locate her, and this zzapping menace needed to be checked out sooner.

Bryce pondered briefly. "I think we need to get faster advice, just in case. Let me see if I can contact Princess Harmony at Castle Roogna. She should either know, or be able to find out."

Rachel looked at him questioningly. "How?"

"I'll try for a magic mirror." He sketched the mirror. "Invoke." It took form, and the spade faded out.

Bryce held the mirror before him. "Can you give me Castle Roogna?" he asked it. "Princess Harmony?" He was not at all sure whether the magic pen could perform magic this potent, by making another magic object. Or how a magic mirror was actually used. He assumed it was like a verbally controlled cell phone.

A face appeared in the mirror. It was an older woman. "Harmony is not in at the moment. Who wants her?"

"Um, I am Bryce from Mundania. One of her suitors. We met yesterday. I have discovered something odd and need advice about how to handle it."

"The Mundanian suitor!" the woman said. "Yes, I know who you are. I am Harmony's mother, King Ivy."

Oops! He had gotten a lot more than he had bargained on. "I apologize, Your Majesty. I didn't mean to bother you. It's not that important."

"Let me decide that. What have you discovered?"

"It's a sort of little worm that hangs in the air, that suddenly goes ZZAPP! And drills through anything in its path. There's more than one of them, I don't know how many. I don't understand it, so I thought I'd better ask someone. I'm alone in the Gap Chasm, with Rachel Dog, collecting puns, and—"

"That's a wiggle," she said, alarmed.

"A what?"

"When the wiggles swarm, nothing in their path is safe. Get yourself and your party out of there immediately. Stanley Steamer too."

"But ma'am, we're not with them. And the walls of the chasm are sheer. We can't get out quickly."

"Oh, bleep, that's right. Run ahead of the wiggles; they don't move rapidly overall. That will keep you safe for a little while. I'll round up a roc." She paused. "Do you know what a roc is?"

"A rock? Yes, there are stones all around here."

"A big bird. When you see it coming, signal it. It will carry you to safety. Now get off the line; I have things to do in a hurry."

"Yes ma'am," he said. "Revoke." The mirror faded.

He turned to Rachel. "It seems we have to race ahead, and then a big bird will pick us up." At this point he wasn't sure what to disbelieve.

He sketched the trike, activated it, and got on. They started moving. He hoped they were leaving the wiggles behind.

A shadow passed over them. Bryce looked up. There was a monstrous bird, the biggest, hugest one he had ever imagined, let alone seen. "The roc!" he cried.

He halted the trike, got off, and waved his arms wildly. "Down here!" he called.

The bird looped around and came in for a landing. It carried a tiny basket in its talons. But when they ran up to it, the basket turned out to be the size of a small house. It was the sheer magnitude of the bird that made it look small.

They piled in, closed the basket door behind them, and sat on the wickerwork floor. They could see through the crevices below and around them. The roc ran along the ground to get up speed, spread its wings, flapped for power, and took off at a sharp angle. The ground retreated at an alarming rate as Bryce and Rachel scrambled to maintain their equilibrium.

"Thanks for the lift," Bryce called.

"Squawk!" the bird replied.

Bryce thought of something. Could he use the magic pen to sketch a translator? He tried, making it a small unit like a cell phone. Then he punched the buttons for HUMAN and ROC.

There was the translation: "You are welcome. I am Roxanne Roc, chore officer of the day."

Well, now. "I am Bryce Mundane, a suitor for the hand of Princess Harmony, and my companion is Rachel Dog. We are pleased to meet you." He pushed the SEND button, and a loud squawk blasted out of the little speaker.

"Squawk!" Roxanne replied. Which translated to "So that's why King Ivy was so urgent to save you from the wiggles! I will rescue Princess Dawn and Picka Bone next."

She did, landing near them, and they scrambled into the basket along with Woofer and Tweeter. Then she flew to Caprice Castle, where it turned out Skully, Joy'nt, and

Mindy had made it on their own, having somehow gotten news.

Caprice moved to a new location, while Dawn explained about the wiggles to the others. "They are a branch of the voles, and normally live well underground in the deep rock. When they spawn the little ones zap out in all directions seeking a new base. In the old days we thought they had to be destroyed, which could be done only by catching them when stationary and chewing them up—they are reputed to taste awful—or crushing them between two stones, or burning or drowning them. Now we know that is unnecessary; leave them alone, they either get where they're going and stop zapping, or exhaust their energy and die. We just need to be out of their way for the few hours they are zapping. King Ivy warned Stanley Steamer, of course, and he fled the Gap Chasm for the day. Tomorrow things will revert to normal."

"That's a relief," Picka said. "We skeletons are practically immune to most threats, having no soft living flesh, but wiggles could riddle our bones and make us most uncomfortable."

"How did we receive timely warning about the swarm?" Joy'nt asked.

"It was Bryce and Rachel who did it," Dawn said. "They spotted the first wiggles zapping, and mirrored King Ivy, who of course knew what to do. That provided the extra hour's leeway we needed to get everyone clear. Bryce saved us all, by that call."

"Well, thank you, Bryce," Skully said. "We wondered where you went so suddenly. Now we know you had more important business."

"It wasn't really like that," Bryce said, embarrassed.

"What was it like?" Mindy asked.

Bryce launched into a simplified version of his adventure. "So when I realized the wiggles were dangerous, I sketched a magic mirror and tried to call Princess Harmony for advice. But her mother King Ivy answered instead, so I told her. It was just spot improvisation. I'm no hero."

"That was one canny use of the magic pen," Picka said. "I would not have thought of that."

"That's because your skull is empty," Dawn said fondly, rapping it with her knuckle. She turned to Bryce. "But it is true that was a clever use of the pen. I had no idea it could be used that way."

"I was desperate," Bryce said. "And lucky. In fact I had remarkable luck throughout that misadventure, surviving the underground river, escaping the sea nymph, foiling the sea monster, and then not getting zapped by the wiggles, as could so readily have happened."

Dawn gazed at him thoughtfully. "Do you believe in luck of that nature?"

"No. I now believe in magic, but that's not the same. I suspect someone or something was guiding our progress."

"The Demon who sponsored you," Dawn said. "That's probably Demon Earth. He must be allowed under the rules to see to your training, and this was part of it: to put you in danger in ways we would not, to force you to exploit your ingenuity and learn better how to handle yourself in Xanth. To learn to use your powerful magic pen. So you may not have been in as much danger as it seemed, though with Demons it is not possible ever to be sure."

"It's really neat, how you figured that pen out," Mindy said. "Making a stink bomb, and a mirror. I never would have thought of that."

"You do seem to have an aptitude for magic," Dawn said.

"Part of my training," Bryce agreed. "That makes sense. The way the goblins attacked Piper could have been another part of it; it certainly educated me about goblins! But I don't think I would care for much more such training, especially if it puts innocent people at risk, as the wiggle swarm did. It must be time for me to go see the Good Magician and get started on the formal Quest."

"And you do seem to be about ready," Dawn agreed. "It has been a pleasure having you and Rachel with us, Bryce; you have been a real help gathering puns."

"And fun to be with," Mindy said.

"You have all been most helpful and kind," Bryce said, touched. "You have taught me a great deal about this magic land. I—" He paused. "When this quest business is over, and I have failed to win the princess, I think I would like to return to Caprice Castle and work with you again, punning, if that would not be an imposition." Rachel made a sound of agreement.

Mindy threw her arms around him and kissed him on the cheek. "You'll be welcome!" Then she drew back, embarrassed. "That is, if Dawn and the folk here agree."

Dawn smiled. "Of course we agree, Mindy."

It occurred to Bryce that Mindy might have become attached to him. She was a nice girl, but she had to know that his love for Princess Harmony made any other romantic interest impossible. Still, once the love spell dissipated, who could say? Yet he would remain an old man, regardless of his body, and that would prejudice any such relationship with anyone so young. So there seemed to be little point in exploring such potential relationships at present. He had a Quest to tackle first.

"Then I suppose it's decided," Bryce said. "Tomorrow I'll head for the Good Magician's castle."

"And tonight we'll have a send-off party for you," Picka said.

They did. It was some party. He danced with Mindy, Dawn, and Joy'nt, the latter two in both skeleton and human form, while Picka demonstrated that he was every bit as fine a musician as Piper had said he was. Bryce really did like these people, and would never forget them, regardless of his own fate.

6

GOOD MAGICIAN

Bryce and Rachel stood before the Good Magician's Castle. Caprice Castle had landed there, let them out, and faded behind them. They were on their own.

"I really didn't mean to drag you into this," he told her. "It's my challenge. You have other interests now."

The dog opened her mouth, but only a sort of growling came out. She looked surprised.

"What's the matter?" he asked. Then he got it: "Mindy told me. She warned me that a person's magic doesn't work around the Good Magician's Castle. We have to get through on our own. So you can't speak, because that's magic, for a dog. Let me verify it for me, too."

He invoked his second sight. There was none. Both eyes saw the same thing. He brought out pen and pad and sketched a mirror. "Invoke." Nothing happened; it remained a simple little picture.

"It's true," he said. "My magic doesn't work either. So let me see if I can translate for you. You were trying to say 'No, you need me.' "

Rachel nodded. She still understood him, but she had brought that ability with her from Mundania.

"How can you be sure of that, Rachel? I'm not handicapped."

She made another half growl. "And I think you are saying that Dawn told you."

She nodded.

"And she knows everything about living things she touches," Bryce said. "Still I regret taking you away from Woofer."

She shrugged. She surely understood that her love for Woofer was similar to Bryce's love for Princess Harmony: the result of a spell. That was magic that had not been nullified.

"Well, let's see what offers here. As I understand it, there will be three Challenges we have to navigate. Only if we make it into the castle proper will I discover what my Quest is to be."

Bryce marched toward the castle, and Rachel paced him. There was a path between brambles, so they used it. It led through a decorative arch within a patch of bamboo trees. Beyond was a pleasant garden area with pretty flowers, shaped cacti, and a fountain feeding into a small stream.

"This is a Challenge?" Bryce asked.

Then his foot caught on a root and he stumbled into a cactus. Several thorns stuck in his arm. "Ouch!" He had to stop to pull them out one by one. "I guess I wasn't looking where I was going. My own fault."

Rachel wagged her tail, agreeing. It caught on another cactus, and she got painful needles in it too.

"Ouch for you too," Bryce said. "Let me help you there." He squatted to remove them, but one foot slipped and he lost his balance and sat down on the path. Where there were stickers.

He got to his feet and felt behind him—and his thumb jammed against another thorn. "A sandspur!" he exclaimed. "No wonder it hurt! Just my luck to sit on a patch of them."

It took a while to get all the thorns, needles, and spurs out. Then they started forward again.

Bryce's foot caught again, and he stumbled into the fountain, soaking the other foot. "Bleep!" Probably he could have uttered a real cuss-word, but he had gotten into the habit of bleeping bad words out.

Rachel tried to help him get clear, but she slipped too, and fell in with a splash.

"We're both suddenly amazingly clumsy," Bryce said as they picked themselves up. "What's got into us? This is more than mere nulling of our magic."

A bulb flashed over Rachel's head. That harmless magic remained. "Rrouff!"

"This is a challenge," he agreed. "A challenge of sheer clumsiness."

They resumed motion, this time being excruciatingly careful. But Bryce's foot came down on a pod that looked like a brown stone. It made a foul-smelling noise and a brown stench wafted out menacingly. "Uh-oh. I think that was something they warned us about: a stink horn. Just our luck to run afoul of it. We need to get away from it fast."

They hastily retreated, while the vapor pursued them. The mere edge of it smelled like badly spoiled poop dipped in vomit. They fled back around the fountain and to the bamboo patch. The cloud roiled up but did not enter the bamboo. It seemed it was limited to the garden.

"Bad luck?" Bryce asked. "The whole garden is bad luck. *That's* our challenge."

Rachel wagged her tail, agreeing.

"So we have to find a way to get through it despite knowing that we'll suffer prohibitively bad luck. In fact we need to nullify that bad luck. Mindy told me there's

always a way to pass a challenge, if a person can only
figure it out."

Rachel agreed.

"Maybe there's a way around it."

They walked around the edge of the garden. There
was a narrow but serviceable path. They didn't slip or
bang into anything. Could it be this simple?

The path led to a small footbridge across the stream
started by the fountain. It was pretty, but neither of
them trusted it. Bryce checked all around and under it,
but it seemed solid. Rachel sniffed the timbers and ground,
finding no problem. It was the only way to cross the
stream, because everywhere else was a dense thicket of
thorns.

"I guess we just have to cross over it and hope for the
best," Bryce said.

They walked up onto the bridge.

Something came flying toward them. They both hastily retreated, and the object thunked into the bridge and
broke open. It was a mess of garbage and feces. Had they
remained on the bridge, it would have struck them, be-
fouling them.

"I am getting a notion," Bryce said. "The path and
bridge are fine, but they are the only way around the
unlucky garden. Something is hurling stinky dirty refuse
at the bridge, so it will strike anyone who tries to cross.
More bad luck for us."

They tested it again. Rachel set a paw on the bridge
while Bryce watched closely in the direction the garbage
had come from. That worked; it did evoke another
bolus, and Bryce was able to spot where it came from.

It was a giant toilet tank.

Bryce groaned. "The pun is almost worse than the garbage! It's a tank that fires refuse. And with our bad luck,
we can't avoid it. It is zeroed in on that bridge we have to
cross."

Rachel looked at him, agreeing. They wended their way back to the bamboo stand.

"So do you have any bright notions?" Bryce asked. "I suspect there is a simple, obvious answer, but my brain is balky at the moment."

Rachel pondered. Then she pointed.

Bryce looked. "You're pointing at the bamboo? But we can't stay here; we have to leave it to get through the garden, one way or another."

The dog went and picked up a fallen length of bamboo. What was she up to?

Rachel carried the bamboo out into the garden. "Watch out," Bryce warned. "You'll stir up more bad luck."

But she didn't. She walked along the path, past the fountain, and to the far side without a misstep.

"Well I'll be darned," Bryce said. "You're immune." He looked at the bamboo. "This must be lucky bamboo, so it counters the bad luck of the rest of the garden."

He fetched another piece, a length suitable for a staff, and ventured out into the garden.

He had no trouble. Rachel had somehow fathomed the solution and gotten them through.

"How did you figure that out, girl?" he inquired as he joined her. But of course she couldn't answer directly. He concluded that she must have realized that if one part of the garden was unlucky, the other part must be lucky. It was elementary, in retrospect.

Now they came to a set of wire-mesh chambers. They were side by side, mounted on concrete slabs. Within each was a creature. One appeared to be a faun, furry, with small horns and goat legs and hoofs. The other was a nymph, with waist-length hair and a shapely bare human body.

Except—there was something wrong. It was the faun that was shapely and female, and the nymph that was male despite the long hair.

"My expertise in Xanth fauna and flora is hardly complete," Bryce murmured. "But I don't think this is correct. What do you think, Rachel?"

The dog shook her head. This didn't make much sense to her either.

"But the two chambers and adjacent bars seem to block off our access to whatever is beyond," Bryce continued. "I see a set of doors in each, front and back. Presumably we need to pass through one chamber or the other. And to do that I suspect we will need the cooperation of their occupants, because those doors are locked from the inside."

Would the faun and nymph cooperate and let them through? Bryce was pretty sure they would not. That was after all another Challenge.

Well, maybe they could ask. Bryce stepped up close to the male nymph. "Hello. I am Bryce Mundane, and this is Rachel Dog."

"Nyet Nymph here," the male said sourly. "What's it to you?"

"We are two folk seeking to enter the Good Magician's Castle. Is this a Challenge?"

"You bet your bootees it is," Nyet said.

Would the nymph actually give answers? "What do we have to do to pass it?"

"You have to fulfill my wildest dream."

"But you're not a visitor, you're a Challenge!"

"That's the challenge, dodo."

Just so. "What is your wildest dream?"

"To get together with my beloved and celebrate."

Bryce glanced at the other chamber. "And your beloved is the—the female?"

"Duh! That's Fauna Faun."

"And you can't simply open your doors and be together?"

"Duh again."

"Why not?"

"Because the moment one of our doors opens in front, the other's front door is locked shut. Only the back door will open, leaving us on opposite sides of the wall. We can't get together."

Bryce considered the chambers. That would bar them, certainly. But how was he to change a fixed setting that they could not? To hide his lack of an idea, he asked another question. "How did you get into this situation? I mean, of course this is a setup for the Challenge, but surely you have a cover story?"

"Oh, yeah," Nyet agreed. "It's that we're two freaks. The storks somehow got confused when they delivered us, and I got placed with the nymphs. But they wanted nothing to do with me, because I'm male. The only males they'll have anything to do with are fauns. I didn't have horns, fur, hooves. I look effeminate to them. So they booted me. I spent years wandering, until finally a giant caught me and put me in this cage. It seems I'm a collector's item: the only male nymph in Xanth. Meanwhile there was my opposite number, a female faun, who got delivered to the fauns. They didn't want to have anything to do with Fauna either, because while she was female, she wasn't a nymph, and all they wanted to do was chase and catch nymphs and celebrate with them. So she was outcast too. Finally the giant caught her, and caged her beside me, as two unique specimens. But that's all we are to the giant: zoo animals, here to be ogled and that's all. So we look at each other, we talk, and we have fallen in love. But we can't be together, unless some traveler comes and figures out a way to unify us."

"That's remarkable," Bryce said, impressed. He glanced across at Fauna. "Is that how you see it too?"

"No."

That took him a moment to assimilate. "No?"

"I was a regular faun, catching nymphs and celebrating with them every five minutes, all day. But I ran into a transformation spell, and it changed me into a female. I was so ashamed that I fled before any others saw me, and diligently hid. All I want is to find another transformation spell so I can change back to the way I was."

"But what about getting together with Nyet, then?"

"He says he knows where such a spell is. He'll take me there if we get out of here."

Bryce had private doubts about that, but did not voice them. This was after all only a setting. "So I need to figure out how the two of you can get out on the same side, so that then he can lead you on." Then he amended it. "To the transformation spell."

"You have it," she agreed.

Rachel sniffed around the base of the chambers. Something interested her.

Bryce inspected the chambers. "These seem to be mounted on circular pedestals."

"They do," Fauna agreed.

"So?" Nyet inquired derisively.

"I wonder if they rotate."

Neither person replied. That gave him a hint that he was on the right track. He put his hands on the wire mesh of Nyet's front wall and pushed. The wall moved. He continued pushing, and it continued moving. It was traveling in a circle, around the axis of the base.

"Well I'll be bleeped," Nyet remarked as the slow motion carried him along.

"Not if I get out first," Fauna said.

Bryce pushed until the front wall became a side wall. Then he did the same for the other chamber, pushing it in the same direction.

"But that's moving my front door away from his," Fauna protested.

"Precisely," Bryce said. "It is your back door that needs to abut his front door."

She nodded, startled.

When the quarter turn was complete, Bryce stood back. "Now open your doors, and you can be together."

"So we can," Nyet said. He opened his front door, and Fauna opened her back door. Now there was a portal between the two chambers.

Bryce was really curious what the two would do next. Would they really celebrate in public?

Nyet stepped through. Fauna met him with a smile.

"Shall we resume where we left off?" Nyet asked as he sat down on her bed.

"By all means," she agreed, joining him.

"As I recall, we were discussing transcendental metabolism."

"Mind over matter," she agreed.

"A tough concept to digest."

"This is how you celebrate?" Bryce asked.

"Oh, we have plenty of time for that between Challenges," Nyet said. "Now we are continuing our interrupted discussion."

"But what about us? Your chambers still block our way."

Fauna shrugged. "That's your problem."

Annoyed, Bryce took hold of Nyet's chamber wall and yanked it around the opposite way from before. It spun around until the door faced forward again. "Come on, Rachel," he said.

The two of them entered the empty chamber. Bryce closed the door behind them. Then he walked across to the back door. He opened it. They stepped out on the other side. They were through.

The nymph and faun didn't seem to notice. They were deep in their discussion of transcendental metabolism.

"Whatever works," Bryce said to Rachel. They walked on forward.

They came to what looked like a room with a number of letters strewn on the floor. There were high fences around it, and lines painted on the turf which served as the floor. A low net crossed the center, and beside the net was a small tower wherein sat a severe silent woman. Bryce thought to address her, but her glare stifled that unspoken.

"What is this, Wimbledon?" Bryce muttered.

Rachel looked at him.

"Never mind, I merely made an irrelevant connection in my foolish mind. Obviously this is the next Challenge. We need to figure it out, and find a way to get beyond it."

Rachel wagged her tail, agreeing.

"So do you have any idea what's what, here?"

Rachel pointed to a chair opposite the grim woman's tower. Across it lay a woman's simple white dress.

"You figure that's a key to the solution?"

Rachel wagged her tail. That was exactly what she figured.

Bryce walked to the chair and picked up the dress. It appeared to be a straight loose-fitting item of apparel, not at all fancy. Did it belong to the woman on the tower? She was already fully clothed, but maybe this was her dress when she went off-duty. "I don't see what to make of it."

He picked up one of the strewn letters. It was an S made of plaster, several inches high. Had it fallen from a wall? There was no suitably solid wall nearby.

He picked up another. It was also a big plaster S. So was a third, and a fourth. Finally he had them all piled on the chair beside the dress. There were ten identical S's. No other letters.

They walked around the edge of the setting, finding nothing. They were confined to this open, netted chamber.

"Whatever the next stage is, let's have it," Bryce said, not expecting any response.

Suddenly balls were flying at him. He grabbed an S and used it to fend off the first one, and that worked, but when the ball struck the S, both puffed up in smoke. He grabbed a second S to block the second ball, and again both destroyed each other. The balls kept coming, so he kept using S's, until all were gone. Then the balls stopped.

"Love Ten," the woman on the tower said.

Then Bryce got an inspiration. A bulb even flashed over his head. "Ten S's! Put them together and you get ten esses, or tennis, complete with balls. This is a Tennis Court."

Rachel just looked at him.

"Well, it's a step," he said. "Now I just have to figure out how to win the game so we can get out of it."

But now his mind was percolating. "If it's a Court, of any kind, by the crazy reasoning of this realm, there must be a way to win my case. Since I have no racquet I don't think it's by actually playing the game. There must be something else. Something fiendishly punny."

His eye fell on the white dress on the chair. He picked it up and studied it. Now he saw that around the hem of its skirt were letters. He spelled them out. "P-A-R-A-D-I-G-M. Paradigm." He paused to ponder. "A paradigm is a technical term meaning a set of forms, all of which contain a particular element. What does that have to do with a dress?"

Rachel was unable to help him.

Bryce got another idea. "This dress—it's a shift. So this is a Paradigm Shift. So maybe it, in proper pun manner, changes the set of ideas that the woman who wears it has. Such as the rules governing a Ten-S Court."

Rachel wagged her tail. He was making sense to her. She was the one who had pointed out the shift.

"And the woman whose mind I want to change is the one governing this Ten-S game," Bryce concluded. "She's here to keep score, but I want her to declare it's over so we can move on. All I need to do, maybe, is to put this shift on her."

He looked at the woman, she looked back, glare ready. He knew better than to approach her. She would not change clothing in public.

But he got yet another idea. "Rachel," he murmured. "Can you growl like distant thunder?"

The dog's ears perked up. She went to a corner, put her head down, and issued a long, low, rumbling growl.

"Oh, my!" Bryce exclaimed. "I think I hear thunder! We're going to get rained out! I hope there's not too much lightning!"

The judge looked around nervously.

Rachel growled again. This time the thunder sounded closer.

"Where there's thunder, there's lightning," Bryce said. "And it generally strikes the highest places first." He gazed assessingly at the little tower. "I'm getting away from there."

There was a third peal of thunder, louder and closer yet. Rachel was really getting into it.

The judge scrambled down from her perch. She picked up the shift and flung it over herself. It melded to her form, replacing her existing clothing.

Sure enough, it changed her mind. "What are we doing here?" she demanded. "We have to get under cover!" She hurried to the wall, and a door opened in it. She passed through.

Bryce and Rachel followed immediately after. They didn't want to get wet either. Or trapped in the S court.

The judge turned to face them. "Very clever," she said. "You have earned your admittance to the castle. I am Wira, the Good Magician's daughter-in-law. This way, please."

"I thought you were a prop for the Challenge," Bryce said, embarrassed.

"That, too. We were short-handed, so I filled in."

They entered a comfortable living room. A veiled woman sat there, her attention fixed on several glass beads.

"Mother Gorgon," Wira said. "They are here."

The woman looked up. "Already?"

"They found a way to shortcut the last Challenge. This is Bryce Mundane and his companion Rachel Dog, also from Mundania."

"How are Mundanes getting into Xanth? I thought the realms separated years ago."

"They did, Mother Gorgon. But this is the result of a Demon contest."

"Oh, bleep! I wish the Demons would just leave us alone." The woman's veil oriented on Bryce and Rachel. "I am the Gorgon, the Designated Wife of the month."

Bryce was taken aback. "Wives are Designated?"

"And you don't know about Xanth," the Gorgon said perceptively.

"We have been learning this past month, staying with Princess Dawn at Caprice Castle. But there always seems to be more to learn."

"Indeed. The Good Magician Humfrey has five and a half wives. Since he is allowed only one at a time, we alternate months, and it's my turn." The veil quirked. "That's actually about all any one of us can handle. Humfrey is over a century old, and chronically grumpy."

"You—you are actually a gorgon?" Bryce asked. "With a—a death gaze?"

"Oh yes. You would not care to look at my bare face. It would turn you to stone. Hence the veil. I was just putting a craze on these glass beads, which will be used for decorations. I can do it through the veil at close range."

"I am at a loss," Bryce said. "Why would the Good Magician want to marry a—a gorgon?"

"He can nullify my face when he chooses," she said. "As for the rest—why do you think?" She whipped away her cloak and revealed a luscious body in a bikini. It almost freaked Bryce out. "Actually, I pursued him before he got his prior wives back, and the castle was sadly disorganized. His socks were piled up in smelly mounds." Her nose wrinkled under the veil. "I put it in order, and he appreciated that. Now tell me more about this Demon contest. I haven't been paying attention."

"It seems the Demons are making a wager on which one can provide the best prospective husband for the Princess Harmony. Each is selecting a promising man, and the several suitors will compete for her hand." He grimaced. "It is not necessarily our choice, or the princess's choice. I was cleaning out my garage in Mundania when I was abruptly brought to Xanth, along with Rachel here. Now I am here to get news of my Quest."

"But Harmony is a child!" she protested.

Bryce smiled. "My position exactly. I was eighty, in Mundania, an old man. But she is sixteen, and it seems the Demons deem that old enough."

The Gorgon toted up years on her fingers. "Why, so she is! How quickly time passes when you're not paying proper attention. Well, what will be, will be. If Harmony chooses you, you will be hers regardless. I wish you well, or ill, whichever you prefer."

"Thank you."

"The Good Magician will see you now," Wira said. She had disappeared during his chat with the Gorgon, and reappeared with the news.

"Then I guess we will see him," Bryce said.

Wira led the way up a narrow winding stairway to a gloomy cubbyhole of an office. There perched an ancient gnomelike man, poring over a huge tome.

"Father Humfrey, here are Bryce and Rachel Mundane," Wira said.

The Magician's spectacles oriented on the dog. "Rachel, you can't stay," he said. "You are an accidental participant in this scene. You belong with the one who needs you most, and Bryce no longer does."

The dog's tail dropped between her legs. She did not like this news.

"There are two others who do need you, one in Xanth, the other in Mundania. Therein lies the problem, since you can't be in both places simultaneously. You may have a difficult choice."

Rachel remained frozen, evidently dreading the verdict.

"However, in consideration for the service you have rendered Bryce, getting him safely into and acclimatized to Xanth, you have been granted a dispensation. You will return to Mundania tomorrow, to be with the one there who needs you most, a woman with a chronic condition, named Mary. You will surely like her. But you will spend the intervening day and night in a state of time dilation, so that for you and your companion Woofer a year will pass. I believe you will enjoy it."

Rachel remained dubious. "This Mundane—will I be old there?"

The Good Magician seemed unsurprised that she could talk. "You will keep your rejuvenated age, then age normally. But you will not be able to talk in human speech there."

"And Bryce—will I see him again?"

"Once, before you depart for Mundania."

Rachel looked at him so forlornly that Bryce got down on his knees and hugged her. "Our association was largely accidental," he said. "It seems it couldn't last. But I will always remember you."

She licked his face, then departed with Wira.

Bryce faced Humfrey. "I want what's best for her, of course, but I had hoped we would stay together."

"Your destiny is in Xanth. You can't return to Mundania at this time. She can."

And that, it seemed, was it.

"So now what is this Quest I am obliged to go on, to win the hand of a princess I have no intention of marrying?"

The Magician's mouth almost quirked. "Even as a Mundane, you surely understand that your intentions relate to your destiny only peripherally."

Bryce found himself liking Humfrey. "I understand you are older than I am, as are Trent and Iris, though they have been rejuvenated. You too, though you don't look it."

"Youthened," Humfrey agreed. "I maintain my physical age at approximately a hundred for convenience. That spares me the foolish passions of youth."

"Such as being spelled into love for a teen princess."

"That, too," the Magician agreed.

"Why are you taking time to talk to me? Your reputation is for unsociable grumpiness."

"I seldom encounter a person worth socializing with."

"And why the oblique compliment? Are you setting me up for something awkward?"

"That, too," Humfrey agreed again. "The future of Xanth is important to me, and Princess Harmony is integral to that future, and you are perhaps the most salient likely influence on her. Therefore you are worth at least a modicum of my attention."

Bryce had to laugh. "Maybe you had better just tell me what I am supposed to do to acquit myself with sufficient dispatch to be worthy of that modicum."

The Magician actually smiled. "That is my present purpose. All the suitors will start off together, the Quest being to locate, obtain, and bring back the thing Princess Harmony most needs to govern effectively at such time as she becomes King of Xanth. You will return with your offerings, and she will decide which gift is most fitting, and choose the suitor who has it. That choice will decide the issue, and the Demon who sponsored the winner will gain status accordingly. Thereafter the others will be free to pursue their own lives."

"She must choose according to the gift? Not from love?"

"A princess marries for advantage, not emotion."

"Princess Dawn didn't."

"Actually she did. She married a male worthy of her, being Xanth's finest musician. The fact that she loved him was secondary."

"Not to her."

"Had he not demonstrated his superior ability, she would have married his rival, Piper. Love was indeed secondary."

"I don't like that."

Humfrey peered over his thick spectacles at him. "You were under the impression that your preferences have more than marginal relevance?"

Bryce was embarrassed. He had been under exactly that evidently foolish impression. But he plowed on. "That's it? No further guidance?"

The Magician looked at him. "You have met the princess, and come to know her somewhat. You must have a notion what she will most need."

"Not enough of one. Maturity comes to mind, however."

"That is not something that can be readily given. What else?"

"She seems to be an apt study. She should be able to choose well."

"From the offerings presented. It is your Quest to return with the fittest one, that will benefit her the most. If you fail, she will have to choose a lesser one, and perhaps cause Xanth to suffer when she is king. Is that your wish?"

This old man was no fool! He was maneuvering Bryce into an intellectual corner. "No! I just don't like aspects of the setup. People should not be treated as pawns in a game."

"We are dealing with Demons here, any one of which could obliterate all of Xanth without even blinking. We must be satisfied to be played as pawns in their game, hoping to survive intact. It is a matter of realism."

"Realism," Bryce agreed, seeing it. "You are, I think, suggesting that I look not only for what the princess needs, but for what the other suitors won't provide. So that she will have a better choice than otherwise. Despite whatever the Demons may have in mind."

"Sometimes it is possible to play a situation for more than those who devise it intend."

That did make cunning sense. "I will make my best effort," Bryce said.

"That may or may not be good enough." Humfrey's gaze returned to his giant tome. Bryce realized that he had been dismissed.

He turned away. There was Wira. "I will show you to your room," she murmured.

He had a room here? "Thank you."

"I don't think the Good Magician ever before spent the amount of time on a querent as on you," Wira said as they walked along dusky halls. "You must be a remarkable person."

"If I am, it is fate or magic responsible, rather than any inherent merit."

"Perhaps."

The castle was surprisingly large, judging by the extent of the passages. But Bryce realized that with magic, literally anything was possible. "How is it I rate a room?"

"All the Suitors will stay the night, and depart together tomorrow," she explained. "That way you can get to know each other."

"Is that wise, since we are in competition with each other?"

"You are not competing," she said. "You are helping each other."

Bryce decided not to argue the point. Maybe the Good Magician wanted to put a positive face on what could become a savage rivalry.

"Here is your room," Wira said, pausing at a door. "Your roommate will be along shortly."

He would have a roommate? Well, why not, considering the free lodging. "Thank you."

The room had two beds, a lavatory, a mirror, and a desk. It would do. Bryce selected one bed and lay down on it. He was tired, and glad to have the rest.

Another person entered. Bryce sat up. "Hello. I am Bryce Mundane. I—" He broke off, surprised.

"And I am Anna Molly," she replied.

"You're a woman!"

"That was my impression," she agreed, smiling.

"I thought you were my roommate."

"I believe I am. You have a problem with that?"

"Yes, I have a problem. Unmarried men and women don't room together." He reconsidered. "At least they didn't in my day."

"Nor in mine," she said. "Let me explain. My brother was selected as a suitor to the princess, but he's busy at this time, so I unexpectedly substituted for him. I have no interest in marrying the princess, but I am representing him so that he can marry her if I win."

"This is unexpected," Bryce agreed.

"That's my talent. I cause the unexpected to happen. Sometimes it's voluntary; sometimes it just happens. So I was assigned to be your roommate. I'm sure we can complain to the management and get it corrected, if you wish."

Bryce saw the pun, Anna Molly, anomaly. But he was no longer collecting puns. "I did not mean to imply any fault in you," he said quickly. "It may be that they are crowded and lack rooms for all."

"Maybe," she agreed. "Certainly it is anomalous, but I have come to expect that. It occurred to me that there could be complications, since I'm sure all the other suitors will be male. I will manage somehow." But she looked uncertain.

"Stay," he said. "We'll manage."

"Oh, thank you!"

They talked, and he learned that her brother was Justin Kase, who could summon things that might be needed in the future. She had been talking with him when he abruptly received a summons from the Good Magician to become a Suitor.

"The unexpected," Bryce said.

"Exactly. It can cost me friends."

Bryce also discovered another element of her nature. She was thin but fit, no beauty but not ugly, with dark hair bound back. She wore a shirt and trousers, with solid shoes. An ordinary woman, except for one thing. She had one blue eye and one brown eye.

"Yes, my direct gaze is the first surprise," she said, seeing him pause with the discovery. "It is disconcerting, I am told."

"Yes. But not bad. My talent is related to my eyes too: my left eye sees ten seconds into the future. That was really disconcerting, the first time."

"You do understand," she said gratefully. "I'm glad I met you."

"We'll be together here only one night. Will you trust me not to look when you are changing clothes?"

"I am going to be among several males for maybe an extended period of time. I have schooled myself not to be prudish. Look if you want to, but don't make a scene."

"That will do," he agreed. "Ditto here."

"It has been a wearing trip. I believe I will wash up and change now."

"Why don't I take a walk down the hall?"

"Please, I'd prefer you not to. Someone less understanding might come in."

"Point taken. Let me mention something else: in Mundania I was eighty years old. I think of folk your age as like grandchildren."

She smiled. "That helps."

She went to the lavatory, and Bryce lay on the bed gazing at the ceiling. He did see Anna as like a granddaughter, but his body was now also of that generation and he didn't trust it not to react. So he wasn't looking.

Anna emerged. Now Bryce looked. She had changed into a simple dress and let her hair down. Her body had progressed from thin to slender. She looked three times as feminine as before. "I like you better this way," he said. "No affront intended. It's that in my day girls seldom wore pants."

"Nor in my day either," she said. "But for traveling, and the Challenges, and all, pants seemed better."

"I agree."

"But for traveling with the suitors, which is better?"

"Pants, I think. Because there may be rough terrain, and a skirt—" He spread his hands. "Could be awkward."

"Because at any time a gust of wind could come and blow up my skirt, and they would see my panties and freak out?"

"Yes. I freaked out myself when a demoness flashed me. It's involuntary. So it seems better not to risk it."

"Thank you. That makes good sense. What about for dinner tonight?"

"Stay with the dress. That way all the suitors will understand who you are."

"I will. I appreciate your advice."

Wira appeared at the door. "Dinner is served."

"Oh, I didn't wash up myself," Bryce said.

"Let me help you," Anna said. She fetched a washcloth and efficiently did his face. She definitely had the female touch. "You look fine."

"Thank you."

"Follow the blue line," Wira said, and moved on.

They followed the line, which neither had noticed before. "I'm not sure it was there until she said it was," Anna murmured.

"I agree."

"You're very agreeable."

She thought he was trying to cater to her? "I will say so if I disagree."

They came to what turned out to be a banquet hall. Different colored lines were evidently to guide the others. The four others were already there. Bryce and Anna took the last two seats.

The Gorgon appeared. "I will introduce you, Suitors. Tomorrow you will travel together, going on your several Quests. Stand as I name you, so that you can recognize each other. Piper the Musician."

Bryce's jaw dropped. Piper was a Suitor?

Indeed he was. The man stood for a moment, then sat down.

"Another surprise?" Anna murmured. "You shouldn't have sat next to me. Too many anomalies."

"You have a question?" the Gorgon asked her.

"She doesn't; I do," Bryce said. "I thought Piper had another interest."

"I do," Piper said. "But that's interim, by mutual agreement. If I win the princess, that will be my future." He sat down.

"The Demon Pose," the Gorgon said. Her veil quirked. "Small d, apart from his formal name. D Pose."

The demon stood. "My interest is in taking over the kingdom from within, displacing the present monarch." He sat down.

Bryce wasn't the only one surprised. This was an ugly ambition. What made him think that Princess Harmony would cooperate in deposing her mother?

"Arsenal," the Gorgon said. "Combat expert."

The man stood. He was stoutly constructed, with muscles to the tips of his fingers. "Don't get in my way." He sat down.

Bryce saw Piper smile faintly. He knew why; the man had no need to fear any ordinary man. Neither did the demon, small d regardless.

"Lucky."

A feckless sandy-haired youth stood. "My talent is to be lucky for a set time." He sat down.

Well, luck probably would count for as much as any talent.

"Anna Molly."

Anna stood. "Yes, I am a woman, standing in for my brother, who is the real Suitor. I cause the unexpected to happen, beginning with my presence among you." She sat. It was plain that she had surprised the others.

"Bryce Mundane."

Bryce stood. "I'm actually an old man, rejuve—uh, youthened, not in this by choice." He sat.

"Enjoy your repast, all," the Gorgon said. Then: "Oh, one more thing: we don't expect most of you folk to be apt housekeepers, foragers, clothing menders, or whatever, so we have a volunteer to travel with you and perform these chores: Melinda."

Mindy appeared, looking dowdy. Bryce realized that

this was deliberate, because she had not been that way when she danced with him. That surely made sense, in this company. "Just ignore me," she said. "I'll be there when you need me."

Again, Bryce was surprised to the point of amazement, once it sank in. Mindy was coming along? She hadn't said a word!

Now they fell to eating, with Mindy serving. She was good at it, having evidently rehearsed this role.

"I don't think I am responsible for all your surprises," Anna murmured. "That last surprised even me. It's a relief not to be the only woman along."

"If you are responsible, your magic is powerful indeed."

She laughed. "It is mostly mischievous, I think."

They finished the meal without much socializing. Bryce was covertly studying the others, trying to judge what kind of competitors they would be, for all that Wira had said they were not competing but helping each other. Wira seemed to be a nice person; she probably thought ill of no one. He was sure the others were assessing things similarly.

The Gorgon reappeared as the meal concluded. "We have no entertainments scheduled," she said. "You will all need a good night's rest, preparing for what may be an arduous excursion commencing tomorrow."

There was a general murmur of agreement. In short order Bryce and Anna were back in their room.

"I'm glad I'm rooming with you and not one of the others," Anna said. "I don't quite trust them, while you're a gentleman."

"And you don't want to be surprised in the night by someone who is unscrupulous."

"Exactly. Maybe on the Quest I'll be able to room with Melinda."

It occurred to Bryce that that just might be why Mindy was added to the party. Still, she must have volunteered for it. What was on her mind? She had to know that there were bound to be frustrations and crudities along the way, things a proper girl would not care to be exposed to. Unless she had become so surfeit with puns that this was preferable.

"I know Mindy," he said. "She's a servant girl at Caprice Castle, where I stayed. She's a nice enough girl."

"That's another relief."

It occurred to Bryce that Anna was another nice girl he would have been satisfied to know better. Maybe when the Quest was done, and he had washed out, and she was free, he would look her up. If by that time he had gotten accustomed to the extreme difference in their ages.

In the morning they went down for breakfast. Anna wore her jeans, heavy shirt, and sneakers, with her hair bound back again, ready for the day. Bryce was surprised again by the thoroughness of the transformation; clothing really did make a difference.

"I know," she said. "I look like a tomboy. That seems best."

"Yes it does."

The others were starting to loosen up as Mindy served them an excellent meal. "Any hint of the actual nature of this Quest?" Arsenal asked. "All I was told was that we are to search for what the teen princess most needs to help her govern effectively. I think she needs a good man, but that does not seem to be the answer."

The others laughed sympathetically. "I think we were all told the same thing," Lucky said. "I find it no more satisfying than you do."

Lucky looked at Anna. "You're a woman, or you were last night. What's your take on this?"

"She's sixteen," Anna replied. "When I was that age, I wanted a captive demon to cater to my slightest whim, a cornucopia that would produce endless tasty nonfattening desserts, and to be three times as pretty as I never dreamed of being. I was pretty shallow. If she is similar, there's no telling what she wants. It could be anything from a bonbon to a pet dragon."

"Perhaps the real question," Bryce said, "is whether we are to look for what the princess might want, or for what she actually needs, which may be something she has no present interest in, like discipline."

"Well spoken," Piper said. "As I understand it, she will choose from among our offerings, of whatever nature, and unless this Quest is unduly extended, she will still be sixteen when she chooses. So I would be inclined to err on the shallow side."

"She did not seem shallow when I met her," Bryce said. "Young, yes, inexperienced, yes, ignorant of the ways of men, yes, but she was learning visibly as we talked. She strikes me as essentially sensible, and she may honestly seek what she deems to be the most useful tool for effective governing."

"Well spoken again," Piper said. "I can see you're not the dullest tooth in the dragon's mouth."

"I could be wrong," Bryce said modestly.

"And you could be right," Arsenal said.

"Maybe we need the luck to find something that appeals to both natures," Lucky said. "Like a lovely gem she can wear, that also gives her the power to read men's minds."

"And who would have the luck to spy that gem?" Arsenal inquired wryly.

"And which among us would want an innocent girl reading our lusty masculine minds?" Piper asked. "She'd kick the whole lot of us out."

Anna laughed. "Maybe my brother is smarter than I thought, having me substitute for him. That protects his mind, which I know is as degraded as any man's, from premature review."

"Except that she'd read your mind, and know the nature of his," Lucky said.

"The answer is easy," Arsenal said. "Don't bring her such a gem."

"But if we find it," Lucky said, "are we going to leave it behind, knowing it might be what she most wants or needs?"

Arsenal nodded. "We might have to draw lots to see who has to bring it to her."

The dialogue continued. Bryce found it edifying as an indication of the thoughts of the other Suitors. None of them were stupid or close-minded. The Demons seemed to have chosen well.

The Gorgon appeared. "The Quest will commence in an hour," she said. "You have the intervening time to relax or make yourselves ready." She looked at Bryce. "Rachel wants to see you."

Arsenal looked at him. "You have a girlfriend?"

"In a manner," Bryce agreed.

"May I come too?" Anna asked. "I'm really curious."

"You can all come," Bryce said.

They followed the stately Gorgon to a chamber where two grown dogs and three smaller dogs stood. "Rachel!" Bryce exclaimed, getting down to hug her. "Who are your friends?"

"These are our pups," she replied.

"That's right. It's been a year for you," he said, remembering. "You had time to—to have a family."

"Yes. Woofer will take them to Caprice Castle. I will return to Mundania now. It is best."

It surely was. "I'll miss you," he told her.

"Have a great Quest, Bryce." She licked his face. Then she faded from view. She was on her way to Mundania.

Woofer and the pups headed off out of the castle. Bryce knew they would find Caprice, or it would find them. The pups would surely become great pun sniffers.

Bryce stood and turned back to face the others. No one said a word.

"Rachel came across from Mundania with me," Bryce explained. "She helped me get oriented in Xanth. But there's someone in Mundania who needs her more. She had to go."

"We understand," Anna said, and the others nodded. Now it was really time to begin the Quest.

7

SUITORS

T hey assembled outside the castle. There was Bryce's trike. "I brought it," Mindy said. "I thought you might have use for it."

"Bless you!" Bryce exclaimed, hugging her. "But the others will need them too." He looked at Piper. "You have your duplication spell?"

"Of course."

"What is this contraption?" Arsenal demanded, eying it suspiciously.

"It's a device to assist rapid travel," Bryce explained. "I brought it with me from Mundania, and it became magic here. Allow me to demonstrate." He got on the trike and pedaled. The trike zoomed forward, cruising through the brush, narrowly avoiding a tree. Bryce circled around and came back to the group. "Anyone can use it."

"I'm not sure I want to," Mindy said.

Bryce looked at her. Unlike Anna, she was wearing a skirt. On the trike, her knees would be almost as high as her head, and her panties would show. "Do you have jeans you can use for this purpose?"

"Oh, I suppose so," she said grumpily. She reached down, pushed her skirt together between her legs, and buttoned it. Now she had what amounted to trousers or culottes. She had come prepared after all.

Piper invoked the duplication spell, and soon there were seven identical trikes.

They all practiced briefly, following Bryce's guidance and example. It wasn't hard, because it was difficult to fall over on the trike, and the magic made brush and rocks no problem.

Only Arsenal hesitated. "This is your device, Bryce. Why are you sharing, when you could have zoomed off ahead and been first to the station? Do you know something we don't?"

"I know nothing," Bryce said. "Least of all where we're going. I just feel we'll all benefit if we share where we can. The trikes will help us all."

Arsenal did not seem convinced, but the others were satisfied.

"So where *are* we going?" Anna asked.

"The Good Magician gave me a scroll," Mindy said. "It will unroll just enough to reveal one site destination at a time. He told me that you will have just one day to find an Object. If you don't, it will dissipate and be forever lost." She unrolled it and read: "Base of Mount Rushmost."

"That's way to the south!" Anna protested. "And there are dragons there."

"Not so much at the base," Mindy said. "They use the plateau at the top for their gatherings. They shouldn't bother us."

"We will need the trikes," Piper said. "Unless we want to camp on the way."

"But we have a deadline," D Pose said.

"The Good Magician said we would be able to make the schedule," Mindy said. "So you should have whatever time you need."

"Let me get this straight," Lucky said. "We each need to fetch one thing for the princess, and she'll pick the one she wants. Suppose someone doesn't get his gift?"

"Then I think he loses," Mindy said. "The Magician didn't tell me that; it just stands to reason."

"So we might as well cooperate and share," Lucky said. "Unless we've got a grudge against one of us."

"I think that's the idea," Mindy agreed. "So Bryce's sharing his trike makes sense. The sooner you all collect your gifts, the sooner the final decision will be made. I doubt that any of you really want to mess up any other. If you did, and the princess learned of it—"

"She will," Bryce said. "She's got a Tapestry."

"And if that one was the very gift she most wanted," Mindy concluded, "where would you be then?"

They considered, and nodded. The point had been made.

"Then let's go," Arsenal said, and forged ahead. He was a natural leader, it seemed.

They triked southward, following one of the enchanted paths. But after a while Arsenal called a halt. "The enchanted paths wind all around. It will take us too long. We need a shortcut."

"That could be dangerous," Piper pointed out. "There are dragons and other menaces we had best avoid if we can."

"I can handle a dragon," Arsenal said.

"But what about the rest of us?" Piper asked.

"Anyone who's afraid of dragons should not be on this Quest."

"Now that's not fair," Piper said. "Anyone who isn't cautious about dragons is a fool."

"Are you saying I'm a fool?" Arsenal demanded, resting one hand on his sword.

Bryce stepped in between them, knowing that Arsenal *was* a fool, because if push came to shove Piper could probably handle both him and a dragon together. But he thought it better for Piper to conceal his nature as long as feasible and for there to be peace in the group as long as possible. "The rest of us may have a different perspective on dragons, lacking your martial expertise," he said to Arsenal. "We are sure you will protect us if we encounter a dragon, but dispatching it would surely delay us, and none of us wish to be delayed." He glanced at Piper. "Isn't that what you meant?"

Piper was privately amused, knowing that Bryce knew his nature. "Yes, I believe it was."

"Well, then," Arsenal said grumpily, realizing that he had been managed, but not able to do much about it.

"And you do have a point," Bryce said. "If we want to reach that checkpoint today, we will need a shortcut." He looked around. "How do the rest of you feel?"

The remaining three Suitors exchanged a three-pronged glance. Then Anna shrugged. "I prefer to get through this as expeditiously as possible, regardless of the deadline. A shortcut will do, provided it's safe."

"Sure," Lucky agreed.

"Right," Pose said. "There will surely be plenty to challenge us, and getting there is bound to be the least of it. Let's take our chances."

"Next question," Piper said. "Do we have a suitable shortcut path to follow? I have seen signs along the way, but mainly for more popular destinations."

"I see a cluster of signs," Lucky said. He was of course the one to be lucky in that respect.

"What's that you're holding?" Anna asked. "You're not wearing jewelry?"

"It's a charm the princess gave me," Lucky said. "To focus my luck for better effect."

"A lucky charm?"

"It charms luck. This is the first time I've tried it."

"That's interesting," Anna said. "She gave me a trinket too. A little magic purse." She held up a postage-stamp-sized mini purse. "It holds more than you might think." She inverted it, dumping out the contents, and a small torrent of items dropped out: a hairbrush, comb, makeup kit, a spare dress, shoes, and a wrapped sandwich. "It's quite handy, really." She picked up her items and packed them back inside.

"She gave me a penknife," Arsenal said. He brought out a small object, and opened it to reveal a small knife blade on one side, and a pen on the other. "It cuts or draws. I haven't found much use for it yet, but I like it."

"She gave me a bottle," Pose said, holding up an ornate little glass bottle. "I can dematerialize and enter it, and it's a perfectly appointed room complete with bed and lamp so I can rest in complete private comfort."

"Unless someone puts a cork in it," Lucky said.

"It locks from the inside, not the outside," Pose said, "I can't be trapped. It's very nice." He put the bottle away.

The others looked at Piper. "Yes, I too," he said, producing a small musical pipe. "A magic piccolo with perfect tone and four keys."

"It looks like a toy," Arsenal said.

"It's no toy." Piper put it to his lips and played a brief and utterly lovely melody whose notes seemed to range far beyond what such a tiny instrument should be able to do. But of course it was magic, not limited as an ordinary instrument might be.

They looked at Bryce. "She gave me a magic pen," he said. "I can sketch objects and make them become physical."

"We are wasting time," Arsenal said. "Better be on our way."

They went to the cluster of signs Lucky had spotted. Sure enough, there was one for Mount Rushmost.

"But can we trust it?" Anna asked. "How do we know it wasn't planted to lead folk like us into a trap?"

"Good question," Bryce said. "We could use some reassurance on that score."

"I agree," Arsenal said, surprisingly. "Unenchanted paths are normally used by land dragons and other monsters for their own convenience; others use them at their own risk. I doubt anyone knew that we would take this particular path, so there is unlikely to be a trap. But we should use it with caution, with every person alert for danger and the women in the middle."

"Hey, I'll pull my own weight," Anna said. "I don't need to be coddled."

"Two things," Arsenal said. "There are trolls and goblins that delight in catching and eating delicate flesh, and human women are prime targets. You look good enough to eat, no offense. You could put us all at risk by being on the edge. And Mindy would surely appreciate the company in the center."

"I would," Mindy agreed.

"Oh. Yes," Anna agreed, slightly disconcerted.

Arsenal glanced at Pose. "And you might invoke your demonly talent to find us something useful, such as ripe pie trees so we can eat while traveling."

"Actually, I prefer to act human, with human limitations, because I'll be courting the human princess and want to seem halfway suitable. She knows I'm a demon, of course; I clarified that when we met. But I assume it will be easier to win her trust and her interest if I at least seem human. So I won't be puffing into smoke or popping instantly from place to place."

Arsenal considered that. Bryce had the impression that he didn't much like the demon, but knew better than to challenge him in too obvious a manner. "Point made. We all want to impress the princess, apart from our offerings to her. But can you help us with the things we need along the way? Such as by popping off invisibly, locating food, and returning to let us know so we can find it ourselves?"

"Can do," Pose said. "I do have a certain demonly awareness that may be helpful." He flickered briefly. "There is food at a nearby house: pie and cake plants growing profusely in the yard. We might ask."

"Exactly," Arsenal agreed. "Let us know when we are in the vicinity of that house."

"I will murmur something," Pose agreed. "Meanwhile I would appreciate it if the rest of you do not make anything of my nature to strangers. Let me pass as a man. It will be good practice for me."

"Readily done," Arsenal said. "You look like an ordinary man to me." His mouth formed a somewhat malignant smile. "Very ordinary."

The demon did not take offense. "Thank you."

Now Arsenal looked at Piper and Bryce. "Are we in agreement, on this and other matters?"

"We are," Piper said.

The others nodded. They might have been nervous about traveling with a demon, but this was reassuring.

Bryce saw that Arsenal really was an effective leader, at least as long as he got his own way. So it was easiest to let him lead. It might indeed get them to where they were going faster. "Yes."

"Then onward," Arsenal said, and stepped off the enchanted path and onto the shortcut path. The others followed, with Pose second, Anna and Mindy next, then Lucky, Piper, and Bryce bringing up the rear.

They followed the path through the forest as it gently curved here and there. Then it came to a tangle of alternate paths radiating out in all directions. There were eight of them, with no indication which one was correct.

"Oh, no, it's probably my fault," Anna said. "An anomaly. They probably all go there, but some will be longer than others, and some may be dangerous."

"We don't have time to dither," Arsenal said. "We need to decide on one."

"But it has to be the right one," Lucky said. "I used my luck finding the original path; I can't be sure to be lucky again so soon."

"We can't afford to gamble," Pose said.

There was a crash of thunder, and a fierce gust of wind blasted them. "Oh, bleep!" Mindy swore. "Fracto was just waiting for us to leave the enchanted path. Now we'll get soaked."

"We can handle rain," Arsenal said gruffly.

"But we girls don't care to get soaked," Mindy said. "It messes up our hair and plasters our shirts and forces us to wring out our underwear."

A significant glance ricocheted around the five men, none of whom would really mind seeing women with plastered shirts wringing out their panties. But it wasn't expedient to say that.

Anna put up her hand, intercepting the look before it could make another loop and squeezing it into nothing. "You should try being a woman, before enjoying a woman's humiliation," she said.

"We apologize," Bryce said quickly.

"I have a raincoat in my purse," Anna said to Mindy. "But only one, and it's not big enough for both of us."

"So we'd just better avoid that storm," Mindy said tightly.

Meanwhile the swirling cloud was looming closer, menacingly dark in the center. The wind was blowing leaves from nearby trees. This would be a deluge.

They pedaled on, but the storm was gaining on them.

"I spy a house," Lucky said.

"And there's something useful in it," Pose said. "That is the house with the food."

They forged toward the house. It was a neat cottage surrounded by a tall hedge. There were a fair number of pie and cake plants growing within the enclosure. Obviously the occupant had plenty to eat.

They stopped their trikes and got to their feet.

"Let me ask," Mindy said. "I may make a better impression."

"To be sure," Arsenal agreed.

Mindy went up to the door and knocked. The wind whipped her hair about and tugged at her clothing, doing a bit of plastering of its own, making her look appealingly wild. In a moment the door opened, showing an ordinary young man. "Yes?"

"He's the one," Pose murmured. "He is what we need, one way or another."

Mindy considered hardly half a moment, absorbing that. Then she made her best effort. "Please, we are a traveling group of two women and five men, not looking for trouble," she said with a nice smile. "We seek refuge from the storm and advice about our route. We are depending on your generosity. May we come in?"

The man considered, gazing at her. She inhaled as a gust of wind threatened to untuck her shirt. His generous nature got the better of him. "Sure."

They hurried in just as the first fat drops of rain came down. Bryce was the last one in, and he pushed the door closed against the battering wind. Angry rain smashed against it, demonstrating the storm's frustration at losing its quarry.

"Thank you so much," Mindy said. "You saved us from a drenching." She tucked her shirt back in, but she was still breathing hard from her exertion. "You are so good to us. We really appreciate it."

"Well, sure," the man agreed, his goodness prevailing in the face of her compliments, his eye on the heaving shirt. Bryce wondered whether she had played him, Bryce, similarly, when he was at Caprice Castle, and he hadn't noticed. She was not the beauty that Dawn was, or even Anna, but she evidently knew how to impress a man when she wanted to. Most women did.

Mindy quickly introduced the other members of the party. Prompted by this, the man introduced himself: he was Andrew, or more fully "Average Magician Andrew."

"You're a Magician?" Mindy asked, breathlessly awed.

"Well, not exactly," he admitted with a bit of bashfulness. "My talent is to answer questions. If I could answer every one accurately, I'd be as good as the Good Magician. But I am right exactly fifty percent of the time. I don't know when I'm right or wrong, just that half of my answers will be in each category. So my friends call me a Magician, but I'm not sure I'm even half of a Magician. If only I could always be right, or at least know when I was wrong, I'd be great. As it is, I'm not much."

"But you are surely just what we need," Mindy gushed, still breathing hard. It seemed impossible that Andrew would not notice how she was overdoing it, but his gaze was caught somewhere between her face and her shirt. "You can tell us which path to take."

"I will be glad to help in any way I can," Andrew said. "But the truth is that few folk find my answers useful. They would be, if they were guaranteed right or wrong, but they aren't. I don't offhand know which path is the right one for you, so I would have to use my talent, which may not help."

Bryce was interested. This just might be an intellectual puzzle he could solve. "You said your answers are right exactly half the time," he said. "Do you mean that they average out in the course of time, so you could have five wrong answers followed by several right ones?"

"No. They are always even. If one is wrong, the next will be right. But I don't know which is which."

"Ah. But if you did know one, that would in effect fix the other, as in quantum mechanics."

"I am not familiar with that magic," Andrew said.

Bryce smiled. "Nobody is. Let me express it more plainly: if you absolutely knew your first answer was right, then the second one would have to be wrong, and vice versa."

"Yes. But of course there is no point in asking a question to which you already know the answer. I can answer only once for a given person. So you could not help yourself by asking more than one question; you have only one chance."

"Yes," Bryce agreed. "But there are six of us with a common objective. We should be able to guarantee a true answer, if we cooperate."

"I'm not sure how," Andrew said uncertainly.

"First things first," Bryce said. "What can we exchange for the use of your talent to help us? We are not beggars."

"Oh, I'd charge a year's service, if I could guarantee my answers, the way the Good Magician does. But as it is, they are practically worthless."

"Nevertheless, we are in a hurry, you can help us, and we will pay."

"Where are you going with this?" Arsenal asked.

"I am crafting an ethical solution to our problem."

"What problem?"

"That we don't know a safe shortcut."

"I told you, I can protect us from dragons."

"What about getting washed into the sea by a deluge, as is threatening now?" Bryce asked. "Carried away by a roc bird? Poisoned by bad pies? Abducted by a goblin horde too big to fight off? There are dangers galore, off the enchanted paths." As he had discovered, thanks to his sponsoring Demon's quick course of education.

"He's right," Anna said. "We need reassurance. Otherwise we had better return to the enchanted path, regardless of the extra time it takes. We may have to pedal all night, but we'll get there." The others nodded agreement.

"Point taken," Arsenal said reluctantly, seeing rebellion in the ranks. "Get it done." Thus making it his directive, preserving his leadership.

"What do you need, that we might provide?" Mindy asked.

Andrew made a gesture of acquiescence. "The fact is, I'm hungry."

"But you have pies growing all around your house," Mindy said.

"I do and I don't. Those food plants are like my talent: you can't trust them."

"They looked good to me," Mindy said. "I'd eat them."

"Let me explain. Take the cake plants: some are angel's food, and some are devil's food. But they look alike."

"Either is bound to be tasty," Mindy said.

"Tasty, yes. But don't eat them."

"I don't understand."

"The angel's food cake makes you behave like a saint for as long as it takes to digest. You can't lie, are easily offended by crude language, and go out of your way to do nice things for other creatures, even if it isn't what you want to do. The devil's food cake makes you the opposite; you will be foul-mouthed and evil for as long as it takes to digest. Neither state is comfortable. Believe me, I know, because when I get too hungry, I have to eat."

"And your last meal was angel's food," Mindy said.

"How did you know?"

"You are being very decent."

"Yes. Had I been normal, I would never have let strangers into my house, storm or not."

"Why don't you simply stop eating when you feel the effect?" Anna asked. "Or take a bite of one, then of another, to counter it?"

"Because it takes a while for the digestion to start, and

the effect doesn't show until then. The cakes are good; once I start one, I have to finish it."

"Well, I think I can solve your food problem," Mindy said. "Suppose we trade that for your answering one question by each of the six others here?"

"That's more than fair, considering."

"Here's how," Mindy said briskly. "Anna and I will harvest several cakes, enough to be sure of getting some of each kind, and mix them together into one composite cake. We're women; we know how to do this sort of thing, in contrast to ignorant men. The effects of the different kinds should cancel out, and we can all have a good meal." She turned to Bryce. "Meanwhile you can organize our questions to be sure of getting the answer we need: how to find a guaranteed safe shortcut path to Mount Rushmost."

"Can do," Bryce said.

"You'd better," Arsenal muttered. "Or we're wasting time here."

The girls went out to fetch cakes. Bryce focused on Andrew. "Six of us will each ask one question. You will use your talent to answer each. We will come at the truth soon enough."

"I told you, I can't guarantee—"

"That's all right," Bryce said. "Arsenal, can you organize our group so that each person asks only the question I suggest? No one must ask out of turn. This has to be done exactly right."

"Yes," Arsenal said gruffly. "I'll keep the discipline. I'll ask the first. What is it?"

"There are eight paths out there," Bryce said carefully. "Let's number them one to eight, beginning left of where the original path intersects them and proceeding until the last one is to the right of the original path. Do you understand?"

"Of course I understand," Arsenal said impatiently. "I'm not a dullard."

"Then here is your question. Is the best path for us, the one that is quick and safe throughout, one of the first four?"

"This is pointless," Arsenal muttered. But he girded his loins and faced Andrew. "I believe you heard the qualifications, and understand the context."

"Yes," Andrew agreed.

"Is the correct path one of the first four?"

"Yes."

"But we don't know whether that answer is correct," Lucky said. "And even if it is, it still leaves us with several choices."

"And you may ask the second question," Bryce said. "Which is, how many women are in our party?"

"But we know that!" Mindy called from the kitchen area, where she and Anna now had a pile of cakes.

"So we do," Bryce agreed. "Ask it, please, Lucky."

"But this is crazy!"

Bryce glanced at Arsenal. "Just ask it," Arsenal said grimly.

Lucky faced Andrew. "How many women are in our party?"

"Two."

"That is a correct answer," Bryce said.

"And you have wasted a question," Andrew said.

"By no means. The answer to the second question is right, so the answer to the first must be wrong. Is that not so?"

"That is so," Andrew agreed, surprised. "Your path is not among the first four."

"We are left with paths numbered five through eight, the second four," Bryce said. "Is our best path one of the first two of those, that is, number five or number six?"

"I'll ask it," Pose said. "Andrew, is—"

"Yes."

"Next question," Bryce said. "Do ogres crunch bones?"

"Anna, will you ask that question?" Arsenal called.

"Consider it asked," she called back. "I've got cake on my hands."

"No," Andrew said.

"That is a false answer," Bryce said. "So the answer to the prior one must be true: it is Path Five or Path Six."

"You are making bleeping sense," Arsenal said, catching on.

"Next question: is it Path Six?"

"I will ask that," Piper said.

"Yes," Andrew said.

"And my own question," Bryce said. "Is your name Andrew?"

"No," Andrew said.

"Therefore the prior answer was true, and it is Path Six. We have our path."

"You did it!" Mindy cried. "You are one smart man!"

"One old experienced man," Bryce said. But he was pleased.

"Dinner is served," Mindy said. "Giant Composite Cake, there on the kitchen table, too big to move. Cut yourselves sections and eat."

They did. It was very good, and they did not suffer inconvenient sieges of Good or Evil.

"You have solved my diet problem," Andrew said to Mindy. "I don't suppose I could persuade you to stay here?"

She blushed. "No man ever wanted me to stay with him before. I can't remain here; I am traveling with the group. But you will have no problem making your own composite cake, now that you know you have to do it before you eat any."

"Oh, I know. It wasn't only the cake that appealed to me."

Mindy blushed worse, finally realizing that she had overdone it with the breathing. "Thank you."

"And you have solved much of my Answer problem," Andrew said to Bryce. "In the course of getting your own answer. Now I have a technique to make it work more reliably."

"Yes," Bryce agreed. "You can finesse it." He smiled. "Maybe you can find a woman whose talent is to ask stupidly obvious questions, to help you set up for the real ones."

"Yes, maybe I can," Andrew agreed thoughtfully.

"We must get moving," Arsenal said. "The rain has stopped."

So it had. They moved out, got on their trikes, and pedaled to the tangle of paths. They counted them off carefully, and took Path Six.

Fracto, as it turned out, had not departed; with cloudy cunning he had eased off, waiting for them to come out. Now he surged back, revving up his wind.

But their path chose this moment to plunge into a cave. They got into it and safe from the storm just before it broke, going single file. There was a faint glow from the walls and ceiling that enabled them to see clearly enough.

"It really is the right path," Mindy said appreciatively.

"No plastered shirts," Lucky said, less appreciatively. The others laughed.

But their relief was premature. The storm still raged outside, and now water was flowing into the cave, threatening to become a torrent. They had nowhere to go to escape it. They had to get off their trikes. "These may be harmed by water," Bryce said. "Certainly it will be a drag on the wheels."

Fortunately the machines turned out to be foldable, and light enough to carry. The several people stood in an uncertain cluster, holding their bundled trikes.

"Fracto is raging," Mindy said. "He's trying to drown us out." She looked at Pose. "I know you'd rather see wet shirts, but could you do us the favor of locating an alcove or offshoot that will keep us dry until the water drains?"

D Pose glanced at her shirt, which was visible through the folds of the trike. She inhaled. He nodded. "I suppose a regular man would do the right thing," he said.

"Which is to safeguard maidens in distress," she agreed, leaning forward to kiss him on the cheek.

Bryce nodded internally. Even a demon appreciated that kind of attention from a woman. Mindy was using her feminine art again, to get her way, but no one objected.

Pose flickered, then spoke. "There's a split ahead. One fork goes high, and will not get flooded. The other goes low, and will flood. It also passes through goblin and troll haunts. But the correct path, which I can verify by its faint glow, is the lower one."

"That doesn't make sense," Lucky said. "The safe path should avoid all natural hazards."

"Not necessarily," Bryce said. "Appearances can be deceptive. We need to study this further."

"But the water's rising!" Anna protested. Indeed, now it was coursing about their ankles, with a lot more on the way.

"Bryce has made sense before," Arsenal said. "We'll take the low route."

"You just want to see wet shirts!" Mindy flared.

"That, too," he agreed. "Now move, or we'll soon see them and more right here."

Mindy glanced down at the water swirling about her calves. The cuffs of her jeans were plastered. She moved.

They splashed along the path, carrying their burdens. Soon they came to the fork. The right-hand one looked tempting as it rose into dry terrain. They could readily ride along that.

"There must be a reason," Piper said. "Pose, why don't you check out the right path more thoroughly, while we slog along the left one?"

The demon flickered for a longer moment, almost a moment and a half. Bryce knew he was zooming invisibly along the path, tracing it to its destination. Then he returned, stabilizing. "It leads to a volcanic vent," he reported. "Burning lava is trickling from it, down toward the intersection." He half smiled. "Wouldn't be good for the tires."

"Reason enough," Piper said. "I think we'd rather see wet shirts than burned ones."

"You would," Mindy muttered. But Bryce's reasoning had been vindicated. They were better off on the low path.

They waded on, the water rising to their knees.

"Goblins ahead," Pose said.

"Oh, no!" Anna said. "They're worse than water."

"Keep moving," Arsenal said gruffly. He was carrying his trike with one arm, leaving his other arm free to wield a weapon.

The passage opened out into a cavern. There were goblins, the ugly males hammering weapons, the lovely females kneading bread. Beyond them was what Bryce presumed was a typical goblin mound, like a giant anthill, with entry holes all through it.

A male looked up and spied them. "Ho! Fresh meat!"

"Keep moving," Arsenal repeated. "We have to trust the path." Then he called out to the goblins. "After us, the deluge!" He gestured with his free hand.

The water chose this moment to surge more vigorously. It splashed into the cavern, covering the floor.

"Eeeek!" a gobliness cried, leaping up, plastered. It seemed she had been sleeping, and gotten caught and soaked. She made a most interesting figure.

"It's flooding!" a male cried. "We had no warning!"

Now the goblins scrambled to get organized, bringing sandbags to block off their village. It seemed they had suffered floods before, and were prepared, but this time had been caught off guard. They were so busy protecting their work area and mound that they entirely forgot about the intruders.

The far side of the cavern rose. They were able to set down their trikes, unfold them, and resume riding. The path here was broad, so they could go two or three abreast. They had been excruciatingly lucky. Bryce saw Lucky holding his charm, and realized why.

"What's ahead?" Arsenal called across to Pose.

"A troll village."

"The flooding won't distract them," Arsenal said. "Because we've left it behind."

"What else do we have?" Lucky asked. "Trolls eat human flesh if they can get it."

"Do male trolls freak?" Bryce asked.

Arsenal was immediately on it. "Girls: off with your jeans, until we pass the trolls. It's an emergency. We won't look."

Mindy started to protest, then changed her mind and quickly drew her jeans down. Anna did the same. Bryce, warned by his second sight, looked away just in time.

Now the girls took the lead. The recumbent trikes caused their knees to be as high as their heads, and their legs really showed as they pedaled. Bryce, well behind, could glimpse only half-glimpses of their lifted bare knees, and that made him slightly faint. A full view from the front or side would surely wipe out any man, goblin, or troll.

Soon enough, but not quite too soon, they reached the troll village. Some trolls were carrying bolts of wood in from the realm above, while others were hanging animal haunches from a framework over an open pit fire. They were about to have a big meaty meal.

A troll spied the approaching trike party. "Ho!" he cried. Then he got a better look at the leading trikes and froze in place, drool dripping from his snout.

The others looked, and immediately were similarly frozen. In a moment and a half all the males were immobile, staring. Bryce was impressed by how effective those panties were. He had been freaked out before, but never had the chance to see others freaked. He hoped he hadn't drooled similarly.

The party biked on by, unmolested. But of course it couldn't be that easy.

There were troll females present, and they were neither freaked out nor amused. "Those human tarts are flashing our men!" one cried. "Spear them! We'll dump them into the cook-pot first, then wake our men. They won't be so hot for human panties when they're boiling in hot sauce!"

Oops. The lady trolls looked as fierce as the men, and they evidently did not like the way their men were reacting to visiting flesh. Probably their panties were not nearly as effective.

But Arsenal rose to the occasion. "Men!" he called. "Off with your pants. Show your undershorts!" He paused in his own pedaling to draw down his own trousers.

Would that work? Bryce was dubious, but there really was no choice. He pulled off his own pants and stacked them in the basket. Then, undershorts showing, he resumed pedaling.

The nearest female troll charged toward them, wielding a club Bryce himself could hardly have managed.

Then she got an eyeful of male shorts and stumbled to a halt, eyes glazing. It was working!

The seven trikes passed the troll village without hindrance, as the trolls, male and female, stood like statues. None of them were proof against the flashing underwear of the human party. Only in Xanth!

When they were well beyond the village, Arsenal called a halt. "Good job, folk. We can dress now. Girls first. Anyone who looks will freak."

Bryce closed his eyes, not looking. It was impossible to cheat on something like that. Plastered shirts might be fun to see, but panties were deadly.

"Okay," Mindy called. "We're decent."

Then the men put their pants on. In two moments they were decent too.

Anna stood staring, not moving or speaking.

"Oh, bleep!" Mindy swore. "She must have looked." She snapped her fingers by Anna's face. "Wake, girl!"

Anna recovered. "Did something happen?"

"You looked, and got freaked out," Mindy said. "Male shorts don't freak as well as female panties do, but they share some of the same magic. Five shorts together make it pretty strong, as those trolls discovered."

"Oh," Anna said, embarrassed. "I never thought—I never saw—"

"Let's move on," Arsenal said. He turned to Pose. "Anything else along the path we need to be wary of?"

Pose flickered. "Another goblin village. Then we're clear to reach Mount Rushmost."

"Already?" Bryce asked, surprised.

"It's a shortcut," Mindy reminded him. "Cuts our time down to what's needed to get there tonight."

Oh. Things were so much more literal in Xanth.

"Can we handle them the same way?" Arsenal asked Pose.

"No. They are forewarned, probably by a goblin messenger, and prepared. It's a tortuous route, requiring careful vision, and they have lovely goblinesses posted at every turn. They mean to freak *us* out."

"Oh, bleep! What can we do?"

Bryce had an idea. "We need a sheer lucky break. Lucky needs to exercise his talent determinedly, not just for spot scenes."

Lucky nodded. "I can do that. I can turn it on for the next hour, and we'll get whatever lucky break is possible. But after that I won't be able to summon any more good luck today."

"After that, we will be at our destination," Arsenal said.

"So luck may somehow nullify the females," Bryce said. "What about the males?"

"This is weird," Pose said. "They have all gone on a hunting trip on the surface. Only the females remain below."

"So no males can be freaked out by our legs!" Anna said. "They *are* prepared."

"Can we men freak them out, same as we did the trolls?" Bryce asked.

Pose shook his head. "They're wearing smoked glasses. They know what they're doing."

"Make your luck good," Arsenal told Lucky.

"I can't control it specifically," Lucky said. "Just turn it on and let it operate in its own fashion. I don't know what will happen."

"Will your charm help?" Mindy asked.

"I'll try," Lucky said, bringing it out and concentrating.

"Just so long as it does happen," Arsenal said. "For a safe path, this one leaves much to be desired."

Bryce emphatically agreed. Evidently few paths

achieved the standards of the officially enchanted ones, where all dangers were prevented.

They resumed pedaling. The path wound through a series of caves and passages, traversing the subterranean landscape.

Then they came to the second goblin village. The path passed right through it, and wound into a mountainous slope beyond. And there, sure enough, were the goblinesses. They were lining the path through the village, and stood at every turn in the dangerous terrain beyond. Even from a distance it was clear that all were in bras and panties, and all were superbly shaped. It seemed that all female goblins were lovely, in sharp contrast to the ugly males.

"Lovely or not, they've got knives," Pose said. "We will have to fight them, but they'll overwhelm us. There are hundreds of them."

"I don't want to fight lovely creatures half my size," Piper said.

"None of us do," Bryce agreed. He hated the thought of having to battle knife-wielding little lovelies. But he knew he would do it, rather than let them kill him and cook him up for dinner. Assuming he wasn't freaked out first by their outfits. Since he had to look to guide his trike, he would surely see their bodies. This seemed to be a lose-lose situation.

Arsenal glanced at Lucky. "Where is your good luck?"

Lucky spread his hands. "All I know is that it will manifest. The charm should have guided it."

"We have no choice but to trust it," Arsenal said. "Move out." He led the way.

The goblins thronged to surround them. In a moment their panties would be close enough to register on male eyeballs. Bryce found it hard to imagine a prettier doom.

One of the goblins was not in panties. She was in full royal dress. She seemed to be the queen.

"Gwenny!" Mindy cried.

All the goblins paused in place.

The queen peered at her. "Do I know you?"

Mindy seemed momentarily confused. "Uh, yes. We met at Caprice Castle when you visited Princess Dawn."

"I am not sure of that," the queen said.

Mindy jumped off her trike and ran toward the queen. "I can explain."

The goblins closed in on Mindy, but the queen gestured them back. The two came together and conversed briefly. Mindy sat on the ground to make her height equal to the standing queen's height.

Then the queen nodded. "I must have misremembered. We did meet. I apologize for my confusion." Then she turned to the goblins around her. "These people are on a special mission for the Good Magician. They must not be interfered with. Let them pass freely."

The goblins stared at the queen, astonished. So did the members of the Suitors' party. What had happened?

"Must I repeat myself?" the queen inquired sharply.

That did it. The goblins retreated, and soon the way was clear.

Mindy and the queen walked to the trikes. "Give my regards to Princess Dawn when you return," the queen said with an obscure smile. Then she turned and walked away.

"Let's get moving," Mindy said. "Before any goblins change their lovely little mayhem-minded minds."

They obeyed with alacrity. They pedaled rapidly through the village and up the far slope. A few goblins remained, but now they were clothed and showed no knives. They were as pretty as ever, but not freakishly exposed. Bryce was glad they had not had to fight these girls, regardless of who won or lost, and suspected he was not the only one.

The path wound up, finding its way through tunnels and along crevasses. Then abruptly it emerged at the surface of Xanth. They were out of the caves!

And there before them was a vertical mountain. They had arrived at the base of Mount Rushmost.

8

DRESS

It was dusk and they were tired from their ride, and hungry. They had been longer underground than it had seemed at the time. Fortunately they were in a pleasant glade, and there was a pie plant in sight, several pillow bushes, and an alcove in the base of the mountain cliff that would shelter them from moderate rain. There was the sound of a river nearby. They had what they needed to camp for a night.

Lucky found some material in the alcove. He folded it into the form of a pillow and lay down, putting his head on it. "My magic is expended and I'm worn out," he said. "I must sleep." Whereupon he slept.

"We're all tired, I'm sure," Arsenal said. "But we can't simply assume that we are safe here. We don't know the habits of the dragons who come to this mountain. We need to post a sentry who will stay awake and watchful while the rest of us sleep. I suggest two-hour shifts through the night, because I have an hourglass that can be turned over for the second hour, making that convenient. The sentry will finish when the hourglass does. Who wants to be first?"

"I'll be first," Anna Molly said. "I'm too wound up to sleep yet anyway."

"Who will relieve her in two hours?" Arsenal asked.

"I will," Piper said. He glanced at Anna. "Wake me when my turn comes."

Bryce volunteered for the third shift, and Pose for the fourth. That would complete the night.

"It is not that I don't trust any of you," Arsenal said. "But I will wake irregularly and verify that a sentry is on duty. If there is any problem, wake me immediately."

"Meanwhile I will fetch pies and water," Mindy said. "The rest of you get off your feet and rest."

"You should be as tired as the rest of us," Anna said.

"I surely am," Mindy agreed. "But I am here to see that all of you are cared for. I'll relax once I've done my duty."

The others did not argue. Soon they were off their feet, eating pies and drinking from the small folding bucket of water Mindy produced.

"Something I would like to know," Arsenal said. "When we faced an ugly situation with the goblins, you somehow managed to defuse it. How did you do that?"

"The goblin queen visited Caprice Castle once," Mindy said. "Such things are routine among royalty; all the princes and princesses know each other, regardless of species. She recognized me, once I clarified the nature of our encounter. Then I told her about the suitors and the mission. Gwenny is Queen of Goblin Mountain, with a number of vassal tribes. She happened to be visiting this one when we arrived. She has authority to direct them, and did so."

"She happened to be visiting," Arsenal repeated. "Right when we encountered them. She happened to know you. That's an incredible coincidence."

"Remember, Lucky had turned on his luck," Bryce said. "So we got one huge lucky break. This was the proof of his power. It never would have happened on its own."

"True," Arsenal agreed thoughtfully. "But after this experience, I believe we should travel by the enchanted paths as much as possible, regardless of the time taken. I was mistaken to want a shortcut. I do not like depending on luck. We surely will have challenges enough without taking unneeded risks."

The others nodded agreement.

Mindy harvested pillows for them all except Lucky, and they lay down in the alcove to sleep. It had been quite a day.

Almost immediately, it seemed, Piper was waking him. "Your shift," he said, handing Bryce the hourglass. "All's quiet."

Indeed, four hours had passed; the moon had shifted significantly in the sky. Bryce stood and took the hourglass. He set it on a rock and saw the sand start filtering to the lower chamber. This was an object that for once was not a pun. "I've got it."

"There's a nymph," Piper said. "She didn't bother Anna, but she tried to tempt me away from my duty. Maybe she's just bored, but she could be trying to set things up for something devious. Do not let your guard down."

Bryce was concerned. "What if she flashes her panties?"

"Nymphs don't wear panties. They run bare. You won't freak. Enjoy the view, but stay vigilant."

"Thanks for the warning," Bryce said. "I'm still new to magic."

"Thank *you* for interceding when Arsenal was trying to browbeat me," Piper said. "It would have been awkward if I had had to turn monster then. I want to save that for real need."

"He's something of a bully, but he's a competent leader," Bryce said. "I was just trying to keep the peace."

"You are doing more than that," Piper said. "You're a good man."

Bryce realized that they were becoming friends, though of course they were in competition for the favor of Princess Harmony. He assumed all the Suitors had been spelled into love for her, as he had. "So are you," he said.

Piper lay down, put his head on his pillow, and slept. He surely had little to fear regardless, because any person or creature foolish enough to attack him in his sleep would soon discover a horrific monster fighting back.

Bryce walked around the glade. He could see well enough, as his eyes were acclimatized and there was a fair amount of moonlight. It was quiet, with no animals or birds in evidence. That was probably because this was dragon country; other creatures would have been scared off. But maybe the appearance was deceptive.

The nymph appeared, walking from the shadows of the forest cover. She was a splendid figure of a young woman, with a perfect figure and lustrously long hair. "Hello, hero," she said dulcetly. "I am Nyla Nymph."

There seemed to be no harm in replying to her, as long as he remained on guard against distraction. "Hello, Nyla."

"A handsome man like you must be popular with the ladies."

"Not really. I'm an old man in a young body."

"Let me show you how much fun I can be, regardless of your age. I have a bower not far from here where we can be alone."

"Alone? I thought nymphs did not care about privacy when they celebrate."

She came to stand directly before him, even more luscious at close range. "That is true for the nymphs of the Faun & Nymph Retreat," she said. "To them each day is a new life; they have no memory of the prior days and no anticipation of future days. They are eternally young, physically, mentally, and emotionally. But those of us who leave the Retreat lose that innocence. We remember, and we are no longer so open about stork summoning, as they put it in the outer world. We age, and we adopt names. We gradually become increasingly human, until at last we are able to marry and raise children of our own. I would like to do that. But first I need to know more about any man I might marry. Come with me to my bower."

"I thought nymphs were essentially empty-headed. You don't seem to be."

"I am becoming human," she repeated. "Are you going to insist that we do it right here?"

"I am not insisting on anything," he said. "I love another."

"Then perhaps just a momentary liaison." She lay down on the ground and smiled up at him. "Will you join me?"

Suspicious of this direct come-on, Bryce invoked his second sight, which he had suppressed when he slept. All he saw was her on the ground and him standing there.

Then he tried an experiment. Suppose he did join her—what else might happen? He pictured himself getting down to embrace her on the ground.

And saw something scuttling close by. He could not make out its details in the darkness, but he distrusted it.

He erased the mental picture, and the scuttler vanished. He had just discovered a new aspect of his talent. Not only could he see ten seconds ahead in real life, he could see ahead in conjectural life. He could run thought experiments to see how something might turn out, provided they were limited to ten seconds. That could help a lot, depending on the situation.

He wanted to know more about the scuttler. So he got down beside the nymph. The scuttling resumed, exactly as he had foreseen it.

"I knew you'd respond," Nyla said, reaching for him.

But his attention was on the scuttler. Now he could see it, as it scuttled right past him toward the alcove where the others slept. It was somewhat like a millipede, except that it had one giant pincer that looked capable of gouging out a coin-sized chunk of flesh.

"It's a nickelpede!" he exclaimed.

"Kiss me," Nyla said, drawing his head down to hers.

"Some other time," he said, wrenching his head away and jumping to his feet. He pursued the nickelpede. When he reached it, he stomped it with his shoe.

"Oh!" the nymph cried as if in pain.

Bryce turned on her. "You were trying to distract me while the nickelpede attacked the others in their sleep. There must be hundreds more, ready to follow if it gets through. But as you see, it didn't get through."

"Bleep!" she swore. "You ruined it. I didn't really like you anyway."

"Then get out of here and take your deadly bugs with you."

She did, and the danger was over. But it could so readily have been otherwise, had he not been alert. Now he felt weak-kneed.

"So you bested her," Arsenal said, startling him. He was standing by the trunk of a tree, almost invisible.

"I didn't know you were up," Bryce said.

"Exactly. I wanted to be sure you really were on guard. Now I can sleep."

Bryce was annoyed, but soon realized that he had no reason. He was relatively inexperienced in Xanth, and Arsenal knew it, so had backstopped him, just in case. It was the sensible thing to do. "Thank you," he said gruffly.

"You know, she would have delivered," Arsenal said. "You could have possessed that luscious creature."

"While the nickelpedes swarmed past to gouge the sleeping Suitors," Bryce said.

"Exactly. You chose loyalty rather than personal bliss."

"Fool that I am," Bryce agreed wryly.

Arsenal clapped him on the shoulder. "I like that kind of fool. It means I can trust you."

"Thank you," Bryce repeated, less gruffly.

Bryce continued his sentinel duty, pondering what had happened. He had acquitted himself satisfactorily, thanks to Piper's warning and his second sight. It could readily have gone otherwise.

At the one-hour mark he turned over the hourglass. When it finished again, he went to wake Pose. But the demon was already awake. "You did well," he said.

"You were watching too?" Bryce asked.

"Demons don't need to sleep. We're not made of mortal stuff. I was merely emulating the mortal style, practicing."

"So those nickelpedes never really had a chance to chomp us."

"True. But there may be more dangerous menaces observing, so we need to be careful how we show our powers."

"Point made," Bryce said. He lay down in his place and soon was asleep again. He was learning more about his companions, and about Xanth.

In the morning Mindy got breakfast ready, and they considered their next step.

"Somewhere, here, is a prize," Arsenal said. "One of us will win it and return to the Good Magician's Castle while the rest of us go on to the next."

"What prize?" Piper asked. "Which one of us?"

"Those are the questions," Arsenal agreed.

"Soup's on, so to speak," Mindy called. She had gathered and assembled and laid out a nice meal for them.

That finally woke Lucky. He got up and joined them. "I needed that rest," he said. "But now I'm recharged and ready for another hour of excellent luck."

"Save it for the Quest," Anna recommended. "We're still trying to figure out exactly what it is at this point."

"Let me try spot luck," Lucky said. "That's much less wearing than continuous luck." He looked around. "Oh, no!"

"No what?" Arsenal asked.

"I think I've been sleeping on it. It must have been the last gasp of yesterday's luck." Lucky walked back to the alcove and picked up the cloth. He unfolded it and shook it out.

It was a dress.

"I don't get it," Arsenal said. "What good is a dress?"

"You're not a woman," Anna said. "Let me see that." She took it from Lucky and held it up against her body. Somehow it amplified her minimal curves, making her look considerably more buxom.

"It's a prize," Lucky said. "I know it. My luck put me right on it, when I paid attention."

"Some prize," Arsenal said. "Only two members of our party can use it. It doesn't look like much."

"I'm going to try it on," Anna said. "Close your eyes while I change."

The men dutifully closed their eyes, knowing that the sight of her panties would freak them out. The ride past the trolls had demonstrated the power of even mediocre panties.

"Okay."

They looked. And stared.

Anna had been transformed from a rather spare female to a lovely woman. Now every part of her torso was aesthetic to the point of fascination, and even the rest of her seemed to have added luster. She was no longer lean, she was elegant; no longer straight-line, but artistically curved. Even her fingers seemed to have become delicately shaped.

"It's a prize, all right," Piper said. "It makes any woman lovely." He paused, then added, "No offense, Anna."

"None taken," Anna said. "I know I'm no luscious creature. That's part of the reason I felt free to substitute for my brother. I don't turn men on unless I really try, and even then it's no sure thing."

"You do now," Arsenal said, impressed. "If I weren't committed to the princess, I'd want to hug you and kiss you." He smiled a trifle ruefully. "In fact I do want to."

"We all do," Piper said. "It's the magic of the dress. Princess Harmony is already pretty; this dress would make her ravishing. She can surely use it."

"Let's try it on Mindy, just to be sure," Lucky suggested. "No offense."

Mindy laughed. "I know I'm no seductress. I do want to try it."

"By all means," Anna said. She pulled the dress off over her head. Bryce, forewarned by his left eye, shut his eyes in time. The other men freaked out.

"Well, well," Anna said, not at all annoyed. She handed the dress to Mindy, who quickly changed into it.

Then Bryce snapped his fingers, and the four men recovered. "You were caught by surprise," Bryce explained. "But I think her panties under that dress were twice as potent."

Now they looked at Mindy. She, too, had been transformed. She had been a modestly pretty girl; now she was phenomenally pretty. "Oh, I like this dress!" she exclaimed.

"Now we know," Piper said. "This is the first of the prizes we have come for. The princess will surely like it. Which of us wants to try for it?"

"Dresses aren't really my thing," Arsenal said. "There must be a more manly prize farther along."

"A dress like this is certainly my thing," Anna said. "But if I had it, I'd be hard put to give it to the princess."

"Well, I like it," Lucky said. "I found it, so it must be mine. I think the princess would be thrilled to have it as a gift."

Piper shrugged. "Then it should be yours to give her. But I'm surprised there is not more challenge to its acquisition than this. Why should such a valuable thing be left lying on the ground?"

"Maybe so that only the sheerest luck would lead a person to it," Pose said. "It selected you, Lucky."

"Then I accept it," Lucky said. "I will give it to Harmony."

There was a subdued kind of flash. The dress fragmented into powder, leaving Mindy standing in her underwear. Again four men freaked out, Bryce having escaped by blinking as his left eye warned him.

He gave Mindy time to get her regular clothing back on. "Okay," Anna said, amused. They snapped the others back to awareness.

"Sorry," Mindy said, though her tone hinted that she was not completely so. "I didn't know it would do that."

"It seems this is not THE dress," Bryce said. "But merely a copy, a demonstrator model, to show us what it is capable of. Obtaining the real one will be more difficult."

"I'll say!" Lucky said, staring into the forest.

They followed his gaze. There, rising above the trees, was a fantastic castle that had not been there before.

"The moment our decision was made," Arsenal said. "This is Lucky's Quest, to win or lose. Shall we leave him to it, and be on our way to the next?"

"No," Bryce said. "Lucky got us here by using his luck on our behalf, to get us past the goblins. We should not desert him now."

"It's his Quest," Arsenal said. "He used his luck to get himself to it; it wasn't just for us. Why should we help?"

"I don't suppose because it's the decent thing to do?" Bryce asked with irony.

"We're in competition! Only one will get the princess."

"There can be no choice by the princess unless we each return with prizes for her to choose from. We need to help each other. The princess will choose, not us. We do not want to preempt her choices by letting any of our number fail if we can help it."

"That makes sense to me," Piper said. "We don't know what the other Quests will be like. We all may need help."

"If Lucky gets his dress, he'll head home with it," Arsenal pointed out. "He won't be helping anyone else."

"True," Bryce said. "But if we don't help him, none of us can be certain of help from others in the future."

"We are not on an individual Quest with Companions," Arsenal said. "We'll be losing people all along. The last one won't get any help regardless."

"Shall we put it to a vote?" Bryce asked.

"Don't bother," Anna said. "We're with you. We'll all help each other."

"Better to be united throughout," Pose said.

Arsenal smiled. "I agree. Let's get on it."

That was interesting, Bryce thought. Discovering himself outvoted, the man readily joined the winning side. That was one way to handle it.

"I see the castle," Lucky said. "But I'm not sure where the real Dress is, or how to reach it."

Pose flickered. "It's in the highest turret. A fairy queen is wearing it. There are guards galore. They're not going to just hand it to anyone."

"Couldn't you just take it and bring it back?" Anna asked. "Saving us a hassle?"

"No. The moment I intruded, the castle's magic alerts

were triggered, and I had to get out of there immediately. I won't be able to pop in there again. I will have to go physically. If I invoke any demonly effect, those activated defenses will nail me."

"The Demons are limiting us," Piper said.

"Then we need a plan of attack," Arsenal said.

"We do," Bryce agreed. "But I wonder."

"Wonder?" Piper asked.

"This is a Demon setup. That sudden castle can't be real. It has to be an emulation. There must be a key."

"A key?"

"The Demons aren't interested in killing us," Bryce said. "If all of us died, there would be no choices for the princess. Instead they want to challenge us to show our mettle. It's bad for a Demon sponsor if any of us don't turn out to be worthy, so we all must have an exactly even chance. It's a game to them. Where I come from, Mundania, there are fantasy games that may seem real to the participants, but aren't really. I suspect this could be similar. The guards probably are mock-ups, not real people. Any of us who get killed here probably won't really die, just be ejected from the game. We should keep that in mind."

"You have an interesting mind," Piper said.

"But he has been right before," Anna said. "I trust his judgment."

"So do I," Arsenal said, surprisingly. "Our challenge may be threefold: first to survive the Quest, second to win a prize, third to have it chosen by the princess." He faced Bryce. "So what should we be alert for?"

"Surprises. Tricks. The unexpected. Brains may count more than muscle." Bryce glanced at Arsenal. "No offense."

Arsenal laughed. "None taken. A true leader learns to utilize whatever is available, including luck and insight. We had best approach that castle cautiously."

Bryce was struck by a thought. "Would a nymph and nickelpedes be part of it?"

Arsenal, Piper, and Pose focused on him, surprised. "We are already in the Challenge," Piper said.

"Nymph?" Anna asked.

"A nymph came to me during my watch last night," Bryce said. "She tried to distract me so that a swarm of nickelpedes could get at the rest of you while you slept. Fortunately I caught on in time, and trod on the first one, which discouraged the others."

"Fortunately," Pose murmured, electing not to clarify that only Lucky, Anna, Mindy, and perhaps Piper had actually been asleep at the time.

"They tried to take us out before we ever knew about the Dress!" Anna said, annoyed.

"An apt strategic ploy," Arsenal said. "But Bryce was alert, and spared us that mischief."

"We do need to support each other," Anna agreed. "Lest we be taken out well before the finish."

"We need to approach the castle," Arsenal said. "We can march there together, which has the risk of something like a roc bird spotting us and taking us out together. Or we can split up and infiltrate the forest separately, so there is no individual target. But that way we would be unable to help each other, and could take individual losses."

Anna looked at Lucky. "This is your Quest. Those nickelpedes were probably after you, while you were sleeping with your luck depleted. How long can you turn your luck on again?"

"Maybe two hours, before it starts losing potency," Lucky said.

She turned to Arsenal. "How long should a campaign to get into the castle and get the Dress normally take?"

Arsenal smiled. "Three hours, I suspect."

"So we need to speed it up, if we can. To get it under two hours."

"You may be a budding strategist," Arsenal said. "What do you recommend?"

"That Lucky turn on his luck now, and we hurry in a group to the castle, saving time on that part of it." She smiled briefly. "If we're lucky, the roc won't spy us. Then consider speed as well as safety when we enter it. Lucky's luck will protect us all, to an extent, since we are supporting him."

"So be it," Arsenal said. "Lucky, get on it. Move out."

Lucky brought out his charm and focused.

They walked swiftly toward the castle. There was a convenient path, which ordinarily would have been suspicious, but they trusted to the luck to nullify whatever threat it might have. They were utilizing what was available, as Arsenal had said.

The first thing they passed was a pit filled with nickelpedes. But the nymph who guided them happened, purely by chance, to be distracted by a game of card solitaire. "I can't get at that king!" she complained as she laid the cards down.

"Eyes front!" Arsenal hissed, as more than one set of male eyes threatened to orient on the fetching aspects of the bare nymphly torso. Fortunately the nymph did not hear him.

They passed on by. Bryce was disappointed not to have gotten a better look, but knew this was best. Had they paused, the nymph might well have looked up and spied several would-be kings to get at. Even so, they were lucky she wasn't wearing bra or panties, which would have freaked them out regardless.

Which was one of the interesting things about this magic land of Xanth, Bryce thought. Panties had magic that bare bottoms lacked. There was probably an interesting story there, could any man but fathom it without freaking out.

Then they came to a region of oddly compressed rocks strewn all around. The explanation was soon apparent: a gross hairy ogre twelve feet tall was hunched over a bucket the size of a bathtub, squeezing reddish juice from stones. His giant muscles bulged horrendously with the effort, but the juice was flowing. "Best drink known, from palm-granite stone," he muttered as he worked. When he squeezed one stone dry, he pried the squished remnant from his palm and picked up a fresh one. Luckily he was so intent on his effort that he never noticed the passing party.

Farther along they passed a nest the size of a house, wherein snoozed a roc, a bird so big it could have picked up an elephant with one claw. Fortunately its sleep was deep enough so that their passage did not wake it.

In fact without Lucky's formidable luck, they never would have made it the length of this path. This was definitely Lucky's Quest.

They came to the castle. This was a towering structure, several times as tall as it was wide, with several lofty turrets. The highest one was well above the trees, perhaps ten stories up. It would be a challenge just climbing all the winding stairs to reach it.

The castle was surrounded by a moat. Anna knelt and dipped a finger in the water. She yanked it back immediately as a little fish with big jaws snapped viciously. Piranhas or the equivalent. There would be no wading or swimming across this trench.

"Maybe we can make a boat or raft," Piper suggested.

Then the moat monster appeared. A horrendously huge greenish snout rose from the water, girt by sharp horns and tusks. The thing could have taken their entire party in its mouth in one gulp, boat and all.

"No boat," Piper concluded.

"Maybe a tunnel under the moat?" Anna suggested.

"Why would they make a tunnel there?" Piper asked.

"It would be an anomaly," she agreed.

Bryce saw the connection. Her talent was the anomaly. "Let's circle the castle, looking for a tunnel. We can't afford to dither long."

They walked around the castle. The moat monster watched them, but made no move. It was obviously waiting for them to try to cross.

They completed the circle. There seemed to be no tunnel. There was a drawbridge, but it was locked in the upright position inside the moat; they could not use it.

Lucky approached the monster's snout, trusting in his luck not to get snapped up and chomped. "What do you say, serpent? Is there a tunnel?"

The monster's mouth opened so wide it seemed ready to swallow the sky. They could see all the way into its throat and beyond.

"Obviously it is not answering," Piper said.

Then Bryce caught on. "Yes it is! You asked the right question, Lucky! That *is* the tunnel!"

The others stared at him. "That's more likely death by digestion," Arsenal said.

Bryce considered. "It could be both. Play it right, we get safely across the moat. Play it wrong, we get digested. Suppose we prop its mouth open so it can't close and trap us inside?"

"That I can do," Arsenal said. He drew his sword, stepped into the monster's mouth, and stood with the sword point lifted high. If the mouth closed, it would come down on the sharp point. The man certainly had courage.

"Then let's go," Pose said, and stepped in, passing Arsenal.

"I can't actually participate in the Challenges," Mindy said. "Not being a Suitor. I will wait here. Please do return, all of you."

"We'll try," Bryce said bravely, and stepped in.

The others followed, though obviously nervous. Pose led the way down the throat, which now seemed like a red-lined tunnel. The monster could drown them by sinking into the water and letting it run down its open mouth, regardless of Arsenal. But it didn't. It seemed they had found the right move.

The far end exited to a pavement beside the foot of the castle. Bryce looked back, after they emerged, and saw that the opening looked exactly like an anus. Well, why not?

Now they were up against a high blank wall, the outer rampart of the castle. Piper tapped a stone. "It's solid. We can't break it down. We may have to scale this wall to find one of the embrasures and climb in a portal."

"Scale with what?" Pose asked. "In an ordinary case, I would be able to assume the form of a ladder. But as I said, I will be canceled the moment I act like other than a mortal man."

"We could unravel our clothing," Anna said. "Use the material to make a rope that we might climb."

"And that would take how many hours?" Piper asked.

"Too many," she agreed.

Suddenly a gate they hadn't seen before clanged open. Armed men charged out. "Uh-oh," Piper said. "I can stop them, but you might not like the way I do it."

Bryce knew exactly what he meant. He would have to turn monster. It seemed better to save that for another time. "Anna," Bryce said. "If you are willing—"

"Don't look," she said. She drew down her jeans.

The castle guardians charged up, and freaked out to a man. Something about panty magic made them keep their feet, but they were caught in all manner of awkward positions, staring.

"Thanks," Bryce said. "We'll return for you." Because she would not be able to accompany them; she had to remain to make sure every castle soldier remained freaked. It was her sacrifice for the cause.

"Go!" she hissed. It was clear that she wasn't pleased, but it was the weapon they needed at the moment.

They went. They passed the soldiers and went to the open gate without looking back. They entered. They had breached the castle wall, through sheer luck of the circumstances. Now what?

They followed the passage through the wall and into the castle proper. They emerged into a kind of drawing room. There were four excellently-garbed ladies sitting at a table, playing some kind of a board game. They looked up, startled, as the men entered.

"Sound the alarm!" one exclaimed. "The castle has been breached!"

That would be disaster. There were surely many more guards, and they now had no panties to freak them out.

Piper stepped forward. "Ladies, allow me to entertain you. I am a musician."

"But—" the first lady said.

Piper brought out his piccolo and put it to his mouth. He played a note. It was rapturously lovely. He moved on into an evocative tune. Bryce remembered how beautifully the man could play. The ladies were of course fascinated.

Bryce touched Pose's elbow, leading him away. Piper was serving as a distraction, using his music instead of his monster form, and that was surely for the best.

They came to the central stairwell. A staircase spiraled up seemingly endlessly, surely leading to the highest turret. They gazed at it with dismay. That was where they wanted to go, but what a chore it would be to get there one step at a time! They could be ambushed at any of the intervening floors.

In the center was a round column with a door. Bryce

opened the door and saw a platform suspended by a stout rope. "A dumbwaiter!" he said. "They must use this to haul food and incidentals up to the top chamber, to save all that stair climbing."

"Too bad we can't use it," Pose said.

"Maybe we can. These things can have counterweights suspended from a pulley so that even heavy objects can be lifted without undue effort." He walked around to the back and spied another door. He opened it. There was a solid metal weight hanging from another rope. "The counterweight!" He pushed on it, and it dropped slightly. He went around to the other side. Sure enough, the platform had raised slightly.

"We need to haul on the counterweight side, to raise the platform to the top," Bryce said. "We can send Lucky right up there. It was fortunate we discovered this."

"Lucky's luck guided us to it," Pose said. "But I'm not sure he's competent to go up alone. You had better go with him."

"I need to haul on this side," Bryce said. "If we both do, we should readily lift Lucky up. The castle guards won't suspect this ploy, so it should be safe."

"I will haul this side down," Pose said. "I will cling to the weight and make myself heavy enough to haul the two of you up."

"You can do that? What of the castle alerts?"

"I'll be heading swiftly down way below. By the time they catch on, you should be up there."

"But they won't treat you kindly when they do catch you."

"I'm a demon," Pose reminded them. "What can they do to me other than confine me to a pentacle? Now get on that lift before we are discovered here."

Pose was doing an undemonly decent thing, sacrificing himself for the good of the spot mission. He would surely suffer for it. "Thanks," Bryce said. He was coming to like Pose, also.

"Okay, let's get in there," he told Lucky. "We're riding to the top."

They climbed in. There was just room for them both, hunched into nearly fetal formation. "Ready!" Bryce called.

The platform shivered. It shook. Then it started rising. Pose was on the counterweight and increasing his weight.

They accelerated. They zoomed upward so fast the air seemed to thin. Floors zipped by.

Then suddenly they stopped. Had something gone wrong? No, Bryce saw the pulley at the top. They were there.

They scrambled out. They were in the single room of the topmost turret. Naturally the fairy queen was there, wearing the Dress.

"Well, now," she said.

They looked at her. She was absolutely beautiful, of course, as any woman in the Dress would be, but on her the effect was verging on devastating. She had flaming red hair that swirled down to her excruciatingly narrow waist. Her figure put Bryce in mind of the hourglass he had used for timing the night, only better proportioned. Her legs and feet below the skirt were perfectly shaped. Her face was so lovely that to gaze on it more than half a moment was to commence the fall into love.

"Don't look at her!" Bryce said, tearing his eyes away though it felt as though he were peeling the lenses off them. "Just get the Dress!"

"But she's so pretty," Lucky protested.

He was farther gone than Bryce. The Dress made the queen's every wish compelling. In a moment she would have them both in her thrall. She would surely be merciless in dealing with them. This would never do.

Bryce launched himself at the queen. She stepped back, but he managed to tackle her knees. "Get the Dress!" he repeated as he clung to those divine joints.

The queen fell against the wall. Bryce tried to yank her legs out from under her, to bring her all the way down, but in the process his head passed under her flaring skirt and he saw up her thighs. She wore luscious pink panties.

Then he was on the floor hanging on to one slipper. He knew he had freaked out, but recovered because his fall had removed his gaze from her underwear and jogged him back to consciousness. Lucky was trying to pull the Dress off over her head. He was succeeding, in her distraction.

But that promoted another danger. "Don't look at her panties!" Bryce cried, slamming his eyes shut.

"Take that, miscreant!" the queen said. Bryce felt power surge. She was using some kind of spell.

Then the queen stiffened and stopped resisting. Lucky drew the Dress the rest of the way off her, though his eyes were closed. "Got it!" he said, wadding it up.

"Bleepity bleepity bleep!" the queen swore, making the window curtains curl.

"Get out of here!" Bryce said, cracking an eye open just enough to see where the dumbwaiter platform was. He lunged for it.

So did Lucky. They jammed onto it in a tangle of limbs. Their weight started it plunging down as the queen, outraged in her underwear, lifted her hands to throw another devastating spell. Fortunately they dropped out of her sight before the spell landed.

"What happened?" Bryce asked as they fell. He hoped Pose was still on the job and would slow them before they crashed.

"I happened to be standing before a full-length mirror," Lucky said. "Her spell reflected and smacked her down."

"You were incredibly lucky!"

"Of course."

Ah, yes. That was the real key to this escapade: the man's incredible luck. They had moved fast enough to stay within the two-hour limit of its potency.

Then things dissolved around them. The tall castle and its attachments were gone. They were sitting on the ground, and Pose was nearby, not buried. Beyond were Piper, still playing his piccolo without an audience, then Anna still flashing her panties before no soldiers, and Arsenal with sword uplifted without the moat monster's mouth to balk.

And there was Mindy. "Congratulations," she said. "I see you won the Dress."

"Cover up, Anna!" Bryce called. She hastily obeyed.

They had won the Dress for Lucky. The first stage of the Demon Quest had been accomplished.

9

RING

I think I need to get on back to the Good Magician's Castle," Lucky said. "Thank all of you for your help. I couldn't have done it without you."

That was so emphatically true that it merited no comment. "It showed us how we can work together to achieve a common objective," Bryce said diplomatically.

"We'll miss your luck," Arsenal said.

"The princess will surely love the Dress," Anna said.

Lucky nodded. "Well, I'll be on my way. I hope all of you win your prizes." He got on his trike. "My luck's worn out for the day. I'll take the enchanted path back." He rode off.

"Now we need to decide where to go next," Mindy said. She produced her scroll and unrolled it another notch. "The western tip of the Panhandle."

"That's far away!" Bryce protested.

"That, it seems, is part of our joint Challenge," Anna said. "We have a lot of riding to do."

"I have an idea," Piper said. "I have traveled these parts. The Trollway passes close by here."

"The what?" Bryce asked.

"The trolls aren't all monsters. One tribe of them maintains a limited-access highway that runs the length of Xanth. For a nominal fee they will let others use it in perfect safety."

"Oh, like the interstate in Mundania, or a toll road," Bryce said. Then he caught the pun. "Tollway! Too bad we can't store that in Caprice Castle! But it's still a long way."

"There's also the Autotroll," Piper said. "We could ride that and take our trikes along. But that costs more. We could roust up the fee for the Trollway, but not the ride."

"They must want business," Arsenal said. "Maybe we could make a deal."

"We can try," Piper agreed. "Failing that, we can cycle the distance; it will still be faster than using the enchanted paths, and safer than any shortcut."

"Not fast enough," Arsenal said. "Even pedaling day and night."

"So we'll try for the Autotroll deal."

"Lead the way."

They mounted their trikes and started off, following Piper. The trikes worked their magic, and they moved smartly along without being bothered by bushes, rocks, or crevices.

Until they came to a fork in the path. "I don't remember this," Piper said. "It must be new."

"Take either one," Arsenal called gruffly.

Piper took the left fork. That led to a man standing in the way. "Halt!" he cried. "This is my path. No intruders."

Piper halted, and the others behind him. "We are merely passing through," he said politely.

"Well, pass some other way. No one uses this path but me."

Bryce could see that Piper was beginning to get annoyed. "No one owns a common path. Please just let us pass."

"No. Go away."

"And suppose we go through anyway?" Piper asked.

"Then I'll use my talent on you."

"And what talent is that?"

"To give anyone a toothache."

"Oh for bleep's sake!" Arsenal snapped, riding forward, passing around Piper. "He's bluffing."

The man merely glanced at him. Arsenal abruptly clapped his hand to his jaw and crashed into a tree. "Mmmmph!"

"It seems it's not a bluff," Piper said, unsurprised. He turned his trike around. The rest followed suit. They rode away, followed by Arsenal. Fortunately for him, his severe toothache abated once he was out of the man's sight.

They returned to the fork, and this time tried the right turn. This brought them to a moderately sized ant mound. They paused. "What kind is that?" Arsenal asked, more cautious after his experience with the toothache man.

"I've seen that type before," Anna said. "We use them to eliminate the smell in our barnyard. But it's not safe to molest their home mound. They're de-odor-ants."

"I wish I was still collecting puns!" Mindy said.

"Why isn't it safe?" Arsenal asked.

"Because they think that messing with their nest stinks. Then they set out to eliminate the smell by consuming what makes it. You won't stink because you will have been eaten down to nothing."

"We'll leave this alone," Arsenal said.

"But that eliminates both forks," Pose protested.

"Not necessarily," Piper said. "This is a region of high-intensity magic. Things change frequently."

So they rode back along the left fork. Sure enough, the toothache man was no longer there. Now there was a young woman blocking the way.

They stopped again. "Who are you?" Arsenal demanded impatiently.

"I am Miss Teak," she answered with a voice that fairly oozed mystery.

"Mistake?"

"Miss Teak. Come fathom my mystery." She stepped toward Arsenal.

"Oh, Mystique," he agreed. "Feminine mystique. But why the pun on wood?"

"I don't trust this," Anna said. "I think she's one-sided."

"One sided?" Bryce asked.

"Turn around," Anna told Teak. "Let's see the other side of you."

But the woman did not turn. She stepped in to Arsenal, putting her arms around him. He did not seem loath, but neither did he respond.

"Kiss her," Anna said. "Turn her around."

Arsenal kissed her and turned her around.

Miss Teak's backside was hollow. She had no flesh there at all, merely the space within a shell. She was literally half a woman—the front half.

"I knew it!" Anna said. "She's a woodwife."

"So she is," Mindy agreed. "I knew one of those once. She was Wenda Woodwife, actually a good person. She married Prince Charming and became whole."

"That doesn't mean that *this* woodwife is a good person," Pose said. "She could be setting us up for an ambush, the way that nymph did."

Arsenal remained in the creature's embrace. "*Are* you?" he asked her.

"You will never know unless you love me," Teak said. "And my sisters."

"Now I *really* don't trust this," Anna said. "All wood-wives want to become real by snaring human men. If they have their way, we'll never get on with our Quest."

"I agree," Arsenal said. He disengaged from the wood-wife.

"You can't pass here without satisfying me and my sisters," Teak said.

Now the other woodwives were appearing, looking seductively eager. From the front they were phenomenally desirable, but now that Bryce had seen the back of one, he was hardly tempted. All they were was wooden forms without internal substance. They formed a tight phalanx across the path.

And some of them were male, eying Anna and Mindy. They were quite robust and handsome from the front. So it seemed there were wood-husbands too.

What would happen if the group tried to barge on through? Bryce suspected that the wooden aspect of the woodfolk would manifest, and they would become very difficult to escape. This was a confrontation best avoided.

Arsenal evidently came to the same conclusion. "Let's get out of here," he said.

They retreated. The woodfolk did not pursue them, evidently being territorial. That was a relief.

They returned to the right fork. This too had changed. Now instead of an anthill there was a graveyard. The path went right across it. There did not seem to be a way around it, as brambles grew thickly right up to the edges.

They paused to consider it.

"I don't like this," Arsenal said. "We shouldn't desecrate someone's cemetery."

"Uh-oh," Piper said.

For a zombie had appeared. His clothing was ragged, his flesh rotten, and worms wriggled where his face should be.

"Whaaash ooo doingg heere?" he demanded of them.

It was not a garden-variety burial place. It was a zombie graveyard. That was more challenging.

"We need to cross your cemetery," Arsenal said.

"Ovverr mmy deead boody!" the zombie said. "Wee haave espreet de corpse."

"Oh, for my pun bag!" Mindy moaned.

Arsenal was frustrated. "We have to do it, otherwise we'll never get beyond those paths, with their constantly changing impediments. But this is ugly business. They might put a rotting curse on us."

The others agreed. They had to get past this challenging region. But at what price?

Then Bryce thought of something. "How can a long-settled graveyard appear where there was an anthill before? Those ants would have consumed the zombies to get rid of the smell. A new impediment could have replaced the prior one, but a cemetery doesn't travel. One or the other has to be an illusion."

"Or both," Pose said. "Illusions are the easiest magic. All the things balking us may be illusions."

"My toothache was no illusion," Arsenal said.

"That was a live man, not a setting," Bryce said. "But the principle remains: things are being sent to balk us."

"Sent by whom?" Arsenal asked.

"That is an interesting question," Piper said thoughtfully. "Could some party be trying to stop us?"

"Who would dare try to interfere with a Demon contest?" Anna asked.

"Maybe another Demon?" Pose suggested.

"I doubt it," Arsenal said. "The Demons are surely watching our progress, to be sure that none of them cheat. There can be no interference by any of them."

"Then it must be simply the ordinary mischief of the region," Piper said. "A routine challenge to us all."

Bryce wasn't sure of that, but let it be.

"So we can ignore the illusions and move on," Pose said.

That seemed to make sense. But Arsenal had a caveat. "Ignoring illusions can be dangerous. They could cover a bottomless pit. This could be a threat of another nature. We need to be sure this path is firm before we risk it."

"Good point," Pose said. "Fortunately I can verify it. I won't be hurt by a pit." He flickered. "No pit. We can proceed."

They mounted their trikes and started forward. More zombies appeared, barring their way. Arsenal pedaled harder and plowed right into them.

The zombies collapsed into a slushy pile of pieces. The trikes rolled right over them. In barely two moments they were across the graveyard and zooming along the path beyond. They had made it through. Even the rotting bits of flesh that covered the trikes faded out, unable to maintain themselves apart from their original illusion.

"I'm glad we didn't have to desecrate a real grave-yard," Mindy said.

"You and me both, honey," Piper said. "A zombie curse could be unpleasant, to say the least."

Bryce agreed. He was still learning things about the devious bypaths of magic. What would a zombie curse do—start turning a person into a zombie? He hoped never to find out.

Now at last they reached the Trollway. There was a gate across the path with a sign: STOP. PAY TROLL. Bryce repressed a smile.

They stopped. "Now we have to decide what we want," Piper said. "I have small change, but not enough for the Autotroll."

"Can we bargain?" Pose asked.

"With what?"

"Our talents," Bryce suggested. "Piper can play music marvelously well. Arsenal could demonstrate military techniques. The girls could dance. We just might be able to put together a—a traveling minstrel show."

They considered. "I have tried to maintain human form and limitations, generally," Pose said. "But I am a demon. I could assume the form of a stage for a performance by the others."

"Or a pet, or monster," Bryce said. "Whatever props are needed."

"So the rest of us have roles," Pose said. "What about you, Bryce?"

Bryce sighed. "Since I have no real talent to contribute, I think I had better be the Master of Ceremonies."

The others laughed. "Then go make our case," Arsenal said.

Bryce approached the troll booth. "We are a group of six who would like to purchase passage on the Autotroll for the farthest tip of the Panhandle. We doubt we have sufficient payment, so we would like to earn our passage by becoming an entertainment troupe. We have assorted skills that may suffice."

"Give a sample," the troll said.

"Piper?" Bryce said.

Piper brought out his piccolo and played a fetching little melody. It was completely delightful and they all listened appreciatively.

"Passage granted," the troll said. "Your party will remain on the Autotroll as long as the travelers are satisfied with your offerings. Thereafter you will be ejected. Fair enough?"

It was evident that the trolls did not fool around with loafers. "Fair enough," Bryce agreed.

"Food and a private chamber with amenities will be provided as part of your fare."

More than fair enough. "Thank you," Bryce said.

The troll's almost lipless mouth quirked in an approximation of a smile. "We were advised you were coming."

Oh? But of course their struggle with the path illusions could have alerted local folk, one of whom could have reported to the trolls. There was no point in being unduly suspicious.

It wasn't long before the Autotroll arrived. It steamed along tracks in the center of the Trollway, a full-blown old-style train of the type seldom seen anymore in Mundania. It had a steam engine, a coal car, six passenger cars, six sleeper cars, a dining car, six freight cars, a car marked REVUE, and a caboose. It was impressive.

It braked to a halt almost where they stood. A set of steps folded down from the front end of the first passenger car. "All aboard!" the trollductor called.

They boarded, carrying their folded trikes. A porter troll put tags on the trikes for storage in a freight car, and they were shown to their chamber. This was a nice if compact room with seats, fold-down beds, a table, and two windows looking out on the landscape that was now moving back as the train chugged back up to cruising velocity.

"But we can't relax yet," Bryce said. "We need to get our act together so we can satisfy the other passengers. Pose, can you form into supported curtains we can open and close to define our acts?"

The demon was replaced by a set of heavy curtains.

"Good," Bryce said. "We can have Piper play pleasant melodies to accompany the acts. Arsenal, can you show off your weaponry without doing damage to the furniture?"

"Oh, yes."

"And the women." Bryce paused. "I was thinking you could don matching dresses and dance, but I don't know if you have them, or whether Mindy should participate."

"I can't participate in your Challenges," Mindy said. "But this is the in-between traveling. I like to dance anyway."

"I don't," Anna said. "I don't like flashing my panties either. I had to do it for the other trolls and Lucky's Quest, but don't want to do it here."

"You don't have to," Mindy said. "The right costume has petticoats that obscure things so that you only *seem* to flash. Let's see whether the trolls have provided what we need." She delved into a chest in the corner. "Yes, they have." She drew out piles of crinkly white material. "Close your eyes, men."

The men did. Bryce thought of how such a stricture was pure courtesy in Mundania, but necessary in Xanth, where panty magic could and did freak out men.

"Okay," Mindy said after two and a half moments.

They looked. Now the girls were in identical outfits, with blue ribbons in their hair, lovely red dresses, and flaring skirts that seemed to be solidly filled with the crinkly petticoats.

"Now we need to work out a dance," Bryce said. "Something that will divert viewers male and female without being too daring."

"No need," Piper said. "I will play dance music."

"But they need to agree on steps so they can be together," Bryce said.

"No. My music is magic. I will demonstrate."

Piper lifted his pipe and started playing. Both girls immediately started dancing. They were in perfect step, and the dance motions enhanced their femininity and made them quite attractive.

"Wow!" Anna said as they finished. "That melody just took over my body and made it perform."

"But it must be limited," Piper said. "Because they are not in condition for a long strenuous dance. But it should do for the brief acts we will put on."

"Indeed it should," Bryce agreed, impressed.

A troll appeared. "Time for your first show," he said. "Follow me to the revue car."

They did. The revue car had seats on one end, while the other end was clear. Evidently there had been acts performed before, so the Autotroll was well set up.

Their first audience consisted of an assortment of humans, elves, and off-duty trolls. This was probably more of a test case, to be sure the entertainment was worthwhile.

"Pose," Bryce murmured.

The demon became the curtains, separating them from the audience.

Bryce parted the curtains and stepped out to face the audience. "First we will entertain you with a fetching melody," he said. "Piper?"

Piper stepped out, and Bryce went back behind the curtains. Piper did indeed play a fetching melody; they could hear the audience's toes tapping to its beat. It was the warm-up for the show, putting the listeners in the mood for more.

But meanwhile Bryce was setting up the next act. "Arsenal, you're next."

"Stay out with me," Arsenal said. "I need a person to demonstrate against, for best effect."

"Okay."

The melody finished. Bryce stepped out. "Thank you, Piper," he said, and Piper retreated behind the curtain. "Our next act is a demonstration of swordcraft." He faced back. "Arsenal?"

Arsenal came out. He drew his sword and stabbed at Bryce before he could move. Bryce suffered a momentary heart seizure, then realized that the thrust had not scored. The audience reacted similarly, thinking they had seen a murder onstage before realizing it was part of the act.

Bryce clapped a hand to his gut where he had not been stabbed. "Thank you for your restraint," he said to Arsenal. "I know my presentation leaves something to be desired, but I didn't think it was *that* bad."

The audience burst into relieved laughter. Bryce, almost without trying to, had made a public joke.

Arsenal swung the sword at Bryce's neck. Again, it seemed like death, but again there was no contact. The man had excellent control. There was another gasp from the audience.

"I'm going to need my head to finish this act," Bryce said. "Don't forget."

There was another burst of laughter.

Thereafter Arsenal attacked Bryce with every kind of stab and cut, never touching his skin. Then he sheathed the sword and drew out a knife. He flipped it in the air, and caught it. Then he drew a second knife, and a third, juggling them impressively while Bryce continued with spot humor. He was a stand-up comedian, something he had never anticipated. It seemed to have been brought out by his nervousness about the attacks.

Finally Arsenal brought out what looked like a small bomb. He dropped it on the floor. It detonated with a loud pop and exploded into a puff of black smoke. Bryce stepped back in mock alarm. "Thank you," Bryce said, fanning smoke away from himself. "I'm glad I caught you in a good mood!"

More laughter. The military exhibit was done, and the audience had evidently enjoyed it.

"Next we have an exhibition of dancing," Bryce said. "Girls?"

Anna and Mindy emerged from the curtains, looking almost like twins in their matching costumes.

"Piper?" Bryce said.

Piper started to play from behind the curtain. The girls danced. It was every bit as impressive as before. More so, because this time they did some brief leg lifts toward the audience, gaining intense attention from the males, though Bryce knew that they were not seeing nearly as much as they thought, because of the obscuring petticoats. Bryce saw that the females were paying as much attention as the males, perhaps for different reason: studying the costumes, the dance, and the effect of the masked leg lifts.

The dance concluded with a deep bow by both women, and Bryce realized that there was a petticoat effect masking their bosoms so that their breasts did not actually show. But the audience thought they showed, and applauded appreciatively.

"Thank you," Bryce said. "You've been a great audience! Perhaps we'll meet again soon."

They retreated behind the curtains to prolonged applause. Their first show had been a rousing success.

Even the truculent troll conceded as much as he guided them back to their chamber. "Good job. Your next performance will be before another audience in an hour."

Back alone, they more or less collapsed. "That was wonderful!" Anna exclaimed. "Never in my dreams did I ever perform like that for anyone, let alone before an audience. That magic piping made it possible." She half flung herself on Piper and kissed him on the cheek. He looked startled but appreciative.

"Your ad libs helped enliven it," Arsenal said. "The more you talked, the more they liked me."

"We make a good troupe," Piper said.

But they had hardly relaxed before the troll was back. "Something has occurred." He looked at Piper. "You are evidently a skilled musician. Can you do a dirge?"

"Maybe," Piper said. "What's the occasion?"

"There is a contingent of Gnobody Gnomes aboard. They are on their way to make a connection with the Soul Train, which is for ailing souls, because one of their number recently died. They are in mourning, and would like to have a dirge. We would like to oblige them if we can. Can you accommodate them? We would be most appreciative."

"They are thinking of the 'Gnobody Gnows the Trouble I've Seen Dirge.' That's an especially challenging one."

"They are, and it is," the troll agreed. "They doubt

that any non-gnome can play it effectively, but I told them I would ask."

Piper glanced at Bryce. "I'll need your help."

"Of course," Bryce said, uncertain where this was going.

Piper addressed the troll. "You have a sound system on this train? So that I could play in one car and be heard in another?"

"Of course."

"Because for such serious music I will need to be by myself, with only Bryce to assist. We'll do it in a freight car, if there is space."

"There is space in the leading freight car, where your trikes are stored."

"Good enough. Tell the gnomes I will play their dirge in half an hour."

"I will. Thank you." It was amazing how courteous a troll could be when he wanted something. He departed.

"We will return after the dirge," Piper told the others. "I recommend that you not listen to it."

"What's so bad about a sad song?" Arsenal demanded.

"Evidently you haven't heard this one," Pose said, who evidently had.

"That's right, I haven't. And I'll bleeping well listen if I choose to."

Bryce and Piper left them in their dialogue as they made their way to the leading freight car. Their trikes were neatly parked there, but there was a fair amount of empty space remaining. "This will do," Piper said.

"What's going on?" Bryce asked.

"This particular dirge requires full organ music. I can't do that on my little piccolo, but can on my big pipes. I want you to stand guard at the entry to make sure no one intrudes. Make sure there's fresh air there for you to breathe. When I am ready, you can announce the dirge."

"But—"

Then Piper started melting into his monster form. Oh.

The monster was considerably larger than the man, as Bryce had seen before. It spread out across the floor in a seemingly eyeless, earless black mass. Bryce barely had room to stand at the entry. At least now he understood why Piper had insisted on privacy. He was protecting his hidden identity, so as not to freak out the girls and perhaps the trolls. That was surely a sensible precaution.

The mass of the monster solidified. Tubes appeared within his substance. Gas hissed through the tubes, thick and dank smelling. That explained why he needed fresh air.

"TURN OFF SOUND," a tube hissed.

Bryce checked the control panel by the entry, and found a switch marked SOUND. He pushed it to the OFF position.

Piper warmed up. First one tube would hiss a note, then another, a different note. The notes became clearer and more melodic. Then there came a tune, played by an assortment of tubes. Bryce realized with surprise that it was a four-part harmony, soprano, alto, tenor, and bass. Some of the notes were piercingly high, others reverberatingly low. This really was an organ!

"READY," the tube said.

Bryce turned the sound back on. "The Musician Piper is about to play the 'Gnobody Gnows the Trouble I've Seen Dirge' for the Gnobody Gnomes," he announced. "This is a somber occasion. Please take your places and do not interrupt the music."

Then Piper started playing the Dirge. It was not unduly loud, but there was amazing power in it. The high notes were penetrating, the low notes authoritative. Overall it was lovely, compelling, and overwhelmingly sad. Bryce felt his eyes sting, not from the gases, but from evoked emotion despite his ignorance of the deceased gnome for whom this was being rendered. The song picked him up emotionally, wafted him through the soft air, ran him through an ill-tempered meat grinder, and finally buried him about two miles and six feet underground.

Bryce slowly came to his senses. The monster was coalescing back into the man. The Dirge was done. "Thank you for your consideration," Bryce said to the unseen audience. "Now the regular programming will resume." He turned off the sound.

"You did well," Piper said as his head molded into shape.

"Me? You were phenomenal! I never heard such power in music of any kind. You say you're Xanth's second-best musician? I find that hard to believe."

"You underestimate the walking skeleton, as I did. He also may be Xanth's finest person."

Bryce did not argue the case, still bemused by the astonishing experience of the Dirge. They exited the freight car and returned to the passenger car where the others were.

Arsenal, Anna, and Mindy were sitting with their heads hanging, their faces tear-streaked. They had listened.

The troll was there too, as forebodingly dark as ever. "The gnomes are impressed and appreciative," he said. "So are we, because we value their business. Each member of your party is hereby granted a lifetime pass to use our facilities free of further charge. We have just one request."

It seemed that trolls could also be generous when pleased. "What is it?" Bryce asked.

"The Dirge was so well rendered that it has put the entire passenger list into nearly catatonic depression. We ask that you play a more cheering melody to bring them out of it."

Piper smiled. He put his piccolo to his lips. He piped a wonderfully uplifting merry little tune. Bryce's depression lifted, and he was sure the effect was similar throughout the train.

The remaining trip was routine. They did more spot shows for audiences that warmly reacted to them, and between times rested and feasted in their chamber. The Autotroll intersected what turned out to be the Soul Train, for ailing souls, running underground, jealously guarded by demons. The party of gnomes transferred to it and were gone. Their naturally dour expressions remained; evidently they had not listened to the upbeat melody, preferring to remain depressed in honor of their lost comrade.

In due course the train drew to a halt at its last stop: the Panhandle. This was of course like a huge pan with an immensely long handle. They debarked with their trikes at the very tip of that handle. The Autotroll chugged around a wide loop of track and moved back the way it had come. The easy part of their journey was over.

Just beyond the end of the track, at the foot of a mountain, was a small pavilion with a table. On the table was a sign: RING OF POWER: DEMONSTRATOR MODEL.

"Just like that?" Anna asked skeptically.

"The Quests have been set up for us," Arsenal reminded her. "The Demons evidently saw no reason to leave us in doubt. Now who is interested in this one?"

"What does it do?" Bryce asked.

"Try it and find out," Pose suggested. He sat down on the big toe of the foot of the mountain. The others sat on the other toes.

Bryce shrugged and picked up the ring. It seemed quite ordinary. It seemed to be made of brass, without decoration. He slipped it on his middle finger. Nothing happened. "How do I invoke it?" he asked.

Pose shrugged. He was improving on his human mannerisms. "Rings differ. Maybe the challenge is to discover the key to its operation."

"Try saying the words 'I invoke you,'" Anna suggested.

"I invoke you, Ring of Power," Bryce said formally. Still nothing happened.

"You may need to figure out exactly what power this ring relates to," Piper said. "Physical, mental, emotional, magic—there surely is something. The Demons would not place a dud."

"And how the bleep am I to know something like that?" Bryce demanded, frustrated. "Do I wish for a mountain to move six inches to the left?"

There was a rumble that shook the ground. The others exclaimed, jumping up.

The mountain foot had moved six inches to the left.

Bryce privately enjoyed their discomfort. They had left him to figure out the Ring, and had gotten jolted because of it. "Well, now. Let's see the mountain rise up a foot."

The mountain foot lifted a foot. Nothing on it changed; the rocks and trees on the slope remained undisturbed. But they were now on a mountain that floated in the air.

The Ring of Power really could move mountains.

"Let's have the mountain settle slowly back to the ground," Bryce said. "Exactly where it was before."

The mountain settled gently down to the ground.

It occurred to Bryce that this Ring could be dangerous if carelessly or improperly used. That made him nervous. It was simply too much power, capable of being exerted too casually. "I think we have a notion of the nature of the Ring of Power," he said, sliding it off his finger. "Who wants to take it? That person can experiment with it on the way to the Good Magician's Castle."

"Weapons are my thing," Arsenal said. "Moving mountains aren't."

"Music is my thing," Piper said.

"Anomalies are mine," Anna said. "I'd prefer to get something that will help me to control them better."

"That leaves it to me," Pose said. "I appreciate power, and believe the princess will too. I'll take it."

The Ring sailed out of Bryce's hand. It flew in an arc to the mountain and landed on it. The mountain puffed into a cloud of smoke. This thinned and dissipated, revealing a wonderland of brass rings. There were stacks of rings forming trees, others forming round houses, others forming paths leading past ring-shaped pools, fields, and hills. It was a nice enough scene, fashioned entirely of rings. The whole was enclosed in one big circle, outside of which the terrain was normal.

"And I think our challenge is to find it," Arsenal said. "At least we know where to look."

"One of those rings must be the one," Piper agreed. "But which one?"

"And it probably can be any size," Anna said.

"Needle in a haystack," Bryce said.

"There must be thousands of rings," Pose said, dismayed. "It could take years to check them all. And how do we know that any one ring is THE ring?"

"I wonder," Bryce said. "This whole scene formed instantly. That suggests it's less solid than it seems." He stepped into the circle and touched a ring-tree.

His hand passed through it.

"Illusion!" Anna said. "Just like the zombie graveyard!"

"Illusion," Bryce agreed. "Cheap magic. That simplifies things somewhat; the ring we need to find will be the one solid one." He swept his hand through another tree.

"That will still take a lot of searching," Pose said. "I could cover more territory by dissipating into smoke myself, but then I wouldn't be able to feel something solid. I'm stuck with man-limitations."

"But it can be done," Arsenal said. "Let's all get on it. We can divide it into sections for each of us to focus on." He waded in, swinging his hands.

The others joined him, taking different sections. Bryce had one with several houses. That was weird, because when he entered one, swinging his hands through its walls, he encountered illusion residents: people made of rings. Before he knew it he was feeling through a young ring woman. She screamed soundlessly and slapped him, but her ringed hand passed through his face.

"Sorry, ma'am," he said, embarrassed. "But I have to check everything here by touching it, or trying to."

She considered. Evidently she could hear him. She turned away and pulled up her ringed skirt to flash her copper-ring panties. She could smite him that way. Fortunately he was warned by his left eye, and closed his right eye. He spanked her on the bottom, and touched nothing. She had the grace to laugh, soundlessly.

After an hour, discovering nothing solid, Bryce paused to reconsider. Could he find a more efficient way to check things? This way would take days that they surely didn't have.

He walked back to the outer rim. Mindy was sitting on it, watching without participating. She was still wearing her dress from the Autotroll, without petticoats, and her knees were carelessly separated. "Um, Mindy, you may want to sit differently," he said, approaching her.

Then he froze.

"I'm sorry; I wasn't thinking," she said, clapping her knees together.

"It's not that," he said. "I didn't see anything. I just realized something. You're sitting on a ring."

"Yes, there are no chairs out here. This lets me watch without participating."

"So that's a solid ring."

"A big one," she agreed, smiling. Then she paused. "The Ring of Power may be any size."

"That's my thought."

"Pick it up and find out."

"No. That's for Pose." Bryce walked back into the circled area, searching out the demon.

He found him in a region with a fancy rock garden made out of rings, with statues of rings, methodically sweeping hands through them all. "Yo," Pose said, spying him. "You finish your territory?"

"Not exactly. Mindy is sitting on the outer rim."

"Yes, I saw her. Almost freaked out, except that demons don't freak the way men do. Someone should tell her."

"I did," Bryce said, and waited.

"So what's your point?" Then the demon did an almost human double take. "She. Is. Sitting. On. A. Ring."

"A big ring," Bryce agreed. "I thought you might want to check it out."

"Why didn't you take it?"

"I believe we agreed that this one is yours to take."

"So you came to tell me."

"Yes."

Pose shook his head. "If this is it, I'll lose your association just when I'm getting to like you."

"That's the irony of our situation."

They arrived at the rim where Mindy still sat, her knees demurely together. "Let's see what we have," Pose said. He bent down, put his hands on the big ring, and heaved it up.

It shrank in an instant back to the size the demonstrator model had been. Mindy fell on the ground, her support abruptly gone. "Oh!"

Bryce went quickly to help her get back to her feet as the illusion setting faded out. The prior mountain was back, with its big foot. "We really owe this discovery to you. If you hadn't been sitting on it, it never would have occurred to me that it was solid."

"And here I was trying to stay out of your Quest," she said. "But you're the one who figured it out."

The other searchers returned, realizing that the problem had been solved.

Meanwhile Pose was donning the Ring and trying it out. He lifted the mountain a few inches, and set it down again. "This is it, all right. I'll experiment on my way back, so that I can demonstrate its full potential to the princess."

They bid each other farewell, and Pose rode his trike away with the Ring of Power. He was still emulating human form and limitations, hoping to impress the princess with his humanity.

Bryce sighed. "Did we do the right thing? He means to depose the present human government of Xanth."

"The princess knows that," Anna said. "She won't choose him."

"Unless she hankers to be King of Xanth much faster than she will be otherwise," Piper said.

"I don't think she's that type," Bryce said.

"Let's hope so," Arsenal said.

"Why don't we all relax before tackling the next Quest," Mindy suggested.

"I'm for that," Piper said. "I'll play a relaxing melody."

He did and they did, making an impromptu camp. Mindy foraged for pies, milkweed pods, blankets, pillows, and even found a tent left by tent caterpillars. They rested and ate, then had Piper play dance music. Bryce and Arsenal danced with Mindy and Anna, and it was all very compatible.

"You know, if I weren't in love with the princess," Arsenal said, "I'd be interested in either of you girls. You're nice people, and fun to be with."

Bryce agreed. There were ways in which these young women were better matches for the men than the princess. But he couldn't say that, because he, too, loved the princess.

They spent the night in the tent, taking turns to do sentinel duty, just in case. The girls obviously were not worried about any intentions the men might have. They had all come to know each other, and to respect each other, and they increasingly trusted each other. They were all, after initial questions, good people. They were becoming friends.

Yet they all knew that this was a temporary association. Tomorrow another would Quest for an Object, and their group would diminish again. All too soon the group would diminish to one Suitor, and then to none. Bryce was almost sorry.

10

SWORD

Bryce woke with a girl in his arms. He was on his back, and she was lying half on his body, her face nestled in the hollow of his shoulder. She must have rolled over in the night and unconsciously over-lapped him. She was pleasantly soft, especially where her chest heaved gently against his.

This reminded him that now he was young again, physically, and had been some time without romantic female companionship. True, he was in love with the princess, but that was a somewhat distant thing. This girl was immediate. He would like to kiss her.

Which was a no-no. She was a Companion on the Quest who had to be treated with respect for her inde-pendence and privacy.

It was morning. Time for them to rise. He needed to wake her without embarrassing her.

He tapped her on the shoulder, silently.

She half woke. "Oh, Piper," she murmured.

Oops. She thought she was with another man. He rec-ognized the voice: Anna Molly.

That was interesting. She had gotten interested in Piper? Probably his music had attracted her. Well, he was a good man, and if he did not win the princess, he could be good for Anna. Assuming that he returned her interest. He might be understandably cautious, because when she learned of his monster aspect that might end any ideas she had. At least he had his relationship with the giantess as a backup.

Then Anna woke the rest of the way. "Oh!"

Bryce made a small show of waking up, pretending he had not heard anything before. "We must have collided in the night," he said apologetically.

"Yes." She sat up, and so did Bryce. Piper was on her other side, and Arsenal beyond him, while Mindy was curled up beyond their feet. It was a good-sized tent, but five people crowded it.

Soon they were all up, washing at a local streamlet, and Mindy was foraging for their breakfast. Bryce said nothing about Anna's words; it wasn't his business.

After the meal, they gathered together for the next unrolling of the scroll. Mindy brought it out and read the line. "Region of Fire."

"That's mischief," Arsenal said. "I've been there. It's north of the Gap Chasm, along with the regions of Water, Air, Earth, and the Void. It's hot."

"I have been there too," Piper said. "It can be navigated, carefully."

"We can take the Autotroll," Anna said.

"Not all the way," Piper said. "It avoids the Regions. But there are paths."

They went to the track circle and waited. Soon the train steamed toward them, as if responsive to their need. It stopped, and the trollductor stepped down. "It is our privilege to serve you," he said. And paused.

"We will entertain the passengers," Bryce said.

That was what the troll had evidently hoped for. "Very good."

They were given what seemed to be the same chamber they had had before. They quickly rehearsed another show, this one minus the curtains. There was no gnome mourning party aboard this time, so Piper would not have to change. They worked out a playlet, in which Arsenal was about to slay an evil sorceress, but Piper played such enchanting music that she reformed, literally, with Mindy becoming Anna, and married him instead. They worked the transformation without magic, by putting the two women together in one dress, facing in opposite directions. When they turned about, in the shadowed corner, it seemed that one became the other. The audience, not entirely fooled, nevertheless loved it.

When Arsenal did his flashing sword demonstration, this time with Mindy as the nervous target, there was applause, then a question. "Did you ever meet your match in sword craft?"

"No," Arsenal said. "It is my talent to be proficient with any edged weapon I encounter. But I did once have a close call. My opponent was an ordinary-looking man whose talent turned out to be the ability to become a flying sword. Every time I swung at him, he assumed sword form and flew at me. I didn't know how to stop him. Then I got smart, grabbed a big ball of cork, and used it as a shield. The blade stuck in the cork and couldn't get free. Before it could change back into the man, I hurled cork and blade into the sea where a hungry kraken lurked. I did not stay to witness the outcome of that encounter."

The audience laughed.

"Did you ever slay a dragon?" another passenger asked.

"Never had to," Arsenal said. "When I encounter a

dragon, I do my little sword-flashing show for it, and it generally backs off. Of course much depends on the size of the dragon. And the reach of its heat. If one tried to toast me, I would hurl a knife down its gullet. Mostly we leave each other alone."

Bryce would have thought this was bravado, but after seeing Arsenal's swordflash demonstration, knew it was not.

"I'm glad to hear it," the passenger said. "Dragons aren't evil, just different. I was raised by a dragon."

Now other passengers were interested. "How so?" one asked. "Dragons normally eat any humans they catch alone without weapons or magic."

"Well, it's a long story I'll condense somewhat. It seems there was this hood just sitting on a bush. Maybe it grew there. A dragonness came and tried to chomp it, thinking there might be a person inside. Somehow she got the hood caught on her head. Then its magic manifested, and she became devoted to Mother Hood."

"Another pun," Mindy muttered.

"There was a human baby lying in the grass," the passenger continued. "No one knows how it got there. The dragonness saw it, and instead of gobbling it down, adopted it. Because of the Mother Hood. The child grew up to have some dragon qualities. When enraged he swells to one and a half times his normal size, his fingernails become claws, his skin turns crimson, and he snorts fire."

The others burst into laughter. "You're some storyteller!" another passenger said. "You should join the troupe."

"But it's true," the man insisted. "I'm that man."

"And I'm the Demon Xanth!" the other retorted mockingly.

The man swelled up to one and a half times his prior

size. His fingernails expanded into talons. His skin turned crimson. He snorted fire. "I will not be mocked!"

Bryce dived in between them. "He didn't mean it!" he cried. "He thought you were joking. He was going along with it. Isn't that right?"

"Uh, yes, sure," the other agreed, daunted.

"Oh. Well, then." The dragon man shrank back into normal human semblance.

"The peacemaker strikes again," Arsenal muttered.

"And now we will return to our show," Bryce said. "Arsenal, girls—the playlet."

They hastily organized and went into it, distracting the audience from what had almost become an ugly incident.

After the show, the dragon man approached them. "I am Dudley Dragonman. Thank you for defusing that situation. People don't like me when I get mad. In fact I wonder whether you could use your persuasion to mollify my girlfriend. She's not speaking to me today."

"A lovers' quarrel?" Bryce asked. "I think you need a counselor for that. Maybe there's another passenger who is good at that."

"There was one," the man said. "A woman with the talent of healing broken relationships. But she got off at the last stop."

"Then I'm not sure how we can help," Bryce said.

"Maybe I can help," Anna said. "May we meet your girlfriend?"

"She is Chandra, with the talent of changing from one humanoid form to another. But as I said, she won't speak to me. I can't approach her."

"We can get around that," Bryce said. He went to the nearest speaker. "Will Chandra please come to talk with the troupe members?" His voice reverberated along the passenger cars.

Soon Chandra appeared. She was a lovely elf girl. "How came you by my name?" she demanded.

"We are trying to be peacemakers," Bryce said. "We understand you are angry with your boyfriend, Dudley."

Her eye fell on Dudley. She became a troll female with an ugly face and uglier glare. "I'm not speaking to him!"

"Please," Anna said. "We are only trying to help. Why are you mad at him?"

"He made fun of me!" she flared, becoming a petite goblin girl.

"I didn't mean to," Dudley protested. "But you assumed ogress form."

"What wrong, that song?" Chandra Ogress demanded. She was small for the species, but still almost banged the ceiling with her horrendously ugly head.

"I remembered the classic description of an ogress's face," he said. "It was so true I had to laugh."

"What is that description?" Anna asked.

"Her face looked like a bowl of overcooked mush that someone had sat on."

Bryce had to stifle a guffaw. That was exactly what her face looked like now. Maybe worse.

"Well of course she didn't like that," Anna said. "You were mocking her. She doesn't like to be mocked any better than you do. She's a perfectly decent ogress."

"But—" Dudley said, beginning to swell.

"Do it, idiot," Anna said. "Turn dragon man!"

"Uh, Anna . . ." Bryce murmured.

"You're as bad as she is!" Dudley Dragonman growled as he snorted fire.

"No, I'm worse," Anna said. "Now apologize to her."

"What?" A ball of fire scorched the wall.

"Gourd style."

"Oho!" Mindy murmured.

"What are you talking about?" Dudley demanded.

"You don't know what a gourd-style apology is? I will demonstrate." She turned to Piper. "You know?"

"Yes," Piper said, bemused.

Anna put her arms around him and kissed him so passionately that little hearts flew out.

That was an apology? It looked like utter ardor.

Anna broke the kiss. "Do you accept?"

"Uh," Piper said, seeming half stunned.

"No? Then I'll have to try harder." She kissed him again. This time medium-sized hearts flew out, and Piper's feet started to leave the floor.

She broke again. "Now do you accept?"

Piper squeezed his head back into shape with his hands. "Well, maybe."

"You are forcing me to take it to the limit," Anna said. She kissed him again. This time a huge single heart formed, enclosed them, and lifted both from the floor. A soft glow reflected off the walls, floor, and ceiling of the car. Also from the watching people. Love suffused the train.

Anna finally broke again. "Now do you—" she started, but paused. Piper couldn't answer. He had freaked out. "I'll take that as a yes," she said. She turned to Dudley. "Keep your present forms. Apologize. The ogress needs to know you take her seriously."

Dudley was catching on. The two of them were similarly ugly now. He enfolded the ogress and kissed her. Little ugly tomatoes flew out to circle their heads.

Dudley broke. His face was flushed beyond the dragon stage, as was hers. "Do you accept my apology?"

"No!"

Bryce was dismayed. It had seemed to be going so well.

"Then I'll have to try again." He kissed her more ardently. This time small ugly gourds circled their heads. And Chandra's fingers behind his back formed a little O circle.

Bryce had to stifle another chortle. She had *wanted* to make him kiss her again.

He broke, both of them looking breathless. "Now do you—"

"Not yet," she said. "Let's return to our room and finish this privately." They quickly departed, ogress and dragon man, hand in hand.

"Works every time," Anna said, satisfied. "No one ever refuses a gourd-style apology." She snapped her fingers before Piper's face, and he came out of his freak. "Thank you for your cooperation."

"You're welcome," he said, eying her speculatively. She had evidently made an impression on him, as she surely had intended. She had accomplished her nominal purpose of reconciling the lovers, and also given Piper a signal he could hardly miss. Bryce was old, but still learning things about women.

It was also, he realized, a demonstration of her talent for generating anomalous situations. The rift of a man and woman had been healed while they were in two different forms, neither attractive.

The ride was only a few hours, and then they were in the Regions section of Xanth. "There are five of them," Mindy explained to Bryce as they set up their trikes. "Air, Earth, Water, Fire, and the Void. They are generally avoided by ordinary folk, as they can be dangerous. But we don't have a choice."

"I don't look forward to this," Anna said. "I never wanted to visit this area. It gives me nervous shakes."

"Is there anything I can do?" Piper asked.

"Just stay close to me."

"You know I love the princess."

"I know. But only one Suitor will win her. It wouldn't bother me hugely if you were not the one."

"I think I could survive such a rejection," he said. "However, there may be something you don't know about me."

"Maybe I'll learn," she said, unconcerned. "I know you're a great musician."

Bryce knew what Piper meant, however. How would Anna react when she saw his monster form? Their dialogue suggested that both understood what kind of relationship they were orienting on, and both were interested, but that was a formidable consideration.

They triked south along a well-defined but unenchanted path. Soon they came to a gentle downward slope. "I think this is the outer edge of the Void," Mindy said. "We do not want to get close to that."

"What is the Void?" Bryce asked, hearing the capital.

"It is the fifth Region. Anything can enter it, but almost nothing ever comes out. We dare not risk passing the Line of No Return."

Bryce shuddered. "We dare not," he agreed. "It's like a black hole with an event horizon."

"A what?"

"Don't you remember from Mundania? A star so dense that not even light can escape from it."

"Oh. Yes," she agreed uncertainly.

They found a path that skirted the Void to the west. Evidently others in the past had made a similar decision.

In due course they came to an area where swamps and lakes abounded. To the east was a rainstorm. "Let me guess," Bryce said. "The Region of Water."

"The Region of Water," Mindy agreed. "I understand it is reasonably pleasant if you're a water creature. But it rains constantly."

"And the next one is Fire? Can we reach it through Water?"

"If we had a boat that couldn't sink."

"We'd better continue triking," he said.

Before long they saw a wall of fire. No need to inquire what that was. "Do we know where in the Region of Fire to find whatever we're seeking?"

"Maybe the scroll will say." Mindy brought out the scroll and unrolled it. "Yes! Now it says at its southernmost point."

"So do we enter it and look for that point?"

"We can try," Mindy said.

But when they approached the firewall it was unbearably hot. "Maybe at the border between Fire and Water we can dip some water and splash out a hole in the wall," Bryce suggested.

"Maybe," Arsenal agreed.

They entered the edge of the Region of Water, then waded through the swamp to reach the border with Fire. Mindy found an old rustbucket tree and harvested several rusty buckets. They used these to splash water on the wall.

It hissed and flared angrily, but they kept at it and soon had doused a hole. They entered the Region of Fire and looked around.

The swamp became a dry field. There was burnt stubble on it, with just a tinge of new growth. A fire was sweeping across it. They had to exit their hole quickly before the fire reached them.

"I guess not," Bryce said. "We're not fire-walkers."

"But we'll save the buckets," Piper said. "We might need them again."

They returned to their trikes and rode around the rest of the Region of Fire. The next was the Region of Earth. This did not look very much more promising. It was largely barren, with volcanic vents issuing smoke and steam. Except for one section where the ground was relatively flat and calm.

"Maybe we can cross here to the southern firewall," Bryce suggested. "If we do it quickly, we may get there before a volcano erupts nearby."

Arsenal knelt and touched a finger to the edge of the

smooth surface. "I think not. This is quicksand, in the Mundane sense."

Bryce didn't inquire what the Xanth sense of quicksand was. The Mundane sense was bad enough. "Then how do we get across?"

"I can do it," Piper said.

"Not in your present form," Arsenal said.

"So you knew," Piper said.

"I suspected. I tried to make you change, to confirm it, but Bryce stopped that. Then when you played the Dirge I knew. No little flute-type piccolo could make those sounds. That was an organ!"

"So it was," Piper agreed.

"Okay, if you can do it, then do it," Arsenal said gruffly.

"Do what?" Anna asked.

"Assume my other form," Piper said. "Before I do, I just want to say I have enjoyed my association with you, and will regret seeing it end. You're a fine woman."

"I'm not going anywhere," Anna said. "I don't know what you're talking about."

"You will," Piper said grimly. He glanced at Arsenal. "Use the trikes." Then he started changing.

Anna stared, horrified. "You're melting!"

"You can handle it," Arsenal told her.

"His other form is the Music Monster," Bryce said. "An angry Demon changed him into it. Now he can assume either form. He is still Piper underneath."

"But he's melting!" she repeated.

"He's changing. His other form is amorphous. Physically he's a monster, but you know his human nature."

She did not respond. He glanced at her. She was immobile, her eyes fixed.

She had freaked out.

"Or maybe not," Arsenal said.

"Let him complete the change," Mindy suggested. "Then wake her."

"You knew too?" Bryce asked.

"Yes. He once lived at Caprice Castle. Dawn spoke of him, when she decided to have him conduct you to visit Castle Roogna. She knew he could protect you."

"He could," Bryce agreed. "He did."

The change was complete. The Music Monster stretched out before them like a thick black rug. Thinner than he had been aboard the train, however.

The rug slid out onto the quicksand. "Look out!" Bryce cried.

"He knows what he's doing," Arsenal said.

So it seemed. The rug thinned further as it moved over the sand, covering it with a black mat. In two and a half moments it was entirely on the sand, floating on it. A vent opened and a note sounded.

"He's ready for us," Mindy said. "Better wake Anna."

Bryce snapped his fingers before Anna's face. "Wake, Anna," he said.

She revived. "What happened?"

"You saw Piper transform to his monster form, and freaked out."

"Yes," she said, looking as if about to freak out again. "He just dissolved into goo!"

"It's just a different form. He's a better musician that way, and a formidable fighter. He can use his music to hurl fireballs at attackers. He protected me from a goblin horde once. He will protect you similarly. He will return to human form in due course."

"He's really—the same person?"

"He really is," Bryce assured her. "He was always a person with two forms. He changed this time to help us cross the quicksand."

"How can he do that?"

"Look," Bryce said, gesturing.

Arsenal and Mindy were on the mat, sitting on their trikes. They were not sinking into the quicksand. Piper's trike was parked beside them, and the four buckets.

"I—I wouldn't recognize him that way," Anna said.

"Think of him as a man who can become a floating rug," Bryce said. "Now we have to board too, if we want to cross the quicksand."

"I—I'm afraid."

Maybe it was time for some tough love. "Piper and Arsenal and Mindy are going. So am I. Do you want to wait here for our return?"

"No!" she cried in fear.

He took her hand. "Then join us. We will live or die together."

"Yes," she agreed faintly.

"Get on your trike and ride it on." Bryce did that himself.

She joined him, seeming dazed. They rode onto the mat. It gave slightly beneath their wheels, then firmed. Once they were fully on it, the black substance closed on the wheels where they touched it, holding the trikes in place.

Then the mat moved. It went slowly out into the pool of quicksand, like a low raft. They were crossing.

But the liquid sand mix did not simply allow them to cross unmolested. It bubbled and frothed angrily. Vents opened, emitting hisses of gas. The pool writhed, forming thick ripples. In fact it quaked, shaking the mat.

Piper forged on, undismayed.

Then a hole formed beside the mat, starting to draw it down. "That's a sinkhole!" Arsenal said, alarmed.

The mat backed off, getting clear of the hole. But then a larger vent opened on the other side, emitting a thick cloud of gas. The smell was putrid.

"And that's a stinkhole," Bryce said, coughing.

The sand rose up in a low mound before them. "That stuff is really out to get us," Arsenal said.

"We've got to help Piper navigate," Bryce said. "He can't see well in this form."

"I'll do it," Anna said suddenly. "Piper! Can you hear me?"

A small vent blew a small affirmative note.

"Veer left to avoid mischief ahead."

The mat moved left, missing the mound.

After that it became almost routine. Anna called out the threats and guided Piper to avoid them. It worked perfectly. Bryce and Arsenal kept quiet, letting her do it. She had a certain rapport with the mat.

They came to the wall of fire. "Throw sand on it," Anna said. "To make a gap."

Bryce and Arsenal got up, took buckets, and dipped quicksand. It was heavy, but when it landed on the wall, the fire hissed and retreated. Soon a hole formed.

The mat forged through. They found themselves on a burned bank of a rocky landscape, with no fire close by at the moment.

They got off the mat. Then the mat humped into a glob, and the glob slowly shaped back into the man. Piper had returned, complete with clothing.

Anna approached him. "I think I owe you an apology."

"No, you were great," he said. "You really helped steer me."

"A gourd-style apology." She put her arms around him. "A real one, this time." Without waiting for his response, she drew him in and kissed him. Hearts flew out, spinning madly.

"He won't mind at all if the princess passes him by," Arsenal remarked.

"Hardly at all," Bryce agreed.

When the apology was accepted, they organized for the next stage. "Where is the Object?" Arsenal asked.

Bryce looked around. "Behind you, I think."

Arsenal turned around. There was a waist-high rock, with the hilt of a large sword projecting from it.

"Was that there before?" Arsenal asked.

"I didn't notice it, but I can't be sure it wasn't," Bryce said. "But this is surely the Object. There's a Mundanian legend about a sword in a stone. Only the rightful future king of the land could draw it out."

"That will be the one who marries the princess," Arsenal said. "Or at least, he'll be her consort. Let's see what this is." He put his hand to the hilt and pulled.

The sword didn't budge.

Arsenal tried harder. Still no success. Finally he put both hands on it and heaved with all his might. The sword remained fixed in place.

"You try it," he said to Piper, with ill grace.

Piper tried it, and got nowhere. Then Bryce did. The sword seemed to be part of the rock it projected from.

"Your turn," he told Anna, smiling.

She did try it, with no success, unsurprisingly.

"This has to be a demonstration sword," Bryce said. "Which means we get to try it. How can we try it if it's stuck in the stone?"

"There must be something wrong," Mindy said. She walked up, put her small hand on the hilt, and lifted.

The sword came up in her hand.

The others stared at her. She stared at the sword. "Does this make sense to anyone?" she asked somewhat plaintively.

"Maybe it requires a gentle touch, rather than force," Bryce suggested. "Such as that of a woman."

"Then why couldn't Anna get it?" Piper asked.

"I think I know," Anna said. "Mindy is the only member of this party who doesn't seek an Object. She has nothing to gain by it, so it didn't resist her. It's tuned to the contestants."

"She's not a Suitor, or in lieu of a Suitor," Arsenal said. "That must be it. But now that it's out, can the rest of us try it?"

"Let's find out," Mindy said. She handed the sword to Anna.

"But I don't know the first thing about using one of these," Anna protested. She gazed at the sword in her hand. "It must be illusion. It's light as a feather."

"Not necessarily," Piper said. "It's magic. It may make it easy for its wielder. Try striking something."

Anna shrugged. She took a clumsy slice at the edge of the rock the sword had come from.

A section of stone sliced off and landed on the ground.

Bryce bent to pick up the slice. It was solid rock. Wordlessly he handed it to Arsenal.

"Already this is some demonstration," Arsenal said, hefting the slice, then setting it down. "It may be feather-light for her, but it has full force at the business end. However, a good sword needs more than that. Let's see what else it can do."

Arsenal drew his own sword and advanced on Anna. "Like our demonstrations," he said. "Only try to block my attack."

"I can't block anything!"

But when he swung his blade at her, her sword leaped to counter it. There was a clang as his sword was re-pelled, while hers seemed unaffected. He swung again, and again was readily countered. "It's doing it," Anna said. "I don't even know how."

"Try attacking me, instead of just defending yourself," Arsenal said.

She aimed a clumsy stroke at him. He readily coun-tered it, but when the two blades touched, his bounced back while hers continued its swing. He had to jump clear to avoid getting cut.

"It has made you a formidable swordsman," Arsenal

said. "That's what I wanted to know. Let's try something else. Suppose you need to pry something open with the point?"

Anna saw a crack in the original stone. She put the point of the sword to it. The sword shrank into the size of a knife, fitting into the crack. Then when she twisted, the crack widened into a split, and the rock broke apart.

"This thing is versatile," Bryce said, amazed.

"But will it work for anyone else?" Piper asked.

"Try it," Anna said, pushing the hilt toward him.

Piper took it and moved it about. "Feels like a thin needle." He touched it to one of the sections of the original stone. The point dug in as though the stone were butter.

Bryce took it next, and was similarly surprised by its extreme lightness. But the moment he moved it, it accelerated far beyond his effort, amplifying his will. He handed the hilt to Arsenal.

Arsenal practiced with it, doing another swordcraft show. He nicked the stone, and saw chips fly out. "Who else wants the weapon?" he asked.

There was silence.

"Then I want it," Arsenal said. "It's the finest sword I have encountered, and will serve excellently as a gift for the princess."

The sword puffed into smoke. They were left standing on the scorched plain.

"And now I have to win it," Arsenal said, satisfied.

A figure appeared, walking toward them. It was in the shape of a man, but fiery red. And it carried the Sword.

"A fire demon," Piper said. "This is mischief."

"This is my Challenge," Arsenal said, drawing his own sword.

"But that sword is dangerous," Piper warned. "I doubt that any mortal can defeat it."

"There has to be a way, or the Quest is pointless. I just have to fathom it."

Arsenal was confident to the point of folly. But Bryce realized that he was right: there had to be a way. They simply needed to figure it out before the man got himself killed.

The fire demon strode to the place where the sword had been in the stone. Now it was a flat area, marked by a circle of little flames. He waited.

"That must be the arena," Arsenal said. "Inside is battle. If I step out I may not be pursued, but neither will I possess the Sword."

"Better to step out than lose your head," Bryce said.

"Defeat is not in my lexicon." Arsenal stepped into the ring.

Immediately the demon attacked. The Sword swung toward Arsenal, threatening to literally take off his head. Arsenal countered, but was pushed off balance by the effort of resisting the awful force of the cut. Immediately the Sword shifted and came at him from another angle, and he seemed to block it barely in time.

Then Arsenal recovered his balance and attacked the demon. But no matter how swift his motions, the magic sword was always there to nullify them, seemingly without effort.

"He's overmatched," Piper murmured. "That's a demon sword."

"Yet if he can't stop it, with all his expertise, what hope have we of advising him of any better way?" Bryce asked.

"There has to be a key," Anna said.

The fight continued, and Arsenal was getting the worst of it. He might be able to handle any mortal warrior, but this was a demon with a magical sword. How could anything handle a weapon designed to magically counter any attack?

Bryce remembered reading a story about a table tennis game wherein one player had a magic paddle that always returned a fair shot, no matter how hard or spinning the ball came. It seemed impossible that the other player could win any point, let alone the game. Yet, in the story, he had.

How had he done it? Bryce strained his memory. How could any player win a point against an enchanted paddle that could not miss? Yet there had been a way.

"He's tiring," Piper said. "The demon of course is tireless."

"He was foolish to get into this," Anna said. "But I don't want to sit here and watch him die."

Bryce racked his brain. What was he missing?

Then it came to him. The other player had placed a hard shot to a spot that the one with the magic paddle couldn't reach in time. The paddle could return anything it touched, but the player had to get it to the point of touching. The paddle could not return what it didn't touch.

But this magic sword had a feature the magic paddle lacked: it moved to intercept the opposing blade. No matter where Arsenal attacked, the magic sword was always there in plenty of time, as if anticipating that very ploy. Maybe that was part of its magic. If Arsenal could attack a part of the demon's body that was out of reach of the Sword, then he could score. But there was no part of the body out of reach. So the table tennis example offered no solution.

Unless . . .

A bulb flashed over Bryce's head. There was a way!

"Arsenal," he said.

"Don't distract him," Anna said. "He's already too hard-pressed."

"This distraction is necessary," Bryce said. "Arsenal, there is a way."

"Um," the man said, acknowledging him.

"You have knives."

"Um." Arsenal beat off another attempt on his head, but not by much.

"Take the knives. Two of them. Use them far apart."

Arsenal paused. He dodged another thrust, barely avoiding it. Then he dropped his sword and caught up two knives, one in each hand.

Demons lacked human emotions, unless they happened to have acquired portions of souls. But the fire demon paused, surprised. Maybe he distrusted this ploy, wherein his opponent seemed to be disarming himself. Maybe he was figuring out how to counter it.

Arsenal gave him no time to ponder. He struck at the demon's head with his right-hand knife. The Sword rose to counter it. It was successful; it knocked the knife out of Arsenal's hand.

Then Arsenal's left-hand knife plunged into the demon's rib cage on the other side. Actually it was plunging even as the right-hand knife was being knocked away. The magic sword could not be in two places at once, so had left the other side momentarily undefended.

The demon did not bleed or crumple. He puffed into smoke and drifted away. The Sword dropped to the ground, landing point first, the hilt raised. Arsenal had won it.

He put his hand to it and drew it out of the ground. "Mine!" he exclaimed exultantly.

"Yours," Bryce agreed, relieved.

"My thanks to you," Arsenal said. "You gave me the key."

"I'm just glad I figured it out in time," Bryce said.

Arsenal nodded. "I will remember."

"Now let's get out of here," Anna said nervously. "Before there's another burn."

Piper changed into his monster form, becoming the buoyant mat. They boarded not long before a wave of fire swept through the area. They heaved buckets of sand at the firewall, making a temporary hole, and pushed through. Anna directed the mat accurately through the waves and heaves. It seemed easier this time, now that they knew the route. But it was also true that Anna seemed to have a feel for this anomalous guidance. Her talent was coming into play.

As they achieved the edge of the Region of Earth, Anna leaned down and whispered to the mat. "Good going!" Then she kissed it.

She had more than come to terms with Piper's other nature.

They camped in the refreshing normal landscape of the path beyond the Regions. Mindy found pies and pods for their dinner. "I will trike back to the station and take the train to the Good Magician's Castle," Arsenal said. "I'm done here." He mounted his trike and rode north. He would be caught by darkness, but he was obviously unconcerned. After all, he had the Sword.

Now they were four, counting Mindy. "Let's rest the night," Anna suggested. "And worry about tomorrow, tomorrow." The others were happy to agree.

Mindy found pillows and blankets, two of each. Piper and Anna took one set, Bryce and Mindy the other. The two couples settled down a little apart, fully clothed under the blankets.

Piper brought out his piccolo and played a lovely evening hymn. The music put them all in a good mood.

"You were great," Mindy murmured to Bryce. "How did you ever figure it out?"

"I worked from a Mundane memory. I was lucky it clicked in time, even if we didn't have Lucky to generate the luck."

"Arsenal was twice as lucky. He'd have been done for, otherwise."

"I do what I can. We have all helped each other, and that has facilitated things for all of us."

"May I tell you a secret?"

"Mindy, I'm not trying to pry into anything that's not my business."

"I think I am falling for you."

He did not pretend to misunderstand. "Mindy, don't do that! I love the princess, and if by some fluke she chooses me, she has the first call. You know that."

"I do know that," she agreed. "And I know I'm just an ordinary servant girl. There's no future in my feeling. But it's there."

"I'm sorry," he said. "I don't think there's anything I can do."

"You can kiss me."

He thought to protest, then stifled it. Emotions did not always follow sensible courses.

He kissed her. She sighed, then went to sleep.

He felt both guilty and relieved. She was a nice girl, but way too young for him even if he became free. Her crush was flattering but foolish.

But it reminded him of the problematical nature of his participation here. He was not about to marry a sixteen-year-old girl, even if the princess selected him, the love spell notwithstanding. But what would be the consequence of rejecting her, apart from his own broken heart? And if she did not choose him, as seemed more likely, then what was he to do with the rest of his life here in this fantasy land? Did he really want to return to Caprice Castle and collect puns with Mindy?

He had no satisfactory answer.

11

GEM

Bryce woke to find Mindy already up and busy. She was here to see to the incidental needs of the party, and she was good at that. Her experience at Caprice Castle seemed to have made her a good servant. All she wanted in return was some affection from him, and he was unable to provide that. He felt guilty again.

Well, maybe he could help her. He got up and joined her where she was setting out pies she had harvested. "Anything I can do?"

She glanced at him, and blushed. "I apologize for what I said last night. I shouldn't have."

"Not a gourd-style apology!" he said, alarmed.

She reflected half an instant, then burst out laughing. "What a mess that would be! No, this is garden variety. I put you in an awkward situation, and I regret it."

"I—accept your apology," he said, still feeling awkward.

Now Piper and Anna were up. Their relationship was really none of his business. He felt guilty again for being intensely curious about it. Piper was old too, and committed to the princess too, but evidently more flexible about peripheral relationships.

They had breakfast, then oriented on the next Quest. "What says the scroll?" Piper asked Mindy.

She brought out the scroll and unrolled it. "The Gold Coast," she said.

"Oh, is that like the one in Mundania?" Bryce asked. "Where affluent tourists go?"

Piper smiled tolerantly. "You forget how literal things can be in Xanth. The Gold Coast is made of gold."

"I'd like to see that!"

"You will," Anna said. "As soon as we figure out how to get there."

"Well, there's the Trollway not far to the north," Mindy said. "Or we can intercept an enchanted path south of the Regions."

"Both of which will take time," Bryce said. "Is there a faster way?"

"Not unless we fly," Mindy said. "And I'm not keen on trying to get a dragon or roc bird to carry us there. They might forget and eat us instead."

"Too bad we don't have magic carpets," Anna said, smiling. "So we could fly right over the Gap Chasm and south."

"I wonder," Mindy said thoughtfully. "Bryce, don't you have your magic pen?"

"Yes, of course. But I don't see how—" He paused. "Could it actually draw a workable carpet?"

"I don't know. Maybe you can find out."

Bryce brought out the pen the princess had given him. He sketched a simple little rug. "Invoke."

The rug slid off the page, expanding, becoming a carpet about three feet wide by five feet long. It sailed up and would have escaped into the air, except that Piper grabbed it and held it down. "A little wild," Piper remarked.

"See if it works," Mindy said.

Piper wrestled the carpet to the ground, spread it out, and sat on it. "Lift," he said.

The carpet jerked upward, tilting, almost pitching him off. He grabbed the edges and hung on. "A little wild," he repeated. "But yes, it works."

"I think they have to be broken in, at first," Mindy said. "Until they learn the signals."

"I understand a well-trained carpet responds to invisible signals by its rider," Anna said.

"Yes," Piper agreed. "I have encountered some in my day. But usually it doesn't take long, because carpets like to fly and carry folk. It's their justification for existence."

Bryce drew another rug. Anna caught this one as it expanded, and hung on to it while it heaved and bucked. Soon it settled down, and she was riding in comfort.

"There's a problem," Piper said. "When you drew the second carpet, mine disappeared."

Oops. But Bryce got an idea.

He drew a third, this one twice the length and breadth of the others. Then they wrestled it down and cut it into four smaller carpets. They had gotten around a limit of the pen. Piper and Anna took the first two and resumed taming them.

Mindy got one of the quarters. She lay on it facedown and flew it as if riding a sled, using fingers and toes to remain anchored, and soon it too settled down. "I'm nervous about heights," she explained. "This keeps me low."

Bryce took the fourth piece for himself. He caught it as it separated from the rest, put a knee on it, and held it down. He sat on it, gripping the two sides as Piper had done.

The thing shook as if trying to dislodge him. It tried to curl up so he had less room to sit. It rose a few feet, then dived. It whirled around, almost flinging him off. But in his youth Bryce had ridden horses, and was wise to its antics. His perch seemed precarious, but he remained seated, and when it saw that it could not readily dump him, the carpet behaved.

They practiced at low altitude, flying in slow circles. Mindy stayed with her sled posture, and stayed low enough so that it was almost like being on a real sled. Then they loaded their folded trikes and tied them down with threads from the edges of the carpets. The carpets supported the additional weight without a problem. Mindy gradually got acclimatized and sailed higher, so as not to hold the others back.

Bryce had a new appreciation for the power of the pen. He was glad that Mindy had reminded him of it.

When they were ready, they sat or lay on their four carpets and took off together, forming a formation. They sailed up to just above treetop level, which was the maximum height Mindy could handle, and moved forward. They hoped in this manner to remain inconspicuous, and not attract the attention of any neighborhood dragons. If a dragon came they would have to land so that they could either hide or Piper could change form and fight. It was better to avoid any such trouble.

They skirted the Region of Air, which they definitely did not want to tangle with, lest they be blown out of the sky. Then, surprisingly soon, they reached the Gap Chasm.

"Oh, no!" Mindy said, shuddering. "I can't do that!"

Yet it would be tedious to try to circle around the chasm, and Bryce wasn't certain they could safely drop down into it either. What could they do?

He thought of something. "Close your eyes. Pretend you're two feet above the ground. We can surround you and steer you right. Soon we'll be across and you can look around again."

She winced, but nerved herself. "Will you hold my hand?"

"I will hold your hand," Bryce agreed. He steered his carpet to float right beside hers, almost overlapping, and took her right hand with his left.

"Thank you," she said faintly. She squeezed her eyes tightly shut.

Piper led the way, and Anna closed in on Mindy's left side. Now they were a formation of one leader, followed by three abreast. They moved forward over the chasm.

Mindy did not move or protest, but her hand was clenching his almost painfully tight. She was trying to pretend, but did know where she was.

They maintained altitude, zooming straight across the gulf that opened out alarmingly below them. Bryce had not seen it before from this elevation, and was mightily impressed. It was different than it had seemed when he was down in it. There was nothing like this in his section of Mundania. He saw trees far below, and rocks and fields, and here and there a small cloud floating between them and the bottom.

"It's awesome," he murmured, trying to alleviate Mindy's tension.

Mindy did not look. "With luck we might even spot the Gap Dragon," she said bravely.

"We've met," he said, laughing. She laughed with him. That was one of the things about her: she loved to laugh. Even when she was terrified.

The crossing seemed interminable. Bryce realized there was a headwind, slowing them. The small carpets lacked power, and were well loaded, so now they were barely making progress. Bryce peered ahead, trying to spot the far edge of the Gap.

That was when he saw the other cloud. Oh, no! That looked like Fracto, the mean-spirited storm they had escaped when they went underground. Would Fracto recognize them? Would he remember? Would he hold a grudge?

Yes, yes, and yes. The cloud swelled up before them. In fact it was the source of the headwind, stopping them from getting safely across.

"We need to turn back," Bryce said tersely. "Drift with the wind, get back to land."

Whereupon the wind stopped. Fog was forming behind them as Fracto flung out misty tentacles to surround them.

"What's happening?" Mindy asked through clenched teeth.

"Weather," Bryce said. Then, to the others: "Then we can descend, and wait it out."

But the wind returned, rocking the carpets. They might get dumped before they could land.

"There's a mesa!" Piper said. "On a mountain."

"In the Gap Chasm?" Piper asked. "How can it be here?"

"It's an anomaly," Anna said.

Oh. Her talent was working for them. They dropped to a landing on the flat surface just before the rain started. Mindy opened her eyes, relieved, and got up off her carpet.

A large snake slithered close. Before they could react, it transformed into a lovely nude young woman. Bryce realized that transformations were hard on clothing unless it was built into the magic. "I am Nara Naga, chief of the Noway Naga," she said. "Who are you and what brings you to Menace Mesa?"

"The storm," Bryce said. "We were flying across when Fracto caught us. We had to land suddenly. I am Bryce, this is Piper, and these are Anna and Mindy. We're on a Quest that takes us south. We'll move on as soon as we can."

"That's all right," Nara said. "These things happen. Come into our parlor." She gestured, and a door appeared in the ground. A sloped ramp led down into a cave. "Quickly, before we all get drenched." She led the way down and in.

They followed, encouraged by the thickening rain. Another naga maiden appeared and closed the door behind them, shutting out the rain just as it was getting heavy. They had escaped Fracto again, barely. Literally bare, for the naga.

"You must be hungry after your flight," Nara said. "We'll feed you."

"Well, actually—" Bryce started, because they had had a good breakfast and it was not yet noon.

"We insist on demonstrating our hospitality," Nara said. "Have some sweet cakes." She showed them to a table that was spread with small cakes of assorted colors.

"Goblin cakes," Mindy said. "However did you get those? Usually the goblins won't share them."

"We live in the upper section of the mountain," Nara said, standing behind the table. She took a breath. She was very good at breathing; possibly it had something to do with her lack of a shirt. Had she worn a bra she would have freaked out the men; as it was she came close. "There is a goblin colony in the lower section. We trade with them. We trade similarly with the harpy roost nearby, and the nickelpede nest on the surface."

"That's interesting," Piper said, observing that breathing. "Usually goblins, harpies, and naga are deadly enemies, and nickelpedes have no friends at all."

"We are isolated here in the mountain," Nara explained. Bryce remembered that she had called it Menace Mountain. He was not entirely easy with that. "We are out of contact with our own kind, and the goblins are similarly separated from theirs. We make the best of it."

"That's nice," Anna said, nibbling on a green cake.

"Very nice," Mindy agreed, trying a blue cake.

What could they do? Bryce and Piper picked up red and black cakes while gazing involuntarily at Nara's impressive torso. The pastries were truly tasty, perhaps rendered more so by the conducive context.

"I will show you to your chamber," Nara said, turning

in a manner that displayed her side and back, which were just as good as her front.

"Oh, we're not staying," Bryce protested. "We only came in out of the rain."

"Perhaps," Nara said. She opened a door to a room with two bunks and a barred window. "This should do."

"But there's no need—" Bryce said.

Nara stepped up and kissed him on the mouth. Bryce froze in place, surprised both by the kiss and its potency. It was not the same as a gourd apology kiss, he thought, as there was nothing apologetic about it, but it had its own authority. "Perhaps you and I will tryst tonight," she murmured.

"Oh, I wouldn't—"

She caught his hand and set it on her finely sculpted bare bottom. That was when he freaked out despite her lack of panties.

"Wake!" Piper said.

Bryce stirred woozily. He was lying on a bunk. "I think I freaked out. That naga woman—"

"She drugged us," Piper said. "Fool that I was, I never suspected. I should have known she was not flashing that luscious body for nothing. She distracted us while she fed us that tainted food."

Bryce began to make sense of it. "That bare body, that breathing. That bottom. She was preventing me from doing any serious thinking, until the cake took effect."

"Exactly," Piper said. "I have encountered that type before, but wasn't alert. We're in trouble."

"I wasn't distracted by her body," Mindy said. "But I suspected nothing. Why did she do it? We were no threat to her folk."

"Where is Anna?" Piper asked.

They looked around. There were only the three of them in the room. "Trouble," Bryce agreed.

"Go to the window," Nara said. She was standing outside the door, which Bryce now saw was a barred gate. This was a prison cell!

They went to the window. It looked out from the sheer cliff of the side of the mountain. There was no purchase above, below, or to the sides, and the drop to the floor of the chasm was horrendous. The cell seemed to be inside a U-shaped curve, so that they could see that cliff curving near the open section of the U.

Enough time had passed so that Fracto had given up the siege. That was not necessarily encouraging.

"We're prisoners," Mindy said, appalled. "But why? We're not criminals. We've done nothing to deserve this."

"Precisely," Nara said. "You are innocent travelers of exactly the kind we favor. We are, incidentally, not a normal tribe of naga. We were banned because of our special tastes. Keep watching, and you will see your companion being displayed."

"Displayed?" Bryce asked, staring at her. He did not like the implications at all.

"For the goblins, harpies, and nickelpedes," Nara said. "I told you how we trade with them. We do it by providing them with live raw meat, which they greatly appreciate. That prevents them from coming after *us* for such treats."

"Raw meat?" Piper asked. "*Anna*?"

"We normally start with the most innocently appealing specimen," Nara said. "But never fear, your turns will come."

Piper was still peering out the window. "There's Anna! They're suspending her from a pole!"

Bryce went to look. There was Anna in a harness, hanging below a horizontally projecting pole. She was evidently just now waking up from the drugging, not yet fully aware of her situation.

Now Piper turned to face Nara. "What is the mechanism of this display?"

"I'm so glad you asked," the naga said. She remained nude, but somehow Bryce did not find her as attractive as before. "First to come will be the harpies, who will pluck out her eyes and tongue and anything else they fancy. Some of them have necklaces of eyeballs. Next the male goblins will arrive, to poke into the parts of her body they fancy. By the time they are sated, the nickelpedes will get there to consume the rest. At that point she will finally die. We all love to hear the screaming."

"I was not angry until this moment," Piper murmured grimly. "Bryce, distract her. Mindy, direct me."

He was going to change into monster form! But he needed to conceal it so that the naga did not understand what was happening.

Bryce went to stand directly in front of Nara, blocking her view of the window. "You said we might tryst tonight," he said. "Did you mean it?"

"That depends," she said, eying him appraisingly. "Exactly how cooperative can you be?"

He knew that no appeal to her good nature would be effective. So he appealed to her bad nature. "To guarantee that I'm the last one displayed? I can be pretty ardent. Maybe I can persuade you to spare me entirely."

"You would have to be. I like truly lusty men."

"I can be lusty." Then, realizing that she might react to his body similarly to the way he had reacted to hers, he took off his shirt.

She was interested. "More."

He took off his trousers and stood in his underpants. She focused intently on them, but did not freak out. Maybe that was because she was only half humanoid. "Yes, I think you will do," she said, and turned away. "Until tonight," she said, making a flirt of her bottom that half stunned him. In another moment she was gone.

Bryce turned to face the others, hoping he had given Piper time. "You did," Mindy said from the window. "Piper is on his way."

"I am disgusted as well as appalled," Bryce said. "That naga has absolutely no conscience. She was talking of a tryst while setting us up for torture and death."

"Piper will rescue Anna."

"Yes. Then we'll have to break out of here."

"Maybe you can draw a device."

"Maybe I can," he agreed. "A crowbar, or a jack."

"Or a pineapple."

"Explosive," he agreed. "Blast us out." Then he thought of something. "But that will replace our carpets."

"We can make new ones once we escape."

Now they both peered out the barred window. The black monster was sliding across the cliff wall toward Anna, but was going low. "Move up slightly," Mindy called. Piper did, and now was headed directly toward Anna.

There was a cry in the sky. "The harpies are coming!" Bryce said. "And Piper's not there yet."

"Piper!" Mindy called. "The harpies are coming. They're out beyond the U. Can you see or hear them?"

There was a note from a vent. "He can," she said. "But he'll need our help for pinpoint accuracy."

"I can do that," Bryce said. "You direct him to Anna; I'll spot the harpies for him."

"Anna's about a hundred feet ahead of you," Mindy called. "Make sure you don't bomb her!"

"A harpy squadron is coming in," Bryce called. "At about nine o'clock, range three hundred feet."

The monster issued a harsh series of notes. A flicker of magic flew out. Then a fireball exploded just ahead of the harpies.

There was a collective squawk of dismay as the harpies drew up short. Then they reorganized and flew on toward Anna. Apparently they thought the fireball was a fluke.

"Look at those eyes!" one screeched. "Dibs on the blue one!"

"Dibs on the brown one," another harpy screeched.

That was right: Anna had different-colored eyes.

"Dibs on the tongue!" a third screeched. It seemed that their normal mode of communication was the screech.

"What horror," Mindy murmured, shuddering.

"Ten o'clock, range two hundred feet," Bryce called.

This time the fireball burst in the middle of the squadron. The dirty birds were blasted out of the sky, feathers burning.

"You're about fifty feet from her," Mindy called.

Then Bryce saw a door open just over the pole, where it stuck in the wall. Goblin males swarmed out and scrambled along the pole toward Anna. "I got first poke!" the lead goblin cried. He reached the end of the pole and started shimmying down the rope toward Anna.

"Second poke!" the next goblin cried, starting down after him.

Now Bryce shuddered. It seemed that the goblins were going to swarm over Anna as she hung, intent on gang rape she could not flee.

"Goblins on pole," Bryce called. "About to get on her." How could Piper blast them without also blasting Anna?

The first goblin reached Anna. He clung to her body, ripping away handfuls of her clothing. But she did not give him the satisfaction of screaming. She was one brave girl.

Harsh music sounded. The first goblin stiffened and fell, screaming as he plunged toward the distant ground. The second clung for an instant and a half, then also fell, also screaming. Those were obviously not the screams they had sought.

"He can paralyze with his music," Mindy murmured.

Oh. Of course. "But what of Anna?"

"She's paralyzed too, but she's tied in her harness. Only the goblins are loose."

Ah. The monster had more tricks than Bryce had realized.

But the goblins, intent on rapine, were slow to get the message. More of them were scrambling along the pole. And were getting stunned, and falling, as more harsh notes sounded.

Then the monster reached the pole. That cut off the goblin approach.

But now a third menace manifested. The face of the cliff scintillated with reflections off moving shells.

"The nickelpedes," Mindy said, horrified anew. "They are excellent climbers."

But Piper had already picked up on them. Ichor welled from his body and flowed across the wall. It intercepted the nickelpedes. There was a sizzling as they curled up and died, burned by the acid.

Piper had single-handedly wiped out all three attacking hordes. "My hero!" Anna cried.

"But how can he get her safely down?" Mindy asked. "He can't safely reach her."

"Maybe there's a way," Bryce said. Then he called to Piper: "Nullify your acid. Make your body sticky!" And to Anna: "Swing!"

Anna swished her legs back and forth, and began swinging. She sailed out from the cliff, then in toward it. Out, in, swinging higher. Soon she managed to bang into the monster's body.

And stuck there.

A pseudopod reached out and touched the rope over her head. The rope separated, burned through. That left Anna sticking to Piper. She was nothing loath.

The monster was rescuing the maiden. There was the singular anomaly of this adventure. Which meant that however helpless Anna had seemed, her talent had been working for her.

But where would they go from here? Bryce and Mindy were still locked in the cell, and they could not turn gelatinous and flow out of it. Piper couldn't bring Anna into it.

"They can go on down to the ground, then up and out of the chasm," Mindy said. "We can join them later."

"Go on down and out!" Bryce called to monster and maiden. "We'll rejoin you south of the chasm!"

Piper issued a note of acknowledgment and started sliding down the cliff. Anna adjusted her tattered clothing and rode along. She would get a better seat when they reached the ground.

"Who put you up to this?" a voice screeched at the window. A harpy was there, either a survivor of the aerial blast or a commander who had had the sense to stay clear.

"It was Nara Naga's plot," Bryce said angrily. "She set us up for this ugly slaughter."

"That's what I thought!" the harpy screeched, and flew away.

"I don't think you answered her question," Mindy said.

"It was Nara Naga who fed us drugged cakes and locked us in here, and had Anna put out for torture and sacrifice," Bryce said. "Definitely her vile plot."

"The harpy must have thought it was a trap for *them*," Mindy said. "With Anna as bait to bring them all in so the monster could destroy them."

Bryce reconsidered. "Oh. I misunderstood. I suppose they could see it as an attempt to clear them all out of the mountain so the naga could have it for themselves and not have to share."

Mindy formed half a smile. "That misunderstanding may cause the Noway Naga some mischief on Menace

Mesa. All three other groups will be mad at them, feeling betrayed."

"I suppose so," Bryce agreed. "But I really didn't mean to lie, even to a harpy. I was just somewhat flustered by the turn of events."

"I understand. Now how do we get out of here? The naga will not be pleased with us."

"The pineapple," he said promptly. He brought out pen and pad and sketched a grenade with a safety lock. "Invoke." It slid off the page into his hand. It had a dangerous heft.

"The pineapple," she agreed, eying it nervously.

"Stand behind me," he said. She did.

He released the safety and hurled the grenade at the door. Then he turned to put his arms protectively around Mindy, not knowing how bad the blowback would be.

The pineapple detonated and blew the door apart. The blast of hot air threw them up against the barred window. Fortunately it was secure.

They untangled and got to their feet. The door was a tangle of smoking metal bars. They had no trouble stepping through and out of the cell.

A serpent slithered up. It changed into Nara Naga, gloriously nude as usual. "What's this?" she demanded.

"It's a prison break," Bryce said. "Don't try to stop us."

"Where did you get a pineapple?" she demanded. "What's all the fuss outside?"

"You haven't been paying much attention, have you," Bryce said.

"I've been busy sweating bullets to get our accounts straight." She brushed a couple of bullets from her shoulder. "Now get back in that cell."

"Or what?" Bryce asked.

"Or I'll freak you out and put you there myself."

"I'd like to see you try."

She tried, impatiently. She stepped in to him, pressing her bare body against him. But before she could freak him out, he put both hands around her throat and squeezed. "Try sweating my fingers off," he suggested.

She fought him a moment, then transformed into serpent form and slithered free. In a moment she was gone.

"You're learning," Mindy remarked.

"Yes. After what she set us up for, I have no use for her, no matter how seductive her shape. Now let's get to the top before the naga organize to stop us. We don't have the firepower Piper does."

They located the stairway to the mesa. They pushed the door up and open and emerged. Then Bryce rolled a large rock on top of it, to prevent the naga from following rapidly.

Bryce drew a large-sized carpet. They wrestled it down, hastily taming it, then piled the four folded trikes on.

Other lids lifted, and serpents crawled out. "They have more than one door!" Bryce said.

"We've got to get off the mesa!"

Mindy got on the carpet on her hands and knees. "You steer. I can't look."

Her fear of heights. He understood the problem, but the snakes were assuming human form and were closing in. Recapture would be doom.

Bryce got on, sat in the center, then put her head up against his chest, holding her close to him so that she couldn't see beyond his body. He started the carpet moving, and sailed off the edge of the mesa just as the naga converged. They had made it!

But the carpet was new, and awkwardly loaded, and they were not properly balanced. They spun about and swooped downward. Mindy screamed and clutched him desperately. Bryce fought to restore balance and elevation, and succeeded after a brief struggle.

They lifted up to regular ground height, and soon were there, since there was no contrary headwind. Bryce landed. "We're safe," he said.

Mindy opened her clamped eyes, then got to her feet. "I'm sorry to be so much trouble."

"It's been rough on you," Bryce said. "But all's well now."

"Except that we need to rendezvous with Piper and Anna."

"Why don't you stay here while I take the carpet down the slope to see if I can spy them?"

"Don't forget me," she said, clearly relieved by the chance to avoid further heights.

"I wouldn't do that!" Then he realized she was joking. She was recovering her humor, now that they were back on solid ground. He unloaded the trikes and sat on the carpet.

He sailed down and cruised along the south wall of the chasm. Before long he spied monster and maiden crawling up the wall. "I can take you up," he called.

"Bryce!" Anna exclaimed gladly. "You escaped!" Her clothing was torn from the goblins' attack, but she seemed to be all right.

"We did," he agreed. "Mindy's waiting. Get on the carpet." He hovered close.

Anna stepped onto the carpet, no longer glued to the monster, and sat beside him. Then Piper transformed and climbed on too. The two embraced, taking up less room on the carpet, and maybe just because they wanted to. Bryce carried them all up, and in three moments they were safe on the brink.

Anna stepped onto land and collapsed into shudders. This was understandable, after what she had been through. Mindy put her arm around her. "I was terrified, but you had it worse," she said. "Those horrible monsters!" Anna clung to her, sobbing, knowing she was referring to the harpies, goblins, and nickelpedes.

"I would have fried them all," Piper said grimly.

"They deserved it," Bryce agreed. He had not appreciated before just how ugly Xanth could get.

After a while Anna recovered, being of a strong emotional constitution. She found a shirt to replace the one the goblins had torn, and put it on. Bryce felt guilty for regretting the loss of the spot glimpses of her torso the torn one had provided. His youthened body tended to notice such things more than his old mind thought proper. Nara Naga had been fiendishly tempting, too, despite his detestation of her nature. Sometimes the impulses of the body warred with the sense of the mind.

"Let's get moving," Anna said.

"We make a good team," Piper said as they reorganized, tearing the carpet into four smaller ones as they had done before.

"Thanks to you," Bryce said. "Without your special abilities, we would have been lost."

"Something should be done about those conniving naga," Piper said.

"No need," Mindy said. "We gave the harpies to understand that the naga planted you there on purpose, to wipe them and the goblins and nickelpedes out."

"I didn't mean to," Bryce protested. "I got confused."

Piper nodded. "So now the others will think the naga are their enemy. Things should get interesting on Menace Mesa."

"That seems likely," Bryce agreed, suppressing a shudder. All four groups of creatures were distressingly bloodthirsty. But he doubted they were typical of the rest of their respective kinds, except for the nickelpedes.

"It couldn't have happened to a more deserving group," Anna said with feeling. They all laughed, albeit somewhat uneasily. It had been a very bad siege.

They decided not to delay, but to fly straight on down to the Gold Coast before nightfall. They wanted no further complications on the way. They had lost too much time on Menace Mesa, putting their schedule in danger.

Bryce was amazed as he saw the color. "It really is golden!"

"Things tend to be literal here, remember," Mindy said.

"I know. But every so often it catches me by surprise anyway. So what are we to find here?"

Mindy rolled down her parchment again, but it had no addendum. "We'll just have to look around."

"What's that?" Anna asked.

It turned out to be a golden pedestal supporting a golden box containing a scintillating large gemstone. Behind it was an enormous gold beetle, an ornately carved scarab whose carapace gleamed iridescently in the waning sunlight. This was obviously a setting of some sort, and surely relevant to their Quest.

"It must be what we're looking for," Mindy said. "The gem, not the big bug."

"You never can tell," Piper said. "It's late; do we want to explore this now, or leave it for the morning?"

Anna looked at him. "What do you prefer?"

"If it is another Object, as seems likely, one of us will win it and depart. It might be you. It might be me."

"Yes," Anna agreed. "That was my thought."

"I'd rather spend this night with you, rather than risk having one of us depart right now."

"Oh, yes!" Then she glanced at Bryce and Mindy. "If the others don't mind."

Mindy laughed. "We don't mind. I'll forage for supper."

Bryce realized that despite the way Piper had rescued her, Anna still needed confirmation that he was personally interested in her. Women were like that. Piper had confirmed it. They would spend a loving night together.

Soon they had eaten golden pies that were nevertheless nutritious, and drunk from golden pods, and had found golden cloth to make two small tents. Piper and Anna disappeared into one, and Bryce and Mindy shared the other, clothed.

"Bleep, I envy them," Mindy murmured, well knowing what the couple was up to.

Bryce could not give her a similar confirmation. "I am not going to molest you."

"I know. Sometimes I wish there were more monster in you. When this Quest is done we may never see each other again. I really wouldn't object if you wanted to—to take advantage of me. I wouldn't tell."

She was not Nara Naga, but she was a young woman, and evidently more than willing. Bryce's young body was tempted. But he knew it would not be right. "Maybe when the Quest is done, and the princess has rejected me, we could get together, if you still want to."

"I will still want to," she said. Then she took his hand, kissed it, and went to sleep with his hand in her possession.

Actually there were ways in which Mindy would be better for him than the princess, setting aside things like the love spell on him and the extreme difference in ages. She was fun to be with, and she helped him a lot with unfamiliar aspects of Xanth. He liked the way she laughed. He thought of the way he had loved one woman in Mundania, but married another, and found the one he married in the end to be the better choice. There could be a parallel. But it was not a decision he was ready to make. He *did* love the princess, artificial as he knew that to be, and was not one for incidental dalliance on the side.

Troubled, he slept, still holding Mindy's hand.

In the morning they tackled the gem, which remained in place. Anna picked it up. "This might look nice on a necklace," she said, then winced.

Bryce understood why. The gem was the size of an eyeball. The harpies collected eyeballs for necklaces, and had wanted hers.

"What does it do?" Mindy asked.

"I don't know. Maybe it has to be invoked."

"Anna!" Piper cried. "Behind you!"

She jumped and turned. The giant gold bug had come to life and was advancing on her.

"I can't handle this," Anna said. She handed the gem to Piper. "Tell it to back off."

Piper held the gem and stood his ground. "Back off," he told the scarab. As Bryce understood it, this was not a particularly vicious kind of beetle, but it was shoulder high and did make Anna understandably nervous.

The bug's progress slowed, then halted. It faced Piper from about a body length away, antennae waving.

"That must be it," Bryce said. "It can make the bug stop."

"Maybe," Piper said. "See if it works for you." He handed the gem to Bryce.

Bryce held it and watched the bug. The bug moved, now coming toward him, orienting on the gem. Bryce was nervous too, but deliberately held back from invoking the gem. He wanted to see what happened.

The scarab came to about six feet from him, and stopped. "I did not invoke anything," Bryce said. "The gem must stop the bug from coming close. Maybe that's its nature."

They experimented, with the others taking turns with the gem, and seemed to confirm it. The scarab was drawn to the gem, but could not actually touch it.

"That seems like a rather limited power," Bryce said. "There must be more to it."

"Maybe it repels or controls monsters," Anna said.

"That we can test," Piper said, and transformed to monster form. Then he advanced on Bryce, who was holding the gem at the moment. And stopped six feet away.

"You can't come closer?" Bryce asked. There was a note of agreement.

"Let's really test it," Anna said. She took the gem and faced the monster. "Come to me, as close as you can."

The monster came to six feet and stopped. He could not get closer.

"A gem that fascinates yet balks monsters," Bryce said. "Like a light for moths. That could indeed be potent, if it applies to all monsters."

"Surely it does," Mindy said. "The Demons have offered potent gifts so far."

"The princess could carry it in her purse, and be safe from ogres, trolls, nickelpedes—" Anna paused. "And maybe rapists. Aren't they monsters too, even if some look human?"

"That seems likely," Bryce agreed. "We can't readily test that aspect at the moment, but it is probably worth assuming."

"So who wants it?" Mindy asked.

Piper re-formed. "I just felt its power. Let me verify something." He stepped up and took it from Bryce. "In my human form I can handle it. That suggests that it is the physical form of a monster it repels, rather than the nature of a person."

"Unless it knows you are no threat to the rest of us, despite your capacity," Bryce said. "In which case, it would be discriminating indeed."

"Do you want it?" Piper asked.

"Not really," Bryce said. "I never saw myself as a monster battler."

"Not me," Anna said. "I don't want to be even six feet near any monsters, no matter how safe I may be." Then she glanced at Piper and reconsidered. "Any *other* monsters."

"Then it seems it is mine to claim," Piper said. "It will make a fine gift for the princess."

The gem vanished from his hand. The monster scarab was also gone.

"The demonstration phase is over," Bryce said. "Now you have to locate and win the genuine Gem, wherever it is now."

"Look!" Anna exclaimed.

There was the gold pedestal with the Gem on it, and the giant scarab behind it, exactly as before.

"I don't trust this," Bryce said. "We made our decision; why is it starting over?"

"It looks the same," Piper said. "But the rules may have changed." He went to the Gem, reaching for it. And stopped. "And they have. I can't reach the Gem."

Anna tried. She couldn't reach it either. Neither could Bryce. Mindy didn't try; she had to sit out the actual Challenge. The huge gold bug remained inanimate, evidently not part of this particular Challenge. It had been for demonstration purposes only.

"So it has reversed," Bryce said. "We are all monsters, as far as the Gem is concerned. The challenge is to get past that."

"I'm baffled," Piper said. "We can't get it by going away from it."

Something nagged Bryce's memory. Then he got it. "Princess Harmony is musical. She plays a harmonica."

"What does that have to do with it?" Anna asked. Mindy also looked askance, but stayed out of it.

"Maybe nothing. But I found her harmonica playing, well, magical. It was literally magic, of course, as that's how she invokes her power, but it was also aesthetically enchanting. I was transported, and insisted on hearing more. Maybe it was just the love spell making me appreciate anything about her. But I always liked music, while not having any talent in it myself, and I can tell a skilled rendition from a poor one. She was skilled."

"She is," Anna agreed. "I still don't see the relevance."

"Music has power, and not merely magical. I am wondering if an ideal gift for the princess could have a musical aspect. Maybe I'm going off in a wrong direction."

"And maybe not," Piper said. "Music does have power; I certainly have found it so. The princess is good with her instrument. She just might use it to tame a resistant Gem." He brought out his piccolo, the gift of the princess, and began playing a lovely little tune.

The others watched and listened. Now that Piper was trying it, Bryce feared that his notion was irrelevant.

Piper, still playing, took a step toward the Gem. Then another. Now he was standing about three feet from it, then two. But that was as far as he got.

He stopped playing, and fell back as if repulsed. "It pushed me away!"

"So the music helps," Bryce said, gratified. "Maybe all you need is a more authoritative melody."

Piper tried another, and the others were enraptured by its beauty. He moved close to the Gem again, closer than before. Now he was only about one foot away. But that was as close as he could get.

He stopped playing, and was pushed away again by the repulsive field around the Gem. "It isn't enough."

"What about your other form?" Anna asked.

"But that's a monster! The Gem repels monsters."

"Has it encountered a music monster?" Bryce asked. "Not the one who can hurl firebombs, but the straight musician."

Piper dissolved into gelatin. This time he wasn't thin like a rug but thick. A number of vents formed. He blew a few practice notes. Then he played an organ melody with a complex harmony. It was impressive.

As he played, he slid forward. He breached the six-foot barrier, and the three-foot one. The music attraction was countering the monster repulsion. But could he actually take the Gem?

A pseudopod lifted and reached toward the Gem. It got to about six inches from it and stopped. The music was still not enough.

"Try the Dirge!" Bryce called.

Piper shifted into the Dirge. The powerful, sorrowful theme swept over them all, bringing tears. Anna dabbed her eyes, and Bryce's vision blurred. The music continued, carrying them all along. It was a truly uplifting grief.

Then it stopped. "But it was working!" Anna protested.

"What happened?" Bryce asked.

"I got the Gem," Piper said, re-forming. He held it in his hand. "It no longer repulses me; once I touched it, the Challenge was over."

"Congratulations!" Bryce said.

"But now you'll be going," Anna said sadly.

"But we will meet again," Piper said. "I really hope for that."

"Unless the princess chooses you," Anna said. "With that music and that gift, I fear she will."

"I don't know what to say," Piper said. "I'd like to stay, but I have to complete my Quest."

"I know," Anna said tearfully. "And I'm glad for you. I really am. I just somehow wish . . ." She didn't finish.

"Believe me, I understand," Piper said. "I thought I wanted to marry a princess, but now I know it is love I truly desire. Even though I am spelled to love another, I know you would be better for me. I know that the moment the spell dissipates, my love for you will flower."

Bryce was struck by the similarity to what he had discovered about himself. First love was not necessarily the best love.

"I never thought I would love a monster," Anna said. "I was wrong. It's not just your music, though I love that too."

"The chances are only one in six she'll take me. I'm gambling on that. Farewell for now, Anna." He kissed her, then got on his trike and rode away as if afraid to delay any longer. That was surely sensible.

"I don't think she will choose him," Mindy said. But her opinion did not seem to be much comfort.

12

BEE

"The day is yet young," Bryce said. "Let's see if we can reach the next Object before nightfall."

Mindy unrolled the scroll. "Lake Kiss Mee."

"That's not far," Anna said. "We can make that on the trikes via enchanted paths."

"Let's do it," Bryce agreed. But privately he wondered. The other Objects had been far apart, requiring them to go to extreme measures to reach them in time. Would this next one turn out to be different?

They located a path and triked north. Soon the golden ambiance faded, and normal colors returned.

They came to a large body of water. "Lake Ogre Chobee," Mindy said. "Generations ago most of the ogres moved from the Ogre fen Ogre Fen in the north, down here. They won't bother us as long as we stay on the enchanted paths."

They paused at a rest stop, where they harvested pies and pods. Beside the shelter was a statue of a small horse. They didn't think anything of it until several small children came by. One got on the statue. "Giddyup!"

The horse started rocking, and loud music issued from it. "That's rock music!" Bryce said.

"From a rock horse," Anna agreed, smiling.

"I keep encountering puns when I can't collect them," Mindy complained with a smile. It was good to relax for a while.

They rode on. After a time, possibly a time and a half, they came to a juncture. One sign said GAP CHASM. Another said CASTLE ROOGNA. A third said LAKE KISS MEE. But below it was scrawled a warning: "Enchantment out of order. Proceed at own risk."

They considered that. "Sometimes the paths get messed up and need to be repaired," Mindy said. "The repair crew must be busy."

"But we need to get there in a reasonable time, lest we forfeit," Anna said. "We don't want to go to the other places yet."

"I vote we take the path, but be on guard," Bryce said. Then he thought of something else. "Maybe this is not coincidence."

They looked at him. "Not?" Anna asked.

"We have been having as much of a challenge getting to the Objects as we have had winning them," Bryce said. "I thought that was just ill chance or the nature of backwoods Xanth. But now it occurs to me that it may not be chance at all. It may be part of the Challenge."

Anna nodded. "We were under time pressure to get to Mount Rushmost within a day, so we took a shortcut. Fracto Cloud attacked and we had to go underground, where trolls and two goblin villages lurked. Only sheer luck got us safely past those."

"And Lucky is no longer with us," Mindy said thoughtfully.

"Then we had trouble getting past roadblocks to reach the Trollway," Anna said. "Until we realized they were illusions."

"And we had to navigate boiling quicksand to get to the third Object," Bryce said.

"And the treacherous Noway Naga of Menace Mesa," Anna said with a shudder.

"Now we face another unenchanted path," Bryce concluded. "I think the Demons are testing us again. They don't care whether we survive the journey; it's part of the selection process."

"I think you're right," Anna said. "This is no innocent treasure hunt. This is dangerous. And we no longer have a warrior or a monster to fight for us."

"Or a demon," Bryce agreed. Then he thought of something. "But we might summon one. What are the chances she'd help instead of hinder?"

"Oh, no!" Mindy said. "You wouldn't!"

"I'd like to throw a monkey wrench into whatever mischief is lurking for us along this path," Bryce said. "That might do it. I'm game if you are."

"She would be as likely to mess it up as to mess us up," Anna agreed. "I'm game."

"It would change the game, certainly," Mindy said with enough of a smile to show that she was conscious of the pun.

Bryce nodded. "So let's see what Demoness Metria has to say about it."

A small cloud formed between them. "Did I hear my Appalachian?"

"Appelation," Mindy said quickly, cutting short the demoness's preferred dialogue. "No mountains or horses here."

The cloud formed into one of Metria's more luscious shapes, with a décolletage that did not quite show too much cleavage and a skirt that just barely avoided baring a panty line. She eyed Mindy crossly. "You've lost weight."

"I'm trying to shape myself into the figure of the

woman I'd like to be," Mindy explained, evidently dis-comfited.

Bryce glanced at her. It was true: she was less solid than she had been. He hadn't been paying attention.

"So are you folk up to anything interesting?" Metria asked.

"Fascinating," Bryce said. "We may be about to walk into a nasty trap."

"Oh, goody! But if you're fooling me, I might flash you like this."

But Bryce's left eye warned him, and he shut his right eye just before her dress went transparent, revealing both red bra and blue panties, both formidably overstuffed. "Don't do that," he said. "I might lose control and do something I shouldn't."

"Do what?" she demanded curiously.

"This." He reached out suddenly and goosed her. He hadn't done that to a girl in sixty-five years, and then he had gotten slapped hard alongside the face and been punished with hours of detention. It had seemed worth it at the time.

"OoOoo!" she howled, sailing into the air.

Both Anna and Mindy stifled snorts of illicit mirth. Bryce's hand was numb. It must have been freaked out by contact with those plush panties.

"Fortunately neither of us would do anything gross like that, would we," Bryce said, flexing his fingers to re-store their circulation. "So it's academic."

Metria floated back down to the ground, faint smoke dissipating. "Academic," she agreed. "So you are a man, deep down under that milky toast exterior." Her dress lengthened, ensuring that nothing daring showed above or below. She had, it seemed, gotten the message. For now.

"What kind of toast?" he asked before he caught him-self.

"Milquetoast," Mindy said immediately, cutting off the routine. "It means a spineless person. And she has you wrong regardless. You've got spine." She giggled. "And maybe a sore hand."

"Sore hand!" Metria said, outraged. "The bleep it is! It's spaced out because of its brief contact with heavenly silk." She eyed Bryce. "Want to try it with your face?"

"Here's the situation," Bryce said, deciding to cut off that particular discussion. "The information is private, Metria, so you must promise not to tell."

"I promise," she said, holding up crossed fingers. At least she was honest about her dishonesty.

"We are on a Quest to obtain magical Objects for the Princess Harmony. The next one is in the vicinity of Lake Kiss Mee. But certain obstructions may be in our way. We need to find a way to handle them."

"Why should I care about that?"

"Because capital D Demons are behind this Quest. Ordinary folk seldom have a chance to witness their games in action. Of course if that scares you off—"

"Let's get moving," Metria said briskly. She floated on along the path.

They followed on their trikes. It was a gamble involving the demoness, but maybe no worse than what they faced otherwise.

Yet the ride was remarkably placid. The path wound between marshes and trees, with no impediments. They pedaled hard and made good progress. Surely Lake Kiss Mee was not far off.

They came to a lovely pool. "Oh, I'd like to take a swim and cool off!" Anna said.

"We can't assume it's safe," Bryce said. "I think we should go on by."

"This is your idea of adventure?" Metria demanded. "Pedaling past pools?"

"We have no idea what kind of water is there," Bryce said. "And not much way to test it. I'd rather keep going until we return to a safely enchanted path with a protected rest stop."

"I will check it out," Metria said disdainfully. She faded.

A man approached them. "Hello, strangers," he said jovially. "I am Demon Flower. Welcome to my spa!" He handed each of them a pretty flower.

"No, we'll be moving on," Bryce said.

"If you insist. But sniff my flowers to appreciate their rare scent. That's only a hint of what my spa has to offer."

They sniffed the flowers. The scent was pleasant and intriguing. "Well, maybe we'll stay an hour," Bryce said, and the two women nodded.

"Excellent! Right this way." Flower led them to a nice cabin beside the lake. "You'll find everything you need here," he said grandly. "Including swimsuits. I know you'll love the experience."

They entered the cabin. It was nicely set up with two bunks and a supply of pies and pods.

"This is an anomaly," Anna said. "A demon should be threatening us or making some other mischief, not treating us like pampered guests."

"That's right," Bryce agreed. "Why are we dallying here?"

Metria reappeared. "The flowers, you idiots. Their odor drugged you."

"The flowers!" Bryce moaned. "We fell for it again, just as we did with the naga cakes."

"We are innocents," Anna agreed. "We just walk into things, assuming everyone means well."

Bryce got a suspicion. "Let me check the door." He tried the handle. Sure enough, it was locked. They were prisoners again.

"This is getting interesting," Metria said. "How are you going to get out? Draw another pineapple?"

So she knew about that. She had been tracking them more closely than she let on. Could she be of help? "What would you recommend?"

"Bombing the whole complex into sickly smithereens."

"That's too extreme for the offense."

Metria glanced at Mindy. "You claim he's *not* toast?"

"There are other ways than bombs to solve problems," Mindy said. "He uses them."

The demoness looked back at Bryce. For an instant her body assumed the form of a giant piece of toast.

"The punishment should fit the crime," Bryce said, nettled. "First we should ascertain exactly what the crime is, if there is one. Maybe the door locked accidentally."

Metria emitted a smell of burning toast.

Bryce, prodded into imagination, got half a notion. "A setup like this should have security cameras. In case anything happens that might reflect badly on the management."

Now there was the smell of butter being spread on the toast.

"So we'll just check the record for the last day," Bryce said doggedly. He brought out his pen and sketched an object with numbers and buttons. He invoked it, and it slid off into his hand. "Remote control," he said.

All three looked blankly at him.

"Like for TV," he said. "Only this one is for the security recording playback." He punched the proper buttons.

A picture formed in the middle of the room. Surprised, they moved to the edges so as not to interfere with it.

"An illusion image," Anna murmured.

"A holographic projection," Bryce said.

"Same thing," Mindy said.

The image was of a rather pretty human girl. She had long fair hair and a sweet face. She was saying something, but there was no sound.

"We have to name her," Mindy said. "Then we'll be able to hear her. That's how this kind of magic works."

Bryce realized that he still had things to learn about magic.

"She looks pretty innocent," Anna said.

"So call her Innocent," Metria said impatiently.

". . . I do hope their healing spring can help me," Innocent was saying to herself. "I'll have to ask the management." She tried the door, but found it locked. "Oh! I must have done it when I entered."

But no amount of twisting of the handle released the door. Alarmed, Innocent pounded on it. "Help! I'm locked in!"

The door opened. Flower stood there. "Yes?"

"Oh, I was about to come to you," Innocent said, apparently unconscious of any other meaning in her choice of words. "I have this problem, and I hope your healing spring can fix it."

"It can, of course," Flower said. "But you will have to bathe in the spring. Change into a bathing suit."

"But you haven't even heard what my problem is."

"Tell me."

"It's that I have dragon breath," Innocent said. "It repels regular men and attracts dragons. I need to get rid of it! I tried getting a tooth brush, with tooth paste, to eliminate the smell, but they didn't work."

"I appreciate the problem," Flower said. "Now change."

"But—but you are *looking*," Innocent protested.

Flower stepped into the cabin. "No I'm not." He turned to face away.

"But you could look any time."

"Of course I won't." Flower turned back and held one

of his flowers under her nose. She sniffed it unconsciously.

Flower turned away again, waiting for her to change.

Innocent hesitated, then decided to trust him. She was a very trusting soul, especially after smelling the seductive flower. She removed her clothing and got into the bathing suit that had been laid out for her. "All right," she said, checking herself in the full-length mirror.

Flower turned back. Now Bryce saw what Innocent evidently did not. The suit was opaque up close, but transparent from a distance. The demon was seeing her full bare body. What a rascal!

"This way," Flower said. He led her out of the cabin and to the shore of the nearby pond.

Bryce nodded appreciatively. The recording was tracking her even outside of the cabin!

Innocent dipped a toe. "Oh, it's marvelous!" she exclaimed. "So refreshing!"

"You must get it up to your face for it to work on your breath," Flower said.

"Yes!" Innocent dropped into the water and swam to the center of the pool.

Flower's clothing puffed away and he dived in after her.

The scene shifted to a goblin and a harpy standing at the water's edge. "They have joint talents," Mindy murmured. "That can be activated only when they act together."

Flower signaled the two. The goblin and the harpy both touched the water. It rippled and changed color slightly. The effect spread quickly out across the pool. What had they done to the water?

The ripple intersected Innocent. "Hoo!" she exclaimed. Then she turned to Flower and swam to join him. The two came together in a fury of splashing.

"What are they doing?" Mindy asked. "I can't see the detail."

"They're stork summoning!" Anna said. "That water was changed into a love spring!"

"What a trap!" Bryce said. "Lure her in, then change the water to make her passionate."

Soon the splashing was done, and the two separated. Flower quickly popped back to shore and his clothing re-formed. He made another signal.

The goblin and the harpy touched the water again. Another slightly colored ripple spread across.

Innocent swam to the bank and waded out. She looked confused. "Where am I?"

"That's Lethe water!" Anna said.

Flower walked across to her. "You have just swum in our healing spring. Your dragon breath has been cured. Now you can go home and have a normal life."

"Ouch!" Bryce said. "He left out a rather significant detail."

"Now I see it," Anna said indignantly. "It started as healing elixir, then became love elixir, and finally dilute Lethe. She has no memory of what she's just done in the last ten minutes."

"But the stork will remember," Metria said.

"Flower doesn't care. He's a demon."

Bryce got it. "Demon Flower. Deflower. That's what he does to visiting girls, and they never know."

Flower ushered Innocent back to the cabin, where she changed back to clothing and departed, as innocent as she had been when she came. The picture faded; the replay had run its course.

"That's what he has in mind for us," Anna said, outraged. "And maybe there's a lady troll waiting for Bryce."

"This annoys me," Bryce said.

Metria eyed him as if expecting something interesting. "And what are you going to do about it?"

"I will need your cooperation," he said. "You should enjoy this. It's your kind of mischief."

"Yes?"

"First find that lady troll, assuming there is one. Tell her there are weeds in the center of the pool to be cleaned out. But put some vapor around her, so she doesn't readily show up to others."

"And?" The demoness was as curious as the other two.

"Assume the form of a mortal girl. Approach Flower. Let him lead you into the pool. But pop out of there the moment he signals the goblin and harpy. Maybe make the mist around the troll resemble you."

"Oho!" Then she reconsidered. "But the demon and troll probably do it all the time anyway, between visits by mortal girls. That wouldn't shame them."

"When you pop out, pop over to the goblin and harpy. Persuade them to turn the water into hate elixir. Can you do that?"

"While the two are embraced in the middle," Metria said, seeing it. "Oh, that's dastardly!"

"Meanwhile we'll be on our way," Bryce said. "So as to be safely out of reach when Flower realizes what has happened." He sketched a screwdriver, animated it, went to the door, and soon jimmied the lock to release. They were making their jailbreak.

"You're right," Metria said to Mindy. "He has a gloriously devious mind." She vanished.

"She loves it," Anna said. "Deception, love, hate—that's her nature."

"I thought she would," Bryce said. "That's why she's cooperating."

They were just out of sight of the spa, pedaling vigorously on their trikes, when the clamor began. First it sounded passionate. Then it sounded violent. Metria was doing her part, and surely reveling in the mischief.

"I hope I don't regret doing that," Bryce said, feeling a bit guilty.

"They deserve it," Anna reassured him.

They arrived at Lake Kiss Mee shortly before nightfall. It was beautiful, with serene water and friendly vegetation.

"Do not drink the water," Mindy warned. "Unless you want to start kissing us. It lacks the potency of a love spring, but it does make a person very affectionate."

"The only man I want to kiss is Piper," Anna said. "No offense."

"In a few days you should be with him again," Bryce said.

"Yes. I live for that. But what if the princess selects him? She could, you know; his music is wonderful."

"I don't think she will," Mindy repeated. "She must know about his prior history as a suitor to Princess Dawn."

"Oh, I hope you're right."

Mindy foraged, finding safe food and drink. They made a tent for the night, and the three of them lay down in it. Bryce was in the center, a girl on either side.

"I can't help wondering about my own future," he said. "As you know, I'm an old man in a young body. Assuming I am not selected, I should try to find an old woman in a young body. She would understand. But I have no idea whom that might be."

"You could find a worthy old woman," Anna said. "And take her to a youth spring."

"I suppose I could," he agreed.

"Public announcement," Mindy said. "If you are free, I am going to try to win you myself, age be bleeped. I don't care how old you are. You're smart and funny and I love you."

Bryce was uncomfortable. "Mindy, you know I love the princess. You're almost as young as she is."

"So you can tell me to get lost."

He couldn't be that cruel. "Can't we just be friends?"

"No."

"Well, we'll see, in due course." He did not want to say that regardless of the love spell, he simply was not turned romantically on by Mindy, and doubted that the abatement of the spell would change that. But as a friend she was well worth associating with.

"I came to love a monster," Anna said. "The problem of age shouldn't be as hard as that."

But it was, Bryce realized. For all her youth, Princess Harmony had made a profound impression on him, hardly needing the love spell. But he intended to turn her down, in the unlikely event she chose him, because of her age. It would not be significantly different with Mindy.

But *if* the princess selected him, would his rationale stand up? He knew he should decline, but what if she begged him? What if she played her music to compel him? He could not be quite certain of his response.

He drifted to sleep, troubled.

In the morning they got up, cleaned up, and scouted for whatever it was they were supposed to find. There was no indication. Only the placid lake and a large quiet meadow where bees busily buzzed among the flowers.

"Did we come to the wrong place?" Bryce asked.

"Or did the Demons forget to place an Object?" Anna asked.

"The Demons wouldn't overlook such a thing," Mindy said. "They surely placed it. We just have to recognize it."

"Maybe that's part of the challenge, this time," Bryce said. "To see what is right before us. Unfortunately, we are not seeing very well."

Mindy rechecked the scroll, but there was no additional information. "I think we have to assume that it's here."

"We don't know its size or nature," Anna said. "Remember how the Ring of Power turned out to be the one Mindy was sitting on."

"I'm not sitting on anything now," Mindy said.

Bryce gazed out across the meadow. "We're standing in the meadow, but I doubt it's the whole meadow. Anyway the Ring of Power was hidden after we saw it demonstrated."

"But different Objects have been set up different ways," Anna said. "Lucky was using the Dress as a pillow."

"So perhaps we're missing the obvious," Bryce said. "Yet all I see here are flowers and bees."

"Ditto," Mindy said.

Then he paused. "I forget how the saying goes, but it may be relevant. When what you seek isn't in a likely place, you have to check the unlikely places."

"What, in Lake Kiss Mee?" Anna asked. "Are we looking for a kiss?"

"I'm thinking flowers," he said. "They are pretty, and they can be useful, at least for bees."

"Bees," Anna said. "One isn't much, but a hive of them can be important. For one thing, there's honey there."

"So maybe we need to find the hive," Mindy said.

But they saw no hive. Wherever it was was not in the meadow.

But Bryce kept thinking about bees. "Maybe we don't need the hive. The bees are here. If only we could talk to them!"

"Let's try," Anna said.

"Well, they have a language of sorts in their dances," Bryce said. "But I don't think we could do their kind of dance."

"Too bad they aren't telepathic," Mindy said.

"How do we know they aren't?" Anna said. "Maybe we should try."

They tried, willing the bees to respond.

Yes.

"I got an answer!" Bryce exclaimed. He looked around. "Are you a bee?"

Yes.

"Are you hearing what I'm hearing?" Bryce asked the others. "In your minds?" Both girls nodded.

Bryce looked again. "Which bee?"

Which one do you think?

"The important one! The Queen Bee!"

Correct. A bee flew up and hovered before him. *Will you offer a lady a seat?*

"Certainly," he said, raising his right hand.

The bee landed on it. *Thank you.*

"So you are the Object we must win?"

Ask for the Demonstration.

"We would like to see it," Bryce said.

"Pretend one of you is an attacking ogre."

"I'll do it," Mindy said. "I can join in the demonstration, not the Challenge." She raised her hands high. "I'm an ogre! I'll pulp your head and crunch your bones."

The bees of the meadow abruptly left their flowers and converged on Mindy. They landed on her body. In three-quarters of an instant she was completely covered.

"No!" Bryce said, horrified.

Don't bee concerned. They are not stinging her. This is merely a demonstration.

Oh. Indeed, Mindy was not screaming in pain, though she did seem quite nervous.

"Note the 'bee' talk," Anna murmured. "She doesn't say 'be.' That's typical of such dialects."

That ogre would bee severely distracted, the queen continued. *Worse, if we stung its eyes and tongue.*

"Eyes and tongue," Anna repeated, shuddering. She had her own horror there.

"The bees can protect a person from an attack by a living creature," Bryce agreed.

Scaly creatures are harder, but many have sensitive noses. Robots are more difficult, but we can jam their air intakes and put out their fires.

"Impressive," Bryce agreed, impressed.

The bees flew off Mindy, leaving her unharmed.

If you are hungry, we can provide honey, the queen thought. A small swarm appeared, carrying a honeycomb. They set it down before the three. *Eat.*

They tried the honey. It was delicious and invigorating.

"So you can feed a person, also," Bryce said. "That could be very useful on occasion."

If you need reconnaissance, we can scout the next valley and report, or delve into a cave, unobserved.

"That too could be very useful on occasion," Bryce said.

And in an emergency, we can carry a person.

Bryce was surprised. "Carry a person? But we weigh so much more than you do."

A bee can carry thirty times its own weight. We will demonstrate again.

The bees returned to cluster on Mindy. This time they formed loops of bees clinging to each other, that circled her arms and legs. Then they buzzed their wings. Mindy rose slowly into the air. They were indeed carrying her.

"That could be useful if a person needed to cross a deep crevasse," Bryce said, as the bees set Mindy gently down again.

I will travel with the one who wins me, and serve the one to whom I am given. That is my role in the Quest.

"It seems like a good gift," Mindy said. "The services of the bees are certainly worthwhile."

"It does indeed," Bryce agreed. He looked at Anna. "Is this one that appeals to you?"

"Yes, actually," Anna said. "I like the anomaly of a small friendly living creature instead of a powerful inanimate object. It's a woman's type of gift. If I win it, my brother can give it to the princess, who may like it enough to choose him."

"Your brother," Mindy said. "That's something I don't understand. Why didn't he come on this Quest himself?"

"It's complicated," Anna said uneasily.

"Maybe it's something we should understand," Bryce said. "You have been putting your health and life in danger to win something for him to use. Why are you doing it?"

"I support my brother. He needs this."

"Won't the princess know that he didn't earn it?" Mindy asked. "Why would she choose him?"

I am curious too. I would like to think that the person who wins me would not pass me on to an undeserving relative.

"Please, I'd rather not discuss it."

"I don't want to cause you unnecessary distress," Bryce said. "But I don't want to collude in setting something up for an unworthy Suitor. I don't see why the princess would choose a man who had to have his sister do the hard work and take the considerable risk. I think you owe us an explanation."

Anna broke down in tears. "You're right. I know it. But I just *can't.*"

Something was wrong. Bryce looked at Mindy, then at the Queen Bee perched on his hand.

There is mischief she can't reveal. I am telepathic, so I know it is there. I can't read it unless she brings it up specifically, but it must be resolved.

"Queen, can we put this Challenge on hold for a while?" Bryce asked. "While we work this out?"

Yes. This is important.

Bryce turned to Anna. "We know something is wrong. How can we make it right?"

"You can't," Anna said, weeping. "I hate it, but nothing in Xanth can make it right."

Bryce got a suspicion. "Queen, I realize this is premature, as we have not yet won you. But will you help in this separate matter, before we actually continue the Quest and try to win you?"

Yes.

So it was another anomaly: the prize working with them before being won. Anna's nature was having effect. "Then please have your bees prevent what we discuss here from getting out. Can they do that?"

Yes. They are telepathic too; it is how we communicate. They will set up a shell through which no outsider can fathom what's inside.

"Thank you. Please do it now."

The queen did not move, and he heard no signal, but the other bees rose up and formed a transparent globe around them. The buzzing of their wings echoed the telepathic interference they were running.

Bryce focused on Anna. "I know something is very wrong, and that you can't tell me directly what it is. My guess is that there is some threat to you and your family that forces you to cooperate in something you don't want to."

"That's not exactly it," she said. "But I can't tell you what it is."

That confirmed that there was something. "So I want you to answer some yes-no questions." He paused. "Falsely."

She gazed at him. "I—I don't understand."

"I want you to lie. To say yes instead of no, and no instead of yes. To never tell the truth, only the opposite."

"But I don't want to lie. I've always tried to be honest."

"And I commend you for it. But this is an aspect of a kind of game where the rules change. It's not really lying when you know I know you are not telling the truth. It is more like an exercise in reverse logic, tricky to do, but part of the game. You won't be admitting anything you're not supposed to; you'll be denying it."

Anna looked at Mindy. "Does this make sense to you?"

"I'm not sure," Mindy said. "But I trust Bryce's judgment. He's been right before, and is probably right this time. I know there are tricky games where the rules are different, as he says. I don't know why he wants to play it now, but that will surely come clear soon."

Anna looked at Bryce's hand. "What about you, Queen Bee?"

It verges on genius.

"Genius?" Anna repeated. "Telling me to lie?"

Trust him.

Anna spread her hands. "Then I'll do it, for whatever it's worth."

"Is your name Anna Molly?"

"Of course it is!" Then she caught herself. "I mean, no, it isn't."

Bryce smiled. "That's the spirit. Think before you answer, to make sure it's not the truth." He paused, then started the serious questions. "Did someone threaten you or your family, to make you do something you didn't want to?"

Anna hesitated. "Yes," she answered slowly.

So it really wasn't that. That surprised him. "Did someone promise you or your family something?"

"No."

"Something phenomenal, that you might get no other way?"

"No."

"Great success?"

Anna hesitated. "No." Then she reconsidered. "Yes."

Bryce pondered. His device was working, but it wasn't giving him the answers he expected. What could be interpreted either way?

"True love?" Mindy asked.

"No!" Anna said.

So that was it. And it had already been paid, because Anna had found love with Piper. That was not success in the sense of winning power or riches, but a woman might well choose love over material success.

So they were making progress. They still needed to ascertain who had done this, and why. Bryce had an idea about the first. "The one who promised you this: was it a Demon?"

"No."

"And if you told, were you threatened with the loss of it?"

"No," Anna said uncomfortably.

She didn't want to lose that love, understandably. But why would a Demon prefer to have a Suitor's sister compete instead of the Suitor? "Is there something you are supposed to do here?"

"No." Then again she reconsidered. "Not exactly. Or I mean, exactly."

Another fudgy answer.

Is it something your mere presence accomplishes? the Queen Bee asked.

"No!"

And there it was. "Because you are female?" Bryce asked.

"No."

This remained perplexing. "Does it relate to another Suitor?"

"No."

"Me?" Because he was the only other Suitor left.

"No."

Suddenly it was getting personal. "Because I would treat a woman differently than a man?"

"No."

"But I try to be fair with anyone, male or female," Bryce protested.

"No."

"You're a gentleman," Mindy said. "You have a somewhat courtly manner with women." She smiled obscurely. "You don't take advantage of them."

"No," Anna said, agreeing with her.

"And if it came to a choice of who would get to try for the Object," Mindy continued, "in this case the Queen Bee, and she wanted to, you would let her."

"No," Anna said.

"Well of course I would. But I would do the same for a man."

"Maybe the Demon didn't know that," Mindy said. "Because Anna's Demon would not have been familiar with you. Just with early indications that you showed before the Quest formally began. So Anna is here to see that you don't take the Bee."

"No," Anna agreed.

"But what difference does it make?" Bryce asked. "There's another Object remaining to try for after this one. I can take that one."

"Yes," Anna said.

Bryce, Mindy, and the Queen Bee looked at her, startled.

"You can take another," Anna said. "You don't have to take this one."

Bryce whistled. "That ups the ante. This is the last Object I have a chance of winning?"

"No," Anna said, smiling sadly.

"But if I take this one, you could still take the next one," Bryce said.

"No." Then Anna amplified. "If you don't take this

one, you can take the next one. You will still be in the game. The princess hates you. She will never choose you."

"Oho!" Mindy exclaimed. "The Demons figure the princess likes you, Bryce, and will choose you if she has a chance. Then all the others will lose. They are trying to see that you wash out, don't have a gift for her, and are eliminated. This is the point where that is decided."

"No!" Anna agreed.

"So it is part of the game," Bryce said. "Not just to get good gifts for the princess, but to eliminate other competitors."

"No," Anna agreed again. "I—I think you stink, and I really like the idea of making you wash out."

"Well, you can have the Bee," Bryce said. "I'll take my chances on the next Object."

Anna nodded, tears flowing down her face. So, oddly, did Mindy, as tearfully.

Oh, my, the Bee thought. *This session must end now.*

"I think we have it straight, at last," Bryce agreed. "No one has told anyone anything true, and nothing is changed. We'll proceed as before."

Anna ran to him and kissed him fleetingly on the cheek. Then she organized. "I will take the Bee."

The Queen Bee took off from Bryce's hand and flew across the meadow. *I will sit atop the Hive,* her thought came back. Now the hive appeared, in the middle of the meadow. *We will allow no one to approach. Any who try will not be stung to death, merely to unconsciousness, so that they lose. Good fortune.*

"Lucky is no longer with us," Bryce said.

"I must stay out of this," Mindy said.

Anna started walking toward the hive. Immediately a

swarm of bees rose up and hovered between her and the hive. That was warning enough.

"It *is* a challenge," Anna said. "I know the Queen bears us no malice, but she has to do her job."

Indeed. If you wash out here, we could use a bee-keeper for sundry chores. You would have all the honey you want, and no one would sting you.

"Thank you," Anna said. "I might take you up on that, as I like you and love your honey. But first I have to try to win you."

Of course.

"Could I make really tight clothing, so they couldn't get at me?" Anna asked Bryce.

"That would be risky," Bryce said. "They could sting through thick cloth, and crawl into any hollows. It would have to be airtight, and then you'd have trouble breathing."

"Could I borrow a carpet and fly over them? Dropping down suddenly from above?"

"Not with creatures of the air like bees," Bryce said.

"Or tunnel under the ground to the hive?"

"If you could get underground, so could they," Bryce said. "Remember, they can squeeze into crevices."

"It's such a simple thing," she said, frustrated. "Yet so hard to do."

"Yet there has to be a way," Bryce said. "We just have to think of it."

"If only Fracto Cloud could come by now, and blow them all away!"

"They'd cling to the hive, and sting when you got there."

"You're very good at objections," she flared. "What do you recommend?"

Bryce considered. "What are we missing? We must be thinking too much inside the box."

"Box?"

"Figure of speech. We're being conventional, and not getting anywhere. But maybe if we could come up with something anomalous . . ."

"That's my specialty," she agreed. "The anomaly."

Then Bryce had an idea. "We've been thinking of Xanth. Maybe it should be Mundania."

"Mundania? That seems irrelevant."

"Precisely. It's anomalous."

"How can that help us?"

"I visited a bee farm in Mundania once. They used smudge pots."

"I don't understand. Dirty pots?"

He smiled. "Smudge pots. They had small fires inside of pots, that burned peat or something, making a lot of smoke. It seems the bees couldn't handle the smoke; it messed up their senses so they couldn't orient to sting."

"Smoke," she said. "I never thought of that."

Bryce looked around. "Maybe we can make a smudge pot."

They foraged in the meadow, and found a solid old root with a hole in it. They stuffed that with dried leaves and stems. Then Bryce used his pen to sketch a lighter, animated it, and used it to ignite the packed leaves. They burned reluctantly, issuing thick smoke.

"I think we've got it," Bryce said.

"Are you sure it will work?" Anna asked.

"No. And that bothers me. You could get badly stung."

Anna was doubtful. "I could."

"Would you prefer that I try it?"

"No. I want to try it, succeed or fail. Getting stung is nothing compared to what the harpies and goblins tried to do to me."

She was correct. "Don't hurry. Stay within the cloud of smoke. If you get stung, retreat."

"I will," she said. Then she took the smudge pot and advanced on the hive.

The bees swarmed. They formed a larger cloud around her, but did not get through the smoke. Anna walked up to the hive and picked up the Queen Bee in her hand.

"Just like that," Mindy murmured. "It looks so easy when you have the key."

"She had to have the nerve to do it," Bryce said.

"She did. She earned it."

They walked to the hive. The bees had returned to their labors with the flowers. All was peaceful.

"Now you can rejoin Piper," Bryce said. "Congratulations."

"I owe it all to you," Anna said. "You knew the score, knew this was your last chance, but still you gave it to me."

"It was the right thing to do."

"If you lose because you did the right thing, then the princess will lose her best prospect. I hate that."

Bryce shrugged. "What will be will be. You have been through more than enough."

"If I didn't love Piper, I would love you," Anna said. "Maybe I do, a little." She paused, reconsidering. "More than a little. Hold still; I'm going to kiss you."

"You kissed me before. No need to—"

She stepped in to him, put her hands to his head, held it in place, and kissed him firmly on the mouth. Bees and tiny honeycombs flew around them.

Then Anna and the Queen Bee mounted her trike and rode off. Bryce, dazed, slowly settled back to earth. Had Anna wanted him, he realized, she could have taken him, anomalous as that might be.

"But what about this business of that being your last chance?" Mindy asked. "What an irony if your better nature cost you that."

"I made mistakes in my Mundane life," Bryce said gravely. "This time I mean to do it right. That means not letting the convenience of the moment override the honorable thing, and not letting others dictate the important decisions of my life even if it is for my own good. The princess will survive without me."

"I'm not sure of that. Especially if it's true she prefers you to the others."

"We don't know that's true." But he wondered.

13

MONOCLE

"Where is the next Object?" Bryce asked.

"You are going to try for it?" Mindy asked.

"Of course. I am obliged to do my best, regardless of whether I expect to succeed. And I'm not at all sure I will fail. I don't see how anyone could know that far ahead. As I understand it, the Demons set things up fairly, then don't interfere."

"They do," she agreed. "But it sounds as if someone peeked into the future."

"The future is mutable."

"Maybe it is in Mundania."

He nodded. "Point made. But I will make my best effort."

She unrolled the scroll. "The Gap Chasm," she said, surprised. "We were there before."

"Not as part of the Quest."

"True. But I dread messing with the Gap, unless it is safely down in the bottom of it."

"At least it is not far from here."

"Short distances can be as challenging as long ones," she said. "Especially when Demons have set roadblocks."

"So we'd best be on our way," he said.

They got on the trikes and followed the path on east, to intersect a northbound enchanted path.

In an hour they reached a pleasant lake. Mindy needed to take a toilet break, and disappeared behind a bush. Bryce, thirsty, dipped out a double handful of the clear water and drank. It was amazingly refreshing.

Mindy returned. "I meant to warn you: don't drink that water," she cautioned. "This is Lake Kiss Mee."

"Oops. I just did."

"Oh, bleep!" Then she changed her mind. "No, maybe it will do. You need a person to kiss."

"I do," he said, surprised. In fact the urge was overwhelming.

"So kiss me." She stood before him, definitely thinner than she had once been.

Bryce didn't hesitate. He enfolded her and kissed her repeatedly. He just had to keep doing it; he couldn't stop himself. It was the power of the water governing him, though she was also pleasant to hold. But she bore up remarkably well.

Several minutes later he was finally kissed out. "Thank you," he gasped. "I'm sorry to have put you through that."

"You forget I love you. I'm happy to have you kissing me without limit."

"But this wasn't love! It was the urgency of the water."

"Yes. But I still enjoyed it."

Maybe she had. But he would be more careful hereafter. Because he had enjoyed it too, and that was dangerous.

They found an enchanted path and rode north. In two hours they came to the village of Kiss Mee. It was getting late and they were tired, so they decided to stop. Kiss Mee was close to the Gap Chasm, and they could readily complete their trip in the morning.

"This should be a friendly town, if they drink the local water," Bryce said.

"It is. They do," Mindy said. "But they're acclimatized to it, so they are merely friendly, not demanding. I will seek the Mare."

"The what?"

"The Mare of this town. She's the one who can approve lodging for us."

"A horse? Or do you mean the Mayor?"

"Yes."

Bryce was silent, realizing that he was missing something.

Mindy went to the central stall. There was a female horse. Mindy talked, and the horse whinnied. Mindy returned. "There is a complication."

"I should think so," Bryce said wryly.

"We are welcome to stay the night, but the Mare has a favor to ask. It seems they have a problem they don't know how to handle, so they are hoping we have an idea."

"Why not? I'm happy to return a favor for a favor."

"It's not that easy. Maybe we should not stay here."

"Now I'm really confused. You talk with a horse to get us a room, and now you don't want to?"

"Here's the situation," she said, not smiling. "People have been mysteriously dying. They know who has a motive, but he's never involved when it happens, so they're helpless."

"Motive is not necessarily murder," Bryce said. "Maybe a friend of his is doing it."

"He has no friends here."

"Who is it?"

"A young man named Brant."

"Well, let's go talk with him, for a start."

"I don't think that would be wise."

Mindy was normally very accommodating. Why was she getting negative now? "Why not?"

"Because if we annoy him in any way, we could be the next to die."

Now it was coming clear. "And just asking about the folk who have died could annoy him, especially if he's guilty."

"That's it," she agreed grimly.

"This smacks of a Demon impediment."

"It does."

"Which means we won't be able to avoid it by riding on."

"Oh! I didn't think of that."

"Let's get more detail on exactly who has died, and how."

Mindy talked with the Mare again, and returned with more information.

"There was a girl Brant liked, but she liked another boy better. A few days later that other boy drowned. He was an excellent swimmer, and his friends don't understand how it could have happened. The girl was grief-stricken and refused to see any other boy. In another week she died in an unusual accident. A halfway-friendly neighborhood dragon had been toasting nuts, and a stray jet of flame happened to burn her as she walked past. The dragon hadn't meant to do it; it was a fluke. Then another boy accused Brant of somehow arranging it. A week later that boy died when a passing roc bird came in for a landing, didn't see him, and sat on him. Again, it was a friendly roc, coming in for a routine package delivery. Another weird accident."

"I see the pattern," Bryce said. "It's as if Brant wishes them evil, and it happens."

"Exactly. Can you figure out a way to prove it or stop it?"

"Maybe. It always seems to be several days before affront becomes vengeance. What does Brant do in the interim?"

"Nothing. In fact he sleeps."

"Sleeps?"

"A lot, day and night. Then someone dies."

"In Mundania this would be sheer coincidence. But here in Xanth, it could be magic. Could he be sending them bad dreams, so that they are distracted and become dangerously careless?"

"Only the Night Stallion can do that."

"The what?"

"The Night Stallion runs the dream realm. They make bad dreams for bad people to experience, and the night mares deliver them to deserving folk. It's an inducement to be good."

"The Night Stallion. He knows about all dreams?"

"All bad ones, yes. The Day Stallion supervises nice daydreams for day mares to deliver."

"Then we should go see the Night Stallion to ascertain what he knows about this."

"We can't do that! He's in the dream realm!"

"Ah, but isn't there an access via the peephole gourd?"

She nodded. "That's right. You did encounter a gourd when we were hunting puns. But entering one has its own dangers."

"Not worse than what we have been facing on this Quest, I think."

She nodded. "You have a point."

She went to the Mare again. Soon they were ensconced in a nice room, with two fresh gourds. A villager was instructed to check on them, and to break their eye contact in an hour so that they did not get trapped in the dream realm.

They sat opposite each other at a table, in couch chairs that held their bodies firmly in place. "We must hold hands as we enter, so that we will find ourselves in the same spot in the dream realm," Mindy said.

"You find ways to kiss and hold hands."

She blushed. "I do," she confessed. "But this is legitimate."

He was sorry. "I didn't mean to tease you. I—I like doing it with you." He condemned himself for his youthful-body reactions. She had become more physically attractive, and he was noticing. He took her hands on the table, outside the gourds. "What's next?"

"We'll encounter the standard dream setting for newcomers," Mindy explained. "This is a haunted house, stocked with ghosts and spooks. Beyond it is a graveyard with zombies and walking skeletons. Scary things."

"Like Picka Bone?"

"Yes. His parents were from the dream realm. They aren't bad folk at all, merely different."

"I understand. It's been about seventy years since Halloween spooks actually scared me."

"Then look into the peephole the same time I do."

"So we'll remain together," he agreed.

They looked. The room was gone. They stood before a badly maintained house in a wretched yard. A full moon hung low overhead, looking moldy. It was surely made of old green cheese.

"This is it," Mindy said. "We don't need to hold hands here; our real bodies are doing that." She disengaged.

"Let's bypass the spook house and go directly to the graveyard."

"Can't. This setting is preprogrammed. We have to enter."

"Let me try something else, then." He brought out his pen and pad, which he did have with him. He sketched a folded map marked HAUNTED HOUSE. He activated it, and the map slid off the paper into his hand.

"You're getting good with that magic pen."

"The princess gave it to me, remember. It's a really nice instrument." He unfolded the map. There was a complete display of the interior of the haunted house, hall by creaky hall and room by gloomy room. Sure enough, there was a shortcut to the rear.

"But you are using it in ways the princess probably never thought of."

"I think that's why she gave it to me. She thought I could make better use of it than she could." He studied the map, then folded it and put it in his pocket. "Onward."

They went to the door and Bryce lifted the huge old corroded knocker and let it fall. "OoOOga!" sounded within the house.

"And maybe a horn would blow a knocking sound," Bryce said, smiling.

The door opened. No one was there, just an empty pair of shoes and an empty pair of gloves. The gloves were moving the door.

"Thank you," Bryce said. "Fine setting you have here." One glove made a little wave of acknowledgment, and the shoes stepped aside.

They entered the house. The floorboards creaked alarmingly.

"The shortcut is an immediate turn to the left," Bryce said. "Through the original maid's quarters."

They turned left. A ghost loomed up before them, a bright white sheet with black eye-holes. That might be the original maid.

"BOO!!" Bryce shouted with doubled exclamation point.

Original Ghost Maid was so surprised she zoomed upward and right through the ceiling, leaving only a cloth dropping to the floor. The cloth was ghostly but peculiarly fascinating.

"You beast," Mindy said. "You scared her right out of her panties." She stooped to pick them up. They were filmy to the point of nonexistence, but nevertheless intriguing. Bryce had never quite fathomed panty magic, but certainly it worked. "We're sorry," she called. "He's from Mundania. He doesn't know proper protocol."

The ghost floated back down through the ceiling. She took the panties from Mindy's lifted hand, her white sheet blushing faintly pink. She faded away.

"Now are you going to stop freaking out the staff?" Mindy asked, suppressing the ghost of a smile. "They're only trying to do their job."

"This way." He proceeded through the maid's quarters and out a side door. A short walk led to the graveyard in the back.

There was a walking skeleton, evidently on sentry duty. It looked male, because it was missing a rib. Bryce walked up to him. "Picka Bone sent me."

"Who?" the skeleton asked, startled.

"The son of Marrow Bones and Grace'l Ossein," Mindy said.

The skeleton's skull illuminated. "We know them," he said. "How are they doing in the mortal world?"

"We'll tell you all about them," Bryce said. "While you are guiding us to the Night Stallion."

The skeleton considered. "We can't make a deal until we know each other. Who are you?"

"I am Bryce, and this is Mindy. We're from Mundania."

"I am White Skeleton. Red Skeleton is my cousin."

"He was a fine humorous fellow," Bryce said, impressed.

"You knew him in Mundania?" Mindy asked.

"Knew *of* him, or his non-pun analog."

"This way." White led the way out of the graveyard and through another setting where a camera crew was recording a bad dream. A pack of werewolves was chasing a terrified nymph into a treacherous bog. "Eeee!" she cried. Bryce noticed how her bare nymphly parts bobbed and jiggled enticingly as she ran. Being physically young again was a nuisance when he was trying to get something done; he was too readily distracted.

"Halt," the director said, disgusted. "The term is 'Eeeee!' Five E's, not four. Now try it again."

They ran it again. The nymph was just as enticing the second time, and breathing harder. "Eeeeee!"

"Halt! Five E's, not six. Try to get it right this time."

"Nymphs are stupid," White muttered as they moved on. "They can't count beyond their chest."

"Chest?" Bryce asked.

"Two," Mindy snapped.

Oh. Maybe that was one reason they ran bare. With clothing they would be limited to counting to one. Not that intelligence was the point of a nymph.

While they walked, Mindy filled in the illustrious history of Marrow and Grace'l Bones in mortal Xanth. It was quite a story. Bryce had not realized that Picka Bone derived from such a remarkable lineage. No wonder Princess Dawn had courted him.

Meanwhile White Skeleton was leading them into an abysmal swamp that was surely fraught with all manner of horrors. Bryce saw bubbling pools of green goo, and tree trunks with huge gnarly eyes, and floating wisps of discolored mists that looked corrosive or poisonous. This would not be a good place to get lost in. The path was so devious that it would be a chore just to locate it for a retreat.

They came to an elegant stall standing on a firm islandlike mound. Within it stood a magnificent dark horse who wasn't exactly black. "That will do, White," the horse said. "I will take it from here." Then as the skeleton respectfully backed off, the horse oriented on the two of them. He looked surprised by Mindy. "What are you doing here—"

"Mindy," Mindy said quickly. "A servant employed at Caprice Castle. And this is Bryce Mundane. He is a

Suitor for the Princess Harmony in a Quest arranged by the Demons."

"I see," the horse said, as if reconsidering. Bryce suspected that he was not ordinarily very tolerant of intruders in his realm, but that the mention of the Demon Quest set him back. He turned to Bryce. "I am the Night Stallion, otherwise known as Trojan, the Dark Horse, or the Horse of a Different Color. I run the Realm of Dreams. What is your business here?"

"One moment," Bryce said.

Mindy sent him a warning glance. "You don't make the Night Stallion wait," she murmured.

"Why not? He's making us wait."

"What are you talking about?"

"This isn't the Night Stallion," Bryce said. "This is a fake, set up to distract us from our mission."

"How can you say that? He looks perfectly real to me." She glanced at the horse, who was standing perfectly still, as was the skeleton. It was like a cartoon where the only animated characters were the ones who were speaking at the moment.

"Appearances are easy to come by in the dream realm, since everything here is imaginary," Bryce said. "It's a mistake to judge solely by looks."

"But what else is there?"

"His actions."

"But all he did was introduce himself and ask your business."

"Precisely. The real Stallion surely knows the dreams of every mortal person, and therefore our business here. He wouldn't need to ask."

"That's right," she agreed thoughtfully. "But why would he let the skeleton lead us into a nasty swamp?"

"Because while he knows everything that goes on in the dream realm, it surely keeps him quite busy. He can't afford to have every Tom, Dick, and Harry wandering in and taking his time with inconsequentials. So he diverts them harmlessly, and most never know the difference. But our business is serious. We can't afford to be put off by the standard diversion. We need the Stallion's personal attention."

Mindy nodded. "We do. But if we can't trust the skeleton to lead us to the Stallion, what can we do? We'll never find him in the infinite reaches of the dream realm."

"I suspect he has been tracking us fairly closely," Bryce said. "Because he evidently recognized you as a person of importance."

"Me?"

"The fake did a double-take when he looked directly at you. He must have been advised. Maybe there's a Demon aura about our mission. So the Stallion knows who we are, but doesn't care to shortcut regular policy, which would be a bad precedent. Demon mission or not, we could still be wasting his time. We need to spot him ourselves."

"How can we do that?"

"By common sense." Bryce turned to White Skeleton. "Hello, Trojan."

The skeleton became the horse. "You are one dangerously smart Mundane."

"No, I've just been around the bend a few times."

"Indeed." The horse's mouth curved with a trace of amusement. "I do know what's going on in the dream realm. But your concern stems from the mortal realm, not the dream realm. It will be more efficient if you simply state it now."

"Gladly," Bryce agreed. "The Demons seem to have put certain obstacles in our way as we seek certain objects. We have to handle them before we can move on. In this case, the village of Kiss Mee has been suffering an unfriendly situation, wherein a young man may be dreaming up odd ways for folk he dislikes to die. I thought I should check with you, because if my conjecture is correct, this is an abusive misuse of dreams."

"Who?"

"His name is Brant. He sleeps a lot, and is never close when a person dies. Maybe his talent is to make a dream come true, once he dreams it."

Trojan flickered in the manner the demon Pose had when zipping momentarily elsewhere. "I have verified it. His power is the Deathwish. You are correct: when he dreams up a death, he can then make it happen. It is limited to dreaming; he can't simply wish a person dead. This is indeed an abuse. What do you recommend that I do?"

"I would not presume to tell you what to do in your own realm."

The equine mouth formed a tolerant smile. "You have a certain diplomatic touch, doubtless acquired in the course of your many years of experience in drear Mundania. I have now picked up on the Demon contest. The Suitors must figure out the answers themselves. So you need to make a feasible suggestion."

Just so. "I think the simplest way to deal with it is to cut off Brant's dreams. That way he will not be able to make them come true. Do you have the power to withhold bad dreams as well as to make them?"

"I do," Trojan said. "So be it." He glanced at Mindy. "I believe the princess has chosen well."

"I wouldn't know," Mindy said. "Bryce still must win the last Object, and there is a prediction that he will not succeed."

"That failure would eliminate him as a Suitor?"

"We understand that the princess will choose the man who brings her the best gift," Bryce explained. "If I don't win the Object I won't have a gift to proffer."

"She may indeed choose," the Dark Horse agreed. "But she's a sly one. She might seek to change the rules."

"Even when Demons make the rules?" Mindy asked.

"Rules are subject to interpretation." The Horse shrugged, throwing off iridescent colors. "All the current generation of princesses are headstrong and naughty, some amazingly so. Princess Eve married the lesser Demon Pluto and is making his existence wax hot and cold despite his power. Princess Rhythm did serious damage to the Adult Conspiracy. There are still dreams relating to that mischief." He shook his head. "Princess Harmony is the smartest and most strongly motivated. That makes her devious. Even Demons may discover that."

"I wouldn't say that," Mindy said.

"Naturally not," the Horse agreed, amused.

Trojan evidently had some private joke. Maybe it was because his control of dreams led him to secrets others could not share. Yet he judged Harmony as the smartest of her generation of princesses? He thought she was devious? She had not struck Bryce that way during their interview. She had seemed like a nice girl despite her royalty. Still, it was curious that the Demons had selected her as the center of their contest. Did they see in her something Bryce had missed?

But his mind was wandering. "Thank you, Trojan Horse," he said. "This will enable me to at least try for my Object."

"There is one other thing. I have cut off all future dreams, but he has one remaining from before. Dragons catch a girl and tear her apart."

Mindy shuddered. "Poor girl!"

"We'll be sure to stay well clear of dragons," Bryce said.

"Pleasant awakening," the Night Stallion said.

Then they were back in the room, facing each other across the table. Their eye contact with their gourds had been broken, though the villager assigned to do this had not yet appeared. The Stallion had done it, showing his power in a minor way.

"Now let's go see the Mare again," Mindy said briskly.

They did, then returned to the room for the night. "Trojan seemed amused," Bryce said. "And I question his judgment of the Princess Harmony."

"Don't. He surely has her pegged."

"But he was calling her devious. She seemed straight-forward to me."

Mindy smiled. "Your experience with women may be limited."

"I'm eighty years old!" Then he laughed. "But yes, it is limited. Let's leave it at that."

A village girl arrived with a basket of food. "Oh— you're off the gourd," she said.

"Yes, a while ago," Mindy said. "But thanks for coming, just to be safe."

The girl set out the food and drink. It was a nice meal for two. Then she departed.

They ate, then took turns washing at the basin in the corner. Bryce did not look while Mindy was washing, though he suspected she would not have minded if he did. This was not entirely politeness; he feared the sight of her body would turn him on. Pajamas and a nightie were laid out, so they donned them.

They lay on the bed, Bryce on the left side, Mindy on the right. She extinguished the candle by her side.

"You know," she murmured in the darkness, "no one would see if you moved across to my side."

"But two people would know," he said, not pretending to misunderstand.

"This is Kiss Mee. Everybody here does it, and they don't stop at kisses. They expect it. That's why there's only one bed."

She was surely correct. But it didn't change his position. He was not about to take something merely because it was available, however infernally tempting it might be. "We have been through this before."

She sighed. "We have."

He feared she was crying. "Mindy, even if I weren't in love with the princess, I still would not be making moves on you. You're almost as young as she is."

"And you won't touch anyone that young, however willing, even if no one else knows."

"Correct." He wasn't sure she would ever really understand. She did not have his extra three-score years of sometimes bitter experience.

She buried her face in the pillow. After a time her muffled sobbing ceased and she breathed evenly in sleep.

Only then could Bryce relax. He knew he was doing the right thing. Why, then, did he feel so guilty?

In the morning they found breakfast already laid out for them; evidently the girl had come and left it without waking them. What had the girl thought about their slumber on the bed? Did it matter?

Soon they resumed their traveling, riding their trikes on out of town. The people ignored them, going about their routine business. Evidently the Mare had not talked about their business here.

Except for one person. This was a young man who stared silently at them as they went by, as if suspecting something.

"Oh, bleep," Mindy said when they were alone. "I wonder if that was Brant?"

"What if it was? He's harmless now, as he must have discovered last night."

"Except for one horrible dream."

That gave Bryce a chill. "We'd better be prepared to fight off dragons."

"What if they're at the Gap Chasm, where we have to go?"

"That could be a problem," he agreed. "But forewarned is forearmed, as they say in Mundania."

She glanced across at him. "If I get torn apart by dragons, I'll never forgive you for ignoring me last night."

That was gallows humor. "I'll find a way to stop them," he said with more confidence than he felt.

He brooded on it as they rode. One dragon might be balked by a pineapple tossed into its mouth, but the dream had several dragons. His pen could make only one thing at a time. What would stop several at once? He racked his old brain.

"Maybe we shouldn't go to the Gap," Bryce said.

"I was joking. Of course we have to go there, so you can get your Object."

"I may not be able to get it anyway. I don't want to risk you regardless, but how much worse to do so in a futile pursuit."

"You have to try. That's the whole point of the Quest. You let all the other Suitors take Objects you could have had. Now it's your turn. I'd *really* never forgive myself if I denied you that. I'm supposed to be helping you, not interfering."

He felt a warm surge of emotion at her loyalty to the mission. "Maybe you're right. But if we see dragons, we're getting out of there."

"Okay." She sounded relieved by the compromise, understandably.

He continued to ponder as they traveled. How could a single man with a ten-second glimpse of the future and a magic pen deal with multiple dragons? Finally he got a notion. It required precision and timing, but ought to work. But he hoped there would be no dragon attack.

Maybe his future sight could help. Ten seconds wasn't much, but on occasion it had made a real difference. Suppose he changed his mind after that ten-second warning, and did something else in one second? Would the sight change?

That intrigued him. "Mindy, I may be wasting my own time, but I want to experiment with my second sight, just in case. I'm going to ride off the path, but change my mind."

"But then you won't do it, will you?"

"That's the point. I want to see how my second sight reacts. I'm warning you so that you know I'm not as crazy as it may look."

"Maybe I can help you. You can decide not to kiss me, then change your mind."

He laughed. "I'll keep it in mind." He veered to the right and invoked his left eye.

It showed him crashing into the adjacent brush lining the path. It didn't upend him, because the trike could handle it, but it was thick going.

He corrected his steering. His second sight changed immediately, showing no crash. So it did track changes on an ongoing basis.

"Let's stop and kiss," he said, knowing that would please her despite her awareness that it was only an experiment.

She halted immediately and got off her trike. She stood expectantly. He got off his trike and approached her. His second sight showed him kissing her. Immediately he changed his mind, and the kiss vanished.

Then it reappeared, even though he had not changed his mind again. Mindy was stepping in to him. Oho!

He turned his face away as she embraced him. The left eye showed her standing there, disappointed. Then he changed his mind, and the kiss resumed. He did kiss her.

"It works," he said.

"Oh, I know!"

"I mean the changes in the second sight."

"That, too," she agreed.

They both laughed. But it was significant. His second sight was more responsive than he had thought, and that might make a big difference in some sensitive situation. Such as where to stand when a dragon breathed fire at him.

"Let's move on," he said.

"Must we?" But she disengaged and returned to her trike.

They resumed pedaling. Bryce was struck again by how nice a girl Mindy was. She had the misfortune to have gotten a crush on him, but she was handling it with grace, and she really was being helpful.

They came to the Gap Chasm. It was as awesome a gulf as ever. "We're here," Bryce said. "But I see no Object."

"Maybe it's on the other side."

"That means we'll have to cross."

"I know. Make a big carpet, and hold me tightly."

He did so. They folded and stored the trikes, then Bryce sat in the center, and Mindy sat before him, closing her eyes tightly. He put his arms around her and willed the carpet forward.

It lifted and floated over the brink. There were no clouds and no dragons. All was serene, and soon they landed on the north verge. "We're across," he said gently.

She relaxed. "Thank you. I hate being such a burden. I just—heights—"

"I understand. Now let's see what offers."

And there before them was a pedestal with a cushion. On the cushion was a lens with a handle.

"What is it?" Mindy asked.

"It looks like a monocle. That's like mundane glasses, only with just one lens. They are used at operas to enlarge the view of a distant stage, as I understand it. I'm not sure what use one would be in Xanth."

She picked it up and looked through it. "It doesn't magnify."

"Maybe it clarifies. Try looking at me."

She peered at him through the monocle. "Oh!" She reeled as if dizzy.

"What's the matter?"

"You—I think I saw into your mind, but it was so complicated I got lost."

"My mind?"

"You try it on me." She proffered the lens.

He took it and looked at her. Her face seemed to fuzz, and he suddenly felt girlish. He saw her face, but also felt her mood, which was one of recent fear and present confusion.

"You're right," he said. "This lens sees beyond the face, into the mind. But it's so general as to be useless."

"Maybe it sees the truth," she said. "Here, I'll speak a lie."

"A lie?"

"Remember that game with Anna?"

"Oh. Yes. The opposite of what you mean."

"I am a naughty boy."

Looking at her through the monocle, he picked up her surface meaning: boy meant girl. "It does seem to work."

"I love heights."

Bryce felt a shudder of aversion. She hated heights. "Somehow the image becomes a thought," he said.

"Let me try it again." This time there was no distortion; she was making an honest request.

He gave her the monocle. She oriented it on him. "Say some things I don't know about, some true, some false."

"Back in Mundania I had three children, two girls and a boy."

"Reversed," she said. "Two boys and a girl. It flickered at the untruth, but it also let me into your mind so I could fathom it without guessing or analyzing."

They experimented further, verifying the powers of the monocle. "The princess could use this when dealing with other rulers," Bryce said. "She would know not only when they were lying, but their whole mind-set. It would be invaluable."

"It's a worthy gift," she agreed.

He shrugged. "I'll take it."

The monocle vanished, along with the pedestal. The game was on.

"But where is it?" Mindy asked.

Bryce looked around. "That little cloud in the chasm— was that there before?"

"I don't know. I never looked."

Oh, of course. "I'm pretty sure it wasn't. It looks as if the pedestal is on it, and the monocle must be on the pedestal. All I need to do is to fly out there and take it."

"I'll bet it doesn't just float there and wait for you."

"The Challenge may be to catch it," he agreed. "It may disappear when I approach, and reappear behind me. Something like that. All I can do is fly out there and try."

"Yes. I'll wait here."

"Of course." It was his mission, and she could not brave the awful depth of the chasm. He hugged her, then got on the carpet and floated out toward the little cloud.

Sure enough, when he approached it, it dodged away as if repelled by his presence. He tried looping around, but it dodged another way. He needed to find a way to attract it rather than repel it.

He got an idea. He sailed up above the level of the cloud and came to hover directly over it. The cloud wavered but did not dart away, as if confused. It evidently oriented on the horizontal, not the vertical. Could he drop down and catch it? It surely would not be that easy, but perhaps he was making progress.

There was a scream. He looked. It was Mindy.

Because three dragons were winging rapidly toward her, rising out of the shadow of the chasm.

He knew what that meant. The deathwish dream.

Bryce propelled his carpet toward Mindy. But he saw he would not get there in time. The dragons were moving faster.

He set his carpet on cruise control, as it were, and brought out his pad and pen. He quickly sketched a box with speaker holes on the sides and a big button in the center of the top. He hoped that it worked as he meant it to, once he invoked it. It was about his only chance to save her.

The leading dragon swooped toward Mindy. She tried to run from it, but had no chance. It caught her in its talons just as Bryce reached the brink. She screamed piercingly, but could not escape.

"Invoke!" he said. The picture slid off the page as the carpet dissolved, dumping him on the ground.

The dragon pumped its wings and heaved Mindy off the ground as Bryce ran up. He was just too late, not that he could have wrested her from the dragon anyway.

He oriented his second sight. He was ready to throw the box, but saw that it would miss within ten seconds. He reoriented, but it missed again. He tried a third and a fourth time in as many seconds, getting it right. "Catch!" he called, and heaved it up underhanded.

Mindy saw him. She saw the box coming toward her. She reached out and caught it, first in his second sight, then in the present as it came true. So far so good. She had trusted him to know what he was doing, even if it seemed irrelevant to her at the moment.

But the dragon was already carrying her out over the chasm. Its two companions were converging, claws extended, ready to tear the morsel apart. Bryce had been narrowly focused on the transfer of the box. Now he had to deal with the dragons.

"Push the button!" Bryce yelled.

She saw the button. She jammed her thumb down on it.

Nothing seemed to happen. But abruptly the two other dragons rocked as if struck by something invisible, and the one carrying Mindy shuddered.

"It's a dragon repeller!" Bryce called. "It radiates a sound only they can hear, that hurts their ears. They must flee it."

"But this one can't escape it without dropping me!" she cried, terrified.

"No. It doesn't realize the source. You must steer it. When it happens to fly toward the brink, turn off the box."

"But then it won't repel the dragon!"

"Yes. Trust me."

"I do!" But she remained understandably terrified.

The dragon swerved in its effort to escape the awful sound. For a moment it was going toward the edge. "Now!" Bryce called.

Mindy pushed the button. The dragon abruptly stopped reacting and smoothed out its flight. It looped back toward the center of the chasm.

"Button!" Bryce yelled.

She was already on it. The dragon reacted as if it had just smacked into a wall. It reared back, which was a good trick in midair. Then, perhaps remembering where it had been free of pain, it started flying back toward the brink.

Mindy pushed the button.

The dragon wasn't stupid. Very quickly it learned that there was just one direction that made it pain-free. It flew toward the edge.

"Now bring it down," Bryce called. "You know how."

Mindy did. The moment the dragon started lifting, on came the repeller. The moment it dropped, off it came. Surprisingly soon it came in for a landing on the ground.

"Let me go!" Mindy said, giving it a one-second nudge. The claws relaxed, allowing her to step free. "Now fly away," she said.

The dragon needed no second urging. It leaped into the air and fled.

Mindy ran and flung herself into Bryce's arms. Only then did she collapse in a nervous breakdown. He held her, immensely relieved that his ploy had worked. He had saved her, literally, from being torn to pieces by dragons. He had voided the curse of the deathwish.

Soon Mindy recovered her emotional balance. She was good in that respect. "But you lost the Monocle," she said.

Indeed, the little cloud with its pedestal was gone. "There was no choice," Bryce said.

"It's my fault! I messed up your Quest!"

"I'm not sure you did. I suspect the Challenge was to save you *and* get the Monocle. I failed to rise to the whole of it."

"But if I had hidden from the dragons, you could have gotten it."

"Not if the Demons set it up to make it impossible to separate the two."

"How could you have done both?"

Bryce considered, still holding her. "Maybe if I had drawn a basilisk, it could have stunned both cloud and dragons."

"And me," she said sourly. "What about this: could you have drawn the Monocle and animated it before the dragons arrived?"

Bryce's mouth dropped open. "I wonder."

"Maybe it's not too late."

He let her go and brought out pen and pad. He drew the lens with the handle, and activated it. It slid off the page and he caught it. Had they found a way?

But when they tested it, it turned out to be an ordinary lens, with no magic. Perhaps if he had drawn it earlier, before the dragons came, he could have had the real one, then focused on dispersing the dragons. He had missed his chance.

"Well, let's return," he said heavily.

"But without the Monocle, you have nothing to give the princess."

"So one of the other Suitors will win her," Bryce said. "They are worthy. I will go and report my failure."

"I don't think you failed."

She was trying to console him. "Thanks. At any rate, I want to see you safely back."

"What will you do after it is decided?"

"Probably return to Caprice Castle and help them gather puns. I'm sure they will appreciate it."

"They will," she agreed. "Dull as it is. Oh, Bryce, I'm so sorry!"

"Don't be. I wasn't planning to marry the princess anyway, even if she asked me, which she wouldn't."

"You keep saying that. But Anna said she likes you."

"She's bound by the rules of the game, as I am. She will do what she has to do, so that she can be the best king when it is time."

"But Trojan said she's devious. She might not."

"At this point conjecture is pointless. Let's start back. We can take enchanted paths so there's no further risk. I believe there is one that crosses the chasm."

"There is. That will be no problem." She took a breath. "If you're not going to marry the princess, then there's nothing to stop you from taking advantage of me along the way."

"You know I wouldn't do that."

She sighed. "Bleep."

Then they both laughed. But it was sad, for more than one reason.

14

DECISION

The return trip was uneventful. By evening they were back at the Good Magician's Castle. They paused just across the drawbridge, at the front gate.

"My job is done," Mindy said. "I'll store the trikes. You go on inside; they'll be expecting you."

"You've been great, Mindy!"

"I cost you your Object."

"As I said, I'm not sure of that. It may have been fated, and you were merely the girl at hand to implement it. But I wouldn't trade it for your life, regardless."

"You're so sweet. I think I'll always love you."

That brought back the guilt. He had not sought her love, or wanted it, but felt responsible for it. What could he do?

She understood his hesitation. "Well, you could kiss me, one last time."

That much was feasible. He took her in his arms and kissed her. She kissed him back, eagerly. She was amazingly easy to hold. But she couldn't change the fact that she was only twenty years old, decades too young for him.

He let her go. "Fare well, Mindy."

"We'll meet again. I hope you aren't too angry." She folded one trike and held it as she sat on the other, then pedaled away. In two moments she was around the curve of the castle wall, heading for what must be the servants' entrance.

Bryce stood there a moment, perplexed. Why should he be angry? She had been a perfect companion, and was a worthy person. He was grateful for her assistance.

Well, he had other business to attend to. He walked on through the gate. Sure enough, there was Wira, the Good Magician's daughter-in-law, ready to conduct him to his lodging.

The same room assignments obtained. Bryce was back with Anna Molly. "Did you get your Object?" she asked.

"No."

"Bleep. I hoped my spoiler mission would fail. Believe me, there was nothing personal in it. I had to do what I was assigned to do."

"I understand that," Bryce said. "For what it's worth, I doubt I was fated to win either the Object or the princess. The larger situation simply is not conducive."

"I don't know. All the rest of us got our Objects, in large part because of your insight and help. It's not right for you to be excluded."

"I will survive. This has been one great adventure for me. Back in Mundania my life was frankly dull. If I return to Mundania tomorrow, this has still been a worthwhile interlude."

"You are generous." She pondered briefly. "Do you know what's happening tomorrow?"

"The presentation of gifts to the princess?"

"No. They tell us that is the day after tomorrow. Tomorrow we have to judge some talent contest. The rest of us have been preparing the stadium."

Bryce was surprised. "People will sing or dance?"

"Maybe. But in Xanth a talent is likely to be magical."

"Oh, of course. But why should we judge such a thing?"

"I think it's to keep us out of their hair for a day while they set up for the finale."

"That makes sense. They don't want us running around and getting in their way. The day a princess chooses her husband is significant. Relatives will need to assemble, arrangements be made for food and lodging, and so on."

She nodded. "Maybe it does, now that you put it that way. We're just part of the show." She pondered again. "Do you think the princess has made up her mind?"

"Theoretically she hasn't, because otherwise this whole Demon contest is pointless. She must decide after she sees the gifts."

She nodded. "True."

"How is it working out with Piper?"

"I hope he doesn't win the princess. I love him. If she doesn't marry him, I will."

"I'm glad."

"But if I couldn't marry him, I would go after you. You're really the best man a girl could get."

"I'm eighty years old!"

"Not anymore."

"I am inside. That's what counts."

"You've got this hangup about age. In Xanth you're twenty-one. If I were to go after you, I'd start by seducing you, and every time you mentioned age I'd seduce you again until I wore you down. You'd change your attitude soon enough."

"I doubt it."

"You think I couldn't seduce you if I tried?"

Bryce remembered her parting kiss two days before. She wasn't bluffing. "Couldn't wear me down," he clarified.

She laughed. "But wouldn't it be fun trying!"

He smiled. "Such a situation would be an anomaly."

"Of course."

Then he remembered: her talent was the anomaly. He had walked into that one.

All the Suitors were at dinner. It was good to see them again. They had been a largely random assemblage, but they had had strong interactions and learned respect for each other.

And Mindy was serving the dishes, as before. Why did she think he'd be mad at her?

Back in the room for the night, washing and changing, Anna remarked, "And you didn't make it with Mindy, either."

"Of course not," he agreed.

She shook her head. "Men can be such fools."

He decided to ask her. "Mindy thinks I'm going to be mad at her. I have no idea why. You're a woman; do you know?"

Anna considered. "I can see why she would be mad at you. She practically threw herself at you, and you wouldn't touch her. Sure you love the princess, but most men will take something on the side if it's free. Just as Piper is doing with me. But you mad at her? That doesn't figure."

"I don't believe she was joking."

"She wouldn't joke about something like that. She's a pretty straightforward girl. There must be something we don't know about."

"Something," he agreed morosely. So the mystery remained.

In the morning after breakfast they went out to the stadium. It was a weak effort compared to a Mundane bowl, with a few rows of seats arranged in a broad semicircle around a central platform. Mindy was still putting out more chairs. People were streaming in, evidently eager to participate in the event.

Bryce and Anna took their places on the platform, where there were more chairs. The other Suitors did the same. Bryce noticed that Piper was at the far end. "You're not sitting with Piper?"

"I wish I could. But we don't want to make a scene before the princess chooses. It would be awkward if she chose Piper."

He could appreciate that.

Soon all the seats were filled. Now a man appeared and stood on the platform facing the crowd. "Trent!" Bryce said, recognizing him. "He's the Master of Ceremonies!"

"Harmony's great-grandfather," Anna agreed. "He's always been great with crowds. They're pulling out all the stops."

"For an incidental talent contest?"

Trent overheard them and turned. "It's a kind of rehearsal for the Princess Betrothal ceremony tomorrow. We want to be sure everything is in working order."

"Will everyone be able to hear what's going on?" Bryce asked.

Trent considered. "What do you think, dear?" he asked a woman who had taken a back seat. That was the former queen Iris.

"I can't heeeer you!" she called back.

"Can you make an illusion reflector wall to keep the sound in?"

"Illusion doesn't work that way," she said as a much more impressive stadium appeared around the real one. "It reflects light, not sound."

"Maybe I can help," Bryce said. He brought out pen and pad, and sketched a megaphone. He activated it, and it expanded to a good-sized cone. "Can you hear me?" he said into the small end.

The folk seated in chairs put their hands to their ears. "You nearly blew my hair off," Iris called.

So it worked. It was surely magically enhanced. Bryce handed it to Magician Trent. "Yes, I remember these from my time in Mundania," Trent said. "Thank you."

Bryce had not realized that the man had been in Mundania. "You're welcome."

Now Trent spoke carefully into the megaphone. "I am King Emeritus Trent, your Master of Ceremonies. We are here to hold a talent contest, and these are the judges." He gestured to the people seated on the stage, without introducing them. "We are looking not for the strongest talent, but for the person who makes best use of his or her talent, regardless of its nature or strength. Thus a weak talent used well will beat a strong talent clumsily wielded. Everyone has a fair chance." He paused to let that sink in. "This will be a largely subjective judgment, but the judges' decision, once they come to it, will be final. A majority vote will determine it. If there is a tie vote, I will break it if I choose to."

He paused. "We promised a worthwhile prize. Here it is." He held up a holder in which three colored vials were set. "These are three precious fluids. One is healing elixir, enough for several doses depending on the severity of the injury. Another is youth elixir, two or more doses depending on how much age is removed. The third is a love potion, two doses, guaranteed to make anyone fall desperately in love for at least a year. Are you interested?" There was a moan of appreciation. These liquids were invaluable.

"Now let's have the first talent." Trent looked over the seated people. "You," he said, pointing to a young man. "Stand up, state your name and talent, and demonstrate the use you make of it."

The young man stood up. "I—I'm Jesse," he said nervously. "My talent is to make things lighter. So I can lift almost anything. I can make myself lighter too, so that I can float." He rose into the air.

"Can you lighten moods?" Trent asked.

"Why, I never thought of that," Jesse said.

"Good enough," Trent said briskly. "Judges, make your notes."

"May we discuss it?" Anna asked.

"Among yourselves," Trent agreed. "Briefly."

"He could have done more with it," Arsenal said gruffly. "If he made even token artificial wings, he could fly."

"That's my impression," Anna agreed.

"Next contestant," Trent said, indicating another young man.

"I am Cutter," the man said. "I can be cut into pieces yet not harmed. Want a demonstration?"

Trent glanced at the judges. "No," Anna said, shuddering.

"What use do you make of your talent, apart from cutting up?"

"Sometimes I help out in a freak show," Cutter said.

This too, Bryce thought, was less than impressive use of a formidable talent.

The next talent was to make any inanimate thing become animate for a while. The man demonstrated by making his chair come to life and walk around on its four legs.

Another was a girl who could walk on beams of light. She used a mirror to reflect a sunbeam, then walked on it. That was striking, but again, not imaginative.

"I'm seeing more wasted talents," Piper muttered. "She could carry a flashlight and scale any castle wall, if she thought to try."

Another's talent was grasping at straws: he always got the short straw. "He should be a gambler," Demon Pose muttered. "And always bet against himself."

Another was anonymous unless he called attention to himself. Indeed he seemed almost to fade out of sight. But again, what special use did he make of his talent?

One man could make figures of speech literal. "When it comes to mealtime, I'm a pig," he said, and became a pig.

"Metaphor," Bryce murmured.

"I've said it a million times." And his words echoed all around the stadium as if a million people were speaking.

"Hyperbole," Bryce said. This talent impressed him more than the others. The man not only had it, he was making clever use of it. He made a mental note to vote for that one if nothing better came along.

Then came a woman who could breathe anywhere. She demonstrated by setting a smudge fire and putting her face in the smoke. Then she put her head into a bucket of water. Then she put her face to the ground and had a friend pile sand on top. It didn't matter; she could still breathe.

Then came a woman who could heal monsters. Nothing else, just monsters. "But who wants to heal a monster?" Trent asked.

"That's the thing," she said. "A monster is as you see it. Some people can be monsters in some ways, such as how they treat their relatives, or the ugly way they wear their hair. I can heal them too."

"This interests me," Piper said. "But I already have a girlfriend."

"That's clever," Anna said. "She could heal almost anyone, just by finding some way that person could be called a monster."

Bryce agreed, and made a note.

There was a woman who could convert her lower body into the legs and tail of any creature. She became a mermaid, then a naga, then a harpy. Then she started getting more creative, developing dragon legs and scorpion legs and stinger. This, too, was impressive, especially when she returned to human form and put on panties.

"Creative variations," Anna said. "But can she use it for anything other than a one-person freak show?"

There was the problem. Great talent, little imagination.

Another woman, Flora, could change the color, shape, and smell of flowers. She could make one flower emulate another.

"Is that all?" Trent asked.

"I can make it become a passion flower," she said. Suddenly the petals turned large and purple, and a passionate odor wafted out. Other people started kissing each other. It was genuine.

"That will do," Trent said quickly. "Try another."

"Forget-me-not," Flora said. "Sniff this and you will remember this flower. Eat it and you will have a perfect memory for anything."

The judges made another note: versatile talent, imaginatively used.

Then came Wayne, a man who could summon magic weapons. Arsenal's interest quickened. Then the man explained magic was everywhere in Xanth, so just about everything was magic, and just about anything could be considered a weapon if used as such. "Like dirt," he said, a handful appearing in his hand. "Thrown in a person's face, it's a weapon. Or water—enough of it can drown a person." He was suddenly drenched with water. "Even a feather pillow, if used to smother someone." A pillow appeared. "So I can summon almost anything, as long as I think of a way it can be a weapon."

"He has my vote," Arsenal said.

"I prefer the flower girl," Anna said.

"We'll vote when we've seen them all," Bryce said.

"It won't be a unified decision," Anna said.

"Who cares?" Pose demanded. "We're just marking time anyway."

That might be the case. But Bryce was increasingly bothered by it. The prior challenges had been difficult, their prizes significant. Why should this be different? An insignificant challenge, with no prize for the Suitors. Could there be a purpose to this seemingly innocent activity? Surely there was more here than merely marking time.

The next contestant had the ability to become an inanimate object, then return to his own form. That was a good one, because normally transforming to, say, a block of wood would leave the person unable to speak or do anything, and he would be stuck. But again, that was all; there was no imaginative use of it, such as becoming a dress for a pretty girl to wear, and thus getting to appreciate her curves from up close.

Then came Mariah, with the talent of turning into a fox. She had devised elastic clothing that could handle either form.

How could this matter of judging a talent contest contribute to an edge for impressing the princess?

Maybe that was the key. Harmony was surely watching, and perhaps judging the judges by their decisions. Could she be looking for a mind rather than a physical gift? Would that put Bryce back in the running despite having no magic Object to offer? If so, he would have to try for it, because he was sure he did not want to suffer the wrath of a Demon for not campaigning hard enough.

Now a woman was demonstrating her talent of befriending birds. She could summon a sparrow to her hand, or get a roc to carry her. It was a good talent, but her use of it was no more than might be expected.

Judge not, lest ye be judged, Bryce thought. But he had to judge, and would be judged. At least he could advise the other Suitors, so they all had the same chance.

Now a man was showing how he could turn anything invisible, or visible. He demonstrated by making a woman's clothing become invisible, so that she stood there in bra and panties. Then he made those invisible too. Fortunately she had a good figure. More fortunately, she was his wife, helping him make the demonstration. Another good talent, insufficiently exploited.

So Bryce had a hint about the importance of the presentation tomorrow. If only he had an Object to present!

Now a man demonstrated his talent of noticeability, making himself almost unnoticeable.

"Didn't we see that before?" Lucky asked.

"That was anonymity," Anna replied. "Similar, but not identical."

A woman described and demonstrated her talent of Perspective. She walked away from her boyfriend until he looked to her to be only a few inches tall. Then she squinted, reached out, and picked him up as if he were a doll. He rose into the air. To others he did not look small, but what counted was how he looked to *her*. It was another potentially potent talent. She could probably move anything merely by standing far enough away from it to make it look small enough.

It occurred to Bryce that it would be best if she never realized the full potential of her talent. She could do a lot of damage if she wasn't very careful.

At last the parade of talents was done. Bryce had made notes all along, not trusting his memory, and found that the magic pen worked perfectly well to write with.

"Now the judges will consult," Trent said. "We will break for half an hour for refreshments, then return for the verdict."

Mindy had set up a refreshment stand loaded with good things. Now she came to serve the Suitors, bringing little cups of tsoda pop from Lake Tsoda Popka, and biscuits.

They formed their chairs into a circle for discussion. "If I may," Bryce said. "I think I have an important insight."

"You have had them before," Piper said. "I'm interested."

"It is this," Bryce said. "We have faced a serious challenge each day, and I'm not sure today is an exception. There may be something we have to learn or achieve today that will help us in our presentations tomorrow. So that it's not the perhaps foolish whim of a teen girl that decides the issue. I suspect the point is not the talent contestants, but *us*. We may be judged as we judge others. We may need to fathom the real challenge, just as we have had to do throughout. The difference is that this one is not presented as such; we have to figure it out for ourselves."

"Makes sense to me," Piper said.

"And me," Anna agreed.

"Well I don't see it," Arsenal said. "So they gave us a day off while they set up, put us to some useful incidental work. We don't need to delve for nonexistent meanings." Pose and Lucky nodded agreement.

Bryce shrugged. "I have said my piece. Let's get on with the judging."

It soon turned out the leading candidates were Wayne who could conjure weapons, and Flora who changed flowers. "Conjuring weapons is a man's talent," Arsenal said.

"And adapting flowers is a woman's talent," Anna said.

"He makes nice use of unlikely weapons, broadening his talent," Pose said. "He could wipe her out."

"She is really clever with the passion flower," Piper said. "She could seduce him."

"Power is what ultimately counts," Lucky said.

"Subtlety can subvert power," Bryce said.

They were unable to come to an agreement. The vote was tied with three for Wayne, three for Flora.

Trent came by. "What is your decision?"

"Tie vote," Bryce said. "Wayne Weapons, Flora Flowers. That's the best we can do."

Trent nodded. "I will take it from here."

Which way would he decide, to break the tie? He was a warrior, but also a man with considerable life experience.

The people returned to their seats, and Trent addressed them. "We have a tie vote between Wayne who summons weapons, and Flora who changes flowers. I am electing not to break that tie. The prize will be split between the two of you."

"But those vials can't readily be divided. What do you expect us to do, fight each other for it?" Wayne demanded.

Flora shook her head. "We can each take one vial, and maybe share the third."

"I'll take the healing elixir, for when I get wounded."

"I'll take the youth elixir, for when I get old."

"That leaves the love potion," Wayne said.

"Maybe we could share that," Flora suggested.

Wayne considered. "You did not try to use a passion flower on me."

"You did not threaten me with a weapon."

"You know, you're good-looking."

"You're handsome."

The two gazed at each other. A small heart formed between them.

"I don't think we need to open the love vial," Wayne said.

"We can share it without opening it," Flora agreed.

They came together. They kissed. A larger heart formed over their heads. Then they walked away together, sharing the complete prize.

The audience burst into applause. Then the assembly adjourned. It had been a successful event.

It seemed that Magician Trent had known what he was doing. Bryce marveled at how straightforward love could be, in this magic realm. Assuming that love match had not been set up as entertainment.

That evening Anna washed and changed without waiting for Bryce to turn his back. "It's our last night," she said. "Tomorrow if I don't win for my brother, I'll go with Piper. If he wins he'll go with the princess. If anyone else wins, he and I will be together. You're a good friend; I feel at ease with you."

"Thank you," Bryce said. "I feel the same." But he averted his eyes at key moments, so as not to freak out.

"She wants to choose you," she continued. "I know it. But you don't have a gift, thanks to my interference."

"She'll be better off with one of the others."

"I don't think so."

He shrugged. "What will be, will be."

"You made good sense today. Something may be up. We don't know what will happen tomorrow."

"We don't know," he agreed. "But you should make sure to make the best presentation you can."

"I will, thank you. What will you do, after?"

"I expect to return to Caprice Castle and help them collect puns. It's useful work."

"We'll be there too. Piper has long experience, and I will be with him, so I'll learn."

"He's a good man, regardless of his form."

Bryce lay on his bed and pulled the cover up. Then Anna blew out the candle and came to join him. "Indulge me," she whispered.

"Anna, what are you up to?"

"There is something I must do. That I must say, but can't. As before."

"You know I won't touch you, any more than I would touch Mindy. Apart from everything else, you're way too young."

"I'm twenty-four. There are worse barriers than youth. Trust me."

"I don't understand."

She's serious, the Queen Bee thought. Bryce was startled; he had forgotten about the Bee she had won. Could that telepathy help?

I can't do this for you, the Bee thought. *She's beeing watched by her sponsor Demon. Not with full attention, not with even a fraction of one percent attention, but if she says something that relates to a key concept, she'll bee in trouble.*

Bryce realized that it was like a computer set to spot a particular word or situation. As long as it did not occur, the machine, or in this case Demon, would not be alerted.

"Play the game," Anna whispered urgently. "The one we did before. While pretending to be using me, so that no one will catch on."

"Using you!"

Kiss her. Feel her. Make it look good.

Oh. There was something serious on her mind that she couldn't tell. She had been trying in her fashion to let him know, but he had stupidly been missing it. He had to make whatever was watching her think she was merely diverting herself with a spot tryst, not spilling secrets.

He braced himself, then kissed her and put a hand on her bottom over her nightie. Both were dangerously conducive. "Tell me how you feel about me," he said.

"I hate you."

That verified the reverse game. She was not his girlfriend, but she certainly didn't hate him. Now how should he zero in on her concern, with her unable to advise him?

"I'm not sure exactly how to proceed," he confessed, stroking that too-evocative bottom. What an anomaly!

Ask her about her brother.

Oho! He was not the one being watched, so he could speak freely though she couldn't. It was another anomaly. "Why hasn't your brother shown up yet? You've won the Queen Bee. You've done your part."

"He can appear any time he chooses."

That had to be a lie, but in what way? Why *couldn't* the man appear to present the gift to the princess? "Is he incapacitated?"

This time she struggled for an answer. "No. Yes. Not exactly."

Bryce's head was feeling strained. "Is he imprisoned?"

"No. Not exactly."

Get more basic.

Bryce got a notion. "Does he even exist?"

"Yes, at the moment."

That was a lie? "Does he just pop in and out of existence?"

"No," she said firmly.

Which meant yes. "Is he like a demon?"

"Yes."

So that wasn't it. "Does he change into something else?"

"No. Yes. Not exactly."

So he did change, but maybe not completely. But why should that prevent him from showing up for this most important occasion?

Then Bryce got an idea that momentarily lighted the room. "He changed into you!"

"No," she said gladly.

"One Demon selected him, but the others needed someone to distract me from winning an Object, so they turned him into you," Bryce said. "You *have* no brother, exactly, because you *are* your brother."

She kissed him hard. "No!"

"And you won't get to change back unless you win the contest. There's your incentive to perform."

"No!"

"But now there's a complication: you fell in love with Piper."

"No!"

"So maybe you no longer want to change back. You prefer being a woman. So long as you can be with Piper."

"No."

"But you can't tell Piper, because of that geis on you, that ban."

"No." Now he felt her tears against his face.

"And you want me to tell him, since you can't."

"No." The tears increased.

Bryce considered. "Anna, I'm not going to do that. Here's why: either you will win the princess, and convert, in which case Piper will know, albeit too late. Or you will not win, and I presume be locked into your female form for the rest of your life. So there's no need to tell him. But if you feel you have to, you should be able to do it yourself, at a time of your choosing. You don't need me for this."

Idiot! She needs to know whether Piper will still want her when he learns. She'd rather die than have him bee repulsed by her. The Queen Bee was thinking in bee dialect, of course, and couldn't spell it "be" even in thought.

"But for what it's worth," Bryce continued, "Piper is a literal monster who has finally found a woman who loves him for himself. Surely he will be similarly tolerant of your situation."

"Would *you* be?" She was able to ask a straight question.

That made him pause. He wasn't sure. "Let me test my feelings," he said. "To see whether I am or am not repulsed, now that I know the truth. I don't want to seem to be making a move on you, but I think my body will not lie."

"Never," she said, taking his hand and threading it into her nightie so he could feel her bare torso.

He felt it, in its assorted curves and contours. He kissed her, and she met him more than halfway. She was completely female, physically. He had to react.

Then she threaded her hand into his pajamas and confirmed his arousal. He was not repulsed. Bemused by the anomaly, but turned on. "Thank you!" she breathed. Now that it was a question of physicality, she was no longer barred from expressing her honest sentiment.

"Now get away from me before I lose control," he said.

She hesitated. "I did not mean to tease you. You have

done me another huge favor. If you wish to—to proceed now, I will cooperate. We both know it's merely an act, not a commitment. I will pretend you are Piper."

"No, I don't want that!"

"You're lying," she said fondly. "Thank you." She got out of his bed and went to her own in the darkness.

He had indeed been lying. She had made him desire her fiercely. But he really appreciated her withdrawal. How would he have lived with himself if he had yielded to the moment and done it with a twenty-four-year-old girl who loved another man?

"I hope this helps you appreciate that there may be mysteries yet," she said from her bed. "The Demons have crafted a truly devious course for us all."

"There may indeed be further mysteries," he agreed. But what surprises could possibly remain? Why did he fear that there was something he should have figured out, and hadn't? Something vital.

They settled down to sleep. In one more day it would be over, one way or another.

"I wish all of you well," Mindy said as she served them breakfast. "It has been great knowing you."

"You also," Piper said. "You made the details easy."

"Thank you."

There was a similar crowd in the stadium. Bryce was surprised that Princess Harmony was not there. Maybe she would make an appearance when the moment was right.

They took the seats that Mindy indicated in the front row before the platform. Bryce knew that he should not be nervous, but he was. He suspected the same was true for the other Suitors. Mindy hovered near, perhaps relieved that her service here was almost done. Maybe she missed Caprice Castle.

King Ivy took the stage, along with two of the triplet princesses. They looked painfully like Harmony, but Bryce was not in love with them. "The Princess Harmony will appear soon," she said. "You will make your presentations to me."

The king paused, gazing at the six Suitors. "Arsenal," she said. "Stand and speak your piece."

Arsenal stood. "My gift for the Princess Harmony is the Sword," he said, drawing it and holding it aloft. "With this she can defend herself against any man or creature. It is feather light to the wielder, but full force to the target." He demonstrated by balancing it on his little finger without effort, then grasping the hilt and cleaving a stone in twain.

"Thank you," Ivy said. "I'm sure the princess is impressed. Be seated." She paused. "Demon Pose."

Pose stood. "My gift is the Ring of Power. With this on her hand, the princess could move a mountain if she chose." He smiled briefly. "No mountain here, but maybe this boulder will do." He walked to it, put his arms around it, and lifted it high. "Virtually unlimited force. She will be able to accomplish great constructions."

"That might someday be convenient," King Ivy agreed. "Be seated." She focused on the next. "Lucky."

Lucky stood. "I have a marvelous magic Dress that will make the princess even prettier than she already is." He held it up.

"Harmony would look pretty in anything," Ivy said. "Let's see it demonstrated." She looked around. "Mindy, try it on."

Mindy came forward and took the Dress. "Please don't make me change in public."

"Melody, Rhythm," Ivy said. "Provide her an illusion screen."

The two princesses hummed and beat a little drum. An opaque circular curtain appeared around Mindy.

In a moment and a half Mindy called, "Okay."

The curtain vanished. There stood Mindy in the Dress. She looked astonishingly lovely, even though Bryce had seen her in it before. Maybe she was further enhanced by the weight she had lost during the Quest.

"You're adorable, dear," Ivy said. "It is effective magic. Now give it back."

Mindy frowned as if reluctant. The curtain surrounded her again, and in two more moments she was back in her own dress, looking relatively plain. The demonstration was done.

"Anna Molly."

Anna stood. "I proffer the Queen Bee, courtesy of my brother. She is telepathic, and so responds to thoughts. Her hive can provide protection, reconnaissance, some transport, and food."

A small swarm of bees appeared, carrying a dripping honeycomb. The king took it and tasted it. "Delicious." The bees buzzed away, leaving the comb.

"And you can comb your hair with it, when you have eaten the honey," Anna said with three-fifths of a smile. The king echoed the smile with another two-fifths, completing it. Then everyone smiled.

"Piper," Ivy said.

Piper stood. "I present the hypnotic Gem that can pacify any monster. The princess will be safe from any monster, including me."

There was general laughter. Most of the audience thought he was joking.

"That is good to know," Ivy said. "Bryce Mundane."

Bryce stood. "I regret that I did not succeed in capturing the magic Monocle that enables a person to fathom the mind-set of anyone it focuses on."

"You failed?" the king asked sharply. "Do you care to explain?"

"No."

There was a murmur of chagrin. It seemed he had committed a breach of manners.

"Please," Mindy said. "May I speak?"

Ivy considered briefly, then decided to be tolerant. "You may, briefly."

"Bryce lost the Monocle because I was being attacked by dragons. He saved me instead. He is trying to spare me a deserved rebuke for interfering with his Quest."

The king eyed Bryce. "What is this servant girl to you, that you sacrificed your mission for her?"

"No Object, however magical, is worth the loss of a human life. I would have done the same for any other person."

The king nodded. "You showed more honor in your failure than others might have in their successes. Make your presentation."

This was the chance Bryce had hoped for. "The Monocle would surely be a useful tool, especially when dealing with possibly hostile or deceptive leading figures. But the princess doesn't need it. What she will be better served by is to develop her own observational and intellectual skills. The judgment to assess any situation, and decide objectively what course to follow. That will enable her to be the best king she can be, when the time comes."

Ivy nodded. "Judgment. I agree. This is worthy advice. Be seated."

Bryce sat. Was he really being allowed to present advice rather than a magic gift?

"Now it is time for the Princess Harmony to choose, completing this occasion," the king said. "Harmony?"

Mindy came forward. As she walked, she shifted, until she halted before the king. "Here, Mother," she said, and turned to face the audience.

It was Harmony.

The jaws of the Suitors dropped, including Bryce's. The princess had been with them all along! What had they said about her, what embarrassing secrets had they revealed, thinking themselves secure from her presence?

Harmony smiled. "I apologize for deceiving you. It was my purpose to get to know all of you Suitors in an informal setting, so as to have a better basis for my decision. I could have watched you via the Tapestry, but that seemed too distant. I have been advised that the small details of routine interpersonal interaction can in time become more important than the more obvious things. So I chose a more personal way."

It was slowly sinking in. It was Princess Harmony whom Bryce had saved from the dragons! How could he not have recognized her? Now he remembered little hints, such as the way bad words were bleeped out, indicating the presence of a person under age eighteen. The Night Stallion speaking of the deviousness of the smartest princess. Trojan had known. And Gwenny Goblin, Queen of Goblin Mountain: she knew Harmony too, and had kept her secret.

Harmony seemed to read his thought. "There was a spell to prevent any of you from fathoming my identity. Otherwise you surely would have caught on. There was also magic protecting me from actual harm. Those dragons would not really have torn me apart."

He had thrown away his chance to get the Monocle for nothing? Bryce could not accept that.

"I thank all of you for your gifts," Princess Harmony continued. "They will be added to the Castle Roogna armory for me to use when the occasion warrants. All of you are worthy Suitors, and I might have married any of you, but I have settled on one. The others will be released from the love spell and allowed to get on with their own lives hereafter."

She paused, gathering her thoughts. Then she addressed Lucky. "Lucky, I gave you a charm to help focus your luck, and you used it well when we needed to escape the goblin women. Your gift of the magic Dress is worthy. But I think I do not want to depend overly much on luck or aesthetic appeal to govern properly. I thank you for your participation, and am releasing you."

Lucky's jaw dropped a second time. "I don't love you!"

"You are no longer spelled," she agreed.

Lucky relaxed, seeming pleased to be released.

Harmony turned to Pose. "I appreciate the Ring of Power, but I hope to govern more by reconciliation than brute force. I would also have to be wary of your private objective."

"Yes," Pose agreed. "You would become subject to my will."

"I doubt it," Harmony said. "You would obey my will."

"I would?"

She leaned down and kissed him. A little anvil appeared over his head, with a sledgehammer smashing down on it. The anvil fragmented.

"I would," Pose said, amazed, and sank into unconsciousness. He was a demon, but it seemed was vulnerable to a mortal kiss. Some things transcended demon nature.

"She's no patsy," Anna murmured to Bryce.

Bryce nodded. Indeed she was not. He had wondered whether there would be more surprises; now they were coming rapidly.

Harmony turned to Arsenal. "Perhaps someday I will use the Sword," she said. "It is certainly a worthy gift. But you are too gruff and imperious for my taste; our union would soon fray. I am releasing you."

Arsenal nodded, accepting the verdict.

The princess turned to Piper. "I was delighted by the way you used my gift to you, enchanting us all with your music. I have also learned to appreciate your monster qualities. You are a worthy person, and I might live with you and come to love you in time. But I have a confession."

Piper wasn't the only one to look at her with surprise.

"Those gifts—all of them—had an ulterior purpose," Harmony continued. "They enabled me to observe each of you at any time. But as it turned out, I was able to learn much directly, by sharing your company as the group of you sought the Objects. I saw that you had come to love another woman despite the spell on you. I saw how gladly you rejoined her after she completed her Quest. I would not care to break that up. You are released."

"Thank you, Princess," Piper said, seeming truly grateful.

Now Harmony turned to Anna. "You too are worthy, having performed remarkably despite being under unkind duress. I think I can't say the same for your brother, who it seems lacked the interest to show up for this occasion." She looked hard at Anna. "Do you care to explain that, Anna? Because I am not going to marry you, regardless of your merit."

There was stifled laughter in the audience.

Anna, flushing, took a deep breath. "I cannot."

"Remember what I said about the tokens I gave each of you. I overheard your reverse dialogue with Bryce, and understood it. Were I to choose you, it will be revealed. I hope you will forgive me for keeping that secret. I hope to keep you as a friend, rather than marrying your brother. You are released."

So Harmony knew Anna's secret, and was keeping it.

"Thank you," Anna breathed, tears flowing down her face. "You are generous." She surely would be Harmony's friend, and not just because of that secret. The two had gotten along well during the Quest.

"No I am not," Harmony said. "Because my decision was preempted some time ago. You see, I fell in love myself."

She turned to Bryce. "Anna was right: I love you, Bryce, and I find your advice on judgment to be as worthy as any magical gift you could have brought me. You made by far the most effective use of the gift I gave you, of all the Suitors. And you did save my life, as far as you knew."

Bryce spread his hands, uncertain what to say.

"Bryce, I respect you and I love you. Now I can say it as myself." As she said those words, she seemed phenomenally sincere and beautiful. "Will you marry me?"

Just like that!

What could he do but answer? "No."

There was a concerted gasp. The entire stadium seemed to freeze in place. This time he had really done it.

Harmony did not seem completely surprised. "Why not?"

"You are too young for me. I am quintuple your age."

"So you are," she agreed. "But you have been permanently youthened to five years over my age. You have the chance to start over, and do it right."

"I do," he agreed guardedly.

"Do you love me?"

"Yes." Because of the spell he was under.

"Then I ask you again: will you marry me?"

He hated this. But he had to do what he had to do, though his heart break. "No."

Harmony scanned the audience. "Magician Humfrey."

The Good Magician stood. "Yes, Princess."

"I have chosen, but he has denied me. Does this acquit the Demon's Quest?"

"I believe it does," Humfrey said, surprised. "The point was for you to choose. Technically he does not have to accept."

"Thank you."

Harmony glanced at King Ivy. "Mother?"

King Ivy returned to center stage. "You little minx!" she said fondly. "You knew he would turn you down despite the love enchantment!"

And there it was. Princess Harmony had known exactly what she was doing.

"Now I am free, am I not?" Harmony said. "To make my own choice, in my own time, free of Demon direction."

"I believe you are," Ivy agreed, smiling with a new respect for her smart but willful daughter.

Her two sisters applauded as Harmony went to join them. The three stood together, like the very similar triplets they were.

"But what do the Demons think?" Ivy asked, somewhat nervously.

A dragon with the head of a donkey appeared on the stage: a dragon ass. Beside him was a beautiful woman.

"The Demon Xanth!" Anna murmured beside Bryce. "And his consort the Lady Chlorine."

"The Demons are satisfied," Chlorine said. "Demon Earth's candidate won the Quest. Demon Xanth is pleased too: Princess Harmony outwitted the Demons, playing by their rules to achieve her freedom regardless. That won Xanth a point."

"Thank you, Lady Chlorine," Ivy said. "We are relieved."

"Welcome. It was superlative entertainment." Dragon and Lady faded out.

"This event is concluded," Ivy told the audience. "Eat, drink, be merry, and go home."

The entire assembly broke into applause. It had been a good show with a surprising outcome.

Bryce felt weak with relief. He had feared possible destruction. Now he was free.

Except for one thing: he still loved Princess Harmony. She had not released him.

15

DEMON WAGER

Caprice Castle came to collect them. Bryce got his old room back. It was mundane, in a manner, after the adventure he had participated in. He was no longer a Suitor, merely a refugee from Mundania with a job to do: collecting puns. He had hardly had time to unwind, yet he was already suffering a letdown. In fact he was bored.

Why had he turned down the Princess Harmony? Yes, she was a fifth his age; yes she was a princess, while he was nobody. But this was a different land with different rules. He could have had a remarkable time with her, had he been willing to unbend.

But he was what he was, an old man who had learned to be governed by common sense, not superficial luster. Despite considerable temptation.

"May I get you anything?"

He jumped. He hadn't heard her come in. "Mindy! But you—you're—"

"I am the real Mindy," she said. "Not the princess. She borrowed my form for the event. I wasn't there."

He saw now that she was different. The Mindy on the adventure had slimmed down, becoming more like the princess. This one was solid. The Mindy on the Quest had dispensed with the glasses; this one still used them. "So you're—"

"I am not in love with you," Mindy said.

"Who was I with, before the Quest?"

"Her. You and I have not met before, directly. I understand it was quite an adventure."

"It was," he agreed. "I'm glad to meet you, Mindy. Will you be helping me cope, out in the field?"

"Yes, if you wish. But I understand you have gotten pretty sharp at handling magic things."

"Not sharp enough, I think."

"Tomorrow we'll start."

There was a bark. "Is that Woofer?"

"Yes, cautioning a puppy. They are barely a week old, too young to be trusted out alone, but they will surely become excellent pun sniffers, as their mother Rachel was."

"I hope she's happy back in Mundania." That gave him an idea. "Could I return similarly?"

Mindy considered. "Maybe you could, unlike me. You didn't die. I'll inquire."

She had died? Oh, yes, now he remembered. Suicide. She, or rather the princess, had told him. He decided not to pursue that further. "Thank you."

But there was one thing he wanted to verify. "What do you know about relativity and quantum mechanics?"

"No more than the average layman. I must confess I took a certain satisfaction from the way Einstein himself found instantaneous action at a distance spooky. If *he* didn't understand quantum mechanics, how could I?"

"My position exactly," he agreed. "How about an event horizon?"

"That's the invisible sphere around a black hole beyond which nothing can escape, not even light itself. It's a scary concept, but actually we're in no danger of encountering one directly. Time dilation would make any approach seem eternal. Astronomers speculate that the fundamental laws of the universe may break down and become null within that sphere."

"Surely so."

"Why did you ask?"

"I just wanted to make sure that you are the real Mindy, from Mundania. The pretend Mindy drew a blank on those subjects."

Mindy laughed. "She would. She's not stupid, she's eerily smart, but Xanthians just don't know about things like that."

"To be sure. Just as Mundanians don't know about the intricacies of magic."

"Or the need to sequester puns," she agreed, smiling.

In the morning they set out, riding duplicate trikes. The terrain was new to Bryce, but that wasn't surprising as Caprice Castle was in a new place every day. "I feel I know you," he said, "though actually I don't. Because of thinking it was you during the Quest." Now he noticed that she no longer wore the glasses.

"That's understandable," she said. "I feel I know you too, having watched you so much. I was in Harmony's room most of the time, tracking you via the Tapestry, though that doesn't have sound."

"Yes. I knew we were being observed. I just didn't realize how closely."

They pedaled on, finding convenient paths.

"I really like the trike, now that I've seen it used," Mindy said. "I saw in the Tapestry how Anna and Harmony, in the guise of me, flashed their panties at the trolls."

"You should have worn jeans today," he said, realizing that she was in a dress.

"No, I'm trying to be more like her, doing naughty

things, and not just by giving up my unnecessary glasses. You have to promise not to look, if you get the chance, and not mean it. I promise not to flash you, and not mean it. Accidents happen."

"But you have no romantic interest in me. Why should you flash me?"

"For practice. I know you won't take advantage of me, and if you freak out I'll know I overdid it. Then when I encounter a man I want to impress without seeming to be forward, I'll know how."

He laughed. "You're saying we can be friends, and offer friendly advice even when it comes to naughty glimpses, despite hardly knowing each other."

"Exactly. I have never freaked out a man, but after seeing Harmony do it with my body, I'd like to try. But not with someone I know well. He might just laugh."

He glanced across at her legs, and found that from this angle he could not quite see her panties. So it was safe for now. "If I freak out, let me roll to a stop and then snap your fingers."

"I will."

They rounded a curve in a narrowing section of the path, and she took the lead because she knew where they were going. When she turned in front of him—

He was no longer moving. She was off her trike, standing beside him. "Oops—did I—?"

"Yes, you freaked out," she said, pleased.

"I did look," he admitted unnecessarily.

She kissed him on the cheek. "My first time! I'm so thrilled."

"Congratulations," he said wryly.

She returned to her trike and resumed pedaling. Curious, he looked again. His vision fuzzed, but he did not freak out. It seemed that the same view was not as effective when immediately repeated. He continued to look, learning to control his reaction. When he caught a glimpse of her actual panties as her legs flexed, and remained conscious, he knew he was getting there.

She glanced back at him. "Are you staring at me?"

"Yes. I'm trying to become immune to panties, so I'm not vulnerable. Do you mind?"

"No. Look all you want. I'm just glad it worked the first time. That means it should work on any strange men I encounter."

"It should," he agreed. He was coming to appreciate how the magic of panties could protect a girl from lascivious strangers, without necessarily interfering with romance.

They reached the punning section. They parked their trikes and unlimbered their pun sacks.

Bryce spied a blinding light in the bush. He shaded his eyes and went for it. It turned out to be a pair of darkened spectacles whose lenses shone like sunbeams. "Sun glasses!" he exclaimed, swooping them up.

"I found one too," Mindy said. She showed her capture. It appeared to be a duck, at least had a duck's head. But its body was a strip of paper. In fact it was a dollar bill. "A Duck Bill." She stuffed it into her bag, heedless of its quacking protest.

Bryce almost groaned. They were definitely back at work.

In the afternoon the three princesses appeared, replete with similar brown, red, and green dresses and similar hairdos.

"Hello, folks," Melody said.

"You asked a question," Harmony continued.

"So we brought the answer," Rhythm concluded.

They were definitely playing their public roles. But the effect was spoiled for Bryce, because of his spelled love for Harmony. He knew her not as a posing triplet, but as a remarkable young woman. "Question?" he asked somewhat blankly.

"Whether you can go back to Mundania," Mindy said. "I asked Dawn, and she must have gotten in touch with them."

"Oh. Yes," he agreed.

"We asked the Good Magician," Melody began.

"We can do that without hassle because we're Sorceresses," Harmony concluded.

"And he said yes, you can return, if the route is marked," Rhythm finished.

"So we marked it," Melody said.

"For twenty-four hours," Harmony added.

"And you have to use it in that time, or lose it," Rhythm said.

Bryce was surprised. Could it really be that easy? "Where is it?"

The three pointed. "There," they said together.

And there it was: a path marked in bright blue. It led through the brush and out of sight.

"I can just ride along it now, and be back home?"

"You can," Melody said.

"If you want to," Harmony added somewhat tightly.

"Do you?" Rhythm asked.

Suddenly Bryce was gripped with acute indecision. "I don't know."

"It will be here," Melody said.

"A full day and night," Harmony said, her gaze fixed on him.

"Then gone forever," Rhythm finished.

Then the three of them faded from view.

Bryce felt weak. "I can return," he said. "But I don't know whether I want to. Over there I'll be eighty years old, alone, with chronic health complaints, and a likely death within a year or two. Yet it is home."

"Home," Mindy agreed, evidently experiencing her own memories.

"I think I need advice. What do you think?"

"I think you need better advice than mine. Why don't you check with Princess Dawn? She'll know who can best help you."

"I'll do that," he agreed, relieved to be able to post-pone the dread decision for a few hours.

Back at Caprice Castle Bryce went to the garden, where Princess Dawn was classifying the rare plants that traveled with the castle.

"Oh, hello Bryce," she said, looking up. "It's a good thing you happened by. It gives me a chance to show off the Lady Slippers I discovered here." She held up a lovely pair she had harvested from a Lady Slipper plant. "There's just one problem."

"They make you slip," he said.

"Exactly. If I tried to wear these I'd soon fall on my rear and show more of my legs than I care to."

"That would be deplorable," he said, though he couldn't help imagining her lovely legs flashing in the air.

She looked at him and laughed, comprehending too well. "What can I do for you, apart from that?"

"I have a chance to go home to Mundania, but I'm not quite certain whether to do it. I need advice."

"Because here you orient on a teenage girl," she said. "And you're afraid that if you stay around, she'll try to seduce you, and just possibly might succeed."

"You understand me too well," he said ruefully.

"I'm really on the other side, rooting for Harmony. But I think I know who might be able to render some perspective. I'll go fetch her. Meanwhile, talk with Picka. He knows about being stalked by a princess."

"He does?"

"And she finally got me," Picka said behind him. "Even though she's obviously not my type. Way too much flesh on her nice bones."

"Way too much," Dawn agreed, and flipped her skirt

up to flash him with her panties. Bryce caught only a peripheral glimpse, but it almost freaked him out. Only his practice with Mindy saved him. Picka, however, was unaffected.

Then she changed momentarily to skeletal form and did it again. This time the walking skeleton did freak out. Bryce was unaffected by her bare pelvis bone. By the time he snapped his fingers to rouse Picka, Dawn was gone. She had made her point.

"What's this about being stalked by a princess?" Picka asked.

"It's not that, exactly," Bryce said. "It's that I have a chance to return to Mundania, and I don't know whether I should."

"I do have an empty-headed thought on that," Picka said. "It is my theory that the Demons have set up another contest. They may be wagering on whether Princess Harmony will nab you after all, and if so, when. Offering you a chance to escape her wiles would be part of it."

"Another Demon bet," Bryce said, seeing it. The skeleton's head might be empty, but he was not stupid. "That could explain it, yes."

"The Demons are all-powerful and immortal. They must get bored, so they divert themselves with these wagers that may be minor to them, but not to us who have little power and limited lives. Not that I'm exactly alive, except when I change to manform. Your refusal of the Princess Harmony's proposal is the kind of thing that should interest them."

"And of course they will not do anything to make it easier for us."

"They're Demons," Picka agreed. "One of them will win or lose, depending on your decision, and any interference on their part would void that. So you are on your own."

"Do you have any thoughts about it yourself?"

"Well, my head is empty. But I understand that no man can say no to a princess indefinitely. She's bound to get you eventually."

"Why should she want me? She chose me so that she could be free to make up her own mind."

"True. But she loves you. Maybe she wants you to accept of your own free choice."

"How can it be free when she will not release the love spell that is on me?"

"Excellent point. Maybe you should ask her that."

"Maybe I will," Bryce agreed.

Dawn returned with an undistinguished older woman. "Electra will talk with you," she said. "Let's leave them to it, love." She led Picka away. It was obvious that their association was exactly like that of other couples in Xanth and perhaps Mundania too: the woman ran it.

"Dawn told me of your concern," Electra said. "She thought my own experience might offer some insight."

"Perhaps," Bryce agreed guardedly. He wondered what possible relevance this woman's case could offer. He almost thought he had heard the name before, but couldn't place it.

"She says your main concern is that Harmony is young, while you are old."

"Yes. She's barely beyond childhood. Any bad words spoken in her presence get bleeped out." He paused. "That explains that!"

"Explains what?"

"The members of our Quest were all of age for bad words. Mindy was the youngest, and she was twenty. Still the words got bleeped. Because she wasn't really Mindy, but sixteen-year-old Harmony, the underside of eighteen. I never caught on, but the Adult Conspiracy knew."

Electra nodded. "That was the case when I met Dolph. I was technically almost a thousand years old, having slept for most of my life. I won't bore you with the details. Dolph was barely coming on to age sixteen, too young for bad words or indeed to know the content of the Adult Conspiracy. Yet we married. He was dreadfully immature, but I loved him, and soon he came to love me too. So the age differential didn't matter. It was our physical ages that counted, and we were fairly close there. We have been happy in our marriage and with our children, both beautiful Sorceresses."

"Your children?"

"Oh, did I forget to mention that? I am Dawn and Eve's mother."

Bryce felt dizzy. "Dawn's mother!" Now he remembered the context of her name.

"I'm glad to see her happily married," Electra said. "I can't say I was keen at first on her man being a skeleton, but she evidently chose well and I like Picka Bone well. He's got a good skull over his shoulder bones, he's a decent person, and he's one fine musician."

"No wonder Dawn wanted me to talk with you! Your age differential was greater than mine with Harmony."

"Technically, yes. But it doesn't matter. Dolph and I were right for each other." She studied Bryce appraisingly. "Just as I suspect you and Harmony are right for each other. It would be a shame if you let a technicality bar your happiness."

"But she's so young!"

"Odd thing about that," Electra said. "She won't stay young. She'll get older every year."

"So will I!"

"From age twenty-one on," she agreed. "That five-year difference won't seem like much after a few years. Age is largely irrelevant in Xanth. Breanna of the Black Wave was only fifteen when she encountered Justin Tree, who was about one hundred. They've been happily married for a decade."

She had given him a new perspective. "Thank you for your advice."

"Oh, you're welcome," she said. "I'm glad to have been of help."

It seemed to Bryce that the others he discussed this with wanted him to marry Harmony. Obviously such a union could work out in Xanth. But he was not a native of this fantasy land. He had standards the natives evidently did not understand.

Next day he went out again with Mindy. But as he saw the changed scenery, he reacted with horror. "We're in a new location! Not near the path to Mundania!"

"Oh, I never thought of that!" Mindy said.

Then the bright blue path appeared ahead of them. Beside it stood the three princesses. "We thought of it," Melody said.

"It originates where we choose," Harmony added.

"Which is right here," Rhythm concluded.

Thus suddenly, again, the decision was upon him. "I believe I should go," he said. "I don't belong here in Xanth."

Harmony broke ranks and stepped out from between her sisters. As she did, her clothing changed, enhancing her individuality. She was no longer an almost identical triplet; she was a lovely young woman. "I will go with you."

"That is not feasible," Bryce said. "Mundania has nothing for you."

"Nothing except you," Harmony said. "I love you and want to be with you."

"Harmony, what you have is a teen crush. It will pass in time."

"No. I've had crushes before. I thought it was a crush, and that it would fade after you turned me down. So that I could truly make my own choice. But it didn't fade. It grew stronger, and filled out, and then I knew it was love. I hate to admit it, but it turns out the Demons did know best. It's ironic that now that I can choose for myself, I'm already committed. You are the one for me."

"Harmony—"

"I am trying to use judgment," she continued inexorably. "To be realistic. I have thought it through. I may be barely out of my childhood now, but I will mature in time. It will help considerably if I have the right influence as I prepare to become king. I can learn a lot from you, and I don't mean just about incidental things, I mean about ethics and judgment and becoming a better person, and that's what I mean to do."

That reminded him. "How do you expect me to make any kind of objective decision about you while I am bound by a love spell? You should release me from it."

"Then will you stay?"

"Then I will make a sensible decision."

"You are released," she said simply.

He felt it shedding away from him, leaving him no longer bound. He was free at last! He was able to view her as a young, smart, determined, and quite lovely princess. "Thank you."

Then, freed of the distraction of spelled love, he felt the emptiness. He was in a foreign land with wildly foreign rules, and he was lonely. His life here had no real meaning. He needed compatible environs, a fulfilling mission, and companionship of his own intellectual and social kind. He had none.

"Are you going?" she asked.

"Yes, I believe I am. Mundania is where I belong."

"Then I will go with you," she repeated firmly. "So you won't be alone."

"Harmony, you can't. You'd be an undocumented person there."

"Un-what?"

"No birth certificate," Mindy said. "They insist that everyone have one, in Mundania."

"They would assume you were a teen runaway," Bryce said. "They would institutionalize you. So you would not be with me anyway. You'd have no magic to escape. So I'd be alone anyway. In two years I'd be dead, leaving you stranded with nothing. You can't go."

Harmony nodded. "I see the problem. It's not the place for me. But is it really the place for you? Do you really want to die rather than suffer the love of a girl one-fifth your age?"

"No I don't. But I am what I am, and must do what I am fated to do. That is not getting cozy with a virtual child."

"Uh-oh," Rhythm murmured in the background. "When a man said that to me, I hauled him into a love spring and tore off his clothing. That shut him up."

"Bleep it!" Harmony swore. "I freed you from the love spell. But I can't free myself. I got my love for you the old-fashioned way, by coming to know you, appreciate you, and falling for you. You may be free now but I am not. If you go, I will go with you. You can't stop me."

"You would be doomed!"

"But I'd be doomed with you. That's the way I want it."

He gazed at her. She stood firmly in the path ahead of him, her little chin raised, her brown hair falling back in shock waves, her brown eyes bright with tears, and infernally beautiful. He was no longer in love with her, so could see her objectively, and know that it was true. He also knew she was deadly serious. He would in effect imprison her for life in a world without magic, surely a fate worse than death for her.

He couldn't do it to her.

"I'll stay," he said.

She held her ground. "And?"

"And I am making no other commitment. I am not taking up with a teen girl."

"Then I will court you. I'm sure I can change your mind, in time."

"Harmony—"

"But I will be fair about it," she said. "Other women can court you too. Attractive women, closer to your age. Maybe Mundane women. If one of them appeals to you, you can marry her. It can be like the Demon Quest to find a man for me, only this will be to find a woman for you. And I will be one of them. Do you agree?"

She was indeed being fair. "Yes," he said, fearing that this would not be nearly as simple as it seemed at the moment.

"Starting tomorrow," she said. "Each day a new woman will accompany you pun hunting. She will also try to seduce you and win your heart."

"Harmony—" he repeated. But she and her sisters were gone.

"I think you're in for it," Mindy said. "She's mad at you. She loves you, but she's mad."

"I'm in for it," he agreed ruefully.

"At least you have today to prepare yourself for the siege."

"I have today," he agreed soberly.

Mindy looked around. "This is supposed to be the pun foraging place, but I don't see any."

"We've been harvesting a lot of puns. Maybe they are becoming sparse."

"In that case we'll need a better way to locate them."

"I'll think about it."

Piper and Anna came by, searching. "We spied a couple of puns, but they flew away," Piper said.

"They can't have gotten far," Anna said. "We're determined to bag them."

"What kind of puns were they?" Mindy asked.

"Flies," Piper said. "We didn't get a close enough look to identify what kind, but they stank of puns."

"He doesn't much like puns, except for me," Anna confided.

"Your name is punnish, but you're a real woman," Bryce said.

"Thank you." She winked. "I told him my secret. You were right. I still turn him on."

"You bet she does," Piper said. "I don't care much about her history. She's fabulous now."

"Am I missing something?" Mindy asked.

"This is the real Mindy, not the princess," Bryce reminded them. "She didn't get to listen in on private dialogues."

"Oh, that's right," Anna said. "I was a man, changed by the Demons to female for the Quest so I could distract Bryce from winning his prize. But maybe I distracted Piper more."

"You bet," Piper repeated.

"But if you were—how could you—?"

That was Bryce's question, but he had hesitated to ask.

"I was Justin Kase, who could summon things that might be needed in the future. As it turned out, he summoned me." Anna smiled. "But to answer your question: Justin really liked the ladies. He couldn't get enough of them, and they liked him too, because he summoned things that charmed them. When I changed, so did my interests. I wasn't looking for a man a day. But I remembered how the women had impressed Justin. It wasn't just flashing panties; it was how they delivered. So when I found a man I really liked, I made sure to be the kind of woman who would have caught and held Justin. So now I am that anomaly, a woman who truly desires her man and who gets pleasure pleasuring him. I don't just lie there and wait for him; I evoke the nuances. It's an art, not an act."

"You bet," Piper agreed a third time.

Bryce nodded. She had demonstrated her ability in

that respect with him. She was perhaps a better woman than she might have been had she never had that other experience. Because she remembered.

Had Princess Harmony had that ability, she would have seduced him without difficulty. But she was innocent, and he preferred her that way.

"That's some romance," Mindy said, almost enviously.

"They are well matched," Bryce said. "Both have or have had completely different other identities, and both understand."

There was a stirring in the brush. "Flies," Bryce said.

They converged on the spot. There under a shelter of weeds were a number of flies doing some kind of dance that formed a globe in the air.

"Fly ball!" Anna said, and swooped them into her bag.

"Good enough," Mindy said, and moved on.

Next day a new woman intercepted him as the group prepared to go out punning. She was strikingly beautiful, with bright yellow hair, bright red lips, eyes bright as diamonds, and a provocative figure. "I am the Yellow Rose of Texas," she said. "I'll be your guide today."

Bryce was taken aback. "I thought she was imaginary."

"Maybe in Mundania," she said, smiling. Her eyes sparkled like the dew. "But this is Xanth." She took his hand. "We have things to do."

Bemused, he suffered her to lead him out to the trikes. She wore a flaring yellow skirt, but that didn't stop her from using the trike. She probably intended to freak him out if she got the chance. Harmony had warned him that the women would be out to seduce him.

They rode out. Bryce let Rose lead the way, both because she evidently knew the route, and because that way he did not risk glancing back and seeing under that skirt. He had practiced panty-magic resistance with

Mindy, but feared it wasn't enough. The Yellow Rose was way too impressive.

Then he remembered his second sight. That should enable him to blink before getting caught. Because he could not be sure what the Rose of Texas would do if she had free access while he was freaked out.

They came to what looked like a golf course, with greens and bunkers and nice weather. There were two golf balls in the rough. "Oh, these must be puns!" Rose said. She got off her trike, walked to them, and bent over from the waist so that her skirt flared up behind her. But Bryce, on guard, closed his right eye as his left eye caught the coming flash of her panties. She would not trap him so readily.

Rose froze in place, her fingers touching the balls. What was she up to? He was the one who was supposed to freak, not her.

Then he realized that it was no act. Something had locked her there. But all he saw were the two golf balls. Two golfers must have hit them here, and would soon come along to play their lies.

Then he got it. This was a pair of lies. "Paralyze," he said. "Abysmal pun." Rose had touched them, and been paralyzed.

Bryce put his bag down over the balls and picked them up through the cloth so that he did not touch them directly. He had collected his first pun of the day.

Rose recovered. "What happened?" she asked, straightening up.

"You went after a pun, but it got you first." He explained about the golf balls.

"Oh, what a groaner!" she said. "I should have known better. I was just trying to—"

"To flash me with your panties, and forgot to be on guard," he said.

She nodded. "You're savvy about my motive."

"Yes."

"So I'll cut to the chase. Let's make out." She put a hand to her blouse as if to remove it. "I can show you how happy I can make you."

Actually it was tempting. But he did not trust this. "I hardly know you. But thanks for the offer."

"Oh, pooh."

They spent the day punning, and collected a number. Rose tried to flash him at every opportunity, but did not succeed. She was marvelously endowed, but not really his kind of girl. For one thing, they never had any conversation that hinted at any depth. He didn't know whether she was shallow or merely too focused on seducing him to bother with intellect.

The following day his guide was Clementine. She was lovely, wearing herring boxes without topses for sandals. She was also demure, not trying to flash him or make suggestive remarks. He learned in the course of the day that she had been driving ducklings to the water, caught her foot upon a splinter and fallen into the sea and drowned. Her little sister Tangelo had gotten her man after that. He liked her, but realized that she was no more than another emulation of a Mundane song. He preferred more realism.

The third day it was Jezebel, with flowing dark hair and a dynamic manner. She stepped in to him and kissed him, and she was devilishly compelling, but she too was really no more than a song.

It was similar with Irene, who bid him a truly alluring goodnight. He was tempted, as before, but declined.

"What do you want?" she asked.

"Someone closer to my own age."

Next day it was Helen, from Troy, she whose face had supposedly launched a thousand ships. That was their idea of a woman closer to his age? "Enough!" he exclaimed. "I don't want any of you!"

"Why not?" Helen asked cannily.

"You're not Harmony!" Then he bit his tongue, too late. He had blurted out the truth before he realized it himself. He had been freed of his spelled love for her, but he still recognized her as a lot more woman than any of these emulations. Harmony was young, but at least she was real.

"Oh, but we are," she said. Helen's classic visage faded, to be replaced by Harmony's.

"Oh, for pity's sake!" he said. "It's been you all along! Just as was the case when you were Mindy."

"I'm trying to be what you want me to be," she said. "Older."

"No wonder they all seemed shallow. You were working from brief descriptions in songs or history. You didn't know enough of those women to animate them persuasively."

"Yes. I asked Mindy for advice on attractive Mundane older women. As you say, I'm young. I don't have the experience to emulate experience."

"Please, Harmony, stop trying! I'd prefer to be fending you off personally, instead of fakes."

"You've got it," she agreed. "It didn't work the first time, when I emulated Mindy. I tried to get you to show me the last detail of the Adult Conspiracy, but you wouldn't."

"I wouldn't," he agreed.

"I just can't get it by watching through my little gifts. People hug and kiss, but it's somewhere else."

"In Mundania they have videos that show everything. But they are forbidden for anyone under eighteen."

"Mundania's as bad as Xanth! But that's only part of it. I want you to love me, however you do it. The physical details don't matter." She paused, reconsidering. "Well, actually they do, because I'm curious as bleep about them. But you know what I mean."

"I suppose it's wasted breath to suggest that you look for a man closer to your own age."

"Yes."

He sighed. "If you were only older."

"We have aging spells. I could invoke one. My sister Rhythm used one. But they last only for an hour. Would that do?"

"No."

"Oh Bryce, I love you and want you so bad! Please take me. You don't have to marry me. Just take me!"

"You're offering to be my mistress?"

"Yes! At least then I could have you with me, and maybe someday win your love. Please!" Now her tears were flowing, and he was sure this was not artifice. She was truly desperate.

"I wouldn't do that to you, Harmony. I respect you too much."

"Your respect is killing me!"

She had a point. He was being unfair. "Please, Harmony, can't we just be friends?"

"No!" There was the passion that had been missing from the others.

He had to give her something. "Maybe when you're older, naturally. So you have more life experience."

She pounced on it. "What's the minimum age you'd accept?"

He cast about for a figure. "Oh, maybe forty."

She sighed. "It's going to be a long twenty-four years."

She was serious! She was going to hang on until he agreed to marry him. He doubted he could hold out that many years. She was already touching his heart.

He tried again. "Give me a reason to associate with you that isn't to let you try to seduce me into marriage."

"I'll think about it." She walked away.

Surprised, he just stood there watching her. Was he in for more mischief?

Mindy came to take her place. "I think you should give up and marry her. It will be easier for us all."

"I refuse to be overwhelmed by an imperious teen."

"You're remarkably stubborn." Her tone was more of admiration than censure. She was from Mundania too; she understood.

Stubborn. That was the way she saw it, and probably the others did too. Yet he reserved his right to make his own choice. "I proffered her a compromise."

"She'll come up with something," Mindy said. "She really loves you. You can't be cruel to her forever."

What kind of an emotional hole had he dug himself into? "I don't want to be cruel at all. I just don't think it's right to stick her with an eighty-year-old man from Mundania. She can do so much better. She's a smart and lovely princess." Yet Electra's words haunted him. This was Xanth, where things were different. Details like age could be changed at will.

Next day Harmony was there to escort him. She was in heavy shirt and jeans, her hair tied back in business-like fashion. But she remained infernally pretty. "I think I have it."

"What is it?" he asked guardedly.

"Let's get out in the field with the puns. I can tell you better there."

"Harmony, I'm not going to—"

"I'm not asking you to!" she flared. "It just will require some discussion."

They rode out to the pun field. No puns were immediately evident. "What is it?" he asked.

"Right now we can go to an area and puns are just bursting out all over," she said.

"Not this morning."

"Silly. I took us to a section where they are rare; Dawn cleaned out this area some time ago. That's the point."

"I don't get it."

"What do we do when puns are widely spaced and hidden? How can we finish the job?"

"We'll have to devise a way to locate them."

"Exactly. When the puppies grow up they'll help sniff out puns as Rachel did. Meanwhile you can draw a pun sniffer or something."

"Maybe a compass," he said. "In Mundania it always points north. Or a metal detector, though that would work only at close range."

"The compass," she said. "And I could fix it so it points instead to the nearest pun, or concentration of puns. My magic won't last more than a day, because such things tend to get out of adjustment, like that path to Mundania, but for that day it should work well enough. Then next day we could make another."

"That might work," he agreed.

"Let's try it now."

He got out his pad and sketched a compass. He invoked it, and it slid off into his hand. There was the needle, pointing north, or whatever the Xanth equivalent was.

"Now I'll reorient it," she said. She brought out her little harmonica and played a few notes. He had forgotten how prettily she played. "There."

The needle was pointing in a new direction. "I don't see anything," Bryce said.

"It's there."

They went in the direction the needle indicated. Soon they came to a path. They crossed it, but the needle spun about to point back to it.

"It seems it's the path itself," Bryce said. "But I don't see a path as a pun."

"Let's follow it."

They followed the path, and soon came to a little sign identifying it: BRIDAL PATH. THIS WAY TO MARRY-GO-ROUND.

"Oh, my!" Harmony said. "I like this path!"

"You said you weren't going to—"

"I'm not! This is a surprise to me. I was just testing the compass."

"Should we put the path in the bag?"

She hesitated. "Do we have to?"

He relented. "Leave it. Let's try again."

They stepped off the path, and this time the needle didn't spin. It was pointing in a new direction. It led them to a pie tree with several ripe pies.

"What's punnish about a pie tree?" Harmony asked. "These look like pumpkin pies."

Bryce picked a pie and tasted it. Immediately he felt his belt tighten. His waist was expanding.

Then he got it. "Not pumpkin—*plump*kin. These are immediately fattening."

"Into the bag!" she said immediately, horrified.

"So it does work," Bryce said.

She faced him squarely. "You may have lacked meaning in your life, here in Xanth," she said. "As I did in mine, before I met you. But if we work together, we can zero in on the hard-to-find puns, like these two we didn't recognize at first. We can do a job others can't readily accomplish. Long-distance detection the dogs can't do. For the good of Xanth. This is meaningful, isn't it? A legitimate reason for us to associate? I promise not to flash you or anything; I just want to be with you on any basis you will tolerate." She shook her head with fleeting bemusement. "I never thought to court a crotchety old man from Mundania, any more than you thought to take up with a teen princess. But we can do this together, as friends, and we should."

Astonished, Bryce realized she was right. He had been searching for meaning without realizing it, and frustrated because he hadn't found it. Here was a good and useful job he could do to improve Xanth, exploiting his drawing talent with the magic pen she had given him. They could indeed work together legitimately.

What about the other things he lacked here in Xanth? Now he remembered that he had no companionship of his own type in Mundania, either; the others had all died. But in time he could surely form a new circle here, maybe including men his own age like Bink and Trent. What about the loneliness? He had not felt it while he loved Harmony; now it seemed to be fading as he considered working with her. He doubted that his life would ever be dull with her nearby, regardless of the nature of their relationship. She was young but smart and motivated, and she had fathomed his need and acted forthrightly to fill it.

He gazed at her as she stood there waiting for his answer. Her eyes were bright as diamonds, her hair twined in lustrous coils, her feet were in herring-box sandals, and her face would launch a fair number of ships. She was unconsciously echoing the women she had emulated.

Harmony would be quite a woman, when she achieved her fully adult status. In fact she was already more than most others he had encountered here in Xanth. Or in Mundania.

"Luck of the draw," he said.

Harmony looked at him, perplexed.

"I always thought I should do more with my ability to draw," he explained. "You made it possible, with your gift." He held up the pen.

"You're welcome," she said a bit uncertainly. "I have another confession about that."

"You told me how you tracked us via the gifts. I think that was a smart move."

"It's that the use all of you made of them was really important in my assessment of you."

"You mentioned that too."

"Don't forgive me before you know where I'm going!" she flared.

So there was something else. "I apologize for presuming."

"Those gifts were suggested by my grandparents. They have enormous potential, but only when properly exploited. They're like talents in that talent contest. They reveal things about their owners. Only two of you really rose to that potential. One was Piper, who played the piccolo in a way no one else could have, being one of Xanth's top musicians. The grandfathers thought I would marry him, and I might have, but for two things: his love for Anna, and you."

"Me?"

"You made superlative use of the pen. Others have tried it, but none came close to the things you evoked. Stink bomb, flying carpet, map of the gourd's horror house, dragon repeller—that demonstrated phenomenal imagination and latent magical power. You became a virtual general-purpose Magician, just as I am a general-purpose Sorceress. My perfect match. I *had* to choose you, and not just because I love you."

"All I did was draw," Bryce protested. "I love drawing, and I was lucky to get it right."

"Luck of the draw," she repeated.

More was required. "Now don't misunderstand," he said. "Or take this for more than it is. I have not changed my mind about marriage."

"Take what?" she asked, perplexed.

"I'm going to kiss you."

"Don't tease me!"

"I am not trying to. You have found something I need, and shown me a way to achieve it, and I am grateful. That is all."

"That is all," she agreed faintly.

Then he embraced her and kissed her. She met him so eagerly that hearts flew out like soft bullets and smacked into the surrounding foliage. It was clear that despite his caution he was beginning to fall for her. The old-fashioned way. She was young, but more than worthy.

Her wish probably would not take twenty-four years to accomplish. But he no longer cared. He had a future in Xanth.

AUTHOR'S NOTE

The prior Xanth novel, #35 *Well-Tempered Clavicle*, was written in the shadow of my daughter Penelope's death, which occurred the day I was ready to start writing. This novel, #36, was written in the lesser shadow of the one-year anniversary of Penny's death. We listened to the recording of the Memorial Service for her, which included our own voices sent for the occasion, as we were unable to travel to Oregon. I try not to let the vicissitudes of my private life interfere with my writing, but this has not been easy. Penny is a part of Xanth, as I modeled Princess Ivy on her as she grew up, and her horse became the Night Mare Imbrium. Now Ivy continues on her own, having retreated mostly into the background as King of Xanth. Little things keep reminding me of Penny, such as wearing a shirt she gave me, or Sunday mornings when she *doesn't* call. She remains in my life.

It is I think coincidence, but death does feature in this novel. A reader, Nicole Good, sent a batch of truly groanable puns that she had literally dreamed up, guided on a tour of Xanth by her daughter Melinda, who had died.

Later when I set up to write the novel, I wanted a tour guide for those puns, so I wrote back and asked permission to use Melinda, who became Mindy in this novel. She served well. Then Princess Harmony got her notion, and Mindy became a major character in the rest of the novel, for all that it wasn't really her. Thus we have the anomaly of a person becoming a significant character without ever expecting it, without being requested. Mindy was simply there at the right time. I hope that if there is any Afterlife, Mindy sees and approves my theft of her identity. Wouldn't it be nice if she encountered Penny, and they groaned together over their roles here.

Meanwhile my own life proceeds in its petty pace from day to day (yes, a paraphrase from Shakespeare's *Macbeth*). I still exercise seriously and watch my weight, because that helps keep my brain healthy. I got partial dentures, an expensive and sometimes painful process that took just about a year all told, but now I have a reasonably full set of teeth even if some of them do come out at night. I discovered that I was starting to gain weight, because now I can properly chew my food and I am getting more from the same amount. I have had to cut back on what I eat, as I mean to maintain my weight at my college level. One of the things about me that relates to both my weight and my writing is discipline.

My writing is slower than it once was, because my wife tripped and fell and fractured her left elbow and right knee. They were hairline fractures that didn't show at all externally, but she was incapacitated for about three months and I took over the household chores again. She's better now, but not completely. I still do most of the meals and dishes, mainly because I can stand on my feet longer than she can, though sometimes I get the impression that she doesn't really *like* eating scrambled cheese omelet on burned toast. I insist on going shopping and to doctors' appointments with her, concerned about her state. I don't want something to happen, and not be there to help. We are old, in our seventies, septuagenarians, and our future is no sure thing. We depend on each other. We've been married fifty-four years and want to try for a few more.

I am of course well into retirement age, but I will never retire. I have not seen the spare time that supposedly comes at this age. I am a workaholic, constantly engaged in new projects, and there is always the flow of letters from my fans, which I still try to answer responsively. That is, I actually read and answer them myself; I have no paid service for such things, just my wife to print them out for me. Should that volume increase, or my health decrease, that may change. I am conscious that the note I hurriedly dash out and forget may be far more important to the person at the other end. Sometimes a routine letter of mine gets framed. Oh, I hope I didn't say anything stupid therein!

Fans constantly inquire whether there will be a Xanth movie. I would like to see a Xanth movie while I'm still alive to enjoy it, and it may happen, but at this writing nothing is set. At present there is a movie slated for 2013 based on *Split Infinity,* the first novel of my Adept series. With luck and magic, Xanth's turn will come.

Fans also ask whether I will be attending fan conventions where they can meet me. No, my wife's condition makes travel difficult. I don't want to travel without her, or to leave her home alone. So the chances of my attending any conventions any distance from home are reasonably remote. However, I can be reached via my Web site, www.HiPiers.com, where there is information about my novels, a monthly blog-type column, and a candid ongoing survey of electronic publishing and related services that is intended to help guide aspiring authors to locate decent publishers. I had some hard knocks when I was coming up, over forty years ago; in fact I got blacklisted for protesting when a publisher cheated me. There are sharks in those waters. So now I try to make it easier for new writers to avoid such mischief. This does lead to some fireworks on occasion as errant publishers attempt to shut me up, but now I have the will and the means to fight back, and I do. Xanth is mostly fun fantasy, but my rough experience makes me an ornery cuss in real life. So though I am among the less accessible authors in person, I am among the more accessible electronically despite being on slow dial-up here in the hinterlands.

Now to the remaining credits for ideas contributed by readers, listed in approximate order of appearance in the novel, grouped by contributors. A number of incidental talents became significant characters because they happened to be there when I needed Suitors. This really was, to a considerable extent, the luck of the draw.

Mundanian on a recumbent trike in Xanth—D J Brown "Deaf Blind Old Goat." Service Dog in Xanth, needed for a Good Magician's Castle Challenge, knows private commands; cat burglar, horse thief, wharf rat, toilet tank; "Over my dead body," zombie esprit de corpse, sweating bullets—Mary Rashford. Demon challenge to find the perfect man for Princess Harmony— Barry David Khelder, who unfortunately died before he could see it as the centerpiece of this novel.

Talent of seeing ten seconds into the future—Donald Dickerson. Escalate Her—Emma Schwarzhans. Hedge-clippers; Sand Stone; lucky bamboo; talent of giving a toothache; talent of changing from one humanoid form to another; ability to breathe anywhere; talent of having the legs and tail of any creature; ability to change flowers' color, shape, smell; talent of befriending birds—Aaron Jackson. Flee Shampoo—Jill King. Gum Tree—Joyce Yang. Water Jacket—Russell Styles. Heretic, poultrygeist, D Pose, rock horse, walk on beams of light, getting the short straw, forget-me-not flower—Thomas Pfarrer.

Shoes with heeled souls—Peggy Forsberg. Mossy rolling stone, Ale Mint, Dear John letter, Paradigm Shift, Pair of Lies—Sean Darrow. Sea-saw, party animals, rain deer, butter fingers—Nicole. Gnome Anne's Land—Kristi M Street. Web Browser, Rolling Hills, Sock Hop—Richard Stanfill. N Villages, V Villages, Beach Bums, Ten S's Court, sun glasses—Cal Humrich. Gas Chasm—Matt Yarnot. Eli Ogre's Moon-stir cheese—pun dedicated to Pattie and Ken—Andrea Thompson.

Caterwaul—Rachel Seppala. Pop Fly, talent of healing broken relationships, fly ball—Tim Bruening. Gold den, enor-mouse, Anna Molly—Robert Green. Sar chasm with sars—Kyle Bernelle. None-chucks, Justin Kase—Gary Scharrer. Female faun and male nymph—Tyger B Dacosta. Arsenal—Ben Kalkwarf.

Talent of being lucky, talent of dreaming up ways to die, talent of making anything inanimate become animate, talent of making figures of speech literal, talent of giving someone bad luck, talent of becoming an inanimate object, talent of turning anything invisible, or visible—Brant Tucker. Average Magician Andrew, angel's and devil's food cake—Greg Miller. De-odor-ant—Aaron Wikkerink. Miss Teak—David Kaplan. Soul Train—David D'Champ. Talent of changing into a flying sword—Noah Goodman. The Hood that makes a Mother or Father, the child with dragon qualities—Maddragon.

Demon Flower and the changeable spring—Benjamin A Forschler. Tooth brush, tooth paste, girl with dragon breath—Robert. Making things lighter—Jesse McBeath. Talent of being anonymous—Nicholas Birchett. Talent of being cut to pieces—Bithor. The ability to heal injured monsters—Peter Hunt. Talent of turning into a fox—Mariah of Arkansas. Talent of summoning magic weapons—Honor. Talent of controlling noticeability—Anthony Keech. Talent of Perspective—Brittany Westly.

Duck Bill, Lady Slippers—Quaid Harsell. Bridal Path—
R J Craigs.

There were some suggestions that simply would not fit
in this novel without bursting its seams; I'll try to use
them next time. The last idea used I received OctOgre
22, 2010.

And I hope to see you here again, next novel.

Turn the page for a preview of

PIERS ANTHONY

ESREVER DOOM

Available in October 2013 from
Tom Doherty Associates

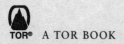

TOR® A TOR BOOK

1

ARRIVAL

Kody woke when the nurse came into his hospital
room. He felt awful. "What happened?"

"Ah, you're awake," the nurse said. "The doc-
tor will be with you shortly. Now if you will just sign this
admittance paper, your insurance will cover it."

"What happened?" he repeated as her hand guided his
numb fingers for the signature.

She glanced at him sympathetically. "You don't remember?"

"I don't," he agreed.

"You were in an accident. A bad one. But they got you
here in time."

"In time for what?"

"The doctor will explain. Meanwhile this will relax
you."

"Don't—" But she was already giving him a dose via
the IV hooked to his arm. He had no choice but to fade
out.

When Kody woke again, he was cautious about speaking. He wanted to know more about his situation before
they dosed him. He had been in an accident? It must

have been a bad one, because his whole body felt washed out. Had a drunk driver hit him? Then what about his car? Was it suffering similarly?

The nurse, morbidly attuned, knew he was awake. "Just in time for the doctor," she said briskly, as if that was all that mattered.

"I just want to know—"

"Not now," she said with impersonal efficiency. "He's here."

So much for any preference he might have. This was, after all, a hospital; they had better things to do than chat with patients.

The doctor was brusque. "You face some serious surgery, Mr. Kody."

"My name's not—"

"Don't be concerned; we'll put you out for the duration. It's called an artificial coma. When you emerge, the surgery will be done and you'll be well on the way to recovery."

"Surgery? What for?"

"So glad you understand." Already the nurse was doing her thing with the IV. He had only moments of consciousness remaining.

"There may be some disorientation," the doctor explained. "It's a known side effect of the anesthetic. A sense of floating, perhaps some temporary mood reversal. Nothing to be concerned about, Mr. Kody."

Mood reversal? He didn't want his mood or anything else reversed. But it was too late to protest; he was going under. Only the doctor's last words lingered. Mood Reverse. Mood. Reverse. Mood reversed was Doom. That did not sound good.

"Boom! Doom!" the ogre cried, hurling the poor creature at the shimmering wall.

Kody reacted before thinking. He put out a hand and intercepted the victim just before it collided. He brought it in to him, unharmed, as the ogre tromped away.

Ogre? Where *was* he?

It got worse. He looked at the creature he had just rescued. It was a bird. No, a cat. In fact it had the head and wings of a bird, and the body and tail of a cat.

The creature, briefly stunned, recovered. "Cheep?" it said.

"You're welcome, I think," Kody said. "I don't know where you were going, but it didn't look healthy."

"Cheep!" the creature looked at the wall, which shimmered in response. The wall was translucent, with an open meadow beyond, but there was a sinister cast to the scene. Kody didn't like it.

"Can you run or fly? I think you need to go home before you run afoul of another ogre."

The thing seemed to understand him. It sat up in his hand, spread its wings, and flapped. It flew up, made a circle in the air, then departed, flying over the jungle.

"You're welcome," Kody repeated, bemused.

Now exactly where was he? Not in the hospital! This seemed to be some sort of fantasy land, with ogres, catbirds, sinister walls, and who knew what else. Kody really wasn't into fantasy; that was his friend Joshua's department. He was at a loss to explain how he had so suddenly come here; the last he knew, he was being put under for some sort of surgery. The doctor said there would be disorientation, maybe mood reversal, and his disoriented mind had translated Mood to Doom.

Could that phrase Mood Reverse be translated into Esrever Doom? That would make about as much sense as the rest of it. He was doomed to be caught in reversal.

And there had been the ogre crying "Doom!" Kody had arrived just in time to rescue a composite creature from likely doom. An incredible coincidence.

But maybe not. Maybe he was in the coma, suffering some sort of mind reversal, and this was a dream deriving from that word. No coincidence at all, if he was imagining it.

Well, he might as well enjoy it while it lasted. He feared he would not enjoy whatever had happened to him in the real world.

He saw a speck in the sky. Something was flying in, and it did not look like a regular bird. Was the composite creature returning? No, this one was rapidly looking larger as it approached. It was the size of an eagle, no, a turkey, no, a horse.

A horse?

It looked like a large winged horse. With the forepart of a man. A—a flying centaur.

The creature landed neatly before him and folded his monstrous gray-brown feathered wings. His muscular human portion was taller than Kody, which was unusual. "Hello, stranger! My friend the catbird tells me you rescued him from a fate worse than death." Now Kody saw that the small creature was perching on the centaur's broad equine back, between the wings.

"I don't know—" Kody said, somewhat at a loss for words.

"Of course you don't know me," the centaur said. "I am Griff the Hipporoc, son of a male centaur and a female roc bird. My parents splashed into each other at a love spring they took for a normal pond. You know how it is; these accidents happen all the time, and account for many interesting crossbreeds. So I share their characteristics, and can speak avian dialects as well as human ones. That's how I came to know the catbird."

That hadn't been exactly what Kody was saying, but it would do. "I'm Kody, from—" He paused, uncertain whether his origin would make any sense to this fantasy creature.

"From Mundania, of course," Griff said. "You have that civilian look about you. Did you die?"

"Oh, I don't think so," Kody said, startled. "At least not yet. They put me in a coma, and I seem to be having a really weird dream."

"Well, that's one way to come to Xanth," Griff said. "We do see Mundanes here every so often, and dreams are important. Look, I really appreciate the way you saved my friend from the Void, so I came to tell you that."

"The Void?"

"The Region from which there's no return," Griff said, gesturing at the wall. "That's the event horizon. If the catbird had gone through that, he would have been lost."

"Oh, I see," Kody said, not really seeing.

"So I think I owe you a return favor. Why don't I take you anywhere you want to go, so you don't have to stumble through the dangerous jungle? Air travel is much faster and safer. You'll soon get eaten by a dragon otherwise."

"I appreciate that," Kody said. "I don't know whether getting eaten by a dragon in a dream would affect me much, but I'd rather not find out. But I have no idea where I want to go."

"Good point." Griff considered favors.

Two mice-like creatures ran along the ground between them. "Oh, bleep!" Griff said. "Don't let them touch you."

Bleep? "Those mice? Aren't they harmless?"

"Hardly! Those are vices. A cross between a vole and a mouse. See those letters on their backs? The one is an AD, the other a DE. If the ADvice touches you it will make you do bad things. Then you'll have to touch the DEvice to become nicer. Better to stay clear of them entirely." He stomped a front hoof. "Get away from us; we don't want any vices." The little creatures scurried away.

"Uh, thank you for the ad—uh, the clarification," Kody said.

"That's not enough of a favor. You saved my friend's life."

The catbird chirped.

"Now that's an idea," Griff agreed. "I'll give him the check her board." He looked at Kody. "Do you play check hers?"

"Well, I—"

"Or cheese. It's adaptable. But it doesn't matter. Just refocus and you'll see the scenes. Touch whichever one you want to go to." He produced a small object and handed it to Kody. "We have to be going now, but thanks again for what you did." The centaur spread his huge wings, trotted along the ground, and sailed upward. In one and a half moments he was gone.

One and a half moments? Evidently that was how time was kept here in Xanth.

He looked at the object. It was a folded mass that unfolded repeatedly to show a checkerboard (check her board?) with the checkers painted on the squares. Each one resembled a buxom young woman in a circular skirt. He touched one, and she moved forward to another square, jiggling.

Intrigued, he touched another, but she didn't move. Then he touched one of the opposing checkers, which resembled a handsome young man in a kilt, and he did move. It was necessary to take turns. Soon Kody was in a game with himself, seeing the check hers jump each other and disappear. When each one jumped, skirt flaring, the other piece looked up, froze in place as if seeing something forbidden, and faded out with an audible huff. They were checking each other out! Thus Check Hers and Check His. This was one naughty magic board!

But checkers was a relatively simple game. Too bad there were not chess pieces. And as he thought of that, the chess pieces appeared, each a little marvel of statuary carved from hard cheese. Which must be why they called it cheese instead of chess; it wasn't just a typo. When he touched a pawn, it stepped forward two squares. Other pieces moved in their traditional ways. So he could play chess on this board.

But what about the pictures Griff had mentioned? Kody focused, and refocused, and in a moment got the range. It was like looking at a 3D picture; focus was everything. Once he had the pictures, they were fascinating. Scenes of assorted magical creatures and things. And if he touched one he would be there?

Better experiment cautiously, because some indeed were dragons. So he oriented on an appealing castle with pleasant foliage and turrets. That should be safe to visit. He touched it.

Nothing happened. Ah, well. He folded the checkerboard, tucked it in a pocket, and looked around.

He was standing before the castle. The change had been so smooth he had not realized it had taken place.

So the game board worked. He could go where he wished, in this fantasy land. There were sixty-four scenes in all; surely one would serve his purpose. If he could only figure out what his purpose was, in this dream.

The front gate of the castle opened. A stunningly lovely young woman stood there, svelte and blonde, evidently the mistress of this castle, as she wore a petite crown. "Why, hello," she said, surprised.

"I apologize for intruding," Kody said. "A centaur gave me a magic device that enables me to travel, and I was trying it out. I think I can as readily depart as I came here."

"First let me touch you," the woman said, approaching him. He stood bemused as she came and touched his hand. "Oh!"

"You see, I'm not from this region," he said. "I don't know the geography or the customs."

"You are Kody, from Mundania," she said. "You were in some sort of accident, and woke in a hospital, where they drugged you, and you find yourself here in Xanth. You think it's all a dream."

Kody's mouth opened, but no words came out. How could she know that?

She smiled, and it was like the rising sun. "I am Princess Dawn. My talent is to know everything about anything living that I touch. You need my help. You must have been guided here. Come in." She turned and re-entered the castle. Her back side was just as impressive as her front side.

Kody followed. He kept being surprised by this dream!

"This is Caprice Castle," Dawn said as they walked. "It has marvelous properties you will discover soon enough. A number of us live here. We gather puns for storage, so that Xanth is not infested worse than it has to be."

"Puns," Kody said. "I believe I have encountered some of those."

"Indeed, it is hard to avoid them. It's a real problem."

"Yes," he agreed. But puns were the least of his concerns at the moment.

"Picka, dear," Dawn said, not loudly.

A spook-house animated skeleton appeared. "Yes, dear," it said.

"This is Kody, from Mundania. He needs help."

"We'll help him," the skeleton agreed. It came forward to shake Kody's hand. He tried not to recoil at the touch of the bare bones. "I am Picka Bone, Dawn's husband. And these are our children." For two small figures had appeared. One was a walking skeleton, the other a cute little girl.

It seemed this crazy realm was destined to keep surprising him. A walking skeleton could marry a princess, and they could have children? Obviously so.

"I'm Piton," the little male skeleton said.

"Hello, Piton," Kody said. "You look a lot like your father."

The boy giggled, complimented.

"I'm Data," the girl said.

Kody realized that Piton was a P name, surely because of his father Picka, while Data was a D name, after her mother Dawn. It seemed that in Xanth men had sons, women had daughters. "Hello, Data. You are lovely like your mother."

The child blushed with pleasure. Kody had not realized a small child could blush. But of course this was a magic land.

There was an awkward pause. Then Dawn approached. "I need to touch you again."

"Welcome," Kody said. "I never mind being touched by a lovely lady." That made *him* pause, because it was not the kind of thing he had ever said before.

Dawn touched him. "It is true. You see us as beautiful."

"Doesn't everyone?" Kody asked, perplexed. "I'm no expert, but if you are not one of the loveliest women extant, and your daughter a beautiful child, this is the most remarkable realm imaginable. Or is it considered bad manners to say the obvious? Have I given offense?"

"No offense," Dawn said. "Far from it."

"He sees you as beautiful?" Picka asked, as if not quite believing it.

"He does," Dawn said. "And Data as really cute."

"Then he's immune!"

Dawn considered. "Not exactly. He's just not reversed in the same way we are."

"Then can he fix it?"

"I don't know. Kody is not completely real, here."

Picka looked at her, perplexed. "Not?"

So did Kody. A walking skeleton found him perplexing? "I don't really understand any of this."

"Come and sit down," Dawn said. "This may take some explaining."

Soon they were ensconced in an appealing living room. Data, thrilled to be appreciated as pretty, came to sit on Kody's lap. But the surprises were not through. For a moment she became a little skeleton, startling him. It was definitely her, because now her dress hung loosely on the bones. She was just as cute in that form as when she had flesh.

"We can change," Data said, her voice emanating from her little skull. "It's part of the magic of Caprice Castle." She reappeared in human form, and squirmed to get her sagged dress to fit properly. "Do you really think I'm cute?"

"Yes, definitely," Kody said.

"That's great!" she leaned forward to hug him.

"Here is the background," Dawn said in a businesslike tone. "About a week ago the Land of Xanth was affected by a malign spell of reversal that caused people to perceive others as the opposite of what they are. That is, handsome or beautiful folk are perceived as ugly, while ugly folk are seen as handsome or lovely. Those in the middle range are affected less, becoming moderately the opposite of what they were. So, for example, others now see me as a hag, while seeing true hags as beautiful. We of the sightly persuasion find this distinctly awkward. We would like to have the old order restored, but we don't know how to do it. The Good Magician Humfrey says that only a person unaffected by the spell has any chance to nullify it. But all residents of Xanth are similarly affected, at least to some degree."

Kody's head was trying to spin. "This is not a literal change? Just one of perception?"

"Correct," Picka said. "I see Dawn as I always have. But now I am repulsed. That complicates our relationship."

"So it's really a mood reversal," Kody said. "Your sight has not changed, just your appreciation of what you see." Esrever doom, he thought: mood reverse. It was almost starting to make odd sense.

"Exactly," Picka agreed. "Even when she assumes skeletal form, I see her nice bones as ugly sticks."

"I don't like being seen as ugly," Dawn said candidly. "No woman does."

"While I, being Mundane, am not affected," Kody said, getting it straight.

"Not exactly," Dawn said.

"I'm not exactly here, yes, as it seems I am dreaming. But apart from that, I see things as they are."

"Not exactly," Dawn repeated.

"I'm not following you."

"I think I need to demonstrate." She glanced at Picka. "With your acquiescence, dear."

The skeleton shrugged. "Of course."

She faced Kody. "Stand."

Data got off his lap, knowing what was coming. He stood, perplexed.

She came to him, put her arms around him, drew him close, and kissed him. He felt almost as if he were floating off the floor. Her wonderful bosom was pressing into his chest, his hands were somehow on her marvelous bottom, and the contact of their lips was sheer rapture. She was an utterly mesmerizing creature. In that moment he loved her, despite knowing that she was not and would never be his. Not only was she a magic princess, far beyond his station, she was a thoroughly married mother of two. He had no business reacting romantically to her.

She drew back, knowing how well she had impressed him. Now it was no mystery how she had conquered a walking skeleton. She could seduce the dead, if she tried. "You liked that."

"God help me, I did," he admitted, shaken. "Please don't do it again."

"So you are reversed."

Now he appreciated her point. "I guess I am."

"Reversed?" Picka asked. "He's a perfectly normal man."

"Indeed he is," Dawn agreed.

Picka and the two children looked at her, puzzled.

Kody changed the subject. "So it may be that I am here for a reason: to get this spell of reversal turned off. So that Mood Reverse is no longer Esrever Doom."

"It may be," Dawn agreed. "The Good Magician will know."

"Who is this Good Magician?" Kody asked.

"He is Xanth's most respected Magician of Information," Picka said. "Anyone who really needs to know something can go to ask the Good Magician. But it isn't easy."

"Not easy?"

"He doesn't much like to be bothered," Picka said. "He is chronically Grumpy, so much so that he has five and a half wives who rotate month by month, a new one stepping in when the old one is worn down. He makes his castle difficult to get into, so that most querents are discouraged and go away without entering. And when he does Answer a Question, he charges the person a year's service, or an equivalent service. Even then, his Answers are seldom obvious; it takes time to figure them out."

"That does seem to be discouraging," Kody agreed. "Obviously I don't want to ask him anything."

"Yet you must," Dawn said. "The welfare of Xanth may depend on it."

The welfare of a purely imaginary magic land he was dreaming about. Yet she surely knew it better than he did. What could he do, but agree? "I must."

"We will have you here as our guest for a few days," Dawn said. "You need time to acclimatize, to get to know more about Xanth. Then we will send you to the Good Magician's Castle."

"But if I am here only a few days, there won't be time for me to do anything, regardless."

"You will be in Xanth as long as you need to be," she said with certainty.

"So be it," he agreed. "But you won't need to help me get there. I have the chessboard." He touched it in his pocket.

"It is best not to depend too much on such artifacts," Dawn said. "Some of them are limited, so that if you use it when you don't need to, you may not be able to use it when you do need to."

"Point taken," Kody agreed.

"Tweeter will show you to your room. You can clean up, then go out to talk with Bryce."

"Tweeter? Bryce?"

"Tweeter is a bird who knows what's what," Picka said. "Bryce is an old Mundane who arrived here last year. Princess Harmony is courting him."

And there was a small nondescript bird hovering in the air before him. "Good to meet you, Tweeter," Kody said.

The bird flew out of the room, and Kody followed. It was apparent that animals were not just animals, here; they were people. They proceeded up winding stairs to a rather nice suite on an upper floor, complete with a made bed, dresser, bathroom, and shower.

"This is all for me?" Kody asked.

"Tweet."

Kody washed up at the sink, noting that the mirror showed him as unchanged from life. Then the glass flickered, and Picka's skull appeared.

"Dawn said you should eat before you go out, as it might be a long afternoon," the skeleton said. "Tweeter will show you where."

He needed food in a dream realm? Evidently so, because he was getting hungry. "Thanks. I'll be there," Kody answered. Then he glanced at the bird. "A magic mirror?"

"Tweet," Tweeter agreed. He was evidently a bird of few words.

In due course they reported to the dining nook, where the meal was already laid out: a sandwich in the shape of a realistic submarine complete with a pickle periscope, and a glass of what looked like root beer. The two children were there. "Yours," Data said expectantly.

He bit into the sandwich, and it was excellent. Then he sipped the drink, and jumped. It felt as if something had kicked him in the rear, though that was impossible, as he was sitting. Both children giggled, and Tweeter made a laughing tweet.

Something was up. "Okay, what's the joke?" he asked them.

"It's boot rear," Piton said. He looked to be barely two years old, assuming skeletons aged at the rate of fleshly folk, but could speak well enough.

Kody contemplated the drink. Root beer, boot rear. A pun that was literal. A kick in the ass. But it was nevertheless tasty and satisfying. "Thank you. I did get a kick out of it."

Children and bird laughed again.

It seemed that this dream realm had a character of its own, and humor was a significant part of it. He could live with that.

After lunch he departed the castle with Tweeter, on his way to find Bryce. The landscape was a hilly jungle with odd looking plants and trees. He spied what had to be an eggplant, because it was growing eggs, and another growing assorted pies.

There was a path curving around and through the scenery, meandering as if enjoying itself. The air was pleasant.

Then Tweeter paused. "Tweet!" That sounded like alarm.

"What is it?"

Instead of answering the bird flew to a large tree by the side of the path, and perched on a massive lower branch. He made a gesture with one wing as if beckoning. So Kody carefully climbed up to join him there. But immediately Tweeter flew to a higher branch, and Kody followed again. Before long they both were on a high branch, peering down at the path. It was a fine view, but what was the point?

There was a motion behind the trees, accompanied by a sort of snuffling. Then a large dark creature, a vastly oversized lizard, came walking down the path, its long body sinuously handling the curves.

"Is that a dinosaur?" Kody asked, amazed.

"Tweet." That was negation.

"Then it must be—a dragon!"

"Tweet." Agreement.

The dragon heard them. It angled its head to peer up the tree. A puff of smoke emerged from its snoot.

"A smoker!" Kody said. Somewhere he had heard that dragons came in several types, one of which was the smoker. If that thing chose to rev up its smoke it could make a cloud around the tree and literally smoke them out. He understood that in house fires, more people died from smoke inhalation than from direct burning. This thing was dangerous!

Then the dragon shrugged and moved on. It had

concluded that they weren't worth the effort. It would have required a lot of smoke to surround a tree this size.

"But if you hadn't warned me, I'd have run right into it on the path. It could have smoked me with one puff, and swallowed me whole."

"Tweet," Tweeter agreed.

"Well look who's climbing trees!" a female voice screeched.

Kody looked, but didn't see anything.

"A silly tweety bird and an ignorant Mundane oaf," the voice screeched.

Now Kody saw the source, perched in a distant tree. It looked like a vulture, except that it had an ugly human head.

"That's a harpy!" he exclaimed, amazed.

"Tweet," Tweeter agreed.

"Lo, the light dawns!" the harpy screeched. "I'm Sniper, mistress of the long-distance verbal attack! What are you two doing there—making love?"

"That's one foul mouth on that creature," Kody remarked.

"Get it straight, idiot!" the harpy screeched. "I have a fowl mouth, not a foul mouth!"

Kody was getting annoyed. "And your face is uglier than your mouth."

This set the harpy back. "Ugly?"

"Repulsive," Kody clarified.

"But since the Curse I've been beautiful!"

Curse? Then Kody caught on: the reversal that made lovely women seem ugly, and ugly harpies seem beautiful. "Too bad, Sniper; I see you as you are."

Tweeter was amused. "Tweet!"

"Oh, yeah?" the harpy screeched. "Well you're another!" Then she spread her motley wings and took off, evidently overmatched.

"Tweet."

"You're right," Kody said. "That was sort of fun."

They dismounted from the tree and resumed travel along the path. Now Kody appreciated his need for a competent guide. It wasn't just a matter of finding a man, but of knowing what dangers to avoid. The bird knew.

They came to a bushy clearing. Tweeter flew ahead, then returned. "Tweet."

"Right. Go this way." He followed the bird to where a young man was kneeling before a melon.

The man glanced up. "Hello. Tweeter tells me you're Kody, a fellow Mundanian, newly arrived, and you want to compare notes."

"Uh, yes, in essence," Kody agreed, taken aback. All that from one tweet? Well, maybe it did fit within 140 characters.

"I'm Bryce. Just let me capture this pun, and I'll be with you."

Now Kody saw that the melon had legs, head, and tail. It was a sadly fat little dog! Bryce opened a bag and put it over the creature. When it was safely inside, he closed the bag and stood up. "That's a melon-collie, a gourd dog. More pun than guardian, I fear. We're trying to capture the most egregious puns first."

"So I see," Kody said.

"So how did you come to Xanth, Kody?"

"I was being anesthetized for surgery, and they warned me there could be side effects, such as mood reverse. I got mood backward and it came out doom. Esrever doom. Things seem to have regressed from there."

"Could you have died?"

"Not that I know of. I'm in a controlled coma."

"So you should return when they bring you out of it."

"Yes. Then the dream will end."

Bryce smiled. "Funny thing about dreams. Some turn

out to be true. Take me: I'm eighty-one years old and in ill health."

Kody repressed a smile. "You don't look it."

"I know. I was magically youthened when I came here, and now am twenty-two, physically, and absolutely healthy. And being courted by a princess. For some men, that would be the stuff of dreams."

"For some men," Kody agreed cautiously.

A lovely teenaged girl approached, accompanied by several young dogs. "Did I hear my name?"

"Princess Harmony," Bryce said. "Kody Mundane."

Harmony smiled, lighting the area. She had lustrous brown hair under her pert crown, glowing brown eyes, and wore a shape-fitting brown dress. "Kody," she repeated.

"Princess Harmony," Kody said. "You look ravishing."

She seemed surprised. "I do?"

He laughed. "I can't think when I've seen a prettier teen, princess or not."

Harmony turned to Bryce. "What do you see?"

"You are the ugliest creature I have ever seen," Bryce answered matter-of-factly.

She looked again at Kody. "Do you want to rephrase your answer?"

"Tweet!"

Harmony looked startled. "True?"

"True," Kody said. "I am not suffering that particular reversal. I see people as they are, and you are almost as beautiful as Princess Dawn."

"Thank you. I think I was, before the gross reversal." She frowned, frustrated.

"So you're here for a reason," Bryce said. "To abolish the Curse."

"I'm not sure about that. I think I'm here by coincidence, or pure imagination. But if I can help, I will."

"I need that Curse to be abolished," Harmony said

seriously to Kody. "You heard him say how I'm the ugliest creature he's ever seen. That means when the curse goes, he'll see me as the loveliest. Then maybe I can nail him. A kiss or two could do it. Certainly a night in the hay. Then he'll have to marry me."

"Stop it!" Bryce said. "You're only seventeen. You know I won't touch a child."

"I know you'll *try* not to touch a teen. But you're weakening."

Kody shook his head. "You're trying to seduce him, and he's resisting?"

She made a cute moue. "He has this foolish Mundane thing about being my grandfather's age and not robbing the cradle."

"I *am* your grandfather's age!" Bryce protested.

Harmony turned to Kody. "See?"

Kody shook his head. "There must be more of a story here than I know."

"There is," Bryce and Harmony said together. Then they laughed. They had evidently been over this ground many times. Obviously they knew each other well, and were probably in love even if they didn't admit it.

"Maybe I can help you collect a few puns while we talk," Kody said. "I need to know more about this land of Zanth."

"Xanth," Bryce said, somehow hearing the spelling. "And yes, you do need to know more about it, if you're to abolish the Curse."

Harmony conjured (perhaps literally) a pun bag for Kody, and they re-oriented on the pun collecting chore. "Woof!" a puppy barked.

"Show the way, Wolfe," Harmony said.

"Wolfe's the son of Woofer, Tweeter's friend," Bryce explained. "He and his sister Rowena are working with us today. Their mother, Rachel, crossed into Xanth last year with me, found romance, but returned to Mundania.

Woofer's was pretty broken up about it, but the pups are doing well."

Kody saw that the male pup had a W name, the same as his sire. The female one had an R name, the same as her mother. "Woofer? That sounds like a loudspeaker."

"Precisely. There are three of them, Woofer Dog, Tweeter Bird, and Midrange Cat. They came to Xanth with a Mundane family, and now live here."

"There seems to be a lot of Mundania here."

"Right around here, yes. Not elsewhere. That's probably why Dawn sent you to me. Mundanes understand Mundanes better."

Wolfe barked. There was a huge-trunked tree that looked like nothing so much as a giant beer mug. Small side branches held out steaming hot dogs and mugs of what had to be beer.

Bryce held up his bag. "Now if we can just fathom the pun."

"Frank 'n Stein," Kody said before he thought.

The monster mug shimmered, dissolved into smoke, and flowed into Kody's pun bag.

"You're a quick learner," Bryce said as Kody stared.

"I had no idea!"

"You could make a good pun catcher," Harmony said. "Of course, it is considered hard labor because it drives people crazy."

"But about this curse," Kody said as they resumed their quest for puns. "I understand I'm supposed to go beg a favor from a certain Good Magician, who will tell me how to go about it. But that he charges outrageously. I don't see why I should do it."

"Because if you don't, you'll be stuck here forever with pundigestion," Harmony said. "Watch where you're stepping. That's crab grass."

Now Kody saw the little green pincers orienting on his

feet. He quickly put down the bag. "In, crabby." And the grass wavered into smoke and flowed in.

Wolfe barked, signaling another pun. A woman was walking toward them. She was of indifferent appearance, which meant the reversal had little effect, but her bosom was curiously cloudy. In fact it was roiling, as if live things were trying to escape. The effect was both fascinating and alarming.

"What is that?" Bryce asked. Kody was similarly perplexed.

"A storm front," Harmony said. "If you men weren't so fixed on bosoms . . ." She opened her bag, and the front dissolved and entered it.

"Ah, here are some nuts," Bryce said. But when he took one it unwound into a wad of paper money. Wolfe barked.

"Cashews," Kody said. "So money really does grow on trees, here." But he was concluding that they were right: he needed to get out of this punfest before it rotted his brain. "How do I get to the Good Magician's Castle?"

"We'd take you there," Bryce said. "But we're pretty busy here, as you can see. We don't want any of these puns to escape, lest they reproduce. Any we don't get today will be lost. But Harmony may be able to help."

"Yes," the Princess agreed as she grabbed a vat of tea that had books floating in it. "Novel-tea." It dissipated and was duly captured. "I can mark a path there. But you'll need a steed, and some protection. Here there be dragons."

"True," Kody agreed, remembering the one he and Tweeter had encountered. "And harpies."

"I will talk to Dawn about it tonight," she said. "I'm sure we can arrange something."

"You could just point the way, and I can go there. I have a good sense of direction."

Both Bryce and Harmony shook their heads. Tweeter tweeted negatively. Even the dog barked No. Apparently they had little confidence in his traveling ability.

Kody sighed. "What must be, must be. I will accept the help I need."

Bryce nodded. "You're learning."

Harmony punched him on the arm. "Now if you were as fast a study, you'd learn that age is irrelevant here in Xanth. Then you'd marry me."

"Unfortunately I'm not that fast a study," Bryce said.

They all laughed.